Clara Braithwaite.
Chris

D1583224

PHILIP J. HAYWARD

Frontispiece

A JOLLY HALF-HOLIDAY

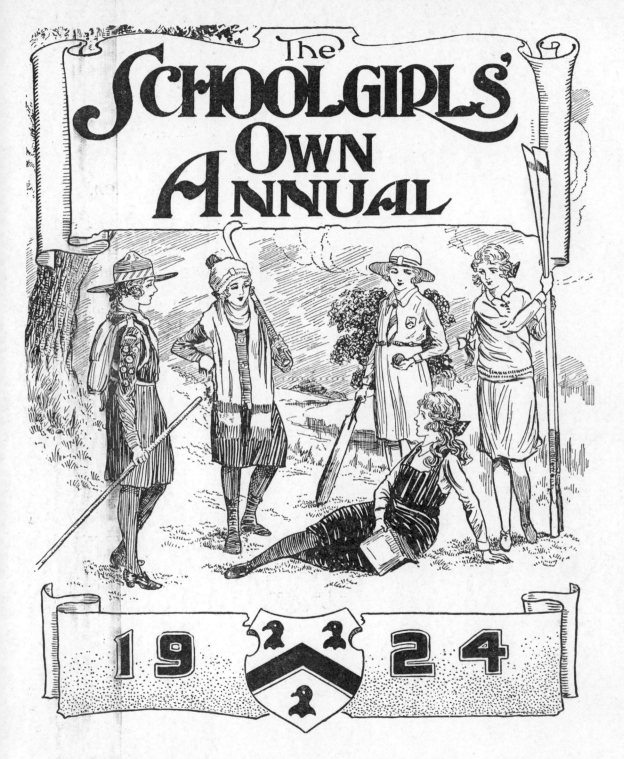

The SCHOOLGIRLS' OWN ANNUAL

1924

ISSUED FROM THE OFFICES OF "THE SCHOOLGIRLS' OWN" AND "THE SCHOOL FRIEND,"
THE FLEETWAY HOUSE, FARRINGDON STREET, LONDON, E.C. 4.

The Fleetway House,

Farringdon Street,

London, E.C.4.

MY DEAR GIRLS,

I here present to your notice the second volume of the " SCHOOL-GIRLS' OWN ANNUAL " with every confidence that you will enjoy it as much—perhaps even more—than you enjoyed the first volume.

Greatly heartened by the thousands of letters I received praising last year's " SCHOOLGIRLS' OWN ANNUAL," I have spared neither time nor trouble in my endeavours to make our second Annual better than the first.

I think you will find in the accompanying pages pretty well everything to suit the tastes of all schoolgirls. School, Adventure, Historical, Home Life—there are stories dealing with all these things; and, in addition, there are articles on subjects which I know cannot fail to appeal.

In the selection of the stories I have gone to the greatest pains to get them as different to each other as possible, so that in glancing through these pages you will find an ever-varying and pleasing contrast to suit all moods.

Some time must, of course, elapse before you can read the contents of this volume, but when you have done so I should esteem it a great favour if you would write and tell me your opinion of the " SCHOOL-GIRLS' OWN ANNUAL." Let me know which is your favourite story, which article you like best—in fact, give me a candid criticism, as so many readers did last year, of everything in the volume.

I am, Your Sincere Friend,

THE EDITOR.

"No Longer" A Madcap!

*A Story of the Girls of
Morcove School*

By Marjorie Stanton

CHAPTER I.

THE CAUSE OF THE TROUBLE

"SHUSH!"

Betty Barton, captain of the Fourth Form at Morcove School, frowned heavily, and side-glanced quickly at the girl who sat at the desk beside her.

Miss Massingham, the Fourth Form mistress, was writing on the blackboard, and from time to time she glanced round sharply to see that the girls were not getting into mischief.

Betty was a conscientious girl, and a hard-worker; but the same could not be said of the girl beside her, who was waggling her own hand out endeavouring to encounter Betty's. For Polly Linton was the madcap of the Form.

It was obvious to most of the girls near by that Polly was trying to pass something to Betty, and several eyes watched anxiously to see what was to happen.

Polly Linton was grinning as she waggled the note about, but a girl who sat behind Polly was frowning seriously. That girl was just now putting her hair to rights. It was rarely indeed that Paula Creel, the most elegant and aristocratic girl in the Form, was not putting her hair to rights. Yet it was always the tidiest in the Form.

Paula was anxious now on account of her friends. She had noticed Miss Massingham half turn her head as Polly, reaching sideways, just saved herself from slipping by grabbing her desk lid and banging it slightly.

"Bai Jove!" lisped Paula, in a dramatic hiss. "Bewlah! Betty darling—Polly——"

Miss Massingham wheeled round suddenly, and Betty became as one frozen. But Paula Creel was apparently intent upon her chum's safety.

Polly Linton, as a last resource, groped for Betty's hand—and dropped that precious note.

"She's dwopped it, y'know!" Paula hissed.

And Polly Linton, frowning, reached her hand back to slap Paula's leg and warn that well-meaning girl that Miss Massingham was an interested spectator of the scene.

It was a fact that the others had smilingly realised—and now Paula realised it, for she gave a faint "Oh, gwacious!" indicative of dismay, and her hand stole nervously to her hair.

"Paula Creel!" exclaimed Miss Massingham in a voice of thunder.

"Bai Jove! Yes, M-Miss Massingham."

"What is the meaning of this whispered conference? I do not write on the board for my own amusement, but for your instruction."

"Yes, wather, Miss Massingham. How-evah——"

Miss Massingham strode forward, for Paula's eyes had been fixed upon the note that had dropped to the floor, and the elegant girl had been vainly nudging Polly to pick it up, a fact that Miss Massingham had not failed to notice.

"Ah!" the mistress exclaimed grimly as she stepped forward, and, stooping, picked up the crumpled note. "This, I presume, was the subject of your discussion?"

"Mum-my discussion? Bai Jove, Miss Massingham, I sincerely hope you do not considah I would hold a discussion. It would be wude——"

3

Miss Massingham ignored the protest, and stared from Betty to Polly.

Polly was tapping her desk, and frowning with engrossed attitude at the writing on the board; and Betty—she was just a trifle flushed and guilty.

Miss Massingham unfolded the note, and her eyebrows raised. She glanced sternly at Polly Linton.

"I see," she remarked grimly. "This is most mysterious.' 'Julius Cæsar in the music-room.' Would you mind telling me what the Roman Emperor in the music-room has to do with the mean annual rainfall of Great Britain?"

"N-nothing," was Polly's hesitating reply.

"Then, pray, what does this extremely mysterious, but doubtless very interesting, message mean?"

"It's—it's only a play we're going to rehearse, Miss Massingham," Polly explained. "We're—we're going to rehearse it in the music-room."

Miss Massingham raised her brows and crumpled the note in her hand.

"You do not enter the Form-room, Polly Linton," she exclaimed tartly, "in order to make arrangements for plays to be acted after school hours. At the present moment you are required to study the rainfall of Great Britain." She whisked back to her desk, and Polly, thinking that the affair was ended, gave a deep sigh of relief.

But it had not ended, as Polly was to know.

"Good-bye, Polly!"

"When lessons are over," the mistress remarked, "you will draw me from memory a map of Great Britain, giving the mean annual rainfall."

She took Polly's text-book, and that girl gave a groan of dismay as what was almost her last hope of knowing the rainfall vanished.

"Poor old Polly!" Paula Creel remarked.

"Paula Creel, you will bring me your text-book, and after lessons you shall remain with Polly."

Betty Barton jumped up.

"Please, please, Miss Massingham," she exclaimed, "I was to blame as well. Polly was trying to pass the note to me."

And then Betty was awarded the same punishment as her two friends.

Madge Minden, Tess Trelawney, and Trixie Hope cast the three unfortunates looks of compassion. They had heard that message Miss Massingham had read aloud, and realised what it meant.

"Julius Cæsar in the music-room."

There were thoughtful expressions then and shining eyes. Madge Minden contrived to give Betty a very serious nod—a nod which might mean anything, but a nod which Betty took to mean that Madge was quite in agreement with what was arranged.

Suddenly the door of the Form-room opened. Polly sat bolt upright, welcoming the interruption. And, indeed, at that moment the Form seemed more animated than it had been during any other period.

At the sight of the page-boy the interest redoubled. For it meant that there was something important—a visitor, or perhaps, the more optimistic thought, that Miss Massingham's presence might be required elsewhere.

But whatever they thought, they were wrong, for after the page-boy had spoken to the Form-mistress, Miss Massingham, with a quite serious frown, looked to her Form.

"Polly!" she exclaimed suddenly; and Polly Linton almost jumped out of her seat.

What was wrong now, she wondered, what escapade of hers had come to light?

She was judging by the serious look on Miss Massingham's face, but the reason for the seriousness Polly quite misinterpreted.

"Just one moment, Polly."

In response to the summons Polly left her place, not without a feeling of some anxiety, and stood before the Form-mistress.

"The page-boy has brought word from the headmistress that your aunt, Mrs. Somers, of Hayten Dell, is ill," Miss Massingham exclaimed. "You have the headmistress's permission to pack your things and go there at once."

Polly Linton opened her eyes wide, surprised and perturbed at the news; for she was fond of her Aunt Sybil, who lived in a little village not far from the school.

"Can I go now, Miss Massingham, please?" she asked.

"As it is a case of serious illness, it is as well that you should."

The page-boy had gone, and Polly, with murmured thanks, made as though to turn to the door. But the Form-mistress laid a restraining hand upon her sleeve.

"One moment," she said. "This does not excuse your detention, Polly, and you must do the punishment when you return." She frowned slightly as she continued: "If only you would pay a little more attention to form work you could easily come very much higher in the lists than you do at present; if only you paid as

4

much attention to school work as you do to games——"

She sighed and left the sentence unfinished, and the madcap of the Form nodded a little vaguely, consoling herself with the thought that the lecture could not be long-lived. For Polly did not take school life very seriously.

It pleased her far more to be the best in her form at hockey than to be the best at any subject in Form work.

"That is all, Polly," Miss Massingham said. "But I may as well tell you that your father has written asking for a report on your conduct——"

"My father has!" Polly exclaimed, aghast.

Many times she had had lectures from her father; but she had taken them rather lightly, because she always felt in her heart that he was lecturing more from a sense of parental duty than from a desire to see her become a swot. In fact, she had had ample proof in the pride he took in her achievements at games.

But since her father had written to Miss Massingham, was it not probable that he was getting agitated on her behalf?

"It only requires you to concentrate on your work," Miss Massingham resumed. "You are high-spirited, Polly. I shall watch you closely during the next few days before I send in a report. Help me send your father a good report by altering your ways."

"I—I'll try," Polly agreed; and into her mind came visions of work left undone—preparations scampered through in a few minutes because she had been wasting time.

Then Miss Massingham made a sign that the discussion was over, and Polly, in none too cheerful mood, hurried up to the dormitory to pack her bag.

She was just kneeling on the suit-case to clip

It was obvious to most of the girls that Polly was trying to pass a note to Betty, and they watched anxiously for what was to happen

the catches when her chums ran into the room, lessons having ended a few moments ago.

"Poor old Polly," Tess Trelawney laughed, placing her hand on her friend's shoulder, "always getting into hot water——"

"And always deserving to," Polly admitted glumly.

And then they accompanied her downstairs, waiting while she went into the Form-room, where Betty Barton and Paula Creel were engaged in map drawing.

Polly kissed them good-bye, told them of the postponed rehearsal, and then took her departure. Not many minutes later she was seated in a train bound for Hayten Dell, and in her mind were tangled thoughts—the forthcoming play that they were to act in aid of charity, the lecture from Miss Massingham, and her aunt, lying seriously ill.

And, as she thought of her aunt, the memory of the last occasion upon which she had seen her came floating back to her mind. It was not a pleasant memory — not on account of her aunt, but because of Vera Somers, her cousin. For Vera was a spiteful girl, and had made unpleasantness.

Polly found herself wishing that Vera might not be there—that, at any rate, she would be a different Vera from the one she had seen on her last visit to her aunt.

And, finally, she consoled herself with the thought that since Vera had now left school she must be different.

And there Polly was right. Vera she would find different—but not an improved Vera! But of that Polly did not suspect. She determined that she would find Vera anxious on her mother's account, and changed for the better.

But what a surprise awaited Polly!

5

CHAPTER II.

AN ENEMY TO FEAR

"You!"

Polly Linton had just entered the hall of Hayten Manor, her aunt's house, when that word greeted her.

She turned and smiled in friendly manner as she saw her cousin upon the staircase. Vera was clothed in a rest-gown, and took Polly's outstretched hand languidly.

"How's aunt?" Polly asked eagerly.

"Eh? Mother—oh, about the same," said Vera easily. "Doesn't vary much, you know; delirious most of the time. But what's brought you here?"

"I came to see aunt," Polly returned coldly, angered by the other's callous words.

"Oh, good! Glad to leave the school for a bit, I suppose, eh?"

"Yes—in a way. Where is aunt's room?"

"Oh, you can't go there yet. The nurse won't let you in. One of the maids will tell you when. How are things at the kindergarten you go to?"

Polly flushed.

"Oh, not so bad," she replied.

"Getting into plenty of scrapes—lectures from the mistresses, and all that?"

"Well, yes," Polly admitted. "I did get a lecture just before I came away."

"Dear old scapegoat, always in trouble," Vera laughed unpleasantly. "Wonder when you'll be expelled? I told your pater I didn't give you more than another term at the most——"

"You—you told pater that?" Polly asked quickly.

"Yes; no harm, I suppose? You've told me plenty of yarns about the things you get up to at school. He didn't seem very amused, though."

Polly choked down angry words, but she glared at her cousin. It was like Vera, she reflected, to do a thing such as that. Now she knew why her father had written.

For several seconds Polly stared at her, then, being informed that she could see her aunt, she hurried to the sick-room.

How quiet, how solemn it was in there!

Tenderly she kissed her aunt's white face, smoothing her cool hand across the hot forehead.

"Poor aunt!" she murmured.

And who would have recognised her now as the madcap of the Fourth—Polly the irrepressible, irresponsible, as she sat beside the bedside of the frail, sick woman, stroking the thin hand that was extended to her?

Betty Barton—the captain of the Fourth

One glance only was needed to realise how ill Mrs. Somers was; and the solemn quietness of the sick-room accentuated matters.

"I am so glad that you have come, Polly dear. I—I feel lonely here, with only nurse as companion," the woman whispered. "Vera is—is very kind, but—but, of course, she has her friends and her social engagements——"

Polly started and, frowning, looked closely into the sad grey eyes of her aunt.

"Social engagements?" she murmured mechanically.

She would have added something, but for once her impulsive tongue was checked, and she tactfully said nothing of what was in her mind.

Social engagements! Was Vera so heartless? Did she speak of social engagements when her mother was so ill?

Just for a moment, while the thoughts were passing through her mind, Polly had glanced away from the sick woman, and when she returned her glance she found that her aunt lay as one in a trance.

A soft footstep sounded beside her, and she glanced up to find the kindly nurse smoothing the counterpane.

"You must go now," the nurse murmured kindly. "Mrs. Somers has been delirious most of the time, and she must not be worried."

She sighed, and Polly, rising, glanced at her wonderingly.

"It would be so much easier," the nurse explained, "if only her daughter —— But there, that's the way of things, I suppose. Those who receive the most affection are the least grateful. To think that this kind, unselfish woman should call for her daughter almost every minute——"

She shook her head sadly and disapprovingly.

"You mean that auntie calls for Vera—and she doesn't come?" Polly cried in absolute amazement.

And then her voice died away, as Mrs. Somers restlessly moved from side to side. Polly, unused to illness, stared, somewhat frightened, with tears of compassion near to her eyes.

"It's a shame," she said indignantly; and she paused again as she heard her aunt unceasingly whispering her cousin's name.

"Vera dear, stay with me, please; don't leave me alone, Vera."

Turning and tossing from side to side the woman repeated that sentence again and again.

"It is always the same," the nurse was saying. "She says little else, and sometimes days have passed when her daughter has seen her only for a moment or so. Even now I think she is dressing for a dance."

Polly was staggered. How any girl could act so cruelly to anyone amazed her, but that Vera should treat her mother so unkindly seemed almost incredible.

Kind-hearted and forgiving, Mrs. Somers indulged her daughter in every way, so that Vera's every wish was granted.

For several moments Polly Linton, with hands clenched and eyes burning, stood staring at the sick woman, then almost abruptly she turned on her heels. and the door closed softly behind her as she hurried from the room.

To reach Vera Somers' room took her but a moment, and she tapped imperatively on the door. The key turned in the lock, and Polly entered even before the door was fully opened.

Vera Somers, amazed at Polly's manner, stared at her, so Polly did not tell her the reason for the visit. For Polly's attention was attracted by the condition of the room. Vera Somers was obviously dressing for one of her " social engagements."

" You're—you're going out ! " Polly exclaimed.

Vera walked back to her dressing-table before replying.

" You're very smart," she said. And she turned to display her beautiful, but rather over-elaborate dress. That it was expensive no second glance was needed to tell, probably it had been designed with that object. " Like my frock ? "

Polly Linton, however, scarcely glanced at it.

" This is not a time to talk of dresses," she exclaimed impatiently. " Your mother is ill—dangerously ill ; can't you realise what it may mean ? "

She spoke more quietly now, and in her voice was a note of pleading.

As she heard the words, Vera Somers threw back her head and her eyes narrowed.

" What do you mean ? " she ejaculated.

" You know what I mean," Polly retorted. " You know that you ought not to go out to dances and theatres while your mother pleads for your presence in her delirium."

Vera Somers shrugged her well-shaped shoulders.

" My dear kid," she returned more calmly and patronisingly, " don't give me your mistresses lectures second-hand. I suppose I can please myself what I do ? "

Polly drew a deep breath.

" You — you mean, then," she exclaimed angrily, "that you are going out this evening ; you can't — you mustn't ! "

Her cousin spun round upon her fiercely.

" Mustn't ! " she exclaimed. " Are you going to give me orders, Polly ? Mustn't, indeed ! You don't seem to realise that one must keep one's social engagements. I should never hear the end of it if I didn't go. All the girls in my set would laugh at me."

" Give me that key ! " fumed Vera. " Give it to me, or I'll take it from you."

" How did you guess it ? "

" Laugh at you for not staying by your mother when she's dangerously ill ? " Polly echoed in sheer amazement. " They must be fine friends indeed ! "

" They re friends I can't afford to lose ! " Vera snapped. " It isn't every girl who gets a chance of going to the Van Hyltons, I can tell you. It will make me socially if I'm seen there. Anyway, I'm going."

7

And she turned back as if the affair were completely finished ; but Polly did not move.

She stood there like a statue, a fierce, angry statue, and the set of her jaw told of determination.

" That is final ? " she asked. " I tell you again, Vera, your mother is ill—dangerously ill, and she wants you by her—even now she is calling for you and yet," Polly added huskily, " you're going to a dance as if nothing were at all wrong."

" I am going, that's sufficient. You needn't go on pleading, making out that I am some sort of criminal ; everybody's doing that," Vera said bitterly.

" Which just shows how wise they are." Polly stepped back to the door and a sharp click from that direction made Vera turn to her.

" What are you doing with that key ? " she exclaimed.

" I have locked the door ! " Polly's voice sounded grim.

" Locked it ! " fumed her cousin. " How dare you ; give me the key."

Polly Linton folded her arms and faced the angry girl who stepped up to her. Vera's eyes were narrowed and her breath came quickly ; her dignity had been flung to the wind.

" Give me that key at once," she stormed, stamping her foot. " Give it to me, or I'll take it from you."

" Don't be absurd, you're not half as strong as I am," Polly retorted coolly. " You are going to stay here until you change your mind and decide not to go to the dance ! "

For several moments the girl stormed and raged helplessly. Then her storming changed to pleading.

" Please, please, Polly," she whimpered. " Think what it will mean to me if I don't go— I must go ! Their car will be here in a minute, and what can I say to them ? It's a chance of a lifetime. I can't miss it."

" If your mother treated you half as unkindly as you treat her," Polly answered, " you'd have no allowance, no money to buy these dresses, and I'd like to know just how long these people will be your friends if you haven't a penny in the world."

But Vera Somers was not listening to her ; she had arisen from the chair in which she had flung herself, and now crossed to the window.

" It's the car," she gasped, turning a white face to her cousin. " It's the Van Hylton's car; they have called for me. Polly, please—I'll do anything for you, honestly I will. I—I——"

But Polly Linton remained as impassive as the sphinx. The door bell rang and the sound of voices came from the drive.

White-faced with anger and humiliation, Vera Somers listened to light footsteps that sounded in the passage outside. In another moment there came a gentle tap on the door, and the servant announced that the Van Hylton's car was waiting their guest. Vera stepped forward, but Polly Linton caught her in a grip of steel, placing a firm hand over her cousin's mouth.

A few moments later the servant's footsteps died away in the distance as she went to tell the waiting chauffeur that Miss Somers's mother had been taken seriously ill, and on that account Miss Somers begged to be excused the dance.

It was all over then, and Vera, white and limp as a rag, fell back into the chair, staring with burning, resentful eyes at the girl who had defeated her.

And not until she had extracted a promise from her did Polly release the thoughtless girl. That promise Vera had to keep—she could not have done

Paula Creel — the swell girl of the Fourth

otherwise—and Polly Linton smiled with a smile of happiness as she watched the girl enter the sick-room. She had won ; but she had made an enemy.

Spiteful to the last, Vera was making the most of things, assuming all credit for not having gone to the dance, even describing how she had not listened when Polly had entreated her to go and to take her, too.

But of that Polly knew nothing.

When, a little time later, she heard that danger was over, and that Mrs. Somers was now in a peaceful sleep, she felt that to gain so much was worth even incurring the enmity of Vera.

That the enmity was very real she learned the next day when she left.

" You saved your mother, Vera," she said warmly as she met the selfish girl coming from the sick-room.

Vera Somers eyed her up and down coolly before replying.

" You think you are very clever, Polly Linton, with your meddling," she said. " But your innings is over—and now it's mine. It won't be very long before you'll be wishing that you had minded your own business ! "

And with those words, so nearly a threat, Vera brushed past Polly and marched down the corridor.

Worried, and puzzled, Polly stared after her ; then, smiling, she shrugged her shoulders. After all, what had she to fear from Vera ? That was the question she asked herself, and it gave her nothing but increased contempt for the girl.

Indeed, so happy was she that her aunt had recovered that she almost forgave Vera and her threats. And when Morcove was reached, Vera was entirely forgotten. Her aunt was on the road to recovery, and in a few days she and Vera would be staying with the Lintons, where she would have friends around her.

Once again Polly was in her old atmosphere, forgetting the lecture from Miss Massingham, and her former, momentary desire to change her ways. Perhaps once she did have a vague uneasiness, but dismissed it from her mind almost immediately, telling herself that it was merely the result of Vera's spiteful words.

Merely ? Ah, there indeed Polly erred, misjudging the extent of her cousin's spite. Vera did not forget, and to her revenge was sweet—how sweet Polly Linton had yet to learn.

CHAPTER III.
POLLY, THE PERFECT !

"ORDER ! "

"Yes, bai Jove, ordah, deah geals. Pway ordah ! "

" Order you, too," said Polly Linton, catching Paula by the shoulders and plumping her down in a chair.

The music-room was crowded with Fourth Form girls, and the door very judiciously had been locked. Girls were sitting round on chairs they had brought ; and those who had not brought chairs had the choice of the window-sill or piano, unless they chose to stand.

" Order for the chair," came Polly Linton's booming voice, and the babble of tongues died down for just a second.

There were cheers as Betty Barton mounted a stool ; for Betty was a popular captain, and the girls were all ready to hear her.

" Ordah ! Pway be silent, deah geals, Polly——"

" Now," Betty exclaimed, when silence had been gained. " This meeting has been called, girls, to decide what we are to do for the Fund Day in Barncombe Town. The Fifth are up to something, you know——"

There were groans for the Fifth, and Betty smiled.

" Never mind. We've got to do something better," she resumed. " Polly suggests playing 'Julius Cæsar'——"

" Because she wants to play Marc Antony," interposed Ursula Wade, the sneak of the Fourth. But no one minded what Ursula said.

" Not a play—a concert," said Madge Minden in her serious way. " We can distribute talent so much better. Play one scene from Shakespeare, if you like——"

" Hear, hear."

Polly Linton—the madcap of the Fourth

" A concert——"

" Good idea——"

And there was a hubbub for some moments, and poor Betty, though she waved her arms ever so, could not gain silence. It was Polly who restored order. Polly thumped the piano till Madge's heart ached, and the piano hummed in protest.

" Now, girls, please don't make so much noise," Betty pleaded, with an anxious glance at the door. " We shall have a mistress arrive on the scene, and that won't do. I take it that you want a concert—shush ! No shouting. Hands up for a concert ! "

Up flew a veritable forest of hands, and Madge Minden elevated two. She felt that she had to do her best.

" Right, then a concert it is, and we'll act some scenes from Shakespeare. As a matter of fact, I think it's a very good idea. We've got heaps of talent——"

" Bai Jove, yaas wathah, Betty darling. I don't mind singing a song y' know."

" Have no concert if Paula's going to sing," said Polly hurriedly; and there was a laugh.

" Weally, Polly——"

And Paula vainly protested. But her voice was scarcely heard. Judging by the noise there wasn't a single girl in the Form who could not do something.

" We can't have you all on the stage," said Betty at last, as, with a rather worried laugh, she put down the pencil which she had used to write down their names. " Madge, Paula, Trixie—I suppose the people can stand a French recitation ? " she asked, rubbing her nose thoughtfully.

" Oui, oui," Trixie hastened to assert, in her alleged French. " Ils l'ameront—they will love it——"

" Have you seen my grandmother's pen——' teased Polly. " No, but I have the garden-roller of my niece's uncle."

Poor Betty sighed hopelessly, and sat down on her chair. There was so much noise that she was afraid lest at any moment a rap should come at the door—a rap that heralded the approach of a mistress.

" We must be quieter," she said anxiously. " For one thing, the Fifth are bound to get to hear of this, and we want to get in ahead of them. Just think," she added eagerly. " If we can score over this play, and beat them at hockey, they'll never be able to hold up their heads again."

" Hear, hear ! "

And that speech received the loyal ovation

9

that it deserved. When the shouting had died down, Betty had her own way. Gradually she made them take seats round the room, and sorted out the performers for the great concert.

"Excellent," she murmured with a sigh of relief when she had finished. "Here's a list fit to beat anything: Madge Minden, pianoforte solo. Paula Creel — er — song. Trixie Hope, French translations, I mean, recitations. Polly Linton, comic song——"

"And me," prompted Dolly Delane, for once putting herself forward.

"Oh, yes, duet Dolly and Tess Trelawney. Then something from me, and last, a scene from 'Julius Cæsar,' with Polly as Marc Antony, and Paula as Julius Cæsar in the Forum scene."

"Good old Paula——"

Paula Creel smiled.

"I wather flatter myself I do that wather well," she admitted, with a shake of the head. "The Cweels have always been good actwesses. I shall soon learn my part y' know."

"You will, silly goose," Polly agreed. "Julius Cæsar's dead in that act. If you can't act as a dead body——"

Polly left the completion unfinished, and the look on Paula's face caused more peals of merriment.

"Order, order!" called Betty again, when confusion broke forth anew. "We must take this up seriously, girls. We shall have to rehearse some of the things——"

Paula Creel was on her feet in an instant, and hurrying to the door.

"Where are you going?" Polly demanded.

"Get my music, Polly dear. I'm going to pwactise, y'know—a Herrin' calling——"

"A—a what?" gasped Polly. "My—my hat, you leave the herrings alone——"

"She means 'Caller Herrin','" Betty laughingly explained. "You go and practise, Paula dear, there's a good girl——"

And when she had gone others went, too. Madge Minden took possession of the piano, and, with a dreamy look on her face, commenced to play her solos.

Round the music-stool a crowd gathered, sorting out songs and duets.

And when, some minutes later, Paula Creel, a thoughtful expression on her face, entered the room, she found that most of the girls had vanished to get their songs.

"I say, Betty dear," she murmured. "I've just been glancin' at my copy of 'Cæsar,' y'know."

"Learnt your part?" smiled Madge Minden dreamily.

Paula nodded.

"I'm goin' to play Marc Antony. I'm wather a good actwess—"

"But—but, Paula dear—your—your—er—

accent," Betty protested cautiously, not wishing to hurt the elegant girl's feelings.

But Paula Creel, fired possibly by the thought of being a prominent actress, had already started.

"Fwiends and Womans, deah geals. Lend me youah eahs—no—that's wrong——"

"Ha, ha, ha!"

"Fwiends, Wemains of countwymen—I mean, womans and countwymen, lend me youah eahs."

"I'd rather not!" cried Polly.

"I come to buwy Cæsar, not to pwaise him. Howevah—er—er—yes, wather. I haven't come to pwaise him, y'know—er—oh, I see—The evil that men do lives after them, y'know; the noble Brutus has said Cæsar was ambitious. It's vewy w'ong——"

"Ha, ha, ha!"

"Weally, Betty dear, I wish you'd give a geal a chance. I feel I should be a success as an actwess, weally I do——"

"You would," Tess Trelawney agreed, choking with laughter. "Poor old Bwutus—still, you'll make a good Cæsar, Paula. You've got just the hair—and—er—the figure——"

"Bai Jove, weally?"

"Y—Yes," nodded Betty, trying not to laugh. "You'll really make an awfully nice Cæsar, Paula dear. Besides, laurels will suit your coiffure."

"Vewy well, then. But I don't mind twying to play Marc Antony. Twy, twy again, y'know. Howevah I'll sing my song."

"Yes, in a minute, dear," Betty remarked tactfully. "Gracious—wh-what's this?"

And the girls about the piano turned suddenly at the new entrant. A girl in a dark cloak had come into the room, and as the dark cloak fell to the floor they saw that it was the madcap of the Fourth.

Polly Linton struck a dramatic attitude.

"Friends, Romans, countrymen, lend me your ears——"

"Yes, wather, Polly dear."

"I come to bury Cæsar——"

"Not to pwaise him, dear geal——"

Polly Linton glared at the well-meaning Paula, and in most un-Antonian manner stepped forward, and took away the tattered copy of Shakespeare.

"Now will you be quiet?" she asked. "You're Cæsar—you don't speak. You're dead. You lie down on the floor."

Polly Linton, once her enthusiasm had been roused, ruled things in her own way, and Betty saw that it was useless to protest. Polly meant to rehearse, and, after all it did not matter greatly, because rehearsal was needed. So Betty took the copy of Shakespeare and attempted to guide her friends.

"Hands up for a concert!"
And up went a veritable
feast of hands

Paula Creel, after smoothing out Polly's cloak as a carpet, placed herself gingerly on the floor, and feigned death.

Then Polly got into her stride, and soon she was rehearsing for all she was worth.

But a moment later the door opened, and a grinning face peered in. It was a Fifth Form girl. The Fifth Form girls were seniors; but they were not above stooping to "tease" and rag the Fourth-Formers.

"What on earth's this?" the girl asked, staring at Polly in her Roman costume. "I say, girls, do come and look at these children——"

Marc Antony's narration ceased suddenly as three smiling faces were framed in the doorway. Keen though she was, Polly was sensitive to ridicule, and she knew that off the stage a Roman in full war kit was rather absurd.

"Go away," she said.

"All right, Mr. Cæsar. Sorry to interrupt. Go on. Friends, Romans and kids——"

Polly made as though to hurl a cushion at them, and the girls vanished.

"Next one will get this cushion," said Polly. "I'm not going to stand that——" And she resumed her speech.

Footsteps sounded in the corridor again, and Polly groped for the cushion. Her hand grasped it tightly as she went on with her speech.

The other girls looked away from the door in order not to warn the entrant, and Polly made a swinging movement with the cushion.

Whiz!

"Oh!"

"Got them!" Polly Linton wheeled round in triumph, and then her hands dropped to her sides and the joy vanished from her face.

For there in the doorway, her hair ruffled, stood Miss Massingham. And the look on the Form mistress' face was not pleasant to behold.

"Oh, I—I'm sorry," stuttered poor Polly.

The mistress advanced to the centre of the room, breathing deeply through her nose.

"No doubt," she said tartly. "So this is the cause of the disgraceful noise that I have heard. It is you again, Polly—goodness gracious, who is this on the floor?"

She stared down at Paula Creel, who was lying quite still on the cloak and cushions.

"It—it's Paula. She's playing Julius Cæsar's death," Polly explained.

"Paula, get up at once. I am surprised to see you acting so foolishly."

But Paula Creel did not move. Steady breathing came from her, and Polly Linton gave a sudden chuckle that was instantly frozen.

"She—she's asleep," she choked.

But Paula was awake an instant later, and rubbing her eyes. When she saw the Form mistress she was on her feet, looking extremely foolish.

"So this, Polly," said the Form mistress severely, "is how you commence to reform, by throwing cushions at mistresses——"

"I—I didn't mean it for you—I—mean—I thought——"

"Possibly you did not. I will believe that. But, anyway, it is not lady-like to throw cushions. Also, you would be better employed doing preparation. Take off that absurd attire at once and return to your study."

And Polly Linton, her hands hanging by her side, stared after the retreating mistress. For now Polly remembered; clearly she recollected the interview with Miss Massingham.

She had been going to reform, and this is how she had begun. Perhaps she would have laughed. But she remembered what the mistress had said.

"Help me send your father a good report."

What report would her father receive now? There was good reason for the madcap of the Form to be silent. Good reason for her to hang her head sorrowfully.

For Mr. Linton, though just, was stern; many times before she had received lectures from him, and now——

Ah! How Polly wished then that she was not such a madcap. But it was too late for wishes!

Had Polly been by the pillar-box half an hour later she would have seen Miss Massingham slip an envelope into it, and the address would have been one that was very familiar to Polly.

As for the contents—perhaps it was just as well that Polly could not see inside that letter!

CHAPTER IV.

THE FOODLESS FEAST.

"SHE's got it!"

That cry rose from the touchline, and there was a yell of enthusiasm from the crowd that gathered round the ropes.

It was not in the ordinary course of events that a large crowd gathered to watch a junior game, but this half-holiday was an exception.

A goalless game was in progress—a ding-dong battle between the Fourth Form at Morcove and the girls of a neighbouring school.

No wonder the crowd round the ropes cheered, visitors and school-supporters too, for Polly

Linton, with a sudden burst of speed, had outwitted the left back of the opposing team, and now she was making a bee-line for the circle.

No wonder there were anxious, long looks on the faces of the opposing side. Only a few minutes' play, and yet in those few minutes all that the girls had battled for might be lost.

And Polly of all girls!

There was a determination in the very way Polly ran. The ball seemed glued to her stick, and the stick might have been a magic wand. The other back, straining every nerve and sinew, was in the circle even as Polly got there.

Now there was excitement indeed. One false move on Polly's part and the ball might be cleared, to remain in mid-field, hacked this way and that, until the game ended.

Already the half-back had fallen back, and Polly's friends in the forward line were standing in strained eagerness waiting for something to happen.

It seemed hours, and yet the whole thing occupied but two minutes.

The ropes were groaning at the crowds that pressed forward against them, and even staid mistresses—even Miss Massingham—watched in breathless anxiety.

"Ah!"

The goalkeeper was rushing out, even as Polly sticked the ball away from the lunging stick of the powerful girl who played back.

A groan of disappointment rose, and also a sigh of gladness, according to the sympathy of the supporters.

And the groans and sighs changed ownership as, with a lightning movement, Polly tipped the ball over the goalkeeper's stick, and the goalkeeper, too late, lunged at it with her padded leg.

Slowly, oh, so slowly that it seemed that even yet one courageous lunge might prevent it crossing the fatal white line!

Defenders and attackers alike stood as though petrified, as though expecting the ball suddenly to turn and fly with invisible wings away from the goal-mouth.

But the laws of momentum were not to be defied, and next moment a yell that was likely to deafen its hearers rose from the crowd that surged round the ropes.

"Goal!"

"Well-played, Polly!"

"Bravo, the Fourth!"

And then Polly could not be seen for wildly excited, cheering girls.

She was chaired, carried shoulder high, and they could see her stick waving wildly above the heads of all.

And then, when the enthusiasm had died down and Polly was placed on her feet, there were cheers for the opposing side—the side

"Fwiends, Womans, and countwymen!" lisped Paula Creel. "Lend me your eahs!"
"Thanks! But I'd rather not!" cried Polly

13

that had fought so well, but with less fortune than their opponents.

"What a game!" Polly exclaimed breathlessly.

And she pushed her arm through Paula Creel's just as that girl was about to praise her for the wonderful game she had played.

"It was the side," Polly said. "The side scored the goal. I didn't do any more than the others."

But she had. As usual, Polly had been the live spirit. Her play had given them heart, even when the tough struggle was at their end of the field.

But it was the game that counted, and not the victory. Now, laughing and chatting merrily, they accompanied their opponents to the gate, where a motor-coach waited to take them back to their own school.

And not until the last cheers were echoed in the distance, and the brilliant tail light of the motor-coach disappeared, did they turn from the gate.

"And now," Betty laughed, "change and tea."

To change was but the work of a moment, and, laughing merrily, they made their way down to the Fourth Form passage. And there was Study No. 12 brightened by the firelight, with Dolly Delane bending before the fire.

"Good, Dolly; you're a brick!" Betty laughed, patting the girl on the shoulder.

"I—I couldn't find anything in the cupboard," said Dolly. "I've brought some things I had, but there isn't much."

Then there were glum faces, indeed. For the match had made them hungry, and they had hearty appetites.

"Oh, crumbs; nothing to eat!" groaned Polly. "This is a bright idea! Who's got some money? Here, Paula; you're a plutocrat——"

But Paula Creel shook her head dismally.

"Bwoke!" she explained, with a gesture. "Clean bwoke!"

"Sixpence!" was Betty's wry but pointed remark.

And Madge Minden brought out two pennies.

"Done—tealess! And no one expecting anything?" Polly asked.

"No, nothing!" Madge said; and the others shook their heads.

"But, I say," remarked Dolly Delane, "there's a letter for you in the rack, Polly. Perhaps there's a remittance."

"Letter for me?" Polly asked excitedly; and her eyes danced. "Is it from dad? You know his handwriting?"

Ursula Wade—the sneak of the Fourth

"Yes, it was——"

But Polly hardly waited to hear the confirmation. She was skipping down the passage light-heartedly. They were saved! She had written to her father for a remittance, and now it had come.

It was indeed an occasion for cheers!

And what joy when she reached the letter-rack and saw the square envelope addressed in her father's clear, well-known handwriting!

She snatched it from the rack, and her fingers trembled as they slit open the flap.

In another second she had drawn out the contents, but there was no remittance. She frowned and opened the single sheet.

She unfolded it, and did not move. Like a rock she stood as she read the contents, and the colour died from her face. The sparkle went from her shining eyes, and she lowered the sheet at last.

Her lip quivered as she looked down the dark corridor, but she made no attempt to move from the spot. The letter was clutched in her hand, and now she screwed it up fiercely. Just for a moment her eyes seemed to burn with a light of battle, and she braced herself.

The report from Miss Massingham had gone forth, and now—now the blow had fallen with a vengeance!

CHAPTER V.

"THE PLAY'S THE THING!"

"POLLY'S been a long time."

Betty Barton made that remark as she glanced through the window on to the dusky quadrangle.

"She certainly has," Madge Minden agreed; "and it's a good sign, too! I shouldn't be surprised if she's gone to the tuck-shop, and she'll come in with her arms loaded!"

"Bai Jove, yes, wather! I'm jolly hungry, so I hope she does!" simpered Paula.

Just then the door burst open, and with such a crash, too, that they thought it must be their chum. But it was Ella Ellgood, one of the Fourth, but not of their particular set.

"Girls, what do you think?" she exclaimed. "The Fifth are giving a concert, too."

"The Fifth are!"

"Yes, and a good one, too," Ella amended. "Strikes me we shall have to alter our plans, Betty. No good having two concerts. The first will score all along the line!"

"Then we've got to be first," said Madge Minden promptly. "I don't see why we should let the Fifth get ahead of us."

But Betty was not so decided.

"It is rather startling," she agreed. "They probably heard our plans, and, of course, if there are two concerts, the first will score. But," she amended, with a look at Madge, "I'm afraid we can't be first. The Fifth have got all the influence."

"We're not going to throw it up?" asked Madge, keenly disappointed.

"Throw up the concert idea—yes," Betty assured her. "But there's no reason on earth why we shouldn't have a play. We've got everything prepared for it, and it will be just as popular."

Then there was debating and discussion. Madge wanted a concert, because of her playing. But the others didn't mind very much which it was, and Madge, not being a selfish girl, very soon gave in.

"Then a play it's going to be?" Betty asked. "I should have liked a concert immensely, but you see how it is, Madge. Perhaps you would play an overture for us?"

And Madge Minden was quickly appeased.

"Polly will be pleased," Tess Trelawney remarked. "She's got the fat part, and she's the best one for it, too."

They were all agreed on that. Marc Antony's part was not by any means an easy one, but Polly knew it by heart, chiefly, as she had often told them, because she had been made to learn it as a small child when she had been disobedient to her governess.

At any rate, she knew the part well, and she acted it well, too. She had a clear-sounding voice, that carried all over a building, so that the words should be heard everywhere.

Madge Minden—the Fourth Form musician

"We shall do it yet!" exclaimed Betty in triumph. "After all, Shakespeare is popular. The mistresses will like it, and everyone will come. Shakespearian shows always draw well. You remember the time when the Ben Greet companies came?"

"Yes, rather. Of course, we sha'n't eclipse them—still, we can do our best," smiled Madge Minden. "And Polly has no stage-fright. It's good to have a lead who is not at all afraid."

"Of course it is. Polly is the girl we rely upon. In fact"—Betty looked seriously at her chums—"it seems that we're relying upon Polly for everything. My word, what chance should we stand against the Fifth without Polly?"

And there was a shaking of heads then. There was no jealousy amongst these chums. They knew only too well their worth, and the worth of their companions. Some things they could do

better than Polly. At French—indeed, at most lessons—Polly was the worst of them all.

But in other things she excelled, and only too willing were they to give praise where praise was due.

"By the way," said Tess Trelawney, suddenly thoughtful, "where is Polly?"

"Mais oui," Trixie Hope agreed in her strange French. "Où est elle? Where is she?"

And there was no Polly to tease her then about the French exercises.

But only a few moments later they heard footsteps in the corridor, and Madge flung open the door.

"Wonder what she's brought?" Tess asked, with shining eyes, as the footsteps sounded nearer.

And they gathered eagerly in the doorway, expecting to see Polly arrive with her arms laden, and her merry eyes laughing.

But what a difference! It was Polly sure enough—but such a Polly! A Polly who walked without the usual sprightliness—a Polly whose face was no longer flushed, whose eyes no longer glinted mischievously.

For a second or two there was silence—a hushed silence that might almost have been felt. Then came from Polly a laugh, a laugh so jerky that it sounded unnatural.

"No luck!" she said in dry tones. "No remittance that post. So we'd better play Mother Hubbard."

"No luck—oh!"

"Well, never—never mind," Betty said with rather an effort. "It doesn't matter. Don't look so down, Polly dear."

"Yes, wather, pway do cheer up, Polly dear!"

"Aren't I cheerful?" Polly asked in hollow tones, her lips trying to smile, but her eyes dull. "It—it's so jolly here, one—one ought to be glad—to be happy that one can be here at all——"

The last words were spoken as if to herself, and the girls stared. Then Betty, always the leader, took her chum by the arm.

"Polly," she said anxiously, "what is the matter, dear? That letter—no bad news? Your father is all right—they're all right at home——"

"Oh, yes. I—nothing like that," Polly assured them; and as she looked from one face to another she tried to brace herself up.

Betty, seeing that nothing was to be gained by pressing the girl with questions, sought to raise the weight from her mind by arousing some fresh interest.

"We've had news," she said. "The Fifth are

getting up a concert in aid of the fund; that means they'll get in first. You know what they are——"

"My word!" Polly exclaimed, really interested now, and forgetting that heavy weight that had so depressed her. "What on earth are we going to do? Get ahead of them? Rag their music?"

Betty shook her head.

"Better not," she advised. "No—we've decided that after all we'll give ' Julius Cæsar.' It's a long time since a play was given at school, you know."

"' Julius Cæsar '? My word, that's great! '

"Yes, we thought that you'd be pleased. Of course, we're relying on you—you know Marc Antony's part so well. It's bound to be a success——"

"Relying on me?" Polly echoed the words sharply, and she seemed to take a step away from them, her face paling.

"Yes, of course; yours is the biggest part, dear," Betty explained, somewhat amazed. "You know it so well, don't you?"

"Know it, yes—but——" Polly Linton gulped, and there was a strained silence in the study while five pairs of eyes were fixed upon her.

"But what, dear?"

Polly Linton's hand clenched and unclenched; she tried hard not to meet their concentrated gaze, and when at last her voice came, it was husky and low.

"But—I—I can't take part——"

Then, before they could stop her, she had turned and fled from the study, leaving her friends staring at the open door, not moving until the echo of her departing footsteps had died away.

"Can't play—Polly can't play——" Betty echoed incredulously. "But she must—I don't understand. There must be something wrong somewhere. Why can't she play?"

"Ah! Why?" Madge Minden agreed. "There is something wrong—someone has been upsetting her. Polly is not a crying sort, but there were tears in her eyes just now, Betty dear, for I saw them!"

CHAPTER VI.

NO LONGER THE MADCAP

ETHEL COURTWAY, captain and most popular prefect of Morcove School, raised her eyebrows in surprise when she switched out the light in the Fourth Form dormitory.

Although not a noisy form, it was seldom indeed that the girls were altogether quiet when Ethel Courtway arrived on the scene to turn out the lights.

To-night was an exception, for there was scarcely a sound, and most of the girls were lying as still as logs. But Ethel said nothing, judging that the exertions of the half-holiday had probably made them tired.

But no sooner had the door clicked to, and Ethel's footsteps died away, than the dormitory, that had been so quiet, was filled with a buzz of talk.

Some girls, laughing, were scrambling out of bed, despite the warning gestures from Betty.

"Not yet," the captain of the Form warned them. "Ethel isn't far away, and if we make too much noise she'll come hurrying back."

"Besides," Madge Minden pointed out, "the Fifth won't be asleep."

Reluctantly the over-anxious girls slipped back into their beds, and contented themselves as well as they could until their leader should deem it prudent to commence hostilities.

It was not the first time that the Morcove girls had raided the senior form, but familiarity with that kind of amusement did not breed contempt of it.

"My word," chuckled Tess Trelawney, "won't the Fifth have the shock of their lives, eh? Just think of them all, fast asleep, and then——"

The manner in which Tess Trelawney gripped her pillow showed only too clearly what was going to happen to the Fifth.

"I believe," said Madge Minden thoughtfully, "that all the best generals attack at dawn, between the dusk and the daylight."

But that suggestion was not received enthusiastically. Betty Barton rested back on her pillow, and looked out of the corner of her eyes at the bed where Polly Linton was lying.

She had not heard Polly's voice, and Polly, as a rule, was the leading spirit in this sort of enterprise.

"Got your pillow ready, Polly?" Betty asked, as her chum turned over in bed.

And Polly Linton nodded rather uncertainly.

"Just think of them," Tess Trelawney resumed. "All snugly asleep, and then biff! biff!"

"Yes, wather, only don't wumple their dresses, deah geals. The Fifth waided us once, and cweased howwibly a dwess of mine that was lying on a chair. A wag's a wag, but——" she added with a serious shake of her head. "But cwumpling a geal's dwess is very sewious."

"Yes, don't start wagging dresses, girls," cautioned Tess seriously. "Creating a draught might give someone a cold."

"Mais, oui. Il fait froid as it is—it's cold already——"

Polly Linton smiled, but made no response. It seemed as though Polly were making an effort not to join in the conversation.

But she was grinning broadly now, and Betty's

heart leapt. This was more like the Polly of old, she reflected.

"My word, Polly," she laughed. "We'll teach them, eh? We're not going to let the Fifth score, are we?"

"I should think not," Polly agreed. "They've got too much cheek. Why, only to-day one of them referred to us as children. Children—us!"

"Like their cheek," agreed Tess Trelawney. "But they'll have a surprise to-night all right!"

Then for some time there was laughter and talking. They were only waiting long enough for the Fifth Form girls to get safely into bed before they commenced the raid.

At last Betty decided that it was time, and she looked at Polly.

"Ready?" she asked, in a whisper. "Now you can show them, Polly!"

But Polly Linton remained in bed, a worried expression on her face.

Betty had slipped on a dressing-gown, and had put her feet into cosy slippers.

She looked in some surprise at her chum, wondering why Polly, usually in the first line in a prank of this sort, should remain in bed.

"Aren't you coming, dear?" she asked.

"I—I—if you don't mind, Betty, I—I'd rather not, please," Polly returned in some confusion, her face red.

At her words other girls turned, amazed and wondering. Polly Linton—not joining in a dormitory raid—what could possibly be the matter?

"But why, dear?" Betty asked gently. "Don't you feel well?"

For a moment it seemed that Polly was tempted to nod her head, and so get out of the matter easily. But it would have been an untruth, and Polly Linton was not the sort of girl to choose the easier path if it were the wrong one.

"It isn't that," she said worriedly; "but—I'd rather not!"

And beneath the bedclothes her hands were tightly clenched.

Ursula Wade, who was standing near-by, laughed in her unpleasant way.

Polly tipped the ball over the goalkeeper's stick, and the next minute the field resounded with, "Goal! Well played, Polly!"

"Afraid?" she asked. "Afraid you might get caught?"

"Ursula!" Betty flared at the girl. "How can you? It's you who would be likely to be afraid, not Polly?"

"Oh, is it?" Ursula's lips curled. "Then let Polly Linton tell us why she isn't coming!"

It was an awkward moment then when Betty glanced in anxious inquiry at her chum.

That Polly Linton, the madcap of the Form should be afraid!

What could be the matter with Polly Linton? Polly the madcap, first in the field and last to leave it!

And only Betty Barton, with her inner insight and greater knowledge of Polly, was able to realise what it meant for that girl to lie in bed while the others were dressing and gathering their pillows.

Now Polly was sitting up, and her eyes were shining.

"That's the style," said Madge Minden "Pack up your troubles till the morning."

With surprising suddenness Polly was out of bed. She had slipped on a dressing-gown and slippers in no time, and now had gathered up a pillow.

"I—I'll come," she said, with a certain amount of reluctance in her tone.

Betty, greatly relieved, nodded her head, and decided that Polly would change her mind also about the play. For if Polly did not act the part of Marc Antony it would mean that Betty or one of the others would have to learn the words; and there was not very much time at their disposal.

They had relied upon Polly. And really she was the last girl in the world to "let them down." That is how Betty looked at it, and she was quite sure, therefore, that Polly would be in the play when at last it should be staged.

Now Polly was moving more slowly, and it appeared almost as though her sudden high spirits had been dampened.

"If—if we got caught, I wonder what 'd happen?" she asked.

"If we get caught—yes, my word! There 'd be trouble," smiled Betty. "Miss Massingham would be annoyed, and perhaps it'd mean a detention. But it wouldn't be the first time the Fourth has been detained. And, after all, we've pulled off pillow fights before, Polly."

But Polly did not reply. She was sitting on her bed, a troubled look in her eyes.

"If—if you don't mind much, I—I'd rather not come."

Polly's voice came tremblingly, hesitatingly.

The brief silence that followed her words was broken by the jeering voice of Ursula Wade.

"Rather not—hark! The brave Polly

afraid of a pillow fight—afraid you may get hurt?" she jeered.

Ursula Wade was always ready to make trouble—always prepared to make some jeering remark at Betty's or Polly's expense.

But Polly was not a girl to take a remark like that lying down.

A gleam of battle was in her eyes as she rose from the bed, gripping her pillow.

"Afraid?" she asked. "Is that what you think, Ursula—that I'm afraid of a pillow fight——"

Ursula nodded, but less certainly now as Polly advanced, swinging the pillow, and she raised her arm in defence as the pillow swung on to her.

Biff!

It landed heavily, and Ursula, yelping, backed away.

"Polly," Betty exclaimed. "Polly—dear——"

But Polly was too enraged to hear her friend; and Ursula, she was backing away, vainly endeavouring to guard herself from that attack.

She swung her pillow about, and swung her hands, but Polly's pillow attack beat them down, and presently Ursula, gasping, collapsed on the floor.

There Polly, breathing hard, let her remain.

"Now perhaps you'll say that I'm afraid?" she asked.

Ursula's small eyes gleamed with malice, but she made no reply. Which was undoubtedly very wise, and extremely discreet.

Polly, without a word, turned on her heel, and went back to her bed.

In another moment she was tucked in. Betty looked at her anxiously, but said not a word, and in a few more minutes Polly Linton was left alone in that long dormitory. Nor did she stir till they had gone.

Then she sat up in bed and blinked about her. For a while she did not move, then from her dry lips came words spoken in anguish.

"They think I'm afraid—if—if only they knew. But I can't tell them—I mustn't. And now—they don't understand. They don't!"

And while in the Fifth Form dormitory there was turmoil and fun dear to the heart of Polly Linton, that girl sat alone in her bed, tears in her eyes.

She could not join them—why?

But that was a question she could not answer —not even when Betty, her dearest and loyalest friend, asked it.

For Polly Linton was bound to silence!

CHAPTER VII.

"I WONDER——"

POLLY LINTON'S strange change of behaviour was the topic of conversation for some days. That Polly was an altered girl was quite

"Hark at the brave Polly!" jeered Ursula Wade. "Afraid of a pillow-fight—afraid you might get hurt, I suppose!"

evident. But what was agitating the Fourth was to know why.

"I'm bothered if I can understand it. What can be the matter with her?" asked Madge Minden. "You know, Betty, we've been relying on her—and she hasn't been at hockey practice or rehearsals."

"I know," Betty agreed in a worried tone, and the captain's brow was wrinkled. "But what can I do? You know how obstinate Polly can be! And besides, she isn't the sort to let the Form down without a reason——"

"No, no, Polly isn't that sort," Madge agreed seriously. "But it really is a mystery."

Others, however, took a more severe view, and were wrath with Polly.

Only one girl in the Form seemed at all pleased. That girl was Ursula Wade. It seemed to Ursula that the loyal friends of Study No. 12 were at last falling out. But even Ursula, cunning and prying though she was, did not know why.

And it was not because she did not wish to find out. Ursula had a score to pay. She had not forgotten the ignominious scene in the dormitory, when she had felt the force of Polly's arm behind the well-aimed pillow.

But Ursula had to wait her time.

And Polly was allowed to go her own way until the time for the match with the Fifth drew near, and Polly was still not at practices.

"I can't understand it," Betty said, as she banged the ball about with a few of the others. "Polly's the last girl to desert the practices. And if she doesn't practise—well, she won't be fit for the match——"

"And we shall lose," Madge Minden finished. "That's evident. Betty, don't you think we ought to go and see her? Why is she moping inside the school all this time, instead of playing games?"

"Don't know. She—she had a French book when I saw her."

"French!" echoed Tess Trelawney. "You don't mean that she was swotting French, Polly?"

19

And there were others who echoed Tess's amazement. For Polly was not given to swotting—and at French she was, to put it quite plainly, a perfect " dud." The French mistress had told her so many times. Polly had once tried to improve her knowledge of the language, and Trixie, who had explained that the friendly spirit of the Entente should be fostered, had tried to help her.

But it had not been much of a success, and Polly's French went " de mal en pis," as the French mistress described it, from bad to worse.

And now—now happy-go-lucky Polly, the madcap of the Form, was staying indoors with a French book as company when she might be playing hockey.

" It can't be," murmured Tess Trelawney with a shake of the head. " She hasn't been detained. And, candidly, it isn't at all like Polly to stay in without a reason."

" Suppose we go and see her, girls," suggested Betty.

And there was a nodding of heads. A few minutes later, hockey-sticks in hand, they were entering the school-house and making their way to the Fourth Form passage.

" Hallo, door's locked," Madge Minden exclaimed when she tried the handle of Study No. 12.

But a rap or two, and they heard the key click in the lock. Polly Linton, slightly flushed, greeted them. The sparkle had gone from her eyes and a troubled frown had taken its place.

" Hallo," she murmured. " Want me ? "

" Yes, dear. Aren't you coming down to practice ? " Betty asked. " You've been deserting hockey. There's the Fifth Form match soon—— "

" Fifth Form match ? " Polly started. " I —I'd forgotten that. "

" Forgotten it ? "

Five voices echoed the words in amazement, and five pairs of eyes regarded Polly as though she were some strange specimen for a museum. Forgotten an important fixture—*the* important fixture, a match which was the talk of the Form ! The match upon which their whole energies had been centred !

And Polly, the best hockey-player in the Form, had forgotten it ! No wonder they stared at her.

" Gwacious ! "

" I—I'm awfully sorry ! " Polly stammered. " But I'm busy ! "

Even as she spoke they could see over her shoulder the litter of books on the table. Papers and books of all descriptions were there, and the sheets of paper had been written upon recently. Polly Linton was swotting.

" Polly—you—you've been working ! "

The madcap of the Fourth gave a laugh that was slightly hollow in its sound.

" Yes—it—it sounds strange. Everyone speaks in amazement that I should do any work. But —but—I must."

" You must ? But why ? I mean we all must to a certain extent," Betty qualified. " But there's no need to swot all the time and neglect sports. The mistresses don't expect that ? "

" The mistresses ? No. But—oh, I can't explain,"

And Polly listlessly turned on her heel. It seemed that there was a lump in her throat— that speaking was difficult ; and awkwardly her friends paused in the doorway, wondering what to do.

Polly was back in her chair now, seating herself heavily. But her attitude was not natural, and though a book was held in her hand the girls could see that she was not reading it.

Puzzled, and perturbed, they could only stand and stare, not knowing what to make of this sudden change. What was there for them to say ? What was there for them to do ?

" Swotting French ? " asked Trixie Hope quickly.

Polly turned her head and nodded.

" Yes. I'm a dud at French. I—I'm a dud at everything," she added half bitterly.

" Oh, Polly, you're not—you—you're not a dud at hockey."

" No ; but what else, bar games ? What am I good at in class ? "

" Oh—oh, heaps of things, f'rinstance —— "

And there Betty stopped, racking her brains to think of some subject at which Polly was good. But what subject was there ? That indeed was a problem.

Just for a second or so the others stood in the doorway watching, then they vanished quietly, closing the door gently.

Left alone, Polly Linton sank heavily into a chair, and then groped amongst the papers at the back of the table drawer.

She frowned as she did so, then pulled out all the contents, examining each paper in turn.

The look on her face told clearly that what she had expected to find was not there, and a look of consternation filled her eyes.

" I—I can't have lost it, surely," she muttered to herself. " But—but—but where can it be ? "

She searched for several minutes—searched everywhere, then gave it up in despair.

Comforting herself with the thought that it must be somewhere in the study, she settled down once more in her chair, to glance gloomily into the dusky close.

But she would not have sat there so quietly had she known that a few studies away another girl was reading the letter for which she had just hunted in vain.

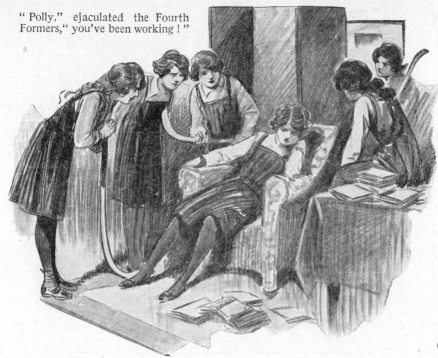

"Polly," ejaculated the Fourth Formers," you've been working!"

"So that is why you have altered, Polly Linton," she said. "No more madcap, no more joining in with the form, for fear you are packed off home."

She glanced down at the letter again, noting the paragraph that warned Polly that she was to say nothing of the matter to anyone, not even to her dearest friend.

"Your father is right, Polly," Ursula nodded to herself. "I haven't forgotten that dormitory scene. You had better take your farewell, for soon it will be good-bye, Morcove, for you."

CHAPTER VIII.

POLLY IS MISSED

And as she read that letter Ursula Wade's eyes gleamed.

"So that's it," she murmured. "I see!"

And she read aloud to herself from the letter.

"'It seems that you are merely wasting your time and my money. Your Form-mistress' report was bad; but I will give you another chance. You may remain at Morcove if during the next weeks I receive from your Form-mistress no derogatory report. And I have instructed her to write to me regularly of your progress. Yet another chance I am offering you of retrieving yourself. In any case, you must pursue your studies hard; but if you succeed in winning the Fisher Scholarship, or show any possibility of doing so, then, of course, the matter will be out of my hands. This will necessitate giving up games and other spare-time occupations. You have called the tune, and now, if you wish to remain at school, you must pay the piper.

"'If not—if you fail to comply with these conditions—then, Polly, much though I regret it, you will have to say good-bye to all that is familiar and dear to you at Morcove.

"'You will find life in an office a change after school, and you must please yourself whether you work at school or in an office. It is for you to decide.'"

Ursula Wade's eyes had in them a peculiar gleam.

"BUT, Polly——"

Betty Barton spoke pleadingly as she looked in bewilderment at the white, strained face of Polly Linton.

"I—I can't, Betty dear. Please don't ask me why."

"Why can't you play, Polly?" Betty insisted, placing one arm about her friend's shoulder. "Why have you taken suddenly to mugging away at dry old school-books instead of joining the form readily? You used to be so keen, Polly dear. Surely you care whether we beat the Fifth or not?"

"Care? Yes, of course I do, Betty. But—well, I'm such a slacker."

In those words there was as much self-condemnation as self-compassion, and Betty Barton, concealing her bewilderment, gripped Polly's arm.

"Well, don't take it to heart so dear," she said. "If it's Miss Massingham you're worrying about, you're just high-spirited—that's all; she ought to know you by this time. Come along, change into your hockey things."

"I am sorry, Betty dear, but—but I can't come."

It was the final decision, spoken as such, and as such Betty took it.

"Very well, Polly," the captain of the Fourth rejoined, a little coldly. "I'm sorry."

And, still puzzled greatly, she went back to the

21

hockey field to tell the others her friend's decision.

To say that they were disappointed would be to express their feelings mildly. Even the substitute, glad though she was to have the chance to play for Morcove, was sorry that Polly could not take her place.

And the Fifth, too, though they wanted to win the match, would rather win it with Polly as an opponent.

It was a glum team that took the field for the Fourth Form. But they were determined to do their best. Some of them were angry with Polly, feeling that she ought to have played, and they in particular were determined to show her—in an independent spirit—that they could get on quite well without her.

Possibly the Fifth Form girls expected it to be " a walk-over " ; but if that were so, they were doomed to sad disappointment.

The Fourth played grimly, and their half-backs hung on to the opposing forwards like leeches.

They fed their forwards well ; but the forwards, without spirited Polly in the centre, seemed lost. Betty was at centre-half, from which position she could act as a pivot for the whole team.

She worked like a Trojan, stemming attacks and starting them by feeding the forwards. Madge Minden, at centre-forward, was playing her best in spirited fashion. But Madge was not so tricky with her stick as was Polly, nor was there the same vim in her smite.

At half-time Betty called her team together. " The score's two nil against us," she said. " But a game's not lost until it's won, you know, girls. Get the ball on their side of the half-way line and they can't score—not if you keep it there."

It was good advice ; for without getting the ball into the goal-circle, scoring was quite impossible, and the closer to their own goal the girls fell back, the nearer to the goal circle were the opponents.

" Clear for all you're worth," Betty advised anxiously to the two backs. " Never mind so much about passing ; if you can get at the ball, smite it for all you're worth to get it right up-field. The forwards should be somewhere around, and they'll get to it first all right——"

" But it's no good banging the ball about anywhere," Tess grumbled. " The Fifth are all over the place."

Betty shook her head.

" Every time the ball leaves your sticks there's the chance of an opponent intercepting it, and you mustn't pass near the goal circle. Get it right away good and hard——"

The whistle went then, and encouraged by their leader the Fourth Form team took the field again.

This time there was grim determination on every face. Polly was missing from the front-line, but there were eleven girls still, and they ought to be able to do something.

The Fifth were smiling rather ; almost as though they regarded the match as too easy ; and Betty noted that fact with an inward chuckle.

If the Fifth-Formers grew careless there was hope yet.

Madge bullied off with the opposing centre-forward fiercely, and the ball was on the Fifth Form's side of the line. Away went the forward up field, passing quickly and accurately.

They were past the half-backs before Trixie Hope, who was playing inside-right, made a mistake.

The tall Fifth Form back was bearing down on them, a sturdy girl who never missed a shot, who was safe if she got within hitting distance of the ball.

Trixie almost mechanically slipped the ball to her centre as the back bore down on her. She had forgotten that Polly was not there.

Madge Minden went to take the pass, got the ball on her stick, and ran. But she had not a sudden burst of speed, and her stick arm was swept aside as the back with outstretched arms banged down on the ball.

Then—biff !

And the ball whizzed upfield towards the Fourth's goal. But Betty with her hand stopped it, and banged it up-field.

But again the Fifth Form forwards got it, and the Fourth retreated. Once again the war was in their half.

What a ding-dong battle it was then ; a battle for victory ; a battle to recover two lost goals and convert them into a third.

But all the time the Fifth kept the ball downfield.

Beyond the half-way line the Fifth Form backs stood, sending the ball back every time that it came their way.

And there was no Polly to rally the forwards, no Polly to charge her way through with a powerful hand and a stick that never wavered.

They knew it—the whole team—that many a time Polly with her unquenchable energy and burst of speed would have streaked up-field on her own if necessary.

Another goal for the Fifth !

Three nil, and the jubilant Fifth Formers returned to the centre line.

Now Betty, her face grim, was waiting for them. How she managed it they knew not, but she kept the ball in the other half. Never once did she miss, but hit with all the vim that was in her.

And it gave the forwards heart. Soon they had the ball, and the backs of the Fifth Form team, surprised, turned languidly—too languidly.

Madge was streaking on, the thudding feet of the panting back close behind her. She stopped suddenly, and the back, unwarned, went careering on, only to find when she did stop that a wing forward had the ball.

She ran to intercept a shot that was coming, and found that instead of a shot the ball had been passed to Trixie, who slipped it to Madge.

Only the goalkeeper to beat—but others running down behind.

Now the goalkeeper, her face tense, was waiting. She rushed, and the ball was slipped to Trixie past the outstretched stick of the back.

And then a deafening cheer shook the ground.

"Goal!"

But before the shouting had died away the shrill note of the referee's whistle told that the game was finished—finished, and lost.

It was long before the cheering died away and the handshaking was finished, and then the Fourth Form team, happy in the knowledge that they had played their best, yet slightly disappointed, returned to the schoolhouse.

"We pulled together wonderfully," said Ella Ellgood. "Madge played centre like a brick——"

"But not like Polly," said Madge quickly. "My word, girls, if we'd had Polly——"

"Yes, if—then truly we should have won," nodded Tess Trelawney. "But apparently she cares more for books than for the honour of the Form."

"Apparently," Betty nodded; but there was a peculiar intonation in her voice; for she knew that when the news of the defeat reached her, Polly Linton would be even more cut-up than the rest. For Polly Linton had set her heart on that match—that match that she could have won, but which through her absence was lost.

Ethel Courtway —the popular head girl of Morcove.

CHAPTER IX.

URSULA GETS BUSY

As the sound of voices came to her ears, Ursula Wade halted and almost instinctively drew into an alcove, pulling a curtain to shield herself.

It was eavesdropping, and distinctly mean; but then Ursula Wade had never been able to lay claim to being honourable.

And now, she was quite anxious to hear the conversation between the two mistresses, only a yard or so away from her.

Their voices gave her their identity, Miss Somerfield, the head mistress, was one, and Miss Massingham, mistress of the Fourth Form, the other.

"I don't know whether it has happened, or whether the prefect who reported it was misled," Miss Somerfield was saying, "but if she is right, and one of the chairs in the Common-Room has been broken, the matter must be investigated at once."

Eagerly Ursula Wade waited for the next words.

"The report is probably correct," nodded Miss Massingham, "and I will investigate and find the culprit."

Ursula Wade knew who the culprit was, for only the previous day she had annoyed Polly Linton with malice aforethought, in the hope that damage would be done. Damage had been done, and the bill would, in due course, be sent to Mr. Linton.

In view of the letter she had read, Ursula could make an accurate guess as to the consequences. But the satisfaction of knowing that her plans had succeeded, that the words she had whispered into the ready ears of a prefect had reached the right place, was completely shattered by the form-mistress' next words.

"I cannot go at once, Miss Somerfield," she said, "I shall be finished with the history papers just before eight. I will go down to the Common-Room at eight o'clock precisely, Miss Somerfield."

And then they parted.

But Ursula Wade remained where she was, drawing a deep breath.

"Good!" she exclaimed, her eyes narrowing as she smiled cunningly. "Miss Massingham will be in the Common-Room at eight."

And then she laughed, as she added the next words.

"And now, Polly Linton, I'm going to play trumps."

Ursula found the Common-Room in a buzz of talk.

There was no need to ask what was their topic of conversation. Voices were raised angrily, and in an arm-chair sat the girl at whom the anger seemed to be hurled. It was Polly Linton.

She had been reading, but at the entrance of the defeated hockey team she had been forced to raise her eyes and meet the accusing glances of her friends.

"Of course we should have won," Tess Trelawney was saying. "Madge Minden played jolly well, but we missed you, Polly."

"I know you did," said Polly rather wearily. "And I'd love to have played; but I couldn't, and there's an end of it."

"That isn't the end of it," Madge Minden returned quietly. "It's all very well to think that the matter can drop there; you've lost us

23

that match. But what about the play? Betty's learning the part the best she can, but it isn't giving her much chance——"

Polly Linton nodded. She was fully aware of that, and she felt it perhaps more keenly than the others did; but she could not help it. It would not do to risk anything now—and it would be risking things if she disobeyed her father's rules.

He would be certain to hear of the play, and he would know that she had taken a big part, the rehearsal of which must have encroached upon her spare time. He would know, then, that she had disobeyed him.

"I'm bothered if I can understand what's the matter with you," Ella Ellgood said impatiently.

Ursula Wade heard all this with evident satisfaction, and now she advanced to the centre of the room. She could see that Polly, unable to explain the reason for her altered conduct, was becoming annoyed at constant questioning.

To be loyal to one's form and yet appear disloyal without even having a chance to prove one's loyalty, was enough indeed to make Polly annoyed.

"You want to know the reason," Ursula Wade asked, "why Polly Linton did not play in the match this afternoon, and why she's backed out of playing Marc Antony?"

The girls wheeled on her, and Polly Linton simply stared.

It was obvious by the look in Polly's eyes that she wondered momentarily if Ursula Wade had found that missing letter.

But if she expected Ursula to tell the whole story, and her true reason, she was mistaken—and relieved.

Ursula Wade gave a glance at her watch, and the corners of her lips twitched slightly.

"Doesn't it occur to any of you," she asked, "that Polly might have a reason for wanting the Fifth to score."

"A reason? What do you mean?"

At that startling suggestion the girls were on their feet, and Polly, too, was staring in as much amazement as anger at her cunning Form-fellow.

Ursula Wade shrugged her shoulders, and pointed accusingly at Polly Linton.

"I mean," she said, "that Polly Linton is being well paid to see that her Form loses."

For a moment or two after that dramatic statement a pin might have been heard to drop. Polly Linton's cheeks flushed, and with blazing eyes she faced her accuser.

"You—you dare!" she choked, "to suggest that I——"

Ursula laughed.

"I have suggested it," she said coldly. "You have been well paid to let the Fifth win that

hockey match, and now you're going to make the play a failure."

Trembling with rage, Polly Linton snatched a cushion from the chair, and Ursula Wade, with much cunning, moved so that she stood in front of the huge clock.

"You dare say that," Polly exclaimed through her teeth. "It's not true, and you know it."

Ursula Wade raised her hand to smooth her hair, and in so doing glanced at the watch on her wrist. It wanted but a minute to eight o'clock.

"I do say it," she said. "You have betrayed your Form——"

The incensed Polly raised her arms, and the next moment the cushion was flying through the air. Like lightning Ursula moved aside, and the cushion crashed against the face of the clock. Next moment there was a mighty noise, as the clock fell—smash!—on to the floor.

"Oh, gwacious, Polly, deah geal!"

"Polly!"

Agitated, alarmed girls stared at the smashed clock, and there was a hushed silence.

But one girl was staring in quite another direction. That girl was Ursula Wade. Ursula's eyes were fixed upon the Common-Room door, which was slowly opening.

And now, as Miss Massingham entered, the girl drew back. Betty Barton, in a last effort to save her chum, stooped to gather up the wrecked clock.

Too late!

As figures in a tableau, the girls stood motionless; while Miss Massingham, horror in her eyes, regarded the smashed clock, looking from it to the rather challenging, flushed, angry face of Polly Linton.

"Polly!" she exclaimed, amazed. "You—— you have done this——"

"I—I—it was an accident!"

"That cushion—you used that as a missile. You recently used me as a target," the mistress remarked acidly. "Apparently my warning was not enough. Follow me to my room."

But she paused, remembering her reason for entering the room. And then—only one question was needed, and Polly Linton, resigned to the hopelessness of her position, admitted to the damage.

Thunderous indeed was the mistress' brow then, and when the Common-Room door closed there was a buzz of talk. And the girl who was the centre of discussion began to wish that she had not been so very clever.

"You planned it," Betty Barton was exclaiming angrily. "This is your doing, Ursula Wade —you stood in front of that clock because you intended that Polly should break it."

"Yes; and what is more, she knew Miss

Massingham was coming," Madge Minden put in, more fiercely than she had ever spoken before.

"I—it's not true," Ursula expostulated, completely flustered.

"I saw you," Madge said in her more usual dignified way. "You cannot deny that you were hiding when Miss Massingham and Miss Somerfield were talking, because I saw you—I wondered why you were listening; now I can guess."

And then, almost without a word being spoken to suggest it, Ursula Wade found herself shunned—found that she had been "sent to Coventry"—sentenced to silence!

That she realised the enormity of that punishment, the slight shiver she gave showed. But for Ursula there was no way out; and she learnt that the way of the transgressor is indeed hard.

Nor was Ursula the only one to learn that hard fact. Polly Linton, as she accompanied the stern-faced Form-mistress, was far from happy. At first she had been resigned to her fate, for that was Polly's happy-go-lucky way.

But now the full importance of it all dawned upon her.

She had failed—failed ignominiously.

What would her father say to her—what could he think of her? How could she induce him to believe that she had tried, tried hard, to alter her ways?

He would not believe it, and she realised that she could hardly expect him to.

No, no, this was the end, without doubt. All her endeavours had been of no avail. She might have played for her Form, and helped them win their match—she could not have had a more ignominious end, anyway.

And before the mistress in the study she stood motionless, not speaking, scarcely moving.

"I am very sorry that this has happened, Polly," the mistress sighed. "But you must realise that I have endeavoured to guide you. What report can I send your father now? The bill for the clock's repairs will be sent to him—also that for the repair of the chair. You understand?"

"Y-yes, Miss Massingham."

The words were heavily spoken, with head bowed; and the mistress, a sympathetic chord in her being touched, gave the girl a kindly glance.

"At least you have the grace to be sorry," she observed. "You may go, Polly; doubtless your father will punish you sufficiently."

And Polly, with those last words still ringing in her ears, went from the room listlessly, to she knew not where.

To go back to the Common-Room to face her chums for perhaps the last time? Oh, it was impossible! Where could she go? What could she do?

As she stood in the cool corridor, facts surged into her head.

She had failed! She must leave the school. That would be her father's verdict—for had he not said as much in his letter?

Her feet guided her to the large door that led into the school grounds, and she wandered towards it. But, as she did so, her eyes observed small, familiar things —things that had become part of her life.

Ursula ducked, and the next minute the cushion sent the clock crashing to the ground

It seemed that every little nook and corner, every chair, picture, and window, had some history that was forged with her own.

These old school steps—how often she had run up them and down! How often her tired feet had dragged up them after a stern game of hockey, or descended them stealthily at some hour when she should have been in the school!

Good-bye—good-bye to all that was near and dear to her! Oh, why, why had she not been different? Why hadn't she set her mind to work in working hours, as others did? If only she were like Betty. If only—and so the vain regrets tormented her; the past, relentlessly unalterable. How clearly, in indelible ink, her small misdemeanours seemed written in those pages. Too late now to turn over a new leaf and start afresh.

Not until lights bobbed up in the dark outline did she realise that it was bedtime. Bed-time, and her last night in the school, of that she now felt sure.

Choking down the lump in her throat, she walked swiftly to the school-house, mingling with the crowd of girls mounting the stairs.

And to her chums' questions she gave but scant replies. To speak at all was difficult. But to tell them the truth—to tell that it was " Good-bye ! "—she just couldn't.

CHAPTER X.

ONCE MORE HER OWN MERRY SELF !

How anxiously Polly glanced through the tall dormitory windows as she dressed the following morning, dreading for the first time in her life the sight of her father, arriving as a moral policeman to capture a wrong-doer.

It was just as she was fixing the ribbon to her hair that she saw him ; and she remained transfixed, only her trembling hands and quivering lip showing that she was not a carved stone figure.

He had arrived—and now the blow had fallen ! Her heart thumped in her throat, and she knew that her pale cheeks had crimsoned. She dared not look at the other girls, but hurried from the dormitory, knowing full well that Betty was following her—yet consciously closing the door in her friend's face.

The blow must fall in private—no one should witness her humiliation. Suppose she cried—what would they say then—what would they think ?

Down the stairs she blundered, only to pause on the bottom one as her father entered the school-house.

Stern eyes—reproachful and unforgiving—they were not the eyes she met !

For about her father's lips a smile played, and his eyes twinkled.

" Polly ! " he cried. " What splendid fortune——"

Dazed, she blinked at him—perhaps he did not understand—perhaps he had not been told all. She must tell him !

He took her hands, and kissed her cold lips. As he did so the twinkle in his eyes gave place to the reflected worry in her own.

" Why, Polly, little harum-scarum—what's the matter ? You look ill—haven't you slept well ? "

" I—I—yes—but—daddy ! " Her voice was hoarse, and she buried her head on his chest, whilst his hand stroked her hair.

And all at once she felt safe—he would understand—he must ! How stupid she had been to regard him as some fierce figure—fierce, her father ! Hysterically she began to laugh ; but he silenced her.

" Come, come, Polly, what is the matter—something is wrong ? Tell me——"

" Your—your letter," she gulped. " Daddy I have tried—I did try to be different. I—I gave up games, and the play, and I've worked ever so hard. Really, I have. Then—then everything went wrong. I didn't mean to break that clock or the chair—it was an accident——"

" Letter—clock—chair——Why, darling, what on earth do you mean ? You talk in riddles. Come, now, what is it ? "

And, really worried, Mr. Linton led his daughter into the cold fresh air.

" From the beginning, now," he said gently."

" This letter—what letter——"

" The letter you wrote me the other day," she cried, puzzled at his manner. " Daddy, you must remember. You—you threatened to take me away and put me in the office if—if I didn't improve. Miss—Miss Massingham sent you a report——"

For several seconds he stared at her as though she were talking in some strange, inexplicable language.

" But, Great Scott ! " he burst out. " I haven't written you a letter, child ! I had a report from Miss Massingham, yes, and I wrote to her—but not to you——"

" Not to me," the bewildered girl cried. " But—but it was typed on your little typewriter, and you signed it—I know your signature, daddy."

He stared at her, round-eyed, and for several seconds did not speak.

" But, gracious, Polly, I've never written you such a letter. I had no such idea in my mind. My poor child—and have you been imagining——" In sheer stupefied amazement he paused, unable to fathom that mystery—as to why his daughter should receive such a letter. " I wrote to Miss Massingham," he continued—" er—quite a different sort of letter. Excusing you for your high spirits, which you—er—possibly inherited from me. But, as for writing you such a letter, 'pon my word, the idea's absurd. Where is the letter ? "

" I don't know, it's lost," Polly cried, her cheeks aglow and her eyes sparkling. She did not trouble to solve the mystery. All that concerned her was the knowledge that her father had not written the letter. She was not going to be taken away from Morcove. She wanted to shout, and laugh, and sing!

But, as though to make assurance doubly sure she turned to him a little anxiously.

"Then you're not going to take me away from Morcove, daddy?"

"Take you away! Great Scott, no—I've just come down to fetch something your aunt left at the Manor House, so dropped in here to see you——"

His next words were smothered—speech was made quite impossible—for, with a relieved, happy daughter clinging to his neck, and kissing, kissing interminably, speech was not easy. It was also not necessary.

.   .   .   .   .   .

Mr. Linton left Morcove that afternoon. He departed with ringing cheers sounding in his ears, and the memory of a very festive tea in Study No. 12 with Polly and all her friends.

As he turned in the lane to wave to the group of girls he smiled, and continued with rejuvenated, springy step. The smile, however, soon vanished, and a steely look replaced it—the grim look, tight-lipped mouth, and set jaw, symptoms that Polly had feared to see.

Those fearsome symptoms were not for Polly, however. Mr. Linton had recalled a certain circumstance that cleared away much that had puzzled him.

Distinctly he remembered writing that letter to Miss Massingham—a letter which, he discovered, had never arrived. In its place had arrived the letter that had caused so much trouble. Who could have changed those letters —who could have wished to change them— but the girl who had taken his letter to post?

Vera Somers—how eager she had been to post that letter—she who always tilted her nose at even the suggestion of meniality in a task. That she should have been eager had struck him as peculiar at the time—but he had merely concluded that it was a sign of a change for the better in Vera.

That it had not been so, he now realised. Also he realised why Vera had been so keen to practise on the type-writer; why she had collected his autograph!

To Polly he had allowed it to remain a mystery, lest the humiliation of the exposure should serve to increase Vera's hatred.

But to Polly, life seemed all sunshine again, and the black cloud had lifted for ever.

Once again she was the happy, care-free Polly whom they had always loved—laughing, joking, teasing.

"And now I'm never going to leave Morcove," she laughed. "When a new girl comes in nineteen sixty, she'll want to know who the distinguished old lady with the aristocratic stoop is."

And Polly placed a hand on her back, stooped, and hobbled across the study, to the merriment of her companions.

"I shall go down to posterity as the only old-aged pensioner prefect of Morcove——"

"Yes, wather! Howevah, pewwaps not the only one, Polly. I fancy I shall wemain heah for many yahs, y'know. Pewwaps in nineteen sixty I shall still be playin' the leadin' parts in dwamatic entertainments—yes, wather! Talking about plays, though, I shall be Marc Antony after all. To be or not to be, y'know—yes, wather! That's the question. Howevah, that it is——"

Betty took her by the arm.

"Oh, you goose, Paula! That speech is Hamlet's, not Horatio's; and, anyway, Horatio is in the play 'Hamlet,' not 'Julius Cæsar.'"

"Good gwacious! Are you quite suah?"

"Quite," said Betty seriously. "Never mind, you shall learn Julius Cæsar's part in the Forum scene, dear. You sit down quietly and learn it."

"Yes, wather. I will wehearse my part now."

"Good!" said Polly, with a chuckle. "We can have a little quiet. Julius Cæsar is dead in that act. So practise being dead—and remember dead men don't talk."

That quiet overcame Paula, and she was actually quiet—"rehearsing."

But when the final rehearsal did come, Paula was up to the mark, and fairly "put her back into it," as Polly said.

What a day it was, too—that play-day! The hall in the village had to be decorated; a thousand and one things had to be attended to.

It was going to be a triumph for the Fourth and a triumph for Polly Linton.

And when the night arrived, and Polly triumphantly played her part, the hand-claps she received were ample compensation for the troubles and trials she had endured.

There was her father in the front row, with her mother beside him, and his applause was the sweetest of music to her ears.

No wonder, then, that Polly's face was flushed, and that at the end of the play she forgot her Roman traditions and executed a war-dance that seemed a combination of a Highland fling and a sailor's hornpipe.

But Polly didn't give a rap for traditions, she was happy. All the clouds had rolled by, and she meant to revel in the sunshine.

"The same old Polly!" laughed Betty Barton happily.

And then the curtain fell, closing the play— and our story.

THE END

YOUR OWN SCHOOL MAGAZINE

I DON'T think there is a schoolgirl in the world who hasn't at some time or another hankered to write either a story or article, and have it published in her very own school magazine.

I know I did, and many and varied were the attempts I and my school friends had at turning out a school "mag." that would reflect credit and glory upon us. But, alas! our efforts almost always turned out failures, principally because we hadn't enough "stickability" to carry our too ambitious schemes through.

However, I was very interested the other day in seeing a magazine that was brought out by a niece of mine and her school chums; and I made up my mind, when the Editor of the SCHOOLGIRLS' OWN ANNUAL asked me, to tell you all about it.

The "mag." that was very proudly displayed to me was absolutely the girls' own work from start to finish. They had contributed the features enclosed, written them out, put them together and had bound the finished thing.

And very nice it looked.

❁ ❁ ❁

THE COVER

The cover—a most important part of any magazine—had been designed by someone apparently of an artistic bent. Yet it was in no way elaborate or out of the ordinary.

A buff-coloured, stiff paper had been employed for the cover, and a simple border made of vivid black and white squares, which stood out boldly, had been employed by way of decoration.

A simple scroll design filled up part of the space inside the border, and the name of the school and the form to which the girls belonged was boldly and effectively printed in old English lettering.

So much for the cover.

On the first page of the magazine was a note by the Editor, stating that this was the first number of the magazine, but that she hoped the "mag." would be a success, and have a long and happy life.

Then we commenced the magazine proper.

❁ ❁ ❁

GOOD TITLES

A story, very well written indeed, came first. I certainly thought this a good idea, for there is nothing that catches the eye so much as an attractive title of an attractive story. This one was called "The Ghost of the Manor," a thrilling title, as I know you will all agree.

As I have said, the story, written by a girl of, I was told, about thirteen, was very good. I enjoyed reading it very much, while picturing to myself the enjoyment the girl herself must have got as she penned those words.

Next came a very interesting feature—the reports of the various platoons of the Girl Guide companies connected with the school.

Next came an article by a girl who compared boys' school tales with girls' school tales. She brought out very clearly the good and bad points in each, and wound up by saying that, though she certainly liked girls' tales best, she had a sneaking admiration for stories written alone for boys.

❁ ❁ ❁

THE SERIAL

Then I came to really what was the choicest thing in the "mag"—the serial! If you want to make a success of your magazine, girls, you must have a really thrilling serial which ends at a really thrilling moment and leaves you longing to know what happens next.

Of course, this most important item of your school mag. should be written by a girl who is thoroughly competent. Just imagine the tragedy if she suddenly announced that she couldn't do a line more of that story, not if you all begged her on bended knees ! And this, I assure you, is the feeling that almost invariably comes to youthful authors when they get so far into a story. They get in a fix and cannot imagine what to write next. It is a tragedy indeed !

So be careful in your choice of a serial writer, for on her depends a lot.

Next came a few illustrations.

A very clever girl had drawn a splendid series of quite harmless little caricatures of various girls on the hockey field. A very tall girl was seen with a tiny stick chasing down the field to meet a tiny goalkeeper who looked most alarmed ! One girl, famous for trying to play golf instead of hockey, was shown with her stick far above her shoulder, shouting " Fore ! " as the ball went sailing up into the air, and so on. Not one of them was unkind, and not one could have hurt anyone. You simply had to laugh at the quaint positions in which some of the girls had been drawn.

A little poem came next which dealt with the behaviour of the class as a whole, respectively in class and in " rec." The girl who wrote it had managed to be very funny over the studious air and silent tongues of the girls in class, as compared with the noise and laughter that went on the minute they were freed from the class-room.

We then came to a story dealing with characters in the school three hundred years ago, when, in place of the modernised building that now stands, there was a convent, where the kindly nuns trained the girls of that day, and taught them marvellous tapestry work, and wonderful embroidery—a very exciting story, that kept me thoroughly interested from start to finish.

❖ ❖ ❖

A WORD OF CAUTION

Just a word here, girls. Don't have anything in your magazine at any time that mistresses may not see. There is no need to say that any allusion to mistresses in your " mag." is not only very disrespectful, but very " bad form."

And so the magazine went on. It represented much honest work, and fun, too, and struck me as being a sensible and very satisfactory effort.

Certainly the girls had every reason to be proud of their first school magazine.

There is no reason why any form or school should not club together in this effort to produce your own " mag."

Admittedly, it's hard work, especially for a poor, harassed Editor who has to exercise both tact and discrimination in her choice as to what shall or shall not go into the magazine.

Naturally, every girl in the form would wish to contribute. At the same time, it is a fact that there are some girls gifted in the literary way, while others couldn't write a story if they tried.

❖ ❖ ❖

THE EDITORIAL CHAIR

It's the Editor's task, then, to pick out the stories, articles, poems, and drawings that strike her as best. Certainly no girl should become annoyed if the Editor sees fit to hold out her effort. A girl who is awfully good at geography may not be able to do composition at all, and therefore, although she has every right to have a shot at a contribution, she must smother her feelings of wounded pride if her contribution is set aside to make room for a better one.

The general appearance should certainly be considered very deeply when the " mag." is being put together. Distribute your stories, illustrations, poems, and articles so that you do not get things of a kind in a bunch together.

As for binding the magazine, the way in which my niece and her friends managed was to connect two pages by means of a narrow strip of white linen-paper, pasted carefully on the right-hand edge of one page and the left-hand edge of another. Thus the separate sheets of paper were bound together, and the whole thing was then affixed by means of a strip of black linen tape between the two cardboard covers, and fixed in position at back and front in the same manner as the pages were.

If you are getting out your own school magazine, aim at working together, putting up with things you don't like and knuckling under to the Editor you have chosen as the best girl to carry out your project.

29

Through Perils to Fortune.

A Story of Two Plucky Girls in the Wilds of Alaska

By Gertrude Nelson

The two girls were muffled in furs. Their ages were sixteen and fifteen respectively, Lucy being the younger.

Though sisters, they offered something of a contrast to one another in looks. Whilst May was inclined to be dark and had long-lashed, steady grey eyes, Lucy had brown hair that would gleam with many amazing tints of gold when caught by the light, and her eyes were a deep blue.

The sisters were, however, alike in their natures. Both possessed sterling courage, a fact that was proved by their having elected to accompany their father into the frozen wastes in search of gold rather than remain behind in Dawson.

His original business had involved the purchasing of furs from trappers. But, forsaking this after a lean period in the way of trade, with his daughters he had joined a rush that had been made some months before in this direction upon rumours reaching Dawson that gold had been struck.

The tales, however, of an Eldorado had proved to be greatly exaggerated.

Many claims had been staked out, but subsequently abandoned in disgust, and upon only one, in addition to that of the Jeffries', was work still going on.

This was situated almost immediately alongside the property of the Britisher and his daughters, so near, indeed, that the boundaries adjoined, and it was worked by a certain Caspar Lefroy, a descendant of French-Canadian trappers, and his daughter, Stella, a girl of about May's age.

Luke Jeffries examined the contents of the pans as his daughters lifted them from the water in the tub. His bearded face had grown haggard

CHAPTER I.

THE NEIGHBOURING CLAIMS

"TIME to go back to the shack for dinner, girls!"

Luke Jeffries tossed aside his spade and re-donned his fur cap and jacket.

He walked to where his two daughters, May and Lucy, stooped over a large tub washing the soil their father's spade and pick had been turning up.

All through the bitterly cold morning the trio had ceaselessly toiled on their claim, which was situated near the last fringe of dwarf pines, fronting slopes of snow.

For, soon, work would be next to impossible for many weeks. Within perhaps only a matter of days now, King Winter would thrust out his icy hand and the great Alaskan Range, which, with its peaks veiled in clinging mist and volcanic fumes, stretched away to their left, would be swept by relentless hurricanes of hail and snow.

And the claim had not paid well enough of late to admit of taking matters easily.

of late, and there were times when a dull despair would creep into it.

May's serious grey eyes became sympathetic as she saw that same hopeless look steal into her father's face now.

For weeks the precious metal obtained from the washings had been growing less and less, and this morning the residue of gold-dust that had remained in the pans after the earth had been washed away had scarcely paid for their labours.

"Don't give up hope, father dear," Lucy said, laying her fingers affectionately upon his arm; for she, too, had not failed to see his glum expression as he looked into the pans. "We may strike it rich, as miners say, even yet."

"I am sure we shall if we keep persevering, when the weather will allow, daddy," May declared, trying to hearten him. "There are parts of the claim you have not yet tested—the part that adjoins the Lefroys' property, for instance."

Luke Jeffries opened his lips to make some sceptical remark, but ere he could do so a step sounded on the thin layer of snow that covered the rocky soil near at hand.

Father and daughters looked round, to find

Then father flourished his whip in response to the loud "Good-byes!" of May and Lucy.

their neighbour, Caspar Lefroy, approaching. Like themselves, he wore the usual furs. His clean-shaven face was swarthy and deeply lined, and his dark hair and brows, his hawk-like nose and thin lips, told of his French-Canadian descent.

When he spoke, however, it was in almost perfect English and with only a very slight accent.

"What luck this morning, Jeffries?" he asked as he raised his heavily gloved hand and removed from his lips a cigarette he was smoking.

"Luck!" Luke Jeffries laughed harshly, bitterly. "We have had the usual luck, and that's about as bad as can be, as you know. And you?"

"Stella and I have not been working very hard this morning," was Caspar Lefroy's reply. "We are tired of slaving and getting next to nothing for our pains. I am thinking, as a matter of fact, of selling our claim, and I wondered if you would care to do likewise."

May shook her head.

"Father is not the sort of man to wrong another," she said a little coldly, for she had always experienced an instinctive dislike and mistrust of their neighbour. "And it would amount to that, Mr. Lefroy, if we sold out to anyone. Our claim is worthless."

A girl whose furs could not quite hide the slender grace of her figure had joined Caspar Lefroy in time to hear the words.

She had an olive-tinted skin and almost vividly scarlet lips. Her wealth of hair was jet black and lustrous, and she carried her small, well-shaped head at a haughty poise.

She was Stella, Lefroy's daughter, and, as her dark eyes fixed themselves upon the face of May, her lips curled scornfully.

"My father was not proposing to defraud anyone," she said, tossing her head. "He would have told you that if you had not interrupted, May Jeffries."

"That is so," Caspar Lefroy nodded, addressing the father of the English girls. "I have a brother, Pierre, in Good Hope Falls, through the Yahna Pass, who would be willing to buy both claims, yours and mine. We discussed the question when I was in the settlement a few weeks ago. Worked as one, they would give one man a fairly comfortable living, and he is anxious to take over my property here when Stella and I leave for Dawson."

"Are you leaving, then?" Luke Jeffries inquired with a trace of surprise, for he had heard nothing of this.

"Yes, and we want to get through before the winter sets in, if it is possible," the other answered. "If you think anything of my suggestion, you can find Pierre at any time in Good Hope Falls, and can fix the business up with him on the nail. I have told him your approximate yield."

"I'll think it over, Lefroy," Luke Jeffries said.

With a nod he turned away, and, followed by May and Lucy, left the claim and walked to the rather spacious log cabin they had built near the pines.

It possessed three rooms, the sleeping quarters of the girls, those of their father, and the living room which was the largest of the three, and heated by a central stove. The air struck warm and cosy after the biting cold outside.

There was also an outhouse, in which eight sledge-dogs and a sledge were kept. Occasional visits had to be made to Good Hope Falls for supplies, and that was a forty-mile journey overland. Travelling by the river, which lay near, some ten miles could be saved, but the river was frozen over now.

May laid a cloth on the rough bench that served as a table, whilst Lucy produced some tinned beef and damper. A kettle was singing on the stove, and the girls' father brewed some tea, making it brown and strong, as is the custom in the frozen North.

The two girls saw that he was deep in thought during the meal that followed, and they conversed together in lowered tones and did not break in upon his meditations. It was not until their father had pushed aside his tin plate and finished his mug of tea that he spoke.

"We will work no more to-day, girls," he said as he rose to his feet and carried his chair near the stove. "It is quite right what Lefroy says. The two claims do not pay when worked separately, but jointly they would give one man a living. I shall harness the dogs to the sledge in the morning and see Pierre Lefroy at Good Hope Falls. If he will buy, he can have our claim. It is starvation for the three of us, and we may as well get rid of it and avoid being snowed in here for the winter months, when, for the most part, we shall be getting no dust at all."

"You know best, daddy," May said, putting her arms round his neck and kissing his cheek. "I think I shall be glad to get away. Although Stella Lefroy never makes herself very sociable, it will be terribly lonely when she and her father have gone."

"I shall be glad, too, to leave," agreed Lucy.

"You, father, will be much happier in business again in Dawson or some other town."

Luke Jeffries nodded.

"I shall indeed, lass," he answered. "It is pretty heart-breaking here at times. I shall start as soon as it is daylight. I shall be back in four days, and, unless the winter—the real winter sets in earlier than usual this year, there should be time for us to pack up and get through to Dawson. Well"—bitterly—"good-bye to our dreams of fortune!"

They went early to bed that night, and were up with the first golden flush of dawn.

After breakfast, which included the inevitable damper and tea, a move was made to the outhouse. The eight wolf-like dogs, with their queer, bushy tails, fawned upon the two girls in delight, for both May and Lucy loved animals and were apt to make much of them.

Luke Jeffries fed them, put a supply of provisions in the sledge for the dogs and himself, then harnessed them. A crack of his whip, and the dogs drew the queer-shaped conveyance out on to the powdery snow that covered the ground.

"Good-bye, dears!" said the girls' father, kissing each in turn. "I'll stop at the Lefroy's shack and just let him know I am going to see his brother. Mind you take care of yourselves whilst I am away."

He climbed into the sledge. Another crack of his whip, and the dogs started forward, drawing the sledge after them on its curved runners.

"Good-bye, father! Good-bye!"

Both girls waved their hands in farewell and, looking over his shoulder, their father flourished his whip in response. They watched him draw up at the cabin of their neighbours and converse for a few moments with Caspar Lefroy and Stella, who came from their dwelling in answer to the "Coo-ee!" he gave.

Then the sledge jerked forward once more, heading for the Yahna Pass, which was easy enough to penetrate now, but which would be impassable when the dread hurricanes and snow-storms of the winter proper began.

May and Lucy continued to look after it until the pine-trees hid it from view. Then they returned into the cabin and busied themselves with washing the crude tin plates and mugs and in tidying the rooms.

That afternoon they took their skates to the river, which was only some ten minutes' walk from the dwelling. The healthy exercise quickly induced a pleasant glow and they did not leave the ice until night was on the point of falling.

Taking off their skates, they put on the snow-shoes they had had strapped to their backs, for, near the river, the snow lay deep and thick.

Chatting and laughing together, happy in the thought of once more returning to comparative civilisation, they turned their faces homewards.

The way led quite near to their father's claim, and, as the two girls came within sight of it, Lucy suddenly gripped her sister's arm.

"Look! What is that light?" she said, pointing.

May halted and stared away through the fast-gathering gloom towards the claim. There certainly was a light twinkling there, and, after standing for a moment with her delicate brows knitted in wonderment, May turned in that direction to investigate.

Her sister followed her, and, with their snow-shoes making no sound upon the powdery snow, they reached the claim and moved forward in the direction of the light.

They could see now that it emanated from a lantern which had been stood upon a boulder. A fur-muffled figure was crouching on hands and knees upon the ground quite near and apparently doing something amongst the rocks that dotted this part of the property.

It was that adjoining the boundary between Luke Jeffries' claim and the property of Caspar Lefroy, the portion that so far remained unworked.

Lucy's snow-shoe came into contact with a loose stone and sent it rattling against a rock. A gasp broke from the kneeling form. Its owner sprang up and spun about, and the two girls uttered exclamations of surprise.

The intruder was Stella Lefroy!

"Why, hallo, girls! How—how you startled me," she exclaimed, obviously agitated but trying to conceal the fact. "Rough, my puppy, has wandered from its mother and I thought it might have strayed into your property," she added, referring to the offspring of one of her father's sledge-dogs of which she had made a pet.

May had trodden upon some object that lay on the ground. She stooped and raised it.

"Do you usually look for lost puppies in other peoples' claims with a pick-axe?" she asked quietly; for such the object was.

"A pick-axe? That is not mine," Stella declared. She gave a toss of her head and took up her lantern. "I hope you do not think I came into your stupid old claim to steal," she sneered. She gave a laugh which, however, did not ring true. "I assure you that I would not rob you of what very little gold there is."

With another haughty movement, she swept past the two British girls and disappeared into the darkness, making in the direction of her father's cabin.

But, although she had left the pick-axe behind, both May and Lucy knew that it must have been she who had brought it there and that she had spoken

A fur-muffled figure was crouching on hands and knees—searching.

S   33   C

falsely. They had helped their father collect up all the tools and appliances on the claim on the preceding day, and carried them to the outhouse adjoining their shack. That no pick-axe had been left there, they were certain.

A sudden suspicion leaped into the mind of May, and although it seemed to her a little wild at first, she turned to her sister and said :

"Go and fetch a light, Lucy ! I want to find out what she was doing here."

Lucy glanced sharply at her sister, surprised at the excitement that was in her tones. She left the claim and went to their cabin, to return a few minutes later with a lighted lantern swinging in her hand.

May took it from her and stood it upon the ground. By its light she saw that the rocky soil had been loosened, and, with her cupped hands, she removed the top layer, which looked as though it had been replaced and patted down with human hands—doubtless those of Stella Lefroy.

A cry broke suddenly from the girl's lips, and she caught at her sister's hand and dragged her down upon her knees beside her.

"Look ! Look !" she cried, almost hysterically. "That is the 'puppy' Stella was searching for."

Lucy stooped nearer and, in her turn, she echoed her sister's excited exclamation. For, in the cavity Stella Lefroy had hewn with her pick, a glittering, yellow vein ran through the rocky soil.

"It's gold—a rich vein without a doubt ! Perhaps a mine of it !" May cried. "It must start on the border of Lefroy's claim and become more extensive in ours. They knew of this when Caspar Lefroy put it into father's mind to sell out to his brother. Oh, Lucy, they have swindled him ! I expect it was just curiosity that brought Stella here to-night. She wanted to make sure of what her father had suspected, and we caught her in the act. She thought, I expect, that as father was away we were safe in our cabin and perhaps in bed !"

Lucy's eyes had filled with indignant tears.

"If we had only known before father started for Good Hope Falls this morning !" she said, clenching her hands. "It's the fortune he has slaved and hoped for, and now he will sign it away for next to nothing, for we have no way of letting him know."

"There is one way—our skates !" May cried, springing to her feet. "By taking to the river and travelling all through the night, there is just the chance that we can overtake him before he reaches Good Hope Falls !"

CHAPTER II.

A RACE AGAINST TIME

LUCY gave a cry of enthusiasm. She realised that what her sister proposed was possible.

The Yahna Pass, which their father had taken with the sledge, took endless torturous turns through the hills, whilst by river a traveller could make in a direct line for Good Hope Falls, and save nearly ten miles.

Then they knew that their father would be compelled to halt at a half-way cabin, to rest his dogs, whilst they would travel all through the night. Lucy thought it likely that they could get ahead of him and intercept him at a point where there was an opening into the pass and the river skirted it at some five miles from the settlement.

They lost no time in preparing for the start. Hurrying to the cabin, they put into knapsacks sufficient provisions to last them the long journey, and with these strapped to their backs, and carrying their skates, they set off back to the river on their snow-shoes.

Reaching the hard-frozen water, they changed their snow-shoes for the skates. By this time the moon had risen and the great crystal-like expanse of the river was made almost as light as if it had been day.

May was the first away, after they had strapped their snow-shoes upon their backs with their knapsacks. Leaning forward, and with her hands clenched and her arms swinging, Lucy shot after her and caught her up. Then, side by side, they skimmed swiftly away over the ice, the steel of their skates giving out a musical ring.

The great race against time, the race that might prevent their father from throwing away a fortune, had begun !

On, on, ever onward over the moonlit ice sped the two girls, the mountain range on their left, and dense pine woods on their right on the far bank of the river.

One mile, two—five, were left behind, yet at present they felt exhilaration born of rushing through the keen air rather than fatigue, and they kept pressing steadily and swiftly forward.

As a matter of fact, their plan was to cover fifteen miles before making a halt for a short rest at a riverside cabin they knew of. Both realised that they must not spare themselves. Every nerve, every muscle would have to be strained, if they were to achieve their object and stop their father reaching Good Hope Falls.

At length, the river grew more narrow, bringing the pine forests on its right bank to within some fifty yards of the girls. May chanced to look in that direction as they skimmed along, and Lucy heard her draw her breath in sharply.

"What's the matter, May?" she asked, slowing down and wheeling gracefully; for her sister had stopped.

"There's something flitting through the trees over on the bank, dear," she said. "Ah, see! There it is! It's some sort of animal, I think."

Lucy followed the direction of May's eyes and saw an indistinct shape creeping along in the confusing shadows beneath the ghostly-looking trees. It was long and light-grey, almost white in hue and——

A long-drawn-out howl floated over the ice, and Lucy caught at May's hand in alarm.

"It's a wolf, May!" she breathed tensely.

May nodded, her face grave. There had been no mistaking the sound, when the prowling animal had given tongue. It was a wolf, and it was seemingly stalking them.

"Let us keep on, Lucy," the elder girl said. "It isn't often that a wolf by itself will attack human beings. It may be hungry and be trying to pluck up courage to pursue and leap at us, but I doubt if it will come to that."

They skated on. But whenever they looked towards the trees it was to see the dim shape of the wolf speeding level with them amongst the trunks, and there was an anxious look in May's eyes. She did not like the howl the animal had given. Although she had said nothing of her misgivings to her sister, she wondered if it had been a call to others of a pack lurking in the forest. And wolves gain courage when strong in numbers.

Abruptly, the stalking wolf again gave tongue, and May's worst fears were confirmed. For distinctly, from somewhere in the forest in the rear, there sounded an answering howl.

"Oh, May, there's more of them—a pack!" cried Lucy, her tone terrified. "What can we do?"

May dashed into the shack and snatched the pen from her father's hand.

"Race on as hard as we can for the cabin where we planned to rest," May answered quickly. "It cannot be more than five or six miles away now."

Necessity lent them wings. They crouched forward like racing cyclists, and fairly flew over the ice. The one wolf kept pace with them, however, and soon other sinister shapes joined him amongst the trees.

How long would elapse before the pursuing pack took the ice and came in direct pursuit?

Mile after mile the girls covered, with the formidable creatures always keeping more or less abreast of them. Then, at last, both girls gave gasps of relief. In the moonlight they could see the cabin between three and four hundred yards ahead on the left bank.

With a last desperate burst of speed, they headed for it. But, almost simultaneously, the night was made hideous by a series of howls, and, glancing over their shoulders, they saw, to their dismay, that the wolves were breaking from cover at last and taking to the ice.

In the one swift look she gave, May judged that the pack numbered a score, and, with the large, almost white wolf they had first glimpsed leading, the animals were now in full cry after them.

"Quicker! quicker!" May panted; and they strove to increase the already whirlwind pace at which they were travelling.

They reached the lone shack, but the wolves seemed to understand that they were in danger of losing their prey, and quickened their onrush. As the girls stumbled in upon their skates, and May slammed to the door, one of the animals flung its body against it and almost dashed it open again.

"Quick! Find the crossbar. There's bound to be one," the girl panted, as she pressed her shoulder against the door. The moonlight streamed in at the one window. Lucy saw the length of wood, caught it up, and placed it in its sockets, barring the door.

It seemed that now the wolves were baffled, and, though one was still scratching at, and throwing itself against, the door, and others were howling hideously in their disappointment, May and Lucy felt that they could afford to take no notice, and they proceeded to build a fire with some of the chopped wood that had been left near the central stove.

Fuel, and provisions, too, if they can be spared, are always left in these lonely shacks by the last traveller to halt at them. It is an unwritten law of the Frozen North.

The fire was soon blazing cheerfully, and the girls removed their skates and sat by it. The faces of both were a little white. The continual scratching and thudding at the door, and the dismal howls of their fierce foes, were beginning to play havoc with their nerves.

Then, suddenly, an unlooked-for danger threatened. The window of the shack was formed of a single sash, hanging upon hinges so that it could be raised from within, and it must have been left unfastened by some former occupant.

The girls heard it creak upon its hinges, and, as they glanced round, to their horror they saw that it was being forced up, and that the head and forepaws of a gaunt grey wolf were actually through the opening.

With his jaws wide, his tongue lolling out, the animal was striving to claw his way into the shack.

Both leapt up. May seized one of the skates and hurled it towards the animal. But it missed, and, had it not been for the presence of mind of her sister, another moment would have seen the snarling creature in the cabin.

Lucy snatched a burning brand from the stove and sprang across the shack. Then, without an instant's hesitation, she thrust the blazing length of wood full into the face of the animal. It uttered a snarling howl of terror, toppled back, and disappeared.

The window fell, and Lucy twisted the wooden button that secured it ; and yet another desperate situation was saved.

For an hour or more the sisters could hear the wolves prowling around the shack, ever and again sniffing and scratching at the door. Then all became strangely silent, and, looking from the window, May saw a sight that surprised her.

The whole pack of animals were making off across the ice. May called Lucy to her side, and the two girls watched the wolves as, at a smart pace, they made for the forest and were lost amongst its shadows.

"It's strange they should give up their attempts to reach us so suddenly," Lucy said. "I wonder what made them tear away like that, and if they will come back ? "

May shook her head. She was as puzzled as her sister, and both were even more surprised when, after they had dozed fitfully by the stove and morning came, they found that there was no sign of their foes having returned.

They were to understand later, however, the grim significance of the sudden departure of the pack. Another and even more relentless danger was imminent as they left the shack, readjusted their skates, and resumed their journey.

CHAPTER III.
THE HURRICANE

MAY and Lucy skated the ten miles to the spot where the hills were broken and the river joined the Yahna Pass in record time. But the hope they had had that they might intercept their father was dashed when, having changed their skates for their snow-shoes, they made their way into the valley.

In the snow were the unmistakable tracks left by a sledge and dogs. Fast though they had travelled, their father was ahead of them.

Progress now was much slower, and anxiously both wondered if they would still be in time to prevent their father signing away his claim. They had journeyed some four miles of the five that had lain between them and Good Hope Falls, when both noticed a sudden change in the atmosphere, and, looking up, they saw little wisps of feathery snow begin to descend and dance along the ridges of the hills that enclosed the pass.

The girls knew dismay, and in a flash they understood why the wolves had beat so abrupt a retreat on the previous night.

Their instinct had warned them of the impending change in the weather that had now arrived, and had made with all speed for some safe lair.

Winter—the real, cruel winter, of the mighty North—was about to descend, accompanied by all its relentless perils. The dancing snowflakes, the icy wind that had suddenly fanned the cheeks of the girls, heralded the coming of a hurricane.

"Lucy, we have not got to lose a moment ! " May said, as she clutched at her sister's arm. "Come ! We must put our best foot forward, or we shall never reach Good Hope Falls at all."

Lucy said nothing, but she plodded along as fast as possible in her cumbersome snow-shoes, knowing full well the danger of being caught in the impending storm of wind and snow.

For half a mile they pressed onward with only a few wisps of snow falling about them. Then a sudden, abrupt rush of icy wind buffeted them, and almost flung them off their feet. It held particles of snow which lashed at their faces like a whip and threatened to blind them. In a second or two their garments were hardened like a shell, whilst the blood began to move sluggishly in their veins ; for, lashed by the wind, the fall had commenced in grim earnest.

The snow whirled ceaselessly about them. Underfoot it quickly deepened. They were soon stumbling through a foot or more of it, and the wind formed treacherous drifts into which one or both would ever and again stumble and fall at full length.

Their sufferings became acute. They were numbed, blinded, almost suffocated by the fury of the blizzard that swept about them. Their faces grew stiff, and every breath they drew became an agony, as if their very lungs were freezing.

But then, as they were almost on the point of giving up hope, they heard shouts from ahead. They had reached the end of the pass ; some trappers had seen them from the window of Good Hope Fall's general store, and had hastened forward to bring them safely into the settlement.

Half-frozen though they were, the girls refused the offers made them to come into the store and partake of hot tea. They asked for the residence of Pierre Lefroy, and were directed to a hut near the store.

Both stumbled through the whirling snow towards it, and May flung open the door. It was to see her father seated at the table with a swarthy-skinned man, who bore a strong resemblance to their neighbour back at the diggings. A pen was in Luke Jeffries' hand, and he was about to append his signature to a paper that lay before him.

"Stop !"

May dashed into the shack, snatched the pen from her father's hand and flung it to the floor. The dark-complexioned man, who was evidently Pierre Lefroy, leapt to his feet, his face paling and his eyes filling with a baffled rage.

"May ! Lucy !" Luke Jeffries stared at them. "How do you come here ? What is the meaning of this ?"

"We followed you to stop your being swindled out of a fortune, daddy," May answered, with a contemptuous glance at Caspar Lefroy's fellow conspirator ; and then quickly she told her father of the discovery of the preceding night.

"I knew nothing of this," Pierre Lefroy declared virtuously. "I vow that I did not, and——"

Luke Jeffries cut him short with a short laugh.

"The good news makes me generous enough to believe you—or to say I do," he said drily, as he tore the agreement he had been about to sign into tiny fragments—"though many might be rude enough to call you a swindler. Girls, you must come to the store and have something hot to drink at once. You look half-frozen."

He slipped an arm about the shoulders of each, and drew them from the shack.

The terrible Alaskan winter has come and gone, and the golden sunlight of summer shines down upon the Jeffries' claim and the near-by log cabin.

May and Lucy are in the living-room, preparing a meal for their father and a mining engineer who a week previously arrived from Dawson, and who is now prospecting on the claim.

Under the floor of the living-room lies sufficient gold to make father and daughters rich for life, and within a few days the mine is to pass into the hands of a company, and they will be setting out for England.

The vein has proved richer and more extensive than the girls could have anticipated even in their wildest dreams.

With packs upon their backs, Caspar Lefroy and his daughter, Stella, emerge from their shack. Their claim has already been taken over by the company, though at nothing like the figure that will be paid to Luke Jeffries, on whose property the bulk of the vein lies, and they are bound for Good Hope Falls.

It is at that moment that May and Lucy step out into the sunshine. Stella sees them and gives a scornful toss of her head before following her father towards the Yahna Pass.

But in her eyes smoulders a baffled anger. She can never forget that, through the pluck of the British girls, her father's plans for colossal wealth came to nought, and that he was prevented from robbing Luke Jeffries of the fortune for which he had toiled and hoped for so long.

THE END

AMATEUR THEATRICALS FOR GIRLS

A USEFUL LITTLE ARTICLE WHICH WILL HELP TO MAKE YOUR PLAY ON "BREAKING-UP" DAY A HUGE SUCCESS

By ALMA BULEY

"EVERYTHING and everyone ready?" asked the stage manager. "Then—up with the curtain!"

And the curtain went up, and the play began.

Quite a simple little affair it was—the actors numbered only about ten, and the whole thing didn't last more than an hour, yet everyone said what a huge success it was, and praised the actors until they were in danger of becoming swollen-headed.

Still, they deserved praise.

I'll tell you why.

The girls who took part in that play had got it up quite on their own, without any adult help at all; and they had made a success of it, simply because they had determined from the first that they would do so. They let **nothing** stand in their way.

Nothing? That included all sorts of things. It included absolute obedience to the four girls they had chosen to give out the parts; it included harbouring no feelings of jealousy when various girls did not get the big parts they expected to have. It included listening patiently to all sorts of criticisms, and taking note of them, and trying to improve.

Those were just a few of the things that were included in that "nothing." But the result was a delightful little play, excellently rendered, which had obviously been well rehearsed, and carefully thought over.

Every girl loves to act; it's one of the instinctive things in a girl's nature to long to dress herself in gowns, grand or unusual, and appear behind the footlights. And there's a lot of good fun to be had out of amateur dramatics—which, on the other hand, mean a lot of hard work, and eating humble pie, too, if you would make them a success.

As I have already told you, these girls of whom I speak had determined to make their play a success.

Their first step was to choose a play that had a suitable number of characters—a not-too-hard-to-accomplish background, since they had in mind the fact that they must make their own scenery, and not too elaborate gowns, since they knew that they must also make these themselves.

There are quite a number of little "playlets" in various elocution books that would serve for this purpose, while some, of course, are printed in books by themselves.

The next thing these girls did was to choose the four girls they considered the best to form a sort of standing committee, which would serve to decide all important matters, such as the choosing of parts, "cuts," and, later, to officiate as producers, criticisers and advisers—in fact, these girls were chosen to "boss the show."

At the same time the other girls had a say in what was, or was not to be, and anything about which question arose they decided by general vote. That decision held good.

It was wonderful what they accomplished in this way. Instead of spending half their time arguing as to who was, or wasn't, most suited to such and such a part, these girls left it to the joint producers, who submitted the list of parts to the rest of the "company." Of course there were some disgruntled ones, who imagined they had a better claim to one of the big parts; but these decided to accept the vote of the majority, and very sensibly made up their minds to make the best of their small parts.

Then every girl set to work to thoroughly learn her part before the first rehearsal was called. That had been insisted on by the "managers," who knew too well the results if any girl "skimped" learning by heart.

Then the rehearsals commenced.

Of course they were hopeless at first. Does anyone ever know their "cues"—where to come in, or go out; how to walk, and how to stand. Backs to the "audience" (which consisted of empty chairs); standing in a slouching, ungainly attitude—these were common mistakes which everyone makes at first.

Of course, every actor should always face the audience, when possible; stand, and walk in an upright manner; unless, of course, the part demands that they should "slouch," as, for instance, in the case of an old woman.

Then the enunciation.

Girls are always inclined to "gabble" their words when they are repeating a thing, especially when they are absolutely word perfect. They want to get it over as quickly as possible, while it is still there in their heads, and the consequence is, very often, that they tuck down their heads, fix their eyes on the floor, and say their "speech" as rapidly as possible.

Of course, that portion of the audience at the back of the hall cannot hear a word, and one is apt to get annoyed if one hears a series of unintelligible mumblings coming from the stage, in place of clear, understandable diction.

Every word should be said, at first, very slowly, and distinctly; the word, if ending with a consonant, should be clipped rather sharply. "G's" are terrible to say clearly, and it sounds very ugly to hear a person talking about "goin'," "singin'," and so on. Also *never* drop the voice at the end of a sentence.

It is very hard, at first, to accustom yourself to perform actions naturally. One is inclined to stiffness and awkwardness, but if the actions are insisted on the whole time during rehearsals, they become far more ordinary and natural.

The next thing to consider will be the frocks and costumes needed.

Of course, it's not wise to choose a play that needs very elaborate "dressing," as probably your actresses will have to make their things at home. Pocket money doesn't go far when there are costumes to be considered, and so it is wisest to try to make the best of what you have at home.

It is wonderful what can be contrived with old lace and coloured curtains, which are of no more use for their original purpose. These make splendid "trains" and "cloaks," and

with a little ingenuity, and the addition of brightly coloured pieces of material, can be given a very convincing air of "richness."

If you want topboots, contrive them by means of a piece of cardboard, carefully rolled, and pasted with shiny black paper, which is obtainable at any stationer's.

Shawls, scarves, big droopy hats, aprons—all these are easily obtainable, and Mother, doubtless, will be sufficiently interested in your schemes to help you here, with all the arranging of frocks and gowns that you cannot do yourself.

By all means have several dress rehearsals, so that you can thoroughly accustom yourselves, and one another, to your novel "get up." You don't want to spoil the show on the night by suddenly seeing the humorous side of some of the costumes, and having a bad attack of the "giggles."

This is a form, by the way, that nervousness often takes with some amateur actresses. They get worked up to a state of high excitement, and then, when they get on to the stage, are incapable of controlling their mirth. This is always a pity, and if you know a certain girl is rather apt to laugh at the wrong moment, I should certainly try to keep her out of the whole thing. Nothing is quite so catching as "giggles." I have seen a whole company of girls simply helpless with laughter about nothing at all, while the audience patiently waited for them to get on with the play.

Use "make-up" with discretion, if you think any is needed at all. It is better to trust to your natural acting ability to carry you through, than to spoil yourselves with too much, or badly applied, make-up. A little powdered rouge may be used on the cheeks, as this is quite harmless, and comes off with a plentiful application of cold cream.

Servant parts and humorous caricature parts should be given to the girls who prove themselves the best actresses. It isn't always the heroine who has the hardest part, or the part which reflects greatest credit upon clever portrayal, you know. The heroine may walk off with a large part of the applause which is really due to some minor character, who has some far more difficult acting to do.

Choose the tallest girls to take masculine parts, if there are any included in your play; and, here is another tip, don't stipulate that your heroine *must* be pretty. If a girl who hasn't so many good looks is more suited to play the part, give it to her. She'll look pretty enough when the night comes, and in putting the question of looks first, you might make a fatal blunder.

Two very important people in your little "company" should be the stage manager and the "property" manager. The former should attend to all such details as the curtain and light arrangements and, too, should have a big say as to the "placing" of the actors on the stage. She is responsible, too, for scenery effects, together with the property manager.

The latter, of course, has to see that every actress is provided with the "properties" necessary. And, I assure you, this is no easy job. Things have a nasty little habit of getting lost—at the wrong moment. The property manager has to keep a keen eye on the play, and must know just when and where the actresses are coming "off," and if they need any "props" when they go on again.

For instance, I once witnessed an amateur show wherein one of the chief characters was supposed to pull a Union Jack out of his pocket and wave it aloft, shouting "Britain for ever! Hurray for the Union Jack!"

He put his hand into his pocket, and the audience saw him hesitate and stammer, whilst a blank expression spread over his face.

We all knew well enough that the "props" manager had forgotten to query whether he had that Small Union Jack or not, and the actor himself had forgotten it.

However, he was resourceful on the whole, and pulled out his handkerchief, and waved it vigorously.

But it didn't seem to have quite the same effect, you know, and, instead of being impressed, the audience badly wanted to laugh!

So you see, girls, it is really important that if a character is required to pick up a letter to read aloud, that a letter should really be lying there; or should a glove, for instance, be the main point of interest, that glove must not be forgotten.

For all these little details, important to the smooth running of the play, the "property" manager is responsible, and therefore, to fill this important rôle, I should advise you to choose one of those methodical, quiet girls, who sets about a job and does it thoroughly and well.

She should make a list of all the things needed for every scene, and make sure before the actors are ready that every single thing is at hand, no matter how small or how large it is.

If you want footlights to your play, it's certainly advisable to consult someone older than yourselves. It's a very dangerous business to contrive them with lanterns, etc., and electric lights are not easy to arrange. On the whole, amateurs would do well to leave out the footlights, since they are not really necessary if the stage is properly lighted in other respects.

For the raising and lowering of the curtain, the stage manager is responsible. She may choose to officiate in this capacity herself, or to employ someone else to do it, but this, like everything else, should be rehearsed. So many times have I seen the curtain refuse to act at the crucial moment.

Here are a few closing "tips."

Don't choose a play that is too long.

Remember that "practice makes perfect."

Try, on the night of the play, to really enter into the spirit of it, and forget your audience.

It's only selfish people who spoil things through self-consciousness—don't think about yourself or your audience. Think of the other actors, and how nervous they're feeling, then your nervousness will vanish.

And remember, that unless you all work together, you'll accomplish nothing.

THE END

HER FATHER'S HONOUR

A SPLENDID GIRL GUIDE STORY

By Mildred Gordon

CHAPTER I.

THE LEADER OF THE ROBIN PATROL.

"I DON'T think it's right," said Sylvia Deakin, tossing her fair hair from her shoulder. "Nothing ever happens in Golden Manor. It's the sleepiest little town in Great Britain. We Guides don't get a chance to distinguish ourselves!"

The usual weekly meeting of the Golden Manor Girl Guides was taking place in the little drill hall in the heart of the town.

Company drill was over, and Miss Ingleby, the popular captain, was marking the attendance book while the Guides stood in little groups conversing for a few moments before they were split up into sections for special study in guide work, such as signalling, basket-making, first aid, and so on.

Sylvia Deakin, the only daughter of Sir Gregory Deakin, the richest resident in the town, was a member of the Robin Patrol, and around her, listening with amused interest and smiling faces, were Amy Pryor, the leader, a dark-haired, rosy-cheeked girl of fifteen, whose sleeves were literally smothered with badges she had won, and three other Robins.

"Why do you sigh for excitement, Sylvia?" asked Amy. "If Golden Manor is a sleepy little place, it is also one of the prettiest. Where can you find a place with a better bay and cliffs and such rugged sea views? Think of our caves and our glorious, bracing air, and our ancient church, and——"

"And our wonderful old hermit who lives in an old railway carriage and has the finest crop of whiskers for miles round!" cut in Doris Meynell, a plump-figured, jolly girl, who found it difficult to be serious about anything.

"I'm glad you mentioned the old hermit, Doris!" cried Sylvia. "He's the only person in Golden Manor that distinguishes it from any other seaside town in the country."

"Even now I don't understand what you mean when you say that we don't have a chance to distinguish ourselves, Sylvia," said the leader of the Robins. "Do you want something exciting to happen in the town?"

"Yes, I do!" said her friend. "I'd like a wreck to occur off the coast, or a fire or a robbery —something to happen so that we Guides could really show the world that we were of some use. I don't mean that I want people to suffer or to be in danger——"

Amy smiled as she shook her head.

"You couldn't have a wreck or a fire without somebody suffering," she interposed gently. "It

41

might provide us with a little excitement for a day or two, but it would soon be forgotten."

"What I was really thinking about was something I read in the newspaper this morning," said Sylvia. "I forget the name of the town, but that doesn't matter. It was about a plucky Girl Guide who dashed out into the roadway and stopped a runaway horse and cart just as the frightened animal was about to dash on the pavement amongst a number of school children. I'd love to have an opportunity like that."

"It was a splendid deed!" Amy exclaimed. "Any Girl Guide would be proud of accomplishing it. I don't suppose the girl thought about the terrible risk she was taking. If she had slipped down in the roadway as she tried to pull up the horse, she might have been run over and killed."

"We'll have to arrange some thrilling exploit in Golden Manor purposely for Sylvia," laughed Doris. "I fancy I can see it in the newspapers already. 'Brave Girl Guide at Golden Manor leaps one hundred feet into the sea to save——'"

"Don't be silly!" Sylvia interrupted her. "I shouldn't think of leaping into the sea to save anybody. It'd be too wet and cold," she added with a merry laugh. "I suppose we'll have to put up with the sleepy old town and make the best of it."

"After all, nobody can make heroic incidents," said Amy. "If anything startling ever did happen in Golden Manor I expect we should all be ready to do our duty."

Miss Ingleby got up from her table at this moment and gave a few sharp commands. The Guides separated into groups for special work. Amy was soon giving demonstrations of the way to bandage broken limbs and the Guides watched their instructress and listened with rapt interest.

When the meeting was over and the Guides were dismissed, Amy, Doris and Sylvia, as was their custom, went home together.

"I've been thinking of what you were saying, Sylvia," Doris laughed. "I know you are dying to be a heroine in something, but if anybody is to be that in Golden Manor, it'll be Amy."

"I don't wish to be a heroine," Amy said, as they laughed. "I'm quite satisfied with things as they are."

"Well, I'm not!" Sylvia exclaimed. "Golden Manor is far too sleepy a place for me."

"Perhaps, after all, if we had the startling adventure you are sighing for, we should wish that nothing had happened," said Amy, as the friends separated.

Amy soon reached her own home. The brass plate on the door announced that "James Pryor, Solicitor," resided there.

Amy's mother had died two years before, and since then she had acted as her father's housekeeper.

The solicitor had felt the loss of his wife very keenly. A gentle, kindly man, immersed in his books, a dreamer and abstracted, he needed someone to keep a close watch on him, as he was always forgetting things and getting into muddles over his business.

As Amy stepped along the little path before the house she could hear her dog, Gipsy, barking violently within the house.

"I wonder what's the matter with Gip?" she murmured. "He doesn't usually make a noise like that."

The front door was on the latch. Amy turned the handle and let herself in. There was a light, she saw, in her father's office, situated in the front of the house.

As she passed into the hall the dog came to her, bounding up to her with delight.

In the doorway stood a man of about medium height, dressed in a shabby green overcoat that reached almost to his heels. A long white beard was hanging from his chin. The old felt hat he wore kept his eyes and face in shadow.

The visitor was old Silas Magson, the eccentric miser, who was said to be wealthy, and who had achieved notoriety by living in an old railway carriage on the cliffs outside the town.

The solicitor, clean-shaven, silver-haired at the temples, with deep-set, dark, dreamy eyes, was sitting at his desk twisting a pencil about in his fingers.

"Good-evening, Mr. Magson!" Amy exclaimed, giving her father's client a genial smile.

"Evening!" grunted the hermit, and turned his back on the girl. "You won't forget to put that business in hand, Mr. Pryor," he went on. "I shall be away for at least a week. I shall expect the conveyance to be ready directly I return."

"It shall be ready and waiting for you," replied the solicitor.

He got up from his chair to usher his client out. Amy was standing in the hall, hanging up her coat and mushroom Guide's hat, as the two men moved towards the door.

"Come here, Gip!" she cried, as the dog ran after the hermit and kept up a noisy barking. "Quiet, you bad dog! Keep quiet!"

She could not understand why the animal was so excited. Whenever the hermit had called before, he had been quiet enough, though, as a rule, he took a dislike to most shabbily-dressed people who came to the house.

"Strange fellow—Silas Magson!" said the solicitor, when he came back along the hall after closing the door. "He seems to get more eccentric every time I meet him."

"I was quite ashamed of Gip," said Amy. "Has he been making a noise all the time Mr. Magson has been here?"

"I suppose so," said her father, his thoughts wandering. "I—I really haven't noticed. Don't bother me now, child. Let me see—what was it I wanted to remember?"

Amy tripped away to the living-room at the end of the hall with the collie running joyfully at her heels.

It was supper-time, and she had a good, healthy appetite. She had the table laid and everything in readiness for the meal when there was a knock at the door.

When Amy ran to open it, she found Sir Gregory Deakin, Sylvia's father, a tall, imposing-looking man, standing on the threshold.

"Hullo, Amy, my lass!" cried Sir Gregory cheerily. "I want to speak to father for a minute."

He passed along to the solicitor's room just as James Pryor came out.

"Good-evening," said Sir Gregory. "I want those title deeds and bearer bonds I left here. Now you've examined them they'll be better in my safe at home."

The appearance of his rich client appeared to make the solicitor more than usually nervous.

"Why, of course—of course, Sir Gregory!" he said. "They're quite in order. I had them here a little while ago. Now, where did I put them?"

James Pryor moved his long, white fingers in confusion amongst the papers which littered his desk.

"Can I help you, daddy?" asked Amy, hurrying into the office. "I remember the papers. They were in a big blue envelope."

"Yes, that's right, child," agreed the solicitor. "They must be here somewhere. Dear, dear! I wish I wasn't so forgetful. I must have put them somewhere for safety, Sir Gregory, and forgotten where it was."

A slight frown crossed the baronet's face.

It was because the solicitor was abstracted and forgetful that he had decided that it would be safer to keep the papers, worth several thousand pounds, in his own home.

"Oh, well, I can't wait any longer," Sir Gregory exclaimed. "Have a good hunt round for them, Pryor, and let me have them first thing in the morning."

"Certainly, Sir Gregory," Amy's father answered. "I'm sorry I've had to disappoint you. Don't be anxious about them, sir. I had them on my table a little while ago."

"Oh, I know they're quite safe with you, Pryor," returned Sir Gregory. "Good night!"

"Good-night, sir!" said the solicitor.

James Pryor closed the door and slipped the bolts into their sockets.

"Come along, daddy," cried Amy, from the sitting-room. "Supper is all ready. There is no need to bother about the papers now. I'll help you to search for them as soon as the plates have been cleared away."

The solicitor stood with bent shoulders, his face pale and troubled, looking towards his clever, cheery daughter.

"No, no, child. I—I've got no desire to eat now," he stammered. "I must find those papers first. They're in here somewhere."

"I'll come in and help you, dad. We'll soon find them between us."

Half an hour was spent in searching the little office. Every drawer was turned out. Piles of papers in the two cupboards were looked through. Amy only paused when there was not another place to search.

"They're not in here, dad," she said at last. "I think you must have hidden them away somewhere out of this room."

The solicitor stood in the middle of the office with ruffled hair and wrinkled forehead, papers strewn on the floor about his feet.

"Good-evening, Mr. Magson!" Amy exclaimed. "Evening!" grunted the hermit.

43

"What ever will Sir Gregory think of me?" Amy heard him murmuring. "But they can't be lost! They must be here—they must! It's really very mysterious and suspicious, too! Now I wonder——"

Amy touched him gently on the arm.

"You are looking tired and overwrought, daddy," she said softly. "Come and have your supper. You'll soon find Sir Gregory's papers when you are fresh and rested in the morning."

Her father pushed her away from him.

"You have your supper, child, and get to bed," he said almost sternly. "Leave mine on the table for me. I'll come when I've finished here."

Amy ate her supper alone. After the meal was over she sat reading for a few minutes, then she went into her father's office to give him the customary good-night kiss.

"Poor daddy," she said gently. "You look worn out!"

Her father forced a smile to his white lips.

"Don't worry about me, child!" he exclaimed. "Go to bed and sleep soundly. I think I know where those papers are."

"Splendid!" cried the leader of the Robins. "I'm so glad, daddy!"

She put her arm affectionately about his neck and pressed her lips to his cheek.

CHAPTER II.

THE MYSTERY OF AMY'S FATHER.

THE sun was shining through her windows and a chaffinch was piping on the laburnum tree outside when Amy roused.

"Good gracious!" she cried, looking at her wristlet watch, which lay on a table beside the bed. "Half-past eight already! I'm awfully late this morning. Daddy will be wanting his breakfast. It's a wonder he hasn't called me."

Amy dressed quickly. On her way to wash in the bathroom, she passed the door of her father's bedroom. It stood wide open.

"Hullo, daddy!" she called out cheerily. "Are you all right this morning? Did you find those papers?"

There was no answer. The house seemed unusually silent and still. The only noise-maker was Gipsy. In his kennel out in the garden, the collie had heard his young mistress's voice, and was barking.

Amy's face became pale. She stepped into her father's room. She started with a little shiver as she saw that the bed had not been slept in!

"Daddy, daddy, where are you?" she cried anxiously, as she ran downstairs.

Her father was not in his office. The floor was strewn with papers, just as she had seen it overnight. She hurried into the other rooms. She saw that the joint of cold meat and the loaf of bread had vanished from the table, though the clean plates showed that the solicitor had not sat down to a meal.

"What ever has happened?" murmured Amy, her cheeks white as snow. "Oh, daddy, where are you?"

As her eyes roved round the living-room, she caught sight of a letter propped up on the mantelpiece before the face of the clock.

She ran across the room and seized it.

"To Amy" was written on the envelope. She recognised her father's thin, artistic handwriting instantly.

With trembling fingers, she tore the envelope open and extracted a sheet of paper. This is what she read:

"My dear Child,—I am afraid you will be very shocked when you read this letter. It will be better for you to think me a coward than to know that I have been sent off to prison. It's all through Sir Gregory Deakin's papers. I can't find them, Amy, although I've hunted everywhere. I know what Sir Gregory and the world will say; they'll say I've stolen them, and that I've run away to avoid punishment and disgrace. But you will believe in your old daddy. You will know, I'm sure, whatever faults I've got that I'm not a thief. I'm distracted and broken-hearted. I can't bear the shame and disgrace of a trial.—YOUR FATHER."

Before she had finished reading the pathetic letter, Amy's eyes were blinded with tears.

She sank down in her father's chair by the table and, in the fulness of her grief, gave way to despairing sobs.

"Why didn't he stay and face the trouble?" she murmured, her emotion spending itself. "If the papers are missing, someone has stolen them; but it was not daddy! Sir Gregory knows that he's not a thief. By running away, daddy's made everyone think he is!"

Amy dried her eyes and set her practical mind to thinking out what was the best thing to do.

She let Gip into the house. It seemed comforting to have the collie with her. She went upstairs to the bathroom, washed, and completed dressing. She made up her mind while she was brushing her soft, luxuriant, dark hair.

"It's only right that Sir Gregory should be the first to know of his loss," she decided.

Without troubling about breakfast, she got out her bicycle and, with the collie trotting behind her, set out for Sir Gregory Deakin's house on the sea-front.

Sylvia Deakin was on the tennis-court at

the side of the house, amusing herself with a racquet and a ball, when Amy sprang from her machine.

"Hullo, Amy!" cried the girl, smiling. "I'm so glad you've come! I was just longing for someone to play with me!"

"I haven't come to play tennis, Sylvia," Amy answered gravely. "Will you ask your father if he can see me?"

"Dad's in his study," said Sylvia. "Of course he'll see you!"

She ran across the lawn and tapped on the French windows. Sir Gregory appeared and talked with his daughter for a moment.

"Bring your bike in here, Amy!" Sylvia cried. "I'll be playing with Gip while you're talking with dad."

Amy wheeled her bicycle into the grounds and stepped through the French windows, and faced the baronet in his cosy study.

"Good-morning, Amy," said Sir Gregory cheerily. "Father is busy, I suppose, so he has sent you with the papers? Of course, I knew——"

"No, sir; I—I haven't got them!" stammered Amy. "I've come to——"

Her voice failed her. Tears appeared in her big, tender eyes.

"Father's gone away, sir!" she blurted out.

Sir Gregory sprang from his chair.

"Gone away!" he cried sharply. "What do you mean?"

Amy pulled her father's letter from her pocket and held it out to him.

Her father was not in his office. The floor was strewn with papers, just as she had seen it overnight.

"I know you won't think father has stolen the papers, sir!" she said, facing him fearlessly. "It's only his nervousness. He couldn't have known what he was doing when he went away. Oh, don't be angry with him, sir!"

Sylvia's father took the letter. He moved to the windows with it, and stood reading it through two or three times.

Amy watched him. She saw Sir Gregory's mouth twitch, and his strong face become hard and grim-looking.

What was he going to say? What would he do? Would he accuse her father of theft? Would he say that the police must look into the matter, and that her father must be hounded down?

Sir Gregory swung round on the girl. Something of these thoughts was in his mind when he looked into Amy's white, troubled face, and the appeal in her eyes found a tender spot in his heart.

The grim look vanished from his face and the old genial expression returned.

"My poor little lass—poor little lass!" he said gently. "If your father had only come to me instead of doing this weak, impulsive thing, we could have put things right."

A heartfelt sigh of relief left Amy's lips.

"Oh, thank you, sir!" she cried. "You know that father has not stolen them. You won't send the police hunting for him?"

"Certainly not. I think he has done a foolish thing, but I know him better than to believe him guilty of a low-down theft! I've looked on him always as a friend, and I will be his friend now."

He received his reward in the look of deep gratitude the girl gave him.

"Oh, I'm so glad—so glad!" she cried, her voice tremulous with joy. "Father is so sensitive, so honourable—this discovery has crushed him. He was afraid to face you, sir, but I knew you would understand."

"There may be no cause for agitation, lassie," said the baronet kindly. "Your father is an absent-minded man. He may have put the papers in some forgotten place. Go home, Amy, and make another search. When I have finished my business I will come to your house with Sylvia. Even if we cannot find the papers a search must be made for your father."

Amy rode back to her home.

45

She had collected up the papers and made her father's office look neat and tidy, but she had failed to find the missing papers, when Sir Gregory and Sylvia drove up to the house in their motor-car.

Sylvia was the first to enter the house. She ran to her friend and embraced her.

"Oh, Amy, dear, I'm so sorry this trouble has fallen on you," she said.

Amy thanked her with a sad smile and turned to Sir Gregory and told him she had been unable to find the papers.

Sir Gregory looked round the office. He showed no desire to search the place. He was quite willing to take Amy's word for it.

"As they cannot be found, let us presume that in some way they have been stolen from the office during your father's absence," he said. "If your father were here, could he help us in this matter? Is there anything else missing besides my papers?"

"No, sir, not that I'm aware of," Amy replied.

"When did you last see the blue packet containing my papers in your father's possession?" Sir Gregory asked.

"Just before I went to the Guide meeting yesterday evening, sir," Amy replied. "Father had been talking about them over tea, and I knew they were yours. He was studying them at his desk when I left the house."

"So the papers disappeared between the time you went to the Guide meeting and returned to the house?" said Sir Gregory. "Did anything suspicious happen during that time? Did your father have any callers?"

"Only Mr. Magson, the hermit," Amy answered. "He called to give father some work to do for him. There may have been other callers, but father said nothing to me about them."

"The inference is that the hermit might have stolen them," said Sir Gregory, "but that, of course, is absurd. That strange-living, eccentric old man is as incapable of committing a crime as a baby."

Amy nodded her head.

"The best plan, I think, at present, will be to keep the loss of my papers a secret," said Sir Gregory after a pause. "But we must search for your father. No need to call the police in to help us to do that. Your father is probably hiding somewhere in the neighbourhood. I'll call on Miss Ingleby, your captain, and ask if the Guides can be organised to make a search."

"Oh, thank you, sir," agreed Amy. "That will be best."

But as soon as Sylvia and her father had driven away an idea occurred to Amy.

She got out her bicycle once more, and,

followed by the collie, she pedalled along the cliff road till she came to the sheltered nook in the headland where the old hermit's railway carriage home was situated.

Gipsy went on ahead over the gorse and barked noisily as he reached the tumbledown house.

The blinds had been drawn to the windows. It was impossible to see inside. There was no sign of life or movement within the place, and Amy hesitated to open any of the doors and look within.

"Of course I ought to have remembered," she told herself. "I heard him tell father last night that he was going away. In any case, I don't suppose he could have thrown any light on the mystery."

And, with the collie beside her, she rode homeward, with a fresh feeling of despair in her heart.

CHAPTER III.

THE SEARCH IN THE CAVES.

THE rest of that day was a nerve-wearing time for Amy. Every step outside, every knock at the door, agitated her. She was afraid she would hear bad news about her father.

Miss Ingleby called just before two o'clock to sympathise with her. The captain was tactful enough not to worry Amy with inquiries.

"You must not distress yourself, dear," Miss Ingleby told her. "It is almost a common complaint nowadays for people who have been working too hard, or who have suffered a great shock, to temporarily lose their memories and to go wandering off into some strange place where they are unable to give an account of themselves. It is necessary for me to be at the harbour office this afternoon or I would join you and the girls in the search. They'll be waiting for you at the drill hall at half-past two."

Directly the captain left, Amy ran up to her room and put on her Guide's uniform. At half-past two, leaving the collie at home, she hurried to the drill hall, and there she found Sylvia, with her fluffy-coated Pomeranian in her arms, Doris Meynell, two girls of the Robin Patrol, and about half a dozen girls from other patrols waiting for her.

"Any news, Amy?" Sylvia asked anxiously, as the leader of the Robins stepped up.

Sylvia had told them that Mr. Pryor was suffering from a nervous breakdown and had gone away, and they were full of sympathy for Amy.

"None at all!" Amy replied. "And now we've met here I hardly know where to begin. Shall we search the fields or shall we go into the caves?"

46

"If I wanted to hide anywhere I should go into the caves, I think," said Doris. "We can buy some candles as we go along, and make torches out of them with strips of paper. Let us search the caves first."

The other girls agreed that this was the best suggestion.

With Amy and Sylvia, her dog in her arms, leading the way, they made their way to the sea front. On the way Doris went into a shop and bought a dozen candles, more than a candle apiece for them all.

"If we all have a candle," she explained, "we sha'n't be afraid of the darkness, and we can wander away from each other if we want to."

The caves were one of the show places to visitors to Golden Manor.

The entrance was down on the beach amidst a cluster of rocks.

Now that the tide was out it was quite easy to get to the entrance.

The girls made their way down "Harbour Walk," a road which had been cut through the rocks to the sea. By walking over the golden sands for a hundred yards or so they came to the first or outside cave.

The origin of the Golden Manor caves was wrapped in mystery. Some of them had been cut out of the sandstone by smugglers a century or so earlier, but the local historian traced them back to the days of the Druids.

The outer cave was one of the smallest of them all. Through a passage at the back it led into a great grotto, its roof adorned with spar and stalactites which flashed back the rays of their candle-lights when the girls stepped within it. It was their colours that made the stalactites so wonderful, blood-red and white and electric blue scintillating from their diamond points.

Here, in the great grotto, where it was said the Druids had met for worship, dances and sometimes dinners were held. But this afternoon, when the Guide candle-

At last Amy neared the edge where the little dog, moaning with pain, was lying.

bearers came in, it was grim and bare, and their lights cast eerie shadows of their figures upon the floor.

Amy knew, of course, that if her father was hiding in any of the caves, they would not find him in the big grotto. Out of this were three tunnels, and these led into many caves, so that it seemed as if the whole cliff-land was honey-combed with hiding-places.

"We'll never find your father in this maze of passages and caves," Sylvia whispered, when the search had lasted half an hour and some of the excitement was vanishing. "He must have heard us calling if he is hiding in here."

"I'm afraid so, Sylvia," Amy replied.

They were ahead of the other girls, and so could not be over-heard.

"I don't think father would come out, even if he saw me, with all the other girls with us," she went on. "It would have been better if we had searched alone, you and I."

"Then we'll get out of the caves by the opening on the rocks and give up the search," suggested Sylvia. "Later on we'll search together, Amy."

And so at length, after Amy had explained to the Guides, they came out on one of the cliff paths that was situated midway between the sea and the top of the cliffs.

It was a difficult climb, up steep, rugged slopes, to the top. More than one girl slipped on the way, and many had to clutch at the gorse bushes to save themselves from falling.

But nothing happened until they were almost at the top of the cliff, when Sylvia's foot slipped, and she would have rolled down the path, with probably dangerous results, had not Doris clutched her in time.

As it was, Tony, her little dog, was tossed out of her arms, fell sheer over the cliff edge, and came to a stop on a ledge of rock thirty feet below them.

47

"My poor little Tony!" cried Sylvia, in great distress. "He might have been killed! Oh, I can't leave him there, and I don't know how I'm going to get at him. What shall I do, Amy?"

They could see the little dog lying on the ledge of rock, wailing, evidently in pain.

"The only thing to do is to climb down to the ledge, and get the poor little thing," said Amy.

"We can't get him!" groaned Sir Gregory's daughter. "It would be impossible for anyone to try to walk along that narrow ledge."

"Oh, I didn't mean by walking," said Amy. "Someone will have to be lowered with a rope. Who was it I saw with a rope this afternoon?" she asked.

"I've got one!" Doris replied, unwinding a rope from under her coat.

Amy took it from her and tested it. She made her way to the top of the cliff, where a post had been planted firmly in the ground.

"I'm going down!" she decided. "If you girls keep the rope twined about this post there won't be any danger. Haul me up when you hear me shout!"

The Guides looked at Amy in amazement.

"Don't do it, Amy!" protested Sylvia. "It's far too risky. Much as I love little Tony, I shouldn't like anything to happen to you."

"But nothing is going to happen to me," said Amy, smiling. "Six of you are surely strong enough to haul me up. Come on, Doris," she added. "You're one of the strong ones."

"It is I who ought to go down, as it's my dog," said Sylvia; "but—but—I haven't the pluck. Oh, do be careful, Amy!"

Amy looped the rope round her waist and under her shoulders. She saw that it was twined around the smooth post and that Sylvia and Doris and four other girls had the other end securely in their hands.

"Lower away!" she cried. "I'm all right. My safety depends on you."

Down she slid, the tight rope squeezing the air from her lungs. When she was free of the top ledge, she began to twist giddily round and round like a joint on a roasting-jack. She clutched at the rope and relieved the pressure about her chest.

Those few moments were a terrible strain, but after that, as she went down more steadily, her spirits returned. At last she came to the ledge where the little dog, moaning with pain, was lying. There was barely room for Amy to rest her feet, so narrow was the ledge. It was a miracle that Tony had stopped there and not crashed to the rocks a hundred feet below.

"Slacken a bit!" Amy called out. "I've got him! Now haul."

She clasped the little Pomeranian in one arm

as she caught at the rope. Steadily she began to rise towards the cliff top, but scarcely were her feet off the ledge when she heard her name called in a hoarse whisper that was strangely familiar.

She looked in the direction of the sound.

Through a hole in the cliff-side about the size of a window a haggard-faced man was looking out.

It was her father!

"Amy!" he cried. "Bring me food!"

CHAPTER IV.

HOW AMY SOLVED THE MYSTERY.

AMY was afraid to call out to her father lest her companions should hear her. She knew that her father did not want a number of girls trooping into his hiding-place.

Indeed, Amy had little time to think about her discovery. Her life was in the hands of her fellow Guides. With one hand holding the little dog to her, Amy was not able to do much for herself when, from the end of the dangling rope, her body struck against the cliff-face every now and then.

Slowly she was hauled up, the girls at the top straining every sinew of the rope. And then, at last, Amy was so near the top that she was able to hand little Tony into Sylvia's arms. She clutched at the edge of the cliff and pulled herself on to the grassy plateau.

"Well done, Amy!" the girls cried. "It was splendid of you!"

Sylvia hugged her as Amy got up.

"You darling!" she exclaimed. "You saved my precious little Tony! It's the bravest thing I've ever known. I only wish dad had been here to see you."

Amy smiled. Sylvia's father had done her a good turn. She was glad she had been able to render his daughter this slight service.

At the top of the cliff road the girls parted to go to their respective homes.

"I'm so sorry we've not been able to find your dad, Amy," Sylvia said. "Perhaps you'll have better news when you get home."

"I don't think we ought to give up searching," Doris said. "If we had lanterns when it gets dark, we might find him in the fields!"

"Let it be at present until I've been home," said Amy. "Thank you ever so much, girls, for coming out to help me."

As soon as she was alone Amy ran all the way to her home. At once she lighted the gas stove and put a kettle of water on to boil. She packed a basket with food, and, when the water was boiling, made some tea and put it into a vacuum flask.

A tea-cloth covering the articles in her basket,

and with the collie as her companion, Amy made her way once more to the cliffs. She had brought a candle with her. When she entered the outer cave she lighted the candle and went forward into the big grotto. She had taken careful notice of the whereabouts of the cave in which she had found her father hiding, but it was a long journey, and it was a weary, worrying time before at length she drew near the place.

"Dad—dad!" she called out. "Are you here? It's Amy!"

Several times she cried out in this way, and had to go on and on, from one cave to another, until at last, as she held the candle above her head and looked about her, and Gipsy barked excitely, she saw a figure come timidly out of the darkness that filled the corners of the cave.

"Amy, is it really you, child?" asked the solicitor excitedly.

The girl put down the basket of food, stood the candle on end in the soft sand, and ran to her father. She clasped him in her arms.

"Oh, daddy," she cried, "why did you run away and leave me? There was no need. Sir Gregory told me that he was sure you had not stolen the papers. He said you ought to have known that he was your friend."

As Amy and her father looked, the door opened and a man's head peeped out

"Sir Gregory said that, did he?" exclaimed James Pryor. "Ah! I knew he would never accuse me of stealing them. None of you guessed, of course, that I had run away purposely to mislead the thief!"

"I don't understand, daddy!" said Amy.

"Of course you don't, dear child," her father said. "I knew that if I ran away my letter would obtain publicity, and the thief be put off his guard. Everybody would think me guilty, and he would consider himself safe."

"Also," continued the father, "I knew I could trust you, Amy, to keep a stout heart and stand by me through thick and thin."

"And so you came away to hunt for the thief?" she asked.

"Yes, lassie," replied James Pryor. "I followed a suspicious-looking man into the caves. He was only a poor, homeless fellow, however, and when I returned to the opening I found my way cut off by the sea."

Amy was satisfied. She bade him sit on the ground while she put out a meal on the little tea-cloth before him. James Pryor ate the food eagerly while Amy talked to him. She told him of her visit to Sir Gregory.

"I'm glad to know that he does not think I've robbed him," muttered her father, "but I shall never have any real peace of mind until the thief has been found."

"I know you had the valuable papers before I went to the Guide meeting," suggested Amy. "When I came back again they were gone. Someone must have stolen them during that time."

"But who, child, who?" asked her father. "Old Silas Magson, the hermit, was the only person who visited me during the evening."

"Then he must have stolen them, daddy!" said Amy with conviction.

"It's impossible, lassie," replied James Pryor, shaking his head. "No, no. Whoever was the thief, I'm certain it wasn't the hermit!"

"Well, let us go back and see Sir Gregory," said Amy. "Perhaps he has made some discovery by now."

Amy gathered up the remains of the meal and packed them in the basket.

Her father was still undecided, but Amy coaxed him and persuaded him.

They began the long journey back along the tortuous windings through the caves with the collie at their heels. It was dark by the time they came out on the beach, and the lights were twinkling along the little promenade.

They were on the top of the cliffs, and had turned their faces homeward, when an idea occurred to Amy.

"Do you remember how excited Gip was last night when the hermit called on us, daddy?" she said. "I've been thinking about it several times since. Gip knows old Mr. Magson quite well, and has never barked like that before. D'you know—*I don't believe that was the hermit!*"

Her father stared at her in amazement.

"I don't believe he was old Silas Magson!" Amy repeated. "I think he was a man disguised to look like the old hermit. Let us go and see."

"But the hermit has gone away," said her father. "He told me he should be absent——"

"That may be part of the trick," asserted Amy. "It won't be much out of our way. Let's go and see!"

She called to the collie, who had bounded on ahead, and then they turned about and made their way to the headland where the hermit had his old carriage home.

It looked very bleak and desolate when they had left the lights of Golden Manor behind them and came out on to the stretch of grassy cliff-land. The roar of the sea on the beach far below came to them on the wind. Here and there a light twinkled from a lightship far out on the waste of waters.

They were within twenty yards of the hermit's home, just distinguishable against a background of dark bushes, when a light suddenly appeared in one of the windows and then vanished again.

"There's someone there, daddy," Amy whispered excitedly. "The hermit cannot be away after all."

Gipsy had seen the light and started barking. Amy would have run forward to the hermit's home, but her father caught her by the arm.

"Wait!" he said, in a low voice. "There may be mischief—if there's someone there. Quiet, Gipsy!"

Amy seized the dog by his collar, and they drew back behind some bushes.

The instant they had done so, a door of old Silas Magson's carriage home was opened and a man looked out. He had evidently heard the dog barking. It was too dark to distinguish his features, but Amy and her father saw that his face was clean-shaven, and that he looked altogether unlike the hermit.

For two or three minutes he stood there looking about him, and then the door closed upon him.

The discovery seemed to stiffen Amy's father, and to make him very alert.

"Wait there, child, with Gip, while I see into this!" he said with determination.

He moved away, and Amy remained crouched near the bushes with her hand on the collie's collar. She saw her father step cautiously to the old railway carriage and peer in through one of the windows.

She would dearly have liked to have joined and have watched with him, but she knew that it would have been impossible to keep the collie quiet on the threshold of the hermit's home.

James Pryor came back to his daughter a few moments later. He was like a man transformed. His face was grave and grim.

"Amy!" he whispered. "When I looked in just now I saw the hermit sitting gagged and bound in a chair. The man we saw at the door just now was standing over him. Hurry away as fast as you can and tell the police to come here. I'm going to stay and protect old Silas Magson as best I can."

"But, daddy, will it be safe?" began Amy.

"Do as I tell you, child! Quick, go!"

The leader of the Robins went away with the collie at her side, but she had not gone very far when she heard shouting voices. Turning about, she saw that the clean-shaven man had rushed out of the carriage and was struggling with her father.

She stood in indecision for a moment, uncertain whether to go back and help her father or to go forward as fast as her legs would carry her in search of the police. But Gipsy knew at once what to do. The collie sprang forward and attacked the solicitor's assailant.

By the time Amy reached the spot, the dog had brought the man to the ground, and would have severely mauled him had not James Pryor called to him.

"Slip inside, Amy," cried her father, "and release the hermit while Gip and I look after this ruffian."

A light was burning in a tiny lamp upon the table when Amy hurried into the hermit's home. The poor man was sitting terrified, tied up helpless, in a high-backed Windsor chair.

"Don't be afraid," she told the old man. "Father and Gip won't let the ruffian get away."

A scarf had been tied about the hermit's mouth. This she removed, first of all.

"It's a mercy you've come, lassie," gasped the hermit, in his soft, gentle voice. "I've been the prisoner of that man for two whole days. He means to rob every wealthy man in Golden Manor."

"I don't think he will!" said Amy, with a little smile of triumph.

As she spoke her fingers were busy untying the knots of the rope that secured the hermit's arms and legs to the chair.

50

"Ay, he borrowed my clothes!" old Silas Magson exclaimed. 'And he has worn a false wig and a beard to make himself look like me. I knew he was at your father's house last night. I can tell you where the scoundrel has hidden certain papers he took. Ah, that's better!"

He gave a sigh of content as Amy unwound the ropes from him, and he was able to get up from the chair and to move freely again.

Amy hurried outside with the ropes. The thief was lying upon the grass, too terrified to move for fear that the collie should spring at him.

Her father took the ropes from her. The man on the grass struggled for a moment when the solicitor began to securely fasten his ankles together, but when Gipsy broke out into fierce barking again he thought better of it, and quietly submitted to his capture.

"Now hurry off for the police, child," cried her father; "and if Sir Gregory Deakin is at home, you might ask him to come along here."

When Amy reached the baronet's home she found Sylvia and her father in the motor-car. They had been about to drive to Amy's house, they told her.

"Well done, Amy!" cried Sir Gregory, when she told him the news. "You have saved your father's honour!"

He bade her enter the motor-car. A quarter of an hour later they pulled up at the headland with two constables in the back seat.

The sequel to the capture was the discovery of Sir Gregory's title deeds and bearer bonds within the hermit's home. As Amy had guessed, the man, an old criminal who had once been an actor, had disguised himself to look like the hermit. Sir Gregory Deakin and the solicitor were not his only victims, they learned afterwards.

The thief, believed to be the harmless and eccentric old hermit, had been given admittance into the houses of several wealthy folk in the town, and had there committed robberies.

Old Silas Magson told how the ruffian had entered his home two nights before and had overpowered him and made him a prisoner.

Amy and her father had not made their capture any too soon. The thief had packed up the stolen property, worth many thousands of pounds, and had evidently intended to take it away with him that night.

"Who would have thought that all these dramatic events were going to happen in Golden Manor since our Guide meeting last night?" cried Sylvia, when the thief had been taken to the lock-up, and Sir George had invited the old hermit and Amy and her father to join his family at dinner. "Last night I was sighing for something to happen. Yet—after all, I think I like the old town best when it's quiet and sleepy."

Amy laughed.

"I'm afraid you're not cut out for a heroine, Sylvia!" said Sir Gregory, smiling. "You couldn't even rescue your own little dog when it was in danger!"

"But Amy is!" Sylvia cried. "She saved little Tony's life!"

"And her father from being a disgraced and ruined man!" added the solicitor, smiling.

And taking Amy in his arms, he fondly kissed the girl who had saved his honour.

THE  END

51

TRICKS AND CATCHES.

THE TORN WALLPAPER

This is not so much a trick as an illusion, and you will find it a very effective one. It can be used as a mild and harmless practical joke.

Take a sheet of thin white paper, fold it in half and tear it as shown in diagram A.

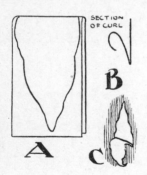

Now take one side, and, with finger and thumb, curl it as shown at figure B, then before anyone comes into the room, wet the back of the non-curled side and stick it on to the wallpaper in a prominent position. See figure C.

Now draw the attention of your audience to it and say that, by a secret process, you will be able to repair the damage. With a handkerchief rub the damaged part of the wall, taking care to conceal the torn paper in the linen folds.

AN EASY COIN TRICK

If you examine the corners of a hem-stitched handkerchief, you will find that the sides are open, and in this trick I am going to show you how these openings can be used. It will be advisable to have a gentleman's handkerchief, the openings being larger.

Before performing the trick, place a coin in one of the corner openings (see A in diagram),

then place the handkerchief on the table, taking care to note where the corner is that contains the coin.

Begin with a few explanatory remarks, such as:

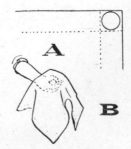

"You will observe that I have not anything in my hands or up my sleeves," then show your hands, empty, and turn up your sleeves to the elbows.

Now take the handkerchief from table, by two corners — one of which must contain the coin—and show both sides to your audience; then take the empty corner you are holding, and throw it over the one that contains the coin (see figure B). You now, under the cover of handkerchief folds, work the coin out of its corner—with finger and thumb—letting it slip into your hand; take handkerchief away and produce the coin, remarking that you have always found this a very useful trick when you have left your purse at home.

THE CHANGING ACES

This is the kind of card trick that appears very clever to an audience, but is simple and easy to perform.

A little preparation is required, as follows: cut from an old card the ace of clubs (see diagram A), and be sure that it is one large enough to cover the ace of diamonds belonging to the pack you are performing with (also see figure B). Now stick it over the diamond with a little soap, and be careful that nothing of the red is showing behind the black.

Having prepared the card, place it carefully under one or two of your conjuring pack and place them on the table. Now, taking the pack in your hand, say: "By the magical influence of my right hand, I can change the colour and suit of a card; as this requires a great amount of nervous strain, I will choose a card with the least number of pips." Pretend to look through the pack, and taking out the faked card, say: "Here is the ace of clubs; this will do nicely." Now hold the card up in your left hand, and making a pass downwards with your right hand (see figure C), knock off the stuck-on club and let it fall to the floor.

NOTE.—Do not forget, when preparing the card, to paste a small piece of paper over top and bottom corners to conceal the suit marks.

THE MAGIC WRITING

This is a more ambitious type of trick, and is used in a more complicated form at public entertainments.

A little preparation is needed, and a blouse or dress with long sleeves must be worn.

Roll up your left sleeve, and on the top part of fore-arm write or paint a name—such as Queen Mary, Lady Curzon, or the name of a friend present—and when the ink or paint is dry pull down your sleeve.

Now write on a slip of paper the same name

you have written on your arm, then fold it and hide it in the palm of your left hand; also, have a number of paper slips, the same size as that contained in your hand.

You are now prepared for the trick, and proceed as follows: Hand round the slips among your audience and ask each person to write the name of a well-known person or a friend; when this is done, give instructions for the slips to be folded up and placed in an empty flower-bowl, or any receptacle handy. When this is done, place your left hand into the bowl and take out a slip; but the slip you take out is the one you have had concealed in your left hand, ignoring the others that have been put in.

Now say (placing the slip on your sleeve, over where you have written the name on your arm): "I am now about to transfer the name on this slip, whatever it is, through my sleeve, on to my arm." Breath upon the slip, open it, read out the name, roll up your sleeve, and show the same name written there. This trick should only be performed when you have a number of people to perform to, and by using a confederate who will acknowledge the name on slip and your arm. It will appear most effective. The confederate can write anything on her slip.

THE MUSICAL CUP

For this trick, start off with something like the following: "Musical sounds can be extracted from iron, wood, glass, tin, and many other things, but the sounds are principally got by tapping the article. I am now going to show you how a note of music can be picked out of a cup, with the fingers and the aid of a fork."

This trick must be performed on a table top without any covering, and the harder and more polished, the better. Place a large cup on the table, and holding a fork (as shown in diagram A), nip the centre prongs with finger and thumb (see figure B). Then put these members into the cup (see figure C), and a musical sound will appear to issue. The secret of this trick is that the sound is caused by resting the handle of the fork on the table (see figure C), after nipping the prongs. Be sure and keep this action hidden by the back of your hand, and after the trick has been done, offer the cup and fork to anyone who would like to try it.

53

A RING AND STRING TRICK

To release a ring that is tied with string, and with the string ends held by another person, seems impossible; nevertheless, it can be done, and under the cover of your own hands, in full view of the audience.

Have a yard and a half of string and a curtain-ring on your table. (This trick can be performed with a finger-ring borrowed from one of your audience.)

Now, handing the string to a friend, ask her to tie the ends; then, tie the ring on to the string, as shown at A in diagram. Give the string ends to a member of the audience and under the cover of your hands proceed to get the string away (see figures B C D). Straighten out the string before showing the ring, and exclaim : " Will you kindly examine the string and the ring ? " Then hand them round.

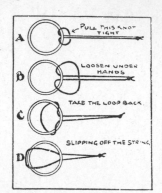

THE COIN, CARD, AND GLASS TRICK

Place a playing-card on the top of a tumbler, and on to the centre of card, a coin ; then, ask a member of your audience if she can get the coin into the glass without touching the card. Undoubtedly the comment will be " Impossible ! " You then explain that, owing to the magnetic influence of your thumb and the top joint of the first finger you will demonstrate how it can be done.

Now take your thumb and first finger and flick away the card (as shown in diagram), and the coin will fall into the glass.

THE GLASS AND SPOON MYSTERY

You must have a confederate for this trick, a younger sister or a small girl friend who can be easily hidden.

The requirements for this trick are a heavy glass tumbler and a teaspoon, with a length of black cotton, one end being tied to the lower part of the handle, as shown in diagram (see figure A). The other end of cotton is held by your confederate, who must be hidden behind a screen or curtain, with the cotton held on a level with the top of the glass (see figure B).

At the words, " I command you to rise," your confederate pulls the cotton, and the spoon rises in the glass.

A little appropriate music and the lights lowered will make this trick very effective ; the black cotton cannot be seen under these conditions. The cotton must be tied to a spoon and resting on the table, with its other end in easy reach of confederate before the performance.

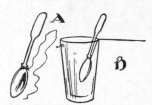

CATCHES

Tell a friend that you can stand with her on a sheet of paper, face to face, and she will be unable to touch you. This seems impossible, nevertheless, it can be done. Now take a sheet of paper, any kind will do, then go outside, and shut the door, push the paper under the bottom, and stand on one half of it, telling your friend to do the same on the other half.

Place five coins on the table, and say to a friend, " Can you make an exact cross with these coins, using the whole five ? " When she gives up trying, you gather up the coins and make the sign of a cross on the table.

There are catches and catches, and the kind that will put you to a lot of calculating trouble, afterwards to find at the end, that you have been caught, is to a lot of people annoying.

On the other hand, many girls enjoy this kind of foolery, and do not mind the laugh against themselves. This is the right kind of spirit, for it classifies a girl as a real sport. I am therefore going to conclude with a catch of the aggravating kind.

The type of girl to work this on is one who is studying, or well up in " Maths." Say to her, " Can you work this out ? " " A train leaving Brighton with fifty people, called at six stations on its way to London. At the first stop, five people got out, and fifteen people got in. At the second stop twenty people got out, and thirty people got in. At the third stop and fourth, sixteen people got out and four persons got in. At the fifth station, nine people got in, and nine got out.

" At the sixth and last stop, fourteen got in, and nine got out. Have you got that ? Well now, can you tell me the name of the engine driver ? "

Betty Barton

The Girl Who Won Through

"Our Betty!"—the most popular girl in the Fourth Form at Morcove School; and, one might almost say, the most popular girl in the *whole* school. Neither are her admirers solely confined to Morcove. There are countless thousands outside, who follow Betty's adventures as they appear each week in the Schoolgirls' Own. To these, Betty needs no introduction; but, nevertheless, they will doubtless be glad to read here, in this compact form, the salient points of our fine little heroine's record.

"I'LL manage!"

Just two little words, but what a lot they stand for! Just a little motto, but with what a wealth of resolve!

This was Betty Barton's motto before her Morcove schooldays when, 'way up North, she had to manage the poor little home—acting the part of a veritable little mother to her little brother and sister, whilst her hard-worked mother did heavy "charring" in the throbbing industrial town.

"I'll manage!" This, and this alone, was brave Betty's answer to every difficulty that arose. She would "manage" at all costs. Betty Barton was the kind of girl who would never be beaten. She would always "manage!"

And how often was that brave little spirit called upon to "manage"! Making ends meet was the daily task of the humble Barton family. But many were the times when ends refused to meet—when the beggarly, varying weekly pittance was not sufficient to provide the nourishing food and warm clothing that the children must have. Then were the wits of Mr. and Mrs. Barton and Betty taxed to their fullest.

For Mr. Barton work was very hard to find and poorly paid work it was when found. Only by means of Mrs. Barton's strenuous drudgery at "charring" was the weekly income of the little

home made equal to paying the rent and feeding and clothing them all.

In those days Betty Barton did wonders for the poor home. All the work of tending to the little ones was taken off the tired shoulders of Mrs. Barton. It was Betty who washed Doris, and Betty who did their mending, and Betty who kept them always entertained and happy. Most of the meals of the home were cooked by wonderful little Betty, too. And the daily shopping that she did, all the shopkeepers had commented, not entirely to their own satisfaction, that Betty could make her shilling go farther than that of many a thrifty housewife! Betty always "managed"!

Creditors were ever a serious factor for the Bartons in those bitter days. In fact, almost the only visitors to the poor home were creditors. And as often as not there was only little Betty at home to face them. And bravely Betty did face them. Creditors who came with threats to have them sold up were so charmed by her manner and her earnestness that they departed comparatively mollified. Perhaps they felt that, somehow or other, Betty would "manage"!

All that is over for the Bartons now. They are well-off. And for Betty in particular both the present and the future are bright and rosy. But never will she forget that wonderful little motto of hers—the motto which alone enabled her to win through those bitter times and emerge in the end with flying colours.

"I'll manage!"

The FORM Against Her!

Betty's Early Struggles at Morcove School

THE Fourth Form at Morcove School, when Betty Barton arrived was not the Fourth Form that it is to-day. Not by any manner of means.

The Fourth was then under the dominant leadership of Cora and Judith Grandways, the sisters. Purse-proud, vain, extravagant, ready to stoop to any mean scheme to further their own ends, these girls were looked upon with admiration and envy by the rest of the Fourth. Cora and Judith were not only their leaders, but their models—their paragons.

How was poor, Betty to fare among the daughters of rich gentlefolk—girls who had been brought up to want for nothing?

But, quite on top of all this, Cora and Judith Grandways had prepared the Fourth for Betty—or, it should rather be said, had prepared them against her. For both Betty Barton and the Grandways sisters hailed from the same town in the North, and Betty's mother had often done charring at the wealthy home of their parents. And the Grandways sisters knew it!

From the first they set out to make Morcove School "too hot" for Betty Barton. They resolved to drive her back to her humble home in the North. And the rest of the Fourth, more out of sheer thoughtlessness and admiration for the purse-proud sisters than any real grudge against Betty, backed them up.

It was heart-breaking for poor Betty Barton. She had thought that all her troubles were over. Alas! she was to learn that the greatest trials of her young life were only just beginning.

Much as she had needed her little motto—"I'll manage!" in her home-life in the North, she needed it more badly than ever now. She was taunted, persecuted, tormented right and left.

Had the Morcove girls thought—and almost all of them have since proved themselves to be sterling girls at heart—they would have realised what a wonderful, spirited heroine Betty was proving herself by standing up to them as she did. But, through the influence of the Grandways sisters, they did not see Betty in this light.

Polly Linton—madcap, high-spirited Polly—was the girl to come forth and stand beside Betty. Polly was the first of them all to see the sterling qualities in Betty Barton—to see that it was her fine, unbreakable spirit that enabled the girl to stand up against the gibes and snubs and persecutions of the Form.

Together they bore the brunt of the whole Form's disapproval of them both. Nothing could shake Polly's friendship for Betty, and nothing, now, could ever drive Betty away from Morcove School. Despicable schemes and plots the Grandways worked to get Betty expelled on wrongful charges. They grew more and more desperate as they found themselves being beaten.

And then Betty found her second loyal friend—Madge Minden!

With two such girls as Polly and Madge supporting Betty, the Fourth Formers at last began to open their eyes. Little as they relished admitting it, they began to feel that they had been doing the poor girl from the North a grave injustice all along. They found that her quiet heroism—the bravery and pluck she kept on showing from time to time—

was making its appeal to them, too. They realised how mean—how despicable—was the part they were all playing.

And, with dramatic suddenness, the whole tide turned. Almost the whole Form deserted Cora and Judith, and came over to Betty's side, to be welcomed with open arms and with complete forgiveness by the girl they had despised.

Such was the force of Betty's fine example upon the Fourth Form at Morcove School. In her first few weeks at school Betty had caused the entire Form to alter its whole course of conduct, to think more of games and the school than it had done previously.

Betty Barton had "managed." She had won through!

56

A Typical Week in BETTY'S Life

Betty Barton's motto, "I'll manage!" is not by any means one which she applies exclusively to herself. That is to say, she is only too willing to "manage" for other people. The description of a typical week of hers will clearly show that. This week is based upon a diary of hers which she kept for exactly one week, and then gave up because, in her own words, it sounded too much like "singing her own praises"!

MONDAY.—On rising, Betty noted with surprise that Ursula Wade and one or two of her bosom cronies were out before her. When she left her bed she knew the reason, for she put both feet into a basin of cold water. This was the reason of the Ursula faction rising so early! And they did not forget to "crow" about it, either!

Betty had stood enough of this kind of thing in the past, and she retaliated in kind. When Ursula was washing, Betty calmly removed her towel, with the result that Ursula went floundering about, shrieking that the soap was in her eyes.

After lessons were over for the day, and prep. finished, Betty spent a pleasant evening in the common room with Polly, Madge, Paula and the rest.

TUESDAY.—Lessons passed uneventfully, save that Betty was once caught whispering the answer to a verbal problem in Miss Redgrave's lessons. Just like Betty again, helping another at her own sacrifice!

In the evening a little council was formed for discussing next Saturday's hockey fixture. The previous week Morcove had lost rather badly, and it was regarded as up to Betty to put on the field a winning side this time.

WEDNESDAY.—The afternoon found Betty not only playing a strenuous game of hockey, but keeping a keen and critical eye on the display of both sides in the practice match. She formed her own opinion as to which were best fitted for the big Saturday match, and that night she posted up her list. The result of her decision was not received too favourably—by those who had been left out, but Betty was not to be swayed by any of their comments.

THURSDAY.—Apart from the ordinary subscriptions, the Morcove Fourth Formers are expected, if they can, to buy their own sports gear. If they cannot afford it, of course, they are at liberty to receive the money from the club fund—providing this "runs" to it!

Betty broke her stick in the practice match, and a remittance arriving, she went into the town to buy a new one out of her own money. There she found a small child weeping over the remains of a rather expensive doll, which she had dropped and broken beyond repair. Again Betty's tender heart was touched, and much as she wanted the new hockey stick, she spent the greater part of the money in buying a new doll for the enraptured little girl. So, after all, Betty had to take most of the money she wanted for the stick from the Fourth Form fund.

As ill fortune would have it, a handbag she had ordered and paid for some time ago arrived just after her purchase of the stick. Of this fact Betty's small band of enemies in the Fourth Form took advantage, refused to believe that Betty had spent her own money on buying a little girl a doll, and declared that she had spent the money on this bag. It was not a condition of things that boded well for the game on Saturday.

FRIDAY.—A brief extract from her diary will be sufficient to describe the Friday of this particular week of Betty's life: "Polly still waging war with girls who disbelieve that I did not spend my money on the new bag, though I keep on telling her to take no notice of them."

SATURDAY.—There were just two events of importance on this particular Saturday. The first, of course, was the game itself. From the first pheep of the whistle Betty Barton played like a trojan.

Seeing that Betty was making every effort to win the game, exerting every ounce of strength and skill, even the girls with least faith in her were stirred to strive their very utmost for the sake of the side. And that was all that was wanted. Morcove won a triumphant victory.

That evening all doubts as to the truth of Betty's story were dispelled—even in the most sceptical mind. A large party of the Fourth Formers obtained permission to see a historical play in the town, and whom should they meet outside the theatre but the little girl whom Betty had helped—and her father! She spied Betty at once, prattled joyously about the occurrence to her father and the girls, and everything was cleared up.

SUNDAY.—The end of a typical, if not exactly a perfect week. Like a heroine Betty has carried herself, without blemish, all along. And we will leave her in the cosy precincts of her study, happily reading her weekly letter from home.

Betty at Sport

BETTY BARTON is a sports girl in the truest sense of the term. This does not simply mean that she ranks with the most adept sports girls of her Form—though, in truth, she does. There is just one thing in sport that is more important than to "shine" at whatever branch of it you are pursuing. And that one thing is to "play the game." Betty Barton plays the game every second of the time.

In a hotly contested match with a rival school, not long ago, Betty showed a large crowd of spectators exactly how the game should be played. Morcove and their opponents were just about equally strong sides, and neither had been able to penetrate the other's defence. Not a goal had been scored, and no more than a few minutes were wanted for the final pheep of the whistle.

Some brilliant individual play brought Betty into a good shooting position, and she shot hard and straight. But one of the opposing backs, a girl who had played a splendidly fine game throughout, and saved her citadel more than once, rushed desperately in to do the same thing once more.

The hard ball struck her knee fiercely, and Betty, who had continued running after shooting, had a superb opportunity of tapping the ball past the goalkeeper almost the second after it had struck the gallant back.

But Betty had seen the girl's face grow white with pain, and she dropped her stick at once and rushed straight to her opponent's assistance. It was a splendid act of sacrifice on Betty's part: very few in her position could have resisted the temptation to score the goal that meant so much.

It was an exhibition of "playing the game" that brought some of the most enthusiastic cheering that had ever been heard at a Morcove hockey match.

In fact, the cheering lasted so long that it merged with that produced by the final blow of the whistle. The result was a draw for Morcove instead of a win, but what mattered the result of the match where "playing the game" was concerned?

A very similar incident occurred in a swimming contest with a rival school from the south of Devon. It was a relay race, and the last lap found Betty Barton racing hard with the captain of the rival school. The latter had a lead of several yards, but Betty was cutting through the water at her very hardest, and overhauling her rival by slow and sure degrees. Neck and neck were they at the finish, and only a yard separated them from the tape, which was stretched across the water at the winning post. It was just a question of which would manage to touch it a fraction before the other.

Even as both were about to make the great effort, Betty heard a strange gasp from her rival. She saw her face twist with pain, and she saw her flounder helplessly in the water. Her rival had, at the last moment, been attacked by cramp! How easy for Betty then to have stretched out her hand, touched the tape, and then to have supported her beaten rival!

But the tape might have been a mile away by Betty's action. She stopped and spun abruptly, seized her rival, and struck out for the nearest bank.

That, in Betty's opinion, was "playing the game," and the swimming contest had no result.

Betty may have superiors so far as concerns competence at sports, but as a true sports girl there is no girl in the whole of Morcove school who can eclipse Betty Barton.

A FEW CONFESSIONS

Supplied by Betty Herself

THE FOURTH FORM CAPTAINCY.—Many girls here have asked me : Will I ever get "fed up" with the Captaincy? Well, I think not! It means a lot of responsibility—it means I must keep an eye on the Form, and at the same time not neglect my own work. It means that whenever the Form is in a fix, it is I who have to think of the way of getting them out of it! But in spite of all this, the post of captain brings its own rewards, and with such chums as Polly and Madge always standing by me I am never at a loss !

SPORT AND LESSONS.—I believe I am very fond of all kinds of sport we indulge in—hockey first, then cricket, swimming, and long distance cycling. Tennis I like, but I am not over keen. As to lessons, I feel rather guilty when I confess to a liking for most subjects we take ! This may not ring true, but, nevertheless, it is a fact.

INDOOR HOBBIES. Needlework and cookery I have always been fond of, but most of what I do in this direction is done in the dark months.

Out of School

□ □ □

CYCLING

CYCLING is not only a recreation Betty Barton loves, but it is the favourite—or very nearly the favourite—outdoor pursuit of her chums as well. They spend a good deal of their spare time cycling together. There is very little of the lovely Devonshire country that they have not explored, and quite a favourite journey of theirs is the long cycle ride to the Lorna Doone country, returning by a different and always beautiful route.

The Betty Barton " on the road " is exactly the same as the Betty Barton in and about Morcove School—ever ready to "manage"! The cyclist with a punctured tyre, or some defect of the machine, has ever a friend in Betty. And fond though Betty is, like any high-spirited girl, of a rushing spin down a steep incline, she is not the girl to frighten children or injure chickens by her recklessness. Betty the cyclist is really just as careful and tender as was Betty the little mother.

PICNICKING

Betty Barton appreciates the joys and excitements of picnicking as much as any junior at Morcove School. All the bustle of packing the things into the big basket, the journey of happy anticipation by boat up river, the laughter caused by the sight of the different aspect of the things when they are unpacked !—Betty enters into all this almost as enthusiastically as Polly Linton herself.

One half-holiday of picnicking in the woods during the last summer, Betty remembers all too vividly. Betty had repaired to a farm-house for water, and on returning she came upon a sight that gave her a shock. Madge and Polly were reclining on the grass, and, squirming forward deliberately and making apparently for Madge's extended arm, was a vicious-looking snake of alarming size !

With great presence of mind Betty threw the contents of the jug at the reptile, which squirmed hurriedly out of sight in angry terror. There was no more picnicking for the chums after that ! And it was not until later, when they learned that the snake had broken free from a neighbouring circus, and that its fangs were poisonous, that Madge realised what she had to thank Betty for !

ON HOLIDAY

Without a doubt it is on holiday that we see Betty Barton at her best. Then we see her as jolly and happy as she is sterling-hearted. Without being so uproariously happy as the madcap Polly, or so wonderfully accomplished on musical instruments as Madge Minden, Betty Barton is yet an asset to any party. That is what all her chums say, and they should know ! But to be happy herself Betty must know that everybody else is happy, too. If there is someone who is not enjoying herself as she ought, it is like Betty to find her out almost at once, find out her reason for not being in tune with the rest, and then not rest until she has remedied matters. Happily, with three such personalities as Betty Barton, Polly Linton, and Madge Minden in their company, there are few who can help enjoying themselves, and holidays with Betty are invariably one round of happiness and good spirits from first to last.

BETTY'S VISITORS.

VISITORS to Morcove School to see Betty Barton are not numerous, but those there are eagerly welcomed by the captain of the Fourth Form. And first and foremost of these are her own father and mother, from the North.

Out rushes Betty as soon as the page announces them, kisses and hugs them in a transport of joy, and then drags them into Study No. 12 to be welcomed by all her friends whom Betty has invited for the occasion. Such afternoons are, in the words of Polly Linton, nothing less than " simply great."

In referring to Betty's visitors, we must certainly not forget to mention little Joe and Doris, Betty's brother and sister. They are bright, cheery children, and great favourites with the chums of the Fourth Form.

One other visitor to Morcove School who is always sure of an uproarious welcome is Betty's Uncle George, who made his fortune in America.

Uncle George's visits are all too rare, for he spends most of his time abroad. But few as they are, Betty and her chums do not forget them in a hurry. Invariably the result of his visit provides the tea-table of Study No. 12 with tasty delicacies for weeks to come.

ADVENTURES BETTY HAS HAD

VERY few girls have had the adventurous life at school that has been Betty Barton's lot, and few have shown such sterling qualities in the face of danger and hardships.

Ever since Betty's rich Uncle George arrived from America, and decided that Betty should go to the great public school for girls in Devonshire, Betty's life has been crammed with adventures—both at the school, and in strange, foreign countries—and she has never once failed to fulfil the part of a heroine.

Through adventure after adventure has she led her loyal chums, and rarely have her plans proved unwise or her decisions wrong.

One can almost marvel at the courage she showed when the members of the Fourth Form journeyed to the land of the Susallah, when those dear chums of Betty's, Madge Minden and Tess Trelawney, were lost.

On this great adventure Betty proved herself a valuable lieutenant to Jack Somerfield, brother of the Headmistress of Morcove, who was the leader of the expedition. Betty's undoubted qualities of leadership were very clearly shown here—courageous as ever, she was as coolheaded as if such an adventure were quite an ordinary occurrence to her!

Again, when members of the Fourth were holidaying in Turania, Betty showed wonderful resolution and steadfastness. The "holiday" was suddenly turned into an adventure of the most thrilling nature when the Morcove party came into conflict with some strange people who were holding prisoners the ex-Queen of Turania and her daughter, Princess Inez, with the object of securing the wonderful crown jewels.

Betty and her chums gained admittance to the gloomy island castle, where the royal prisoners were, and the courageous Form captain led a spirited resistance to the would-be robbers' efforts to recapture the castle. It was like Betty to be always to the fore—always in the thick of the dangers that confronted them—to show a spirit that never wavered, and to put a new heart into her chums.

Later, it was Betty who, alone and unaided, explored the underground passages of the Old Priory, where the Fourth and Fifth Forms had temporary quarters owing to the destruction of Morcove School by fire.

It was during that terrible fire at Morcove School that Betty Barton performed a deed that demanded the very highest order of courage, and, incidentally, placed a Morcove scholar under a very deep obligation to her. And the girl in question was none other than the aristocratic Paula Creel, who was overcome in the Fourth Form dormitory by the smoke and fumes.

At the undoubted risk of her life, Betty fought her way through the flames to where Paula lay insensible and helpless, and brought her to the window, where staunch Polly Linton helped her chum to carry the unfortunate girl to safety.

It was a deed the nobleness of which was only equalled by the modesty with which Betty —and Polly, too—tried to hide the splendid part they had played.

No matter what arises, Betty Barton faces the situation calmly and effectively. She is a loyal friend and a dangerous enemy. Dangerous, not in the sense of being vindictive, but as being exceptionally shrewd and far-seeing.

Brave as she is, she is gentle, too, and with a charm of manner that endears her to those who appreciate all that is highest and best in a schoolgirl and the name of "Betty Barton" will always stand for what is best at Morcove School.

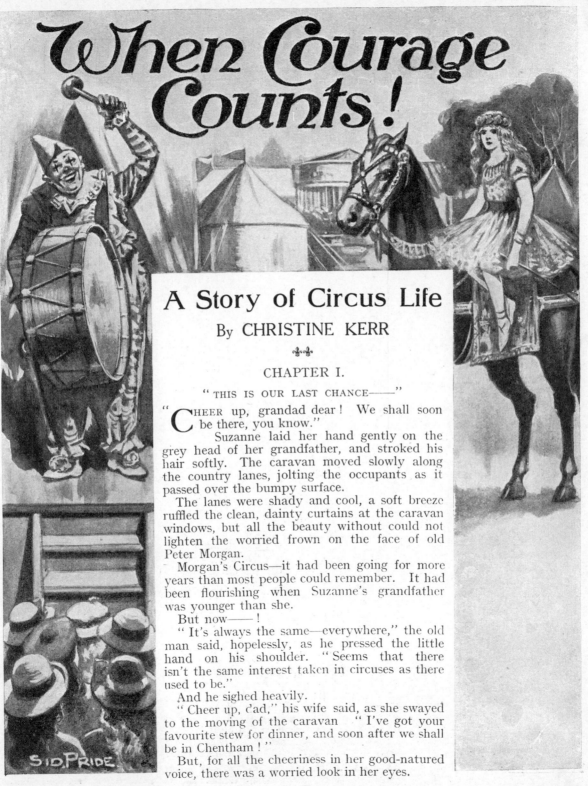

When Courage Counts!

A Story of Circus Life

By CHRISTINE KERR

❖

CHAPTER I.

" THIS IS OUR LAST CHANCE——"

"CHEER up, grandad dear! We shall soon be there, you know."

Suzanne laid her hand gently on the grey head of her grandfather, and stroked his hair softly. The caravan moved slowly along the country lanes, jolting the occupants as it passed over the bumpy surface.

The lanes were shady and cool, a soft breeze ruffled the clean, dainty curtains at the caravan windows, but all the beauty without could not lighten the worried frown on the face of old Peter Morgan.

Morgan's Circus—it had been going for more years than most people could remember. It had been flourishing when Suzanne's grandfather was younger than she.

But now——!

"It's always the same—everywhere," the old man said, hopelessly, as he pressed the little hand on his shoulder. "Seems that there isn't the same interest taken in circuses as there used to be."

And he sighed heavily.

"Cheer up, dad," his wife said, as she swayed to the moving of the caravan "I've got your favourite stew for dinner, and soon after we shall be in Chentham!"

But, for all the cheeriness in her good-natured voice, there was a worried look in her eyes.

61

"Why, yes, grandad dear. Chentham! You've always said what a splendid little place it is—how everyone comes to see the circus. We can stay there for a week, perhaps, and that will set us straight again, won't it?"

"Maybe, maybe, little lass." The old man slipped his hand round Suzanne's slim body and hugged her gently. "It won't be your fault if it doesn't, I know. There was never a little rider like you."

He gazed fondly on the pretty face and the long golden curls of his granddaughter.

"You get more like your mother, I declare you do, every day." And he sighed again, as he thought of his dead daughter.

Suzanne's father had died when she was but a baby, and ever since, for nearly fourteen years, Suzanne had been lovingly cared for by her grandparents, whom she loved dearly.

And now—now they were worried and sad, because the circus had not been successful lately, because people did not seem to care for Timmy, the clown, Billy and Bob, the trapeze artists, and the other folk whom Suzanne thought the most clever and lovable in the world.

She glanced out of the window of the caravan, and the green trees seemed to beckon her. Calling a few words to her grandparents, she opened the door of the caravan, and tripped lightly down the steps.

"Hallo, hallo, hallo!"

A booming, lusty voice hailed her, and a lightly thrown spray of leaves landed on her shoulder.

"Hallo, Timmy! Isn't this a lovely lane? Are we near Chentham?"

She waited until the caravan bearing Timmy and some other members of the circus came level with her. A big hand stretched down to help her, and she vaulted lightly into the seat beside the big clown.

"Chentham! Why, great jumping snakes, we're a couple of hours' journey, yet! Bless us, does the fairy think this is an aeroplane?" And Timmy raised his voice in a hopeless appeal to the two horses who jogged stolidly along in front of them.

"No, you silly old Timmy, of course I don't." And Suzanne laughed heartily. "But I do so want to get there—Timmy."

He looked down at the flushed face of the girl beside him, and his lined face became tender.

"Why are you so eager, little ladybird?" he asked.

"Timmy," Suzanne lowered her voice, and glanced at the open door of her grandparents' caravan, as it moved along at the head of the procession. "Do you think Chentham'll be a good ground?"

The old clown raised his eyebrows and shrugged his shoulders.

"Can't say, little one," he answered. "All I know is that it was jolly good ground the last time we came here. And, I hope it is now," he added, in a serious tone.

She nodded, her big eyes gazing dreamily up at the blue sky.

"You see, Timmy, they're—they're so worried, and—and I can't bear to see grandad looking like this! And it isn't as though it's his fault,"—her voice choked a little—"it's the best circus in the world—I declare it is, and I—I think it's just horrid that people don't come." Her voice rose hotly, and the old man beside her looked at her with a whimsical smile.

"Sure, it's the best show that ever was," he agreed. "Cheer up, my ladybird. Chentham will see us right!"

Suzanne nodded her head vigorously. It was too bad that the circus was failing, she reflected—but she was going to ride to-morrow as she had never ridden before. The circus should be a success—it must be, and she would do her best to make it so.

"Oh, Timmy—look! A kingfisher! Isn't he a beauty?"

There was a flash of blue and green, a swishing of wings, and the bird that had caused Suzanne's cry of admiration flashed across the river beside the road, and disappeared among some reeds.

"Yes—and look at those fine rushes!" The old clown pointed with his whip to a mass of flowering reeds. "We're just striking the river Chent—it runs right through Chentham."

"O-oh!" Suzanne drew in her breath delightedly. "Then we must be getting near——"

"Goodish way yet—and the river gets mighty wide at Chentham—dangerous, too." And Timmy shook his head seriously as he remembered how nearly every year some younger member of the circus had to be warned of the river's dangers.

"Why, Timmy? What's wrong with it?" Suzanne asked, glancing roguishly up at the sombre face.

"Rocks—little ladybird. Great big lumps of rock just below the surface—and when folks that don't know 'em jump in to bathe—well, there have been some nasty accidents there. You be careful, now, won't you?"

Suzanne laughed, and promised not to bathe in the River Chent, though, truth to tell, the idea of bathing in a river did not appeal to her at all.

The circus drew to a halt, and its various members gathered round in a little group on the grass. Whilst the women prepared the midday meal, old Peter Morgan, Timmy, and a few others, sat smoking their pipes, and discussing the prospect in Chentham.

"Cheer up, guv'nor," said Timmy, smacking his hand on the old man's knee. "Are we downhearted?" he demanded, glaring at a harmless-looking little man smoking a short pipe.

"Er—er—no, Timmy, old man. No, I—er—don't think so!" he replied, blinking.

"You what? You don't think so! I should say not. We're going to have the biggest show in Chentham we've ever had. So that's that!"

And so emphatic was Timmy that some of the seriousness seemed to lift from the party, and it was quite a cheery, hopeful band that entered the little market town of Chentham in the early afternoon.

A crowd of children, on their way to school, called an enthusiastic welcome, and Suzanne, smiling and waving, answered them.

"Here we are, here we are, here we are again!" shouted Timmy, from his seat on the front of the caravan, and a hearty laugh greeted his remark.

"It's going to be splendid," Suzanne whispered to her grandmother. "I can just remember it—the village, you know, grannie dear. But it's such years and years since I came here——"

"Yes, it seems years to you, dearie," the old woman replied. "But to me, why it seems but yesterday. Look, Susie dear—there's the place we pitch."

And she indicated a broad, green expanse at the end of the main street.

"The circus has got to move off!" shouted the man as Suzanne walked dejectedly towards the gate.

The caravans drew to a halt, there was a general hustling and scurrying, and in a few seconds Morgan's Circus had definitely pitched in Chentham.

Suzanne hurried round to take charge of Mavourneen, her pony. The animal greeted her appearance with a whinny of delight, and she kissed him on his polished nose, and murmured tender little words in his sensitive ears.

"Boo'fullest," she whispered. "You're going to be the most wonderful pony in the world, to-night, aren't you? We've got to ride as we never did before, my precious, for—for this is almost our last chance——"

Her voice faltered and broke.

The pony whinnied softly, and rubbed his head against Suzanne's shoulder. She put her

63

arms round his neck, and in a moment spoke again, her eyes dim with tears.

"Darling little Mavourneen, if—if the circus isn't a success here, grandad'll have to close down, and then—and then—oh! Mavourneen darling, I couldn't bear to lose you!"

A tear rolled on to the pony's nose, and he looked wistfully at his little mistress as though he quite understood, and was prepared to do his best.

For a long time Suzanne stood there, watching the hasty erection of the tents, and she saw them stick the boards bearing the huge placards into the ground.

And as she watched, the old eager joy, the excitement that she always felt before a show in a new town, crept into her veins, and her sadness left her.

"It's going to be all right, Mavourneen," she said. "We're going to——"

She broke off, her hands fell from the pony's neck, and she started forward. A man, dressed in riding breeches of a rather large checked pattern, had ridden on to the fair-ground, and was talking and gesticulating angrily.

Suzanne hurried forward. She heard her grandfather's voice, and the voice of the stranger, raised in annoyance.

"It's preposterous—perfectly outrageous," the man was saying. "To come and pitch here, on my ground, without my permission. Pshaw! Do you realise who I am, my man?"

"No, sir, that I do not," answered old Peter Morgan. "But Morgan's circus has come here for fifty years or more, ay — and longer, too, and I reckon I didn't think anyone's permission was necessary."

"Well, you know now. I am the owner of this land, and I utterly refuse to allow your noisy circus to stay here. As I own most of the other land here, you need not consider pitching anywhere else. You understand?"

Old Peter Morgan went a trifle pale, and his hands clenched.

"You—you mean," he stammered. "You mean that we can't stay here—not—not at all?"

"Not at all," answered the man, his face growing red with anger.

A girl, dressed in a beautifully cut riding habit had cantered up, and she sat by, staring sneeringly at Suzanne while the altercation ensued.

"Sir!" There was a note of entreaty in Peter Morgan's voice. "I—I—it means so much to us. Let us stay just for one day, sir. Miss, can't you persuade——"

He turned beseechingly to the girl, who drew herself up haughtily.

"I shall not try to influence my father," she answered. "I consider that circuses are nasty,

noisy affairs, and we do not wish Chentham to become noisy. Mr. Derriden, my father, owns practically all of Chentham," she added superciliously.

Suzanne gasped. But no word came from her lips.

For a long time old Peter Morgan stood there, urging, beseeching, pleading, but Mr. Derriden was adamant, and his last words came to Suzanne as she stood by her grandparents' caravan, white and trembling.

"You understand—I will not allow it!"

Suzanne could hardly believe it—that anyone could be so cruel. She thought of the girl's face, how proud and haughty it was. Oh, it was cruel —cruel! It had meant so much to them, and now——

"That's the end of everything!"

Peter Morgan's voice was broken and trembling.

"We've got to face it, old girl, but—but—it's mighty hard."

And to Suzanne, standing silently by the side of the caravan, came the sound of her grandmother's crying.

———

CHAPTER II.

"THE RIVER'S JUST AHEAD!"

SUZANNE sat alone on the front of the caravan in which she slept. It was drawn a long way away from the others, and she stared dreamily out at the roaring, rushing stream some little distance away.

A mass of rock in the centre of the river caused a miniature waterfall, and the noise of it came distinctly to the little circus-rider as she sat there, her chin in her hands, a wistful look in her blue eyes.

It was scarcely an hour since they had reached Chentham, their hopes high and strong, and now—now there was nothing but sorrow in the circus!

Some of its members were wildly indignant, but the blow seemed to have crushed her grandparents, and Suzanne had crept away, unable to bear the sight of their hopelessness.

"And all because of that man on the horse," she reflected, bitterly. "We shouldn't hurt his land—it's waste land, anyway. Oh, surely— surely he must let us!"

So she pondered, watching the play of the sunlight on the little ripples of water at the end of the field. And as she thought, a sudden idea came into her head.

The light sparkled in her eyes, and, a look of resolution on her face, Suzanne jumped down from the caravan, and sought Timmy.

She found the old clown, looking broken and

Facing page 64
THE STAR OF THE CIRCUS

A crowd of children had gathered round the ground, eagerly asking the time of the first performance. A group of schoolgirls were talking to Timmy, who was making them laugh with his droll remarks.

There seemed to be an air of business about the ground that had not been noticeable when Suzanne left, and she spoke to the little man whom Timmy had chided at dinner-time.

"Joe," she said, softly. "What—what's going on ?"

He winked, and jerked a thumb towards Timmy.

"Here's a rare plucked one," he answered. "He's fixed it—we're going to give a show—and forget what that old fillibuster on the horse says. But we've got to do it mighty quick. Tim's just telling the youngsters out there —it's to be at six."

Suzanne's heart leapt. A wild desire to ride Mavourneen once more had surged through her; she longed, as she had never before longed, for the hot, well-known atmosphere of the circus, for the sea of faces around her as she flashed by on her pony's back.

"Oh, gorgeous !" she answered. "I'll get along and look out my clothes."

And she ran off towards her caravan. She almost sang as she went, yet there was a touch of wistfulness in her face. For to-night was to be almost their last night, and then——

But she wouldn't think of it afterwards. Perhaps they would let her keep Mavourneen, though it would be hard enough to part with her other friends.

Inside the caravan she set to work, shaking out the white, spangled frock she wore for her first " turn." Then she turned out her stockings.

"Bother," she said suddenly, "there's a hole and, goodness, there's another ! And I don't believe I've any silk to mend them."

She hunted around, and, after some ten minutes' searching she found the silk. It was hot in the little caravan, and she took up her mending and went outside.

Suzanne climbed to her favourite seat on the roof of her caravan, and sat there, her fingers busy with her mending, but her thoughts far away. The river hissed and gurgled, and from her perch she could see the water, eddying and swirling around the rocks.

The first hole was mended, and the other almost finished, when something made her turn to look up the hill toward the big house she had visited that afternoon, and her heart sank as she did so.

For coming down the hill at a fast pace was Mr. Derriden, riding a big, brown horse ; while beside him, on the sleek, black horse she had ridden that morning, came Dorothy.

"Oh, my gracious !" breathed Suzanne ; and her face grew pale. "They—they've heard about the performance to-night, and they're coming to stop it !"

She knelt up, peering at the oncoming figures.

She wondered what she should do, but, she reflected, nothing she could possibly do would be of any use.

And, stiff with suspense, she waited.

Mr. Derriden rode on to the fair ground, his face an angry red. He dismounted, and strode toward her grandfather. Dorothy touched her horse's flank, and moved up to the two men.

"What, not made a move yet ?" thundered the owner of the ground. "I thought I gave you to understand that you were to go ?"

"Yes, sir, that is so." Old Peter Morgan's voice was not very loud, but the breeze blew it to Suzanne, and she thrilled with pride at the dignified answer. "But a circus requires a certain amount of moving, sir."

Suzanne wondered if her grandfather had known about the hastily arranged show ; but his next words made her realise that he had not known.

"I have no intention of staying longer than is strictly necessary, Mr. Derriden. I should not like to—to spoil your ground," he added ; and the sarcasm in his voice made the squire furious.

"Why, man——"

He turned and cracked his whip sharply. The end of it cut against the side of Dorothy's horse, and a wild cry rent the air.

For the restive animal had taken fright, and, with wide-open nostrils and staring eyes, was bolting down the field at a terrific speed.

Shrieking, Dorothy clung to the animal's neck, helpless in the face of this emergency.

"Help ! Help !"

"Great Scott ! What can we do—what can we do ?" The squire's voice came frantically. "Oh, my goodness, the river's just ahead !"

66

CHAPTER III.

"ONLY" A TRICK RIDER!

"THE river's just ahead!"

The dread shout rang through the air, and Suzanne started to her feet.

She saw the frantically waving crowd, and saw the maddened horse tearing across the intervening green.

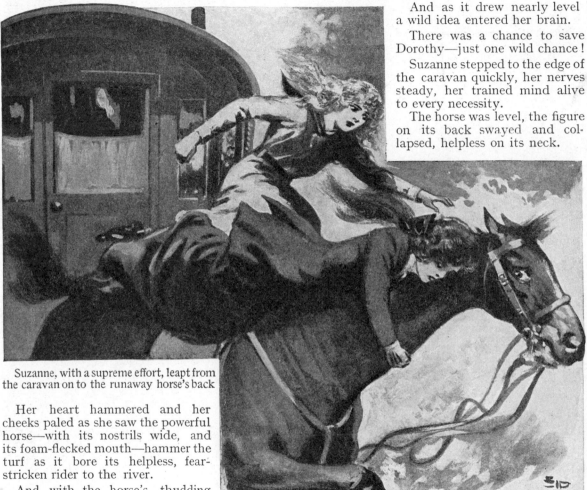

Suzanne, with a supreme effort, leapt from the caravan on to the runaway horse's back

Her heart hammered and her cheeks paled as she saw the powerful horse—with its nostrils wide, and its foam-flecked mouth—hammer the turf as it bore its helpless, fear-stricken rider to the river.

And with the horse's thudding hoofs mingled the roar of the treacherous river, the river to which the horse was tearing, and into which it must surely fling its rider.

"Help! Help!"

Gone now was Dorothy's dignity as she wildly clutched the horse's mane. Her face was white, her eyes starting.

"Help! Help!"

And between the horse and the river there was only the caravan on which Suzanne, petrified with suddenness of the happening, was perched.

What was there that could save the unfortunate girl from the river into whose rocky torrent she would be flung head first?

Already the squire had covered his face; already others had forsaken hope.

On came the horse nearer to the caravan, so that Suzanne could see the terror in its eyes, the wild look that she had seen before in the eyes of a frightened, maddened horse.

And as it drew nearly level a wild idea entered her brain.

There was a chance to save Dorothy—just one wild chance!

Suzanne stepped to the edge of the caravan quickly, her nerves steady, her trained mind alive to every necessity.

The horse was level, the figure on its back swayed and collapsed, helpless on its neck.

Then, with teeth clenched and every muscle supple, little Suzanne the trick rider had leapt from the caravan. A shout went up from the crowd, a shout of alarm.

But Suzanne had not failed.

She was on the horse's back, steadying herself by an effort, just saving herself from a heavy fall. With all her strength she clutched the rein, and all her strength was in her wrists, all her craft and skill was uppermost.

But they were near to the river, near to the

size you require $1\frac{3}{4}$ yards of insertion and 4 yards of lace.

Join the handkerchiefs and insertion as shown in the sketch.

This could be done in two ways. The simplest method is to oversew the handkerchiefs and insertion together, the oversewing being on the wrong side of the cloth.

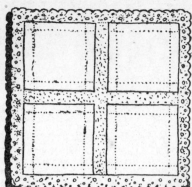

The other way would be to join them together by fancy stitching, using white embroidery cotton for the purpose. You would have to tack the handkerchiefs and insertion on to a large sheet of paper, which would keep the cloth quite flat, while you did the fancy stitching. The lace is sewn to the edges of the cloth, and " fulled " at the corners.

Be sure that you make small stitches, and fasten the cotton on and off very securely.

If you are clever at crochet-work, you can make the insertion in crochet cotton, also the lace for the border of the cloth, and instead of " fulling " on the lace, make a properly fitting corner.

There are several other ways in which this cloth can be made.

If you have no handkerchiefs, and don't want to buy any, you can use any odd pieces of linen you happen to possess. The idea of the insertion lends itself so well to the joining of small pieces.

An old linen sheet, good in parts, could be quite easily used for making the cloth.

If you have only quite small cuttings of linen, and short pieces of insertion and lace, you can make a traycloth or table-centre on the same lines as the cloth.

The same idea, carried out on a larger scale, could be converted into a cot quilt. A sideboard cloth could be made from the same design.

A TINSEL PURSE

A crochet safety purse with a long chain, so that it can be worn round the neck, is just the thing for school wear, and nothing could look prettier than the one sketched on this page, when made up in the new tinsel thread. These crochet purses are as easy-as-easy to make, and the thread for working can be bought at any fancy-work store.

With a steel crochet-hook cast on 36 chain, or more stitches when a larger purse is desired. Turn with 4 chain and work 4 treble into next 4 chain. Miss 2 chain and work 4 treble into following 4 chain ; repeat until end of row.

2nd row : Turn with 4 chain, work block of 4 treble into 2 chain, work 2 chain, miss block of previous row and do 4 treble into next 2 chain ; repeat this to end of row. Work 1st and 2nd rows alternately until the purse is about three inches long. Cast off. Turn down one inch for flap, and join the two sides.

Along the top of the flap on each block crochet a loop con-

sisting of 60 chain. These loops are then pulled through the open spaces opposite, and fastened to a small bone ring, which is then covered over with double crochets. To finish off, add length of chain long enough to fit neck.

HOW TO MAKE AN AT= TRACTIVE BOOK COVER

It is an excellent idea before lending a book to cover it, so that when anyone is reading it it does not become soiled and knocked about. Of course brown paper covers serve the purpose quite well, but they do not look so attractive as one of the kind sketched here. These covers are easy to make and are well worth the trouble.

HOW TO MAKE THE BOOK COVER

Required : A piece of washing material—holland or linen are suitable—and embroidery silk.

First of all, measure the book for which you are making the cover, cut the material, and allow turnings.

The cover when cut will be an oblong shape. To neaten the edges, make a hem all round or scallop them. To make the scallops strong, after you have traced them, run a cotton thread round the tracing, and then buttonhole the scallops.

In one corner of the cover embroider a spray of flowers in silk. Lilies or daisies look quite well, or a butterfly is very pretty.

To finish off this cover, make two handles, and attach as shown in the sketch.

These handles should be made of the same material as the cover. To make them, cut two strips of material 12 ins. long and $1\frac{1}{2}$ ins. across. Turn in the raw edges, fold in half, and sew all round, thus making a strap 12 ins. long, and about $\frac{1}{2}$ in. wide.

The handles are useful when carrying the book, but if you like you can omit them. Just hem the edges of the cover, and turn them over the cover of the book the same as you would with a paper cover.

These covers of material, besides looking much nicer than a paper cover, last much longer, and when they are soiled they easily wash and appear as new.

A DAINTY D'OYLEY CASE

A novelty gift such as the d'oyley case illustrated on this page will always prove welcome to mother or an engaged sister who is busy filling her " bottom drawer." Here again the " piece " bag will come in useful, as odd lengths of silk or sateen can be used for the making.

Cut two circles of stiff cardboard about ten inches across. Smear with paste, and attach your circles of silk, leaving enough for turning in. Line the circles with a contrasting shade of sateen, but before attaching the lining, slip in your ribbons, so that when the d'oyleys are placed between, the circles can be held in position by the tying of the ribbons.

Decorate the top circle by stamping to it the word "D'oyleys" and outlining in chain stitch The newest cases have sprays of fruit stitched flatly to them, as indicated in the illustration.

A USE FOR GOVERNMENT LINEN

A dainty table-centre can be made from an odd length of Government linen, that economical material with its fascinating "drawn thread" effect.

To make, cut the linen the desired length and width, and draw the threads at the edges to give the effect of a fringe to the finished article. Line with sateen, or any odd piece of material you have by you.

Appliqué your flowers to the linen in groups at the corners, or entirely smother the edges of the centre, as the taste desires.

A more elaborate centre for special occasions can be made in exactly the same way by using silk net, and flowers cut from silk or satin, instead of the linen and cretonne. When net is chosen, scallop the outside edge, as shown in illustration.

A DAINTY BASKET

A basket for holding fancywork, or even for carrying home shopping, can be decorated with appliqué motifs. Purchase a small rush straw or bast bag—the type which can be purchased for a few pence at any oil shop—and this forms the foundation. When a really elaborate basket is desired, gild the outside with gold paint. Line inside with a gaily patterned cretonne or silk, ruching along the top to give an effective finish.

To the outside of the bag appliqué your flowers, cut from the same material as the lining. These flowers can be grouped in the centre of the basket in a "set" design, or placed just at random.

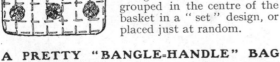

A PRETTY "BANGLE=HANDLE" BAG

A pretty bag never fails to fascinate us, does it, girls? We all agree that they're fascinating to wear, but I think they are no less fascinating to make.

The "bangle-handle" bag illustrated looks very smart when made up in Navy-blue silk, lined with rose pink, and trimmed with rose pink beads. Another pretty combination is to make the bag of a bright shade of blue, trim with silver beads, line with grey, and attach to grey "bangle" handles.

These handles, round pieces of bone or coloured wood, can be bought at any large store.

Quarter of a yard of double-width material and the same amount of lining are necessary for the making of the bag; a pair of "bangle" handles, and beads to trim.

Cut the bag diamond shape, leaving the top part, which is attached to the handles, quite straight. Join up the side seams, leaving them open at the top part of the bag for about 3 ins. Before attaching the lining sew on your beads in the same design as the bag illustrated.

Place the lining in the bag, attach to the side openings, and stitch the two top parts securely to the handles.

When beads are thought too expensive a trimming, quite a good effect is given by placing in their stead stitches of different coloured silk.

AN ATTRACTIVE EGG COSY

The pretty egg cosy illustrated on this page was made from a scrap of yellow silk, a length of black cord, and a piece of coloured silk ribbon, from which the chickens were cut.

Cut the cosy pyramid shape, pad with cotton-wool, and line with a contrasting shade of material. Outline the bottom of the cosy with the cord, or buttonhole stitch.

Cut your two chickens from coloured ribbon, and appliqué one to each side of the cosy with yellow silk.

These little egg cosies make attractive little presents, and there is no doubt that mother would thoroughly appreciate having a few, for they look charming, and are useful as well.

"FIRST SIZE BOOTS"

A pair of "first size" boots make a charming little gift to a new baby. On a bone crochet hook cast on a chain of 21 stitches. Turn with 1 ch., and work 20 d.c. into the next 20 ch., always remembering to insert your hook at the back loop of the stitch, to give that effective raised appearance to the finished article.

2nd row: Turn with 1 ch., working 2 d.c. in 1st and last stitch of row; the other stitches are worked plain.

3rd row: Turn with 1 ch. as in 2nd row. Work 1 d.c. into previous row.

Repeat 2nd and 3rd rows until there are 30 stitches. Finish boot with plain row.

Next work on 30 stitches for 20 rows. Fasten off, and join to front part of boot. Attach to sole, and neatly gather a few rows at the heel to give shape.

Fold the seam of sole to middle of 1st row. Stitch up on wrong side, and turn to right side. Begin in centre of heel.

* 1 tr., 2 ch., miss width of 2 ch.; repeat from * all round.

MAKING YOUR WINTER PARTY A SUCCESS

EDNA put her head in the door and pushed another guest into the drawing-room.

"This is Freda Johnson, girls," she called out. "Gracious! There's that door-bell again!"

And she disappeared once more, leaving Freda standing in the centre of the drawing-room. She looked round rather shyly, at a circle of faces which were, for the most part, totally unfamiliar to her.

"There's a chair here," one of the girls said, trying to make the newcomer feel at ease.

"Thank you," said Freda; and, with a little nervous twirl of her pretty frock, she sat down.

Then came another rather long pause in the conversation.

Nobody had anything to say, everyone looked at everyone else, and wished Edna would come back. It was all right when Edna was there. But there were several strangers present, and, although some of Edna's school chums knew each other, not all the girls were acquainted.

A half-hearted conversation started amongst a little group, something about one of the mistresses at school; then it died away and, in the silence, someone giggled. It sounded dreadful in the stillness.

At last Edna came back, accompanied by several other girls, and her mother as well.

"Why! How silent everyone is!" Edna exclaimed merrily.

And her mother added.

"Yes. Come along. We'll go in to tea, and not wait for the others."

During tea Edna's mother made very strenuous efforts to set everyone talking and at ease, and so far succeeded that at the end of the meal there was considerably more noise than had been noticeable before.

Nevertheless, when the guests rose from the table, and went back to the drawing-room, an awkward pause came before Edna at last proposed playing a game.

Everyone agreed, it was a capital idea.

"What game?" was the next question.

"How about 'The Stool of Repentance'?" someone suggested.

But they did not like that. You see, to play the "Stool of Repentance" everyone has to know everyone else, and know, too, their little points so that they are able to make teasing remarks about the person on the "stool." So that was no good.

Well, to cut a long story short, it wasn't until it was nearly supper-time that Edna got her party really "going." She had no idea of really "running" things so as to make them feel at home, and make things go with a swing.

"Making your party a success." These are mere words, but how to carry out the idea conveyed behind them is quite another thing.

It's not altogether an easy matter.

To be able to say, "This has been a really successful party" you must be able to feel, too, that from the very first minute your guests entered your door they enjoyed themselves. A party must "go" from the first if it is to be a successful party.

That's why it needs thinking out first.

So many girls seem to send out their invitations, get mother to provide a nice tea and supper, and then—leave matters to chance.

The truth is, girls, that your part of the evening needs every bit as careful preparation as does mother's, which is mainly concerned with culinary matters.

An excellent idea is to provide yourself with a programme of games and "notions" to fill the evening, so that there is never an awkward pause when people look at each other and think, "What are we going to do now?"

Personally, I should never advise the lucky party giver to make her guests start off with a set game. First of all, you want to think of some idea that will introduce all your guests to one another, provide a bit of fun and laughter, and so do that most important of all things—"break the ice."

Quite a good idea is to make everyone "find their partner." This may be an old idea, and some of you quite possibly have heard of it before, but it certainly provides plenty of fun.

Before the night of the party you should prepare a number of slips of paper; the number, of course, tallying with the number of guests you have invited.

You must then get out a double list of well-known characters, such as "Cinderella," whose partner would be the "Glass Slipper." "Red Riding Hood" and the "Wolf," "Humpty-Dumpty" and the "Wall," and so on. Of course, if you can get out any humorous ideas, so much the better.

74

Your next move is to write on these slips of paper the names you have chosen, and provide a box of pins.

When you welcome your guests and take them upstairs to take off their outdoor things, pin one of the slips on the back of each girl, and tell them to "go down and find their partner."

Of course, they cannot see the name that is pinned on their back, and it's great fun circulating round the room, turning people round to see what's on their backs, and trying to elicit information from them, without giving anything away.

Then when each guest has found her partner, they must take each other in to tea. Take care, by the way, to put two people together who do not know each other too well, thus you will get your guests well distributed and nicely introduced, with all their shyness gone during the first half hour or so.

It is always wise to have tea quite early, as this undoubtedly does a great deal to make the atmosphere merry and bright, and does away with the strangeness of meeting.

Tea over, back you all tear to the drawing-room and commence the real fun of the evening!

As I've already said, you should have a programme of games all ready, so that there's never a dull moment. Doubtless you all know heaps of games yourselves. "Charades" is an old favourite, and dull, indeed, would be the party which did not include it. There's no end to the fun that can be got out of dressing up in old curtains, old hats of father's and mother's—only mind they *are* old ones! While the efforts of some girl to imitate a man's voice always provokes roars of laughter.

Just a word about charades, however. Have them properly organised.

So often heaps of valuable time is wasted while two or three people wrangle over what parts they shall take! Why not pick a "captain" for each side by vote, and allow her to distribute the parts as she thinks best, while the others implicitly obey her directions. If it is preferred, the "captaincy" could be changed for each word.

Now that dancing is so popular, it isn't at all a bad idea to get someone to play a tune or two on the piano while you perform a fox-trot or one-step. Of course, you want someone who can keep strict dance-time, and someone, too, who is not easily tired. If you are the lucky possessor of a gramophone, so much the better.

Have you ever played "Musical Cushions"?

It's very much on the lines of "Musical Chairs," that well-worn favourite of all parties, only that it doesn't require half so much arranging and shifting of furniture.

Sit down on the floor, in as large a circle as the space will allow, and get mother to lend you a cushion that will stand a good deal of knocking about. For the sake of the room, it isn't wise to have one that is losing its stuffing.

Next, instal someone on the piano stool, and tell her to play a bit, and then stop, exactly as in musical chairs. Then start the cushion on its journey. You can throw it at anyone, and it's wise to throw it directly you get it, for the person who holds the cushion when the music stops is—out!

You can just imagine the shrieks of laughter when some poor girl fumbles wildly after the cushion and catches it just as the music stops! Then, too, when numbers still "in" begin to thin, the delight of the spectators is great as each unlucky girl receives the cushion in her face, and tries to grab it quickly and hurl it away again.

Keep the cushion low and mind the ornaments, by the way!

After that wild scramble, you'd better have something quiet and sedate for a change, and the old "Guessing What's on the Tray" comes in useful for this.

A number of articles of household use are brought in, on a tray, numbering, say, twenty or twenty-five in all, and everyone is allowed a thoroughly good look at them.

Then, after the tray has been either covered or taken from the room, everyone is provided with a sheet of paper and a pencil, and is told to write down the names of everything on the tray. It's amazing how many you can forget!

Of course, the one who has remembered the greatest number should be presented with a little prize of some sort.

Another game of this sort, if you have a musical person present, is to request her to play snatches of this or that popular tune, and ask your guests to write down the names of these as they are played. Last time I played this I couldn't think of the name of "Home, Sweet Home!"

For another quiet game "Coffee-pots" is quite amusing.

Two conspirators put their heads together and choose a word which has, if possible, three or four different meanings. "General" is a good one, since it can mean a military general, a general servant, a General omnibus, and, of course, an adjective qualifying a noun.

When the two have agreed on their word, they commence an animated conversation, bring in the word in its various meanings as often as they possibly can, but substituting the word "coffee-pot" for it whenever it occurs. Thus you get a sentence like this, taking "general" as the chosen word:

"D'you know, our coffee-pot opened the door the other day to a very famous coffee-pot, and told him to wait on the doorstep while she went and fetched mother, and a coffee-pot going by splashed him with mud."

Of course, the idea is for the others to guess the word and join in the conversation, to the utter bewilderment of the poor unfortunate people who don't "get it." Sometimes these people think they've got it, and then something else crops up, and the word they have in mind doesn't fit in a bit. So

"I'm not wearing my pearl necklace. You can have it instead of that plain gold chain, if you like," she said to Daisy.

Daisy Dean shook her head.

"I mustn't part with my key to fortune," she laughed, drawing a small golden key from beneath her dress.

Nellie had often seen this key.

"It must be awfully thrilling to carry the key to fortune always about with you," she murmured. "Daisy, I wonder what lock it fits?"

Daisy Dean dangled the golden key before her eyes, and gazed thoughtfully at it.

"I've no idea," she replied, "When the lawyer who acts on behalf of my guardians pays his yearly visit, his first question is always: 'Key all right, I hope, Daisy Dean?' and laughs, sometimes I think with good-natured contempt, when I show it to him."

"I do wonder what it all means!" cried Nellie. "It may be some pirates' gold, or long-hidden treasure—or perhaps some miser's hoard."

"I sometimes think——" began Daisy, when the door was opened, and a sweet-faced, handsome woman, whose light brown hair was but slightly touched with grey, entered.

"Now, you dawdlers, hurry up. The car is at the door," she announced with a laugh.

"I'll be ready in a minute, dear Mrs. Waine," returned Daisy, as she put a few finishing touches to her costume.

Five minutes later they were ripping along the road in the smooth-running car.

About midway between Planel Court and Nellie Waine's house Daisy noticed a huge, gaunt, lonely-looking house standing some distance back from the road.

It would have looked dismal and depressing even on a bright summer's day, but now, surrounded on all sides by untrimmed twigs, and straggling bushes laden deep with snow, it had a peculiarly weird and ghostly appearance.

"What place is that?" she asked, conscious of an unwonted interest in the gloomy pile.

Nellie Waine laughed.

"What does it look like?" she asked, gazing half fearfully at the many gabled roofs, above which towered a number of quaintly shaped chimneys.

"The Haunted Grange," laughed Daisy.

"And that's exactly what it is," declared Nellie. "It's real name is Dellbrooke Hall. It's the largest house in these parts, and all the land you can see as far as the eye can reach goes with it. Save for an old caretaker and his wife, it is quite empty."

"Has it a ghost?" asked Daisy excitedly.

"Rather! There's a white lady whom, the villagers declare, roams the rooms on certain nights, particularly on Christmas Eve. I say, Daisy," she added, "wouldn't it be thrilling to creep up to the house on our way home. We might see the White Lady."

Daisy Dean smiled somewhat absent-mindedly. Then, turning her head, she looked back until a bend in the road hid the old house from view.

"Hasn't it an owner?" she asked at last, referring to the house.

"Oh, yes, it belongs to the Countess of Dellbrooke," said Nellie. "But she will neither let it nor allow it to be occupied. You see, the heir to the property has not been heard of for years and years. Strangely enough, there is a legend that the Hall will be given up to owls, rats, and other unpleasant creatures until the rightful owner enters by the Heir's Door."

"Won't it do as well if he or she enters by the front door, as a well-conducted heir should?" laughed Daisy Dean.

"My dear girl, you're spoiling the whole legend," remonstrated Nell. "You see, there is a real door in the side of the house that has neither lock nor handle. According to local report, no one can open it but the heir. But here we are at Planel Court," she added as the car turned in through a pair of large, wide-open iron gates.

Alighting from the car, the two girls passed into a magnificent entrance hall, ornamented with antlers, foxes, masks and brushes, trophies of arms, and lined with magnificent suits of armour.

Nellie Waine was greeted on all sides in a way that proclaimed her popularity. She passed one girl with a laughing remark, stopped to exchange a few words with another—introduced Daisy to some particular friend—and thus they made their way to the cloak-room where they left their wraps. Afterwards they entered the anteroom, where Sir William and Lady Planel were waiting to receive their guests.

The baronet, a stately, grey-haired old gentleman, stared curiously at Daisy.

"Haven't I seen you before, my dear?" he said as they shook hands.

"I do not think so, Sir William," replied Daisy. "So far as I know, I have never been in this part of the country before."

"It's strange—very strange—but I certainly seem to recognise you. Do you see a likeness to anybody, Phillipa?" he added, turning to his wife.

Lady Planel turned a pair of kindly grey eyes on the girl, and for a moment her forehead grew furrowed with a thoughtful frown.

"I think not, William. And yet there is something strangely familiar about you, my dear," she added. She turned to greet another guest, whilst Daisy and Nell passed into the large ballroom, where an orchestra was playing a fox-trot.

Thanks to Nell, Daisy had no lack of partners, and the evening passed on flying wings.

The Planels were not the only ones to whom Daisy Dean's face seemed familiar. Now and again she found herself being regarded with a look of semi-recognition by some of the more elderly people present.

Once, as she passed out of the ballroom with her partner, they came face to face with a stout old gentleman wearing the ribbon of a distinguished order, and escorting a tall, aristocratic lady of about his own age.

The gentleman started and gazed at Daisy in surprise.

" Pardon an old man's presumption, my dear, but may I ask your name ? " he said courteously.

He shook his head, and passed on with a word of courtly apology when Daisy satisfied his curiosity, and she heard him say, half to himself, half to his companion :

" It's strange—very strange. But, of course, she cannot be connected with the——"

He passed out of hearing before Daisy could catch the conclusion of the sentence.

About half-past eleven, their dancing-shoes changed for stout walking-boots, the two girls left Planel Court and walked down the drive, chatting gaily over the events of the evening.

It was a glorious night. The snow-clouds had rolled away, leaving the full Christmas moon shining in all its splendour from a canopy of gold and silver stars.

On trudged the two girls, stepping aside now and again to allow cars laden with guests from the Court to sweep by them, from out of which young voices shouted merry Christmas greetings.

After a time they walked on in silence, Nellie busy with thoughts of the presents which she knew would await her the following morning, Daisy conscious of an unaccountable feeling of excitement. It was almost as though some unknown influence was drawing her towards Dellbrooke Hall.

As the gloomy pile loomed in sight, Daisy instinctively quickened her steps.

" Hold on, Daisy. This isn't a Marathon, you know," remonstrated her companion.

With a slight laugh, Daisy Dean slowed down.

" Sorry, dear," she apologised. " I don't

The baronet stared curiously at Daisy. " Haven't I seen you somewhere before, my dear ? " he asked.

know what possesses me to-night. I feel exactly as though something strange was going to happen."

" Just in the mood for a spook hunt, eh, Daisy ? " chuckled Nellie.

CHAPTER II.

THE WHITE LADY

DAISY DEAN made no reply, but moved almost unconsciously towards the long, sweeping carriage-drive beyond which the old house stood, a black blotch to its background of driven snow.

A yard or so from the gates Daisy Dean came to an abrupt halt, and gazed in amazement at the crumbling heraldic device that ornamented either carved stone post.

" Don't be frightened, dear; that isn't a ghost," laughed Nellie.

Daisy Dean made no reply, but the colour fled from her face as she moved with firm, though swift and hurried, step through the open gateway.

Her heart was beating rapidly. The unaccountable excitement that had thrilled her frame was increased tenfold before instinctively she raised her hand to her neck, and laid her trembling fingers on the key, the chased handle of which bore the same crest as that which ornamented the pillared posts between which she had just passed.

As she neared the old house the excitement was driven away by an unwonted sense of coming disaster. Her steps lagged, so that now Nellie Waine was leading the way.

The old house presented a forbidding appearance, for the moon shining on the uncleaned windows was reflected back in a strange, bluish sepulchral glare.

It was, or had been, a fine, half-timbered old Elizabethan mansion, and its many gables rendered it extraordinarily picturesque.

Suddenly Nellie Waine, grasping Daisy by the arm, brought her to an abrupt halt.

"I—I don't think we'll go any farther, Daisy," she stammered. "It's getting late, and —and this place is a bit too spooky for me."

But Daisy seemed scarce to hear her. Her eyes were fixed in an intense stare upon one of the downstair windows.

"What is it, Daisy? What can you see?" demanded Nellie Waine in an awe-stricken whisper.

Daisy Dean drew her hand across her eyes.

Then a forced laugh burst from her lips.

"It's gone now, dear," she reassured her companion. "It must have been my fancy, but I seemed to see a tall figure clad all in white, with a pale, colourless face, and a pair of eyes that seemed to shine like points of fire."

"The White Lady of Dellbrooke Grange!" murmured Nellie, clinging to Daisy's arm. "Oh, come back, Daisy! Don't go any farther! It was stupid to come at all!" she urged.

But her companion moved slowly towards where a furrow in the snow proclaimed a hidden path.

"Let me go, Nellie; I must!" she murmured. "The figure seemed to point in this direction."

"No, no, Daisy! Don't—don't!" pleaded Nell. "Oh, I wish I'd never told you about the Haunted Grange!"

"Don't be afraid, dear. Most likely it was all fancy. Anyhow, it's stupid to be afraid of ghosts; they can't hurt us, you know," muttered Daisy.

Nellie Waine suffered herself to be half-led, half-dragged along the ill-defined path.

Scarce heeding the masses of snow that fell from the tall shrubs between which they passed, the two girls moved onward until at length they reached a raised terrace that occupied the whole front of the house.

Either the spirit of adventure had driven out her fears, or she was emboldened by her companion's courage; at any rate, Nellie Waine rapidly regained her wonted high spirits.

"Where are you going now, Daisy?" she asked as, the terrace reached, Daisy Dean passed round the western wing of the house.

As Daisy glanced around she saw—

"I don't know, dear. Something seems to tell me to go in this direction," she said, with a puzzled frown.

"You're going straight to the Heir's Door," whispered Nell. "Look, here it is!" she added, indicating a pointed archway blocked up by what seemed to be a solid mass of oaken timbers.

"As I told you, 'No admittance, even on business,' is the motto here."

As she spoke she leaned against the door and pressed it with all her strength.

"One might as well try to push through a solid wall," she commented.

Then both girls started violently and clung tightly to each other as, from somewhere close

80

at hand, came the deep booming of a clock striking the midnight hour.

Breathlessly the two girls listened as the slow, regular strokes quivered through the air.

"Nine—ten—eleven—twelve!"

Then faint shrieks of terror burst from their lips as, from somewhere beyond the door, came a loud click, as short, sharp, and incisive as a pistol shot.

For nearly a minute they stood gazing with staring eyes at the door, half expecting to see it swing open and some strange form emerge.

But nothing happened.

Presently Daisy Dean started violently, shook herself, as though shaking off the vague terror which had gripped her heart, and, disengaging her arm from Nellie's timid grasp, moved towards the door, and pushed it gently with one hand.

A long-drawn "Oh!" burst from Nellie Waine's lips as, to her amazement, she saw the heavy door swing slowly open in response to her companion's touch.

"Daisy, come back! It's a trap—oh, it's a trap!" she cried in a hoarse whisper.

But Daisy Dean had already crossed the threshold. After a moment's hesitation, Nellie Waine followed.

Immediately before her Daisy found a short flight of steps, up which she stumbled in the darkness, moving on with a swiftly beating heart, but one from which all fear had vanished.

Another door swung open at her touch, and she found herself in a large room, the walls of which were lined with shelves filled with dust-covered books.

Dust lay everywhere—on the antiquated chairs, the solid tables, and the hard, uncomfortable horse-hair couches which our grandfathers loved.

For a little while she stood looking round the moonlit room; then, shaking off Nellie's detaining arm, tripped lightly across the dust-covered floor to an open door, beyond which lay a magnificent hall.

She recoiled in terror as she saw rows of silent, motionless figures standing on either side of the spacious hall.

The next moment she moved forward with renewed courage, her lips curling in a slight smile of self-contempt, as she realised that the figures which had so startled her were nothing more terrible than suits of armour similar to those she had seen at Planel Court.

Nellie Waine had darted back into the library at her friend's ejaculation of alarm, and thus it happened that she failed to see the mysterious, white-clad form which, appearing at the head of the wide, oak-balustraded staircase that occupied the whole end of the hall, beckoned with one long, white hand ere it glided, as though floating

—a mysterious white-clad form

through the air, along the corridor at the head of the stairs.

Without a moment's hesitation, Daisy Dean crossed the hall. Then she paused at the foot of the stairs.

"Daisy! Daisy! Don't leave me!" cried Nellie Waine, hastening after her.

"It's all right, dear. Stop here till I return," said Daisy, winding one arm protectingly round her companion's waist, but never for a moment removing her fixed gaze from the spot where she had last seen the figure in white.

"Oh, Daisy, don't—don't! Let us go! Let us leave this awful place!" almost sobbed Nellie Waine, throwing her arms round Daisy's neck and burying her face in her shoulder.

Very gently Daisy Dean disengaged herself from the other's clinging grasp.

"I *am* going, dear—I must! Something more powerful than I can resist forces me onward," she said.

Breaking free from Nellie's grasp, she ran lightly up the stairs.

"Stop for me, Daisy. I can't let you run into unknown dangers alone!" cried Nellie. "Besides, I daren't be left by myself."

But Daisy Dean had already reached the top of the stairs, and had traversed half the long, magnificent corridor, the walls of which were hung with age-stained oil paintings of bygone Dellbrookes, ere she overtook her.

Suddenly both girls came to an abrupt halt, and stood gazing at where Daisy Dean's spectral guide stood, an awful white, ghostly figure, between a pair of heavy, moth-eaten curtains that hung on either side of an alcove a little distance away.

Paralysed with terror, Nellie Waine stood as though turned to stone as, in obedience to the spectre's beckoning hand, Daisy Dean advanced with quick, yet steady steps towards the alcove.

In vain Nellie Waine tried to cry out—to beg —to command her friend to come back.

But only hoarse moans escaped her lips until, when Daisy was within a few feet of the apparition, the white-clad form turned and, glancing over her shoulder upon the advancing girl, disappeared beyond the curtains.

A moment later Daisy Dean had followed her fearful guide, and Nellie Waine found herself alone in the picture gallery.

CHAPTER III.

"AFTER MANY YEARS"

How long Nellie stood transfixed with terror and dismay, gazing at the spot where she had last seen Daisy Dean, she never knew. It was probably only seconds, but every second seemed an age, until, her fears submerged in love for her friend, she sprang forward and passed beneath the arch.

She found herself in a bare room less than four feet in width, cased in wainscotting and lighted by a small window, through which the bright beams of the moon shone with sufficient light to reveal the fact that she was all alone.

Daisy Dean had disappeared as completely as though she was the ghost she had followed.

"Daisy! Daisy! Darling Daisy, where are you? Oh, come to me! Daisy!" shrieked Nellie Waine as she beat frenziedly upon the oak-covered walls.

But there was no response, and, with a moan of terror, she covered her face with her hands and sank in a huddled heap on to the floor.

But she did not remain there long.

The place was full of those mysterious sounds which haunt all old houses at night-time.

Vague and indistinct moans, cries, and even voices, seemed ringing in the prostrate girl's ears.

Feeling that even the terror of the picture-gallery, the dimly lit hall, with its silent sentinels of armoured men, the ghostly, dust-covered library, were more easily to be borne than that awful spot where her dearest friend had disappeared, Nellie Waine sprang to her feet.

Shrieking wildly, she sped down the stairs and into the open.

The cool night air partly restored her shattered nerves, but she had almost reached the broken entrance gates before the thought that she was leaving Daisy Dean in peril brought her to a standstill.

It spoke well for Nellie Waine's courage that, after a severe fight with the terror which seemed to have turned the very blood in her veins to ice, she retraced her steps.

Slowly and reluctantly at first, but as the knowledge that Daisy Dean was alone in that strange house came upon her with increased force, she broke into a swift run, which carried her to the mysterious entrance through which Daisy Dean had so strangely gained admittance into the Haunted Grange.

To her dismay the door was closed, and though she thrust at it with all her strength and beat upon its panels until her hands ached again, it remained as fast as when she had first found it.

"Oh, why did I leave her?" moaned Nellie. "She would never have left me alone in that awful place."

Anxious to get help and return to her friend's rescue, she ran as fast as her anxiety and fear could force her through the snow on to the high road.

She continued her headlong flight until she reached her home, where she found her father, mother, and elder brother had just reached home; in fact, were in the act of alighting from their car.

Nellie flung herself like a living bombshell, into their midst.

"Mother! Father! The Haunted Home! Daisy Dean! That terrible White Lady!" she panted disconnectedly.

"Good gracious, Nellie, have you gone mad?" cried Mr. Waine.

But her mother had taken the excited girl in her arms and, laying the child's head on her shoulder, bent protectingly over her.

"Steady, dear. Try to be calm, and tell us what has happened," she said in low, soothing tones.

"It was all my fault, mother," began Nellie. "It was I who suggested we should creep into the Haunted Grange on our way home from Lady Planel's, and——" Then, unable longer to fight down the misery that welled up in her overcharged heart, she cried: "Oh, Daisy! Bright, loving little Daisy! I'll never see you again—never!"

"Oh, yes, you will, dear. Daisy has only wandered into some part of the old house and got lost," comforted Mrs. Waine.

"And is most likely frightened half out of her

wits at finding herself alone," interposed her father. "Take Nellie in, mother. Charlie and I will go back and look for Daisy. To the Haunted Grange, James, as quick as you can drive," he added, re-entering the car, closely followed by his son.

"Take me with you, dad!" pleaded Nellie, turning with outstretched arms towards her father. "Please, please, take me with you! I feel as if I will never be happy again until I know what has happened to dear little Daisy."

"Nonsense, Nellie, we will——" began Mr. Waine.

But the mother settled the question by snatching Nellie in her arms, and following her son and husband into the luxuriously appointed vehicle.

As the car sped, as swiftly as the state of the roads would allow, towards its destination, Nellie gave a somewhat confused account of her adventure in the Haunted Grange, and Daisy's mysterious disappearance.

Indeed, her hearers had but a hazy idea of what had occurred when the car drove up the neglected drive leading to Cairn Court.

"Bless me, the house is on fire!" ejaculated Mr. Waine. "No, by all that's wonderful, there are lights in all the lower rooms," he added, and, together with his companions in the car, sat gazing at the brilliantly lighted windows of the old house, until the chauffeur brought the car to a standstill before the front door.

Almost ere it had stopped, Nellie Waine had flung open the door, and was running lightly up the broad, stone steps, whilst, anxious to protect the girl from harm, her brother sped swiftly after her.

As they reached the top of the steps, the doors swung open of their own accord, and Nellie came to an abrupt halt, gazing in wonder at the brilliantly lighted hall before them.

Although dust still lay thick upon everything, it looked a very different place, beneath the light of the candles from a big glass chandelier that hung from the ceiling, from what it had done in the uncertain moonlight, dimmed by the dusty panes of glass through which it had to force its rays.

"This is certainly the most surprising Christ-

mas adventure I ever had," commented Mr. Waine. Then started aside and grew pale, as a white-clad form slowly descended the broken oak stairs before him.

"The White Lady!" screamed Nellie, whilst even her mother uttered an alarmed cry.

The next moment Mr. Waine had moved swiftly forward.

"Lady Dellbrooke! What is the meaning of this masquerading?" he demanded.

The tall, stately, white-haired lady, whom Nellie Waine had not unnaturally taken for the spectre of Cairn Court, smiled as she advanced towards them.

"The White Lady!" screamed Nellie, and clung to her mother.

"I have yet to learn, Mr. Waine, why one may not do what she wishes in her own house. If the superstitious rustics choose to regard me as the White Lady, I cannot help it," she returned.

"But I understood you were in the North, Countess, and that the house was shut up for good, or——."

"Or until the heir returned," smiled the lady.

Then, unable to remain silent any longer, Nellie moved impulsively forward.

"What have you done with Daisy Dean?" she cried. "Oh, please, please take me to her. I have been so unhappy since she followed you through the wall of the alcove."

"Come and see," said the Countess with a kindly smile.

Then, with a courteous sign to the others, to follow, she led the girl up the creaking stairs.

Wonderingly, Nellie found herself once more in the portrait gallery. Ahead lay the alcove, but now bright lights came from behind the curtain, and when, clutching tight hold of the Countess's hand, she passed through the archway, it was to find that what she had taken for a solid wall was a large door.

It now stood wide open, and beyond it Nellie could see a fair-sized apartment, surrounded with dusty shelves, filled to overflowing with ancient manuscripts, and bound, ledger-looking books.

But Nellie scarce noted the contents of the apartment, for she saw Daisy Dean, a little pale and very bewildered, standing in the centre of the room.

"Daisy! Daisy!" cried the relieved girl, bounding forward and clasping her friend in her arms.

"Oh, Nellie, I've such a lot to tell you," cried Daisy. "The White Lady——" she stopped and glanced into the smiling face of the Countess. "I mean, grandmother told me you would soon come back."

"What's this!" ejaculated Mr. Waine. "Daisy Dean called you grandmother!"

"And so I am," cried the Countess, winding her arm round Daisy's waist. "She is the daughter of the son whom I disowned and drove from home twenty long years ago. He declared he would never cross my threshold, nor look me in the face again—and he kept his word," cried the Countess.

A look of deep seated misery banished the loving smile which she had turned upon Daisy.

"And the Key to Fortune?" Mr. Waine demanded.

"Will open the casket which contains the title-deeds to the estate. None but those who know the secret can move the lock," explained the Countess. "Come, dear, remember the instructions given by those who have been your faithful guardians for so many years," she added, turning to Daisy Dean.

Somewhat abashed by the prominent position in which she found herself, Daisy Dean advanced to the table on which stood a large, beautifully chased, though tarnished, silver casket.

Taking the key from her neck, she inserted it in the lock with trembling hands.

When it was about half-way in she turned it about a quarter way round, then thrust the key forward to its farthest extent, and continued the turning movement.

The next moment the lid flew back, revealing a number of age-stained papers, tied with discoloured ribbons.

"Ah, the rightful heir has returned!" cried the Countess. She held out her arms to Daisy Dean, who, with a glad cry, sprang into them and kissed her new-found grandmother again and again.

"But I don't understand!" ejaculated Mr. Waine for perhaps the twentieth time as they stood amongst the canvas-covered furniture in the drawing room, where the old caretaker had lighted a huge fire.

The Countess smiled.

"There are some things beyond understanding. Yet so far as I can explain I will try to do so.

"The happiest hours of my life were spent in this old house, and I have been accustomed to come here at Christmas time, unknown to anyone but the faithful old servitor who has acted as caretaker ever since the quarrel with my son. My passage from room to room has doubtless given rise to the report that the Grange was haunted by a White Lady. But what I cannot understand is the strange instinct that induced my dear granddaughter to come to the Heir's Door just as I was about to open it in response to somebody's knocking.

"I was in the dark, she in the moonlight. I saw her face, and recognised a Dellbrooke. My heart told me who she was, and keeping up the character of the White Lady, I led her to the Muniment Room, for I knew that if it was indeed the long expected one she would have the Key of Fortune on her."

"Oh, Daisy—then you are actually a Countess!" cried Nellie.

"But always Daisy Dean to you, dear," returned the other, passing her arm round her neck and kissing her fondly.

THE   END

84

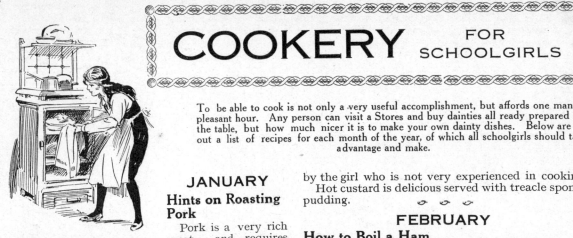

COOKERY FOR SCHOOLGIRLS

To be able to cook is not only a very useful accomplishment, but affords one many a pleasant hour. Any person can visit a Stores and buy dainties all ready prepared for the table, but how much nicer it is to make your own dainty dishes. Below are set out a list of recipes for each month of the year, of which all schoolgirls should take advantage and make.

JANUARY

Hints on Roasting Pork

Pork is a very rich meat, and requires plenty of cooking. Allow twenty minutes to each pound of meat, and twenty minutes over.

Weigh the meat, put it into a baking-tin with plenty of dripping, and place the tin in a hot oven.

Lower the heat after the first ten minutes, and baste the meat frequently while it is cooking.

Roast leg of pork is very nice if stuffed with sage and onion stuffing.

Remember that pork is in season in all the months which contain the letter R.

How to make Sage and Onion Stuffing

Required : One pound of onions, four ounces of breadcrumbs, one dessertspoonful of finely-chopped sage, one ounce of dripping, and salt and pepper.

Peel and chop the onions into small dice. Put them into a saucepan, cover them with cold water, bring them to the boil, and boil for five minutes.

Strain away the water, and drain well.

Melt the dripping in a frying-pan, add the onions, and fry them for fifteen minutes. *Don't* brown them.

Add the breadcrumbs, sage and seasoning, mix well, and the stuffing is ready for use.

Treacle Sponge Pudding

Required : Eight ounces of flour, four ounces of suet, one teaspoonful of black treacle, one egg, two ounces of sugar, half a teaspoonful of bicarbonate of soda, and a little cold milk.

Chop the suet finely and put it into a basin with the flour and bicarbonate of soda. Add the sugar and treacle, and stir well.

Beat the egg, and add it to the other ingredients.

Pour in sufficient cold milk to mix the pudding into a fairly stiff paste.

Grease a pudding-basin, pour in the pudding mixture, cover the basin with greased paper, and steam the pudding for two hours.

This is an inexpensive pudding, and one which can be easily managed

by the girl who is not very experienced in cooking.

Hot custard is delicious served with treacle sponge pudding.

FEBRUARY

How to Boil a Ham

It is more economical to boil your own ham than to buy it ready cooked from the shop.

Hams are usually very salt, and require soaking before they are cooked.

Put them into a large pan or saucepan, cover them with cold water and allow them to stand for twelve hours. The water should be changed two or three times. If the ham is very hard, it should be soaked longer.

Scrape away all the smoked parts, put the ham into a boiler and cover with cold water. Bring it gradually to the boil, and remove the scum.

Keep the ham simmering very gently until it is tender, and be sure that it does not boil quickly, or stop boiling altogether.

A ham weighing eight pounds requires three and a half hours' boiling.

Remove the ham from the boiler, and peel off the skin.

Sprinkle over some bread raspings, or grated nutmeg, and wind a paper frill round the knuckle.

If the ham is to be eaten cold, let it stay in the water in which it is boiled until it is cold. This keeps in the juices, and the flavour of the ham is better.

Brazil Toffee

Required : Six ounces of brown sugar, half a gill of water, one ounce of butter, one ounce of brazil nuts.

Put the sugar and water into a saucepan, heat it gradually, and boil for twenty minutes.

Add the butter, and boil until a little of the toffee if dropped into cold water turns brittle.

Turn the toffee into a greased tin, and when it is beginning to set, mark it with a knife into square pieces.

Remove the nuts from the shells, cut each nut into quarters, and before the toffee is set, press a piece of the nut on to each portion of toffee.

Stand aside to harden.

MARCH

Fish Patties

Required : One ounce of dripping, one ounce of flour, half a pint of milk, salt and pepper, a little lemon juice, one pound of cold cooked fish, and short paste

Melt the dripping in a frying-pan, add the flour, and stir until the flour is cooked. Add the seasoning and lemon juice, and pour in the milk slowly, stirring all the time.

Remove the skin and bones from the fish, break it into small pieces, and add it to the milk. Mix well, and make hot. Prepare a short paste, and line some patty-pans with it. Put some of the fish mixture into each patty-pan, cover with a lid of paste, knock up the edges of the patties, and bake them in a quick oven until they are a golden brown.

These can be served hot for breakfast, and are a real treat. The only difficulty experienced in making the patties is in adding the milk to the flour. It must be added very slowly and stirred well, otherwise the flour will go " lumpy."

Daffodil Buns

Required : Four ounces of flour, one ounce of butter, one ounce of castor sugar, half a teaspoonful of baking powder, half a teaspoonful of finely grated lemon rind, one egg, and a few drops of essence of lemon.

Put the butter and sugar into a basin, and beat them to a cream. Beat the egg, and add it to the butter.

Mix the flour, lemon rind and baking powder together, and add them gradually to the butter, etc.

Add a few drops of essence or lemon, stir the mixture, put it into greased patty-pans, and bake the cakes in a moderate oven for ten minutes. Remove the cakes from the tins, and when they are cold, cover them with lemon icing.

APRIL

Curried Cod

Required : One pound of cod, one ounce of dripping, one dessertspoonful of sugar, one teaspoonful of curry powder, one small onion, half a pint of white stock, and salt and pepper to taste.

Wash and dry the fish, and cut it into pieces about two inches square.

Melt the dripping in a saucepan, and fry the cod slightly on both sides. Remove the fish from the saucepan, and stand it aside.

Peel and slice the onion, put it with the flour and curry powder into the saucepan, and fry for ten minutes. Stir all the time to prevent the onion from becoming browned.

Pour the stock into the saucepan, stir until the contents boil, then simmer for fifteen minutes.

Strain through a sieve, and return the soup to the saucepan.

Add the fish to the soup, season, and allow the saucepan to stand over a very gentle heat for twenty minutes. Stir occasionally to prevent the fish from burning to the bottom of the saucepan.

Serve hot with a border of plain boiled rice.

Baked Sultana Pudding

Required : Eight ounces of flour, three ounces of sugar, four ounces of sultanas, four ounces of margarine, two ounces of candied peel, half a teaspoonful of mixed spice, one teaspoonful of baking powder, and a little cold milk.

Put the sugar and margarine into a basin and beat them to a cream. Chop the peel, clean and pick the sultanas and add them to the margarine and sugar.

Add the spice, baking powder, and flour, and mix well.

Pour in sufficient cold milk to mix the pudding into a stiff paste.

Grease a piedish, pour the pudding into it, and bake in a moderate oven for one and a quarter hours.

MAY

Cold Meat Omelette

Required : Half a pound of cold meat, three ounces of flour, one egg, half a pint of milk, salt and pepper, and one teaspoonful of baking powder.

Mince the meat very finely. Put the flour into a large basin, beat the egg, and add it to the milk. Make a hole in the centre of the flour, gradually add the milk and egg, and beat well until a batter is formed. Grease a piedish. Add the minced meat to the batter, sprinkle in a little salt and pepper, and stir in the baking powder.

Pour the mixture into the greased piedish, and bake in a moderate oven for forty minutes. Turn the omelette on to a hot dish, and serve hot, brown gravy with it.

Springtime Biscuits

Required : Three ounces of flour, one ounce of butter, one ounce of castor sugar, one ounce of currants, one egg, and a quarter of a teaspoonful of mixed spice.

Put the butter and flour into a basin, and rub the butter into the flour until no lumps remain.

Wash and dry the currants.

Add the sugar, currants and spice to the flour, etc., and mix into a stiff paste with the beaten egg.

Roll the paste out on a well-floured board, cut the biscuits into fancy shapes and bake them in a moderate oven until they are slightly browned.

Just before the biscuits are baked, brush them over with a little milk, sprinkle on a little castor sugar, and return them to the oven to brown.

JUNE

Tomato Soup

Required : One and a half pints of stock or water, one pound of tomatoes, one dessertspoonful of fine ago, half an ounce of dripping, one small onion and one small carrot, a small bunch of mixed herbs, salt sand pepper.

Peel the onion, scrape the carrot, and cut them into slices. Slice the tomatoes. Put the dripping into a saucepan and melt it. Add the carrot and the onion and fry for a few minutes, but do not brown them. Add the tomatoes, and cook for a further ten minutes. Pour in the stock or water, and cook until the vegetables are tender. Rub the vegetables through a sieve, and return the soup to the saucepan. Bring to the boil ; add the sago and seasoning and simmer until the sago becomes transparent. Serve very hot.

Bakewell Tart

Required : Four ounces of short paste, a little jam, one ounce each of ground almonds, castor sugar, butter, one egg, and a few drops of essence of almonds.

Prepare a short paste, and line a plate with it. Spread on the jam.

Separate the white from the yolk of the egg.

Put the butter and sugar into a basin and beat them to a cream.

Beat the yolk of egg and add it to the butter and sugar. Then add the almonds and a few drops of essence of almonds. Whip up the white of egg, and add it to the other ingredients. Beat the mixture for one minute.

Spread the mixture lightly on to the paste, and bake in a moderate oven for twenty-five minutes. Serve either hot or cold.

Be sure your tart *is* a bake(d)well tart.

JULY

Cornish Pasties

Required : Four ounces of flour, one and a half ounces of dripping, half a teaspoonful of baking powder, a pinch of salt, two ounces of beef, two ounces of parboiled potatoes, one small parboiled onion, seasoning, a pinch of mixed herbs, and a little gravy.

Cut the meat, onion, and potatoes into small pieces. Put them into a basin and add the gravy, mixed herbs, and seasoning. Mix well.

Put the flour, dripping, and salt into another basin. Rub the dripping into the flour until no lumps remain, add the baking powder, and mix into a paste with a *little* water. Roll out into a strip about a quarter of an inch in thickness.

Cut the paste into round pieces, put some of the meat, etc., into the centre of each round, damp the edges of the paste with cold water and press the edges firmly together on the tops of the pasties.

Place the pasties on to a baking sheet and bake in a moderate oven for twenty minutes.

Walnut Dainties

Required : Short pastry, one ounce of castor sugar, one ounce of butter, one small egg, a few drops of flavouring and one and a half ounces of dried walnuts.

Chop the walnuts into small pieces.

Beat the butter and sugar to a cream, add the walnuts and flavouring and stir well.

Beat the egg, and add sufficient of it to the butter, etc., to form a stiff paste.

Line some patty-pans with short paste, half fill them with the walnut mixture and bake in a moderate oven for fifteen minutes.

Sprinkle the cakes with icing sugar, and place half a walnut in the centre of each. These little cakes are always sure of a welcome on the tea table.

AUGUST

Sunshine Fancies

Required : Three ounces of flour, one and a half ounces of castor sugar, one egg, one and a half ounces of butter, quarter of a teaspoonful of baking powder, one tablespoonful of cold milk, and one ounce of candied cherries.

Put the butter and sugar into a basin, and beat them to a cream.

Separate the white from the yolk of egg, and beat them separately. Add the yolk of egg and milk to the butter, and mix.

Mix the flour and baking powder together, and gradually add them to the butter and egg, and beat well.

Gently stir in the white of egg, and put the cake mixture into greased patty-pans.

Decorate the cakes with the cherries, and bake in a moderate oven for fifteen minutes.

Marzipan Fingers

Required : Four ounces of ground almonds, white of an egg, four ounces of icing sugar, and a few drops of vanilla flavouring.

Rub the icing sugar through a sieve, put into a basin with the almonds, white of egg, and flavouring, and pound together into a firm and smooth paste.

Sprinkle a pasteboard with sugar, and roll out the mixture half an inch in thickness.

Cut into strips about two inches long, and dry very slightly in a cool oven.

SEPTEMBER

Salmon Cakes

Required : One small tin of salmon, four ounces of rice, one egg, seasoning, and a few breadcrumbs.

Boil the rice in water until it is tender, strain and dry. Break the salmon into small pieces, and mix it with the rice. Stir in the *yolk* of the egg, and the seasoning, mix well, and stand over a gentle heat until the mixture is quite hot. Stir occasionally, to prevent it from burning. Turn the mixture on to a large dish, sprinkle a board with flour, and make the mixture into small, round, flat cakes. Beat the white of the egg and dip each cake into it, sprinkle them with breadcrumbs, and fry in the hot fat. Drain, and serve hot.

These cakes are nice, either for supper or breakfast.

SPECIAL TIP.—Be sure that the fat in which you fry these cakes is really smoking hot.

Baked Apple Dumplings

Required : Four ounces of flour, two ounces of dripping or margarine, half a teaspoonful of baking powder, two large cooking apples, and brown sugar.

Prepare a short paste with the flour, dripping, and baking powder. Roll out the paste into a long strip.

Peel the apples and cut them into thin slices.

Cut the paste into squares, put some apples in the centre of each square, and add a little sugar.

Turn the four corners of the paste to the centre of the square, thus covering the apples ; press so as to keep them in position.

Bake on a baking sheet in a good oven till the paste is a pale brown.

Sprinkle the dumplings with castor sugar before sending them to table.

OCTOBER

Meat Patties

Required : Eight ounces of flour, three ounces of lard or dripping, a pinch of salt, a teaspoonful of baking-powder, four ounces of beef, quarter of a teaspoonful of mixed herbs and a little gravy and seasoning.

With the flour, dripping, pinch of salt, and baking powder, prepare a short paste.

Mince the meat, or cut it into very small pieces, put it into a basin with the mixed herbs, and mix together. Add a little seasoning.

Cover six or eight patty-pans with paste, and cut lids of paste to fit.

Put some of the meat into each patty-pan, and cover with a lid of paste.

Knock up the edges of the patties with a knife, brush over the top with a little milk, make a hole in the centre of each patty, pour in a teaspoonful of gravy and bake in a hot oven for twenty minutes.

Date Tart

Required : Short paste, half a pound of dates, four ounces of breadcrumbs, and one teaspoonful of golden syrup.

Remove the stones from the dates, and chop the fruit very finely. Put the breadcrumbs and sugar into a basin, add the dates and syrup, and mix.

Cover a plate with short paste, spread over the dates, and cover the tart with a lid of paste.

Bake in a quick oven for twenty minutes.

This is a good method of using up pastry cuttings, and makes a nice tart 'for supper.

NOVEMBER

Ham Toast

Required : Thin slices of lean ham, a little grated cheese, thin slices of bread, boiling fat for frying.

Remove the crusts from the bread, and cut it into oblong shapes. Fry these in a pan of hot fat, until they are a golden brown, and drain on white kitchen paper. Place on each piece of bread a slice of ham, sprinkle over a little grated cheese, and cover over with another piece of fried bread. Put the ham toasts into the oven for a few minutes, and serve when thoroughly hot. Garnish with parsley.

Use up the meat on the ham bone this way. I'm sure that you will like it better.

Jam Puffs

Required : Puff paste, and any kind of jam.

Prepare a puff paste, and roll it out into a large thin strip.

Cut the paste into round shapes, the size of a large saucer, and into the centre of each piece put a heaped teaspoonful of jam.

Fold over the paste from three sides to the centre. Damp the edges of the paste, and press them down firmly, so that they stick together.

Fold the edges so that they lap over. This will prevent the jam from oozing out.

Place the puffs on to a greased tin, the folded-over edges of the paste underneath.

Bake the puffs in a moderate oven for about fifteen minutes, and just before they are baked, brush them over with a little beaten egg and milk, and return them to the oven until the surfaces are a pale brown.

DECEMBER

Roast Turkey

Required : One turkey, sausage-meat, veal forcemeat, a few slices of fat bacon, gravy, bread sauce, and plenty of fat for basting.

Fill the crop of the bird with sausage-meat, and the body with veal forcemeat. Place the bacon over the breast of the bird, and fasten it on with a skewer.

Place the turkey in a large baking-tin, and add plenty of fat for basting. Put the tin into a hot oven, and cook from an hour and a half to two hours, according to the size of the bird.

Baste frequently. Fifteen minutes before the bird is cooked, remove the bacon from the breast and allow the breast to brown.

Serve on a hot dish. The gravy and bread sauce should be served in separate sauceboats. Preparing the veal forcemeat, bread sauce, assisting with the stuffing of the bird, and the basting, are all duties which the schoolgirl cook can easily manage.

Christmas Pudding (Plain)

Required : Four ounces of flour, four ounces of breadcrumbs, eight ounces of chopped suet, eight ounces of raisins, four ounces of sultanas, four ounces of currants, four ounces of mixed candied peel, four ounces of sugar, two or three eggs, and sufficient milk to mix the pudding.

Stone the raisins, chop the candied peel, and pick, wash, and dry the sultanas and currants. Chop the suet finely. Rub the breadcrumbs.

Put all the dry ingredients into a large basin and mix well together. Beat the eggs and add them to the dry ingredients. Pour in sufficient milk to make the pudding moist, but don't make it " sloppy." Stir well.

Grease one or two basins, and use plenty of dripping for this purpose. Fill the basins quite full with the pudding, and cover the tops with greased paper.

Tie the basins in pudding-cloths, and boil for four hours

THE GIRL QUEEN of CAMPANA

by Ada Crundall

A Story of a Plucky British School Girl.

CHAPTER I.

CAUGHT IN THE STORM.

"SHALL we reach Campana to-night, Phil?"

"Not to-night, Bell, dear—midday to-morrow I hope."

The young girl stifled a sigh of fatigue, and set her little mouth firmly as she trudged along by the side of her big brother Phil.

She knew she was pretty nearly done; but until her legs gave way not one complaint would she utter. No; she would go on and on as they had been doing all day, all yesterday, and all the day before, through this mountainous region that skirted the boundaries of the South American State of Paraguay.

The first stages of their desperate trek had been marked with incessant rain; the second stage—that was yesterday—the sun had shone with the intensity of a furnace; to-day, the air was stifling and humid like a vapour bath.

Now came faintly the roll of distant thunder, and occasionally the darkening sky near the horizon was rent by a momentary flash of lightning.

Bell Constantine forced up her drooping head. Not a human being to be seen anywhere; not a habitation; only the mountains on either side dotted here and there with wild straggling clumps of trees and coarse vegetation.

Her brother suddenly turned on her and whipped her up in his strong arms.

"Let me carry you just for a few minutes," he pleaded.

"No, no Phil!" she protested.

"But you're dead beat — you must be!"

"I'm not. I can go on for h-h-hours."

Bravely Bell attempted to keep her voice firm, but tired nature proved too strong. Her weary arms sought her brother's broad shoulders and she clung to him weeping.

"Oh, we shall fail!" she muttered brokenly, "we shall not arrive in time, and it is all through me."

"Quite so, Bell," returned Phil Constantine with a cheering laugh. "It is entirely your fault that you are only fourteen and not thirty-three like I am. Then you'd be able to walk *me* off my legs. But on the other hand, I'm a mere

infant in arms when it comes to talking Spanish, while you're a grown-up in the lingo. When we get to Campana you'll carry me along, and rescue poor old father into the bargain, with your clever patter—so hang on until I tell you I'm tired."

Thus lightly he spoke; but had she seen his eyes she would have read in them the growing anxiety as he gazed at the heavy banking of advancing cloud that was rapidly wiping out the last vestiges of the streaky, angry sunset.

Two minutes later a flash of lightning darted through the sky and for a moment lit up the scene around them. It was followed by a clap of thunder so closely, indeed, that both knew they would very shortly be in the very heart of the tempest.

Then came a mighty rush of wind sweeping into their faces so that Phil was forced to stop. But with the exception of a drop or so there had, as yet, been no rain.

"Phil," cried Bell, gently sliding from his arms—she had to shout to make herself heard— "I am *quite* rested, really, honour bright. There seems to be some sort of track down——"

A further gust of wind tore at them and her voice became mingled with its shrieking onslaught. The storm now commenced in earnest. Big drops of rain followed each other in rapid succession until it seemed as if sheets of water were falling from the skies.

They were, of course, quickly drenched to the skin, and this, added to the fact that they had scarcely eaten anything that day, produced a coldness and shivering which was almost unendurable.

The sounds which filled the air had an awful effect upon their senses, and Bell could not tell which was the most terrible —the loud thunder-clap or the roaring of the wind.

A more than usually vivid flash of lightning broke over on their left and, for a brief second, details stood out for miles with photographic distinctness. The track Bell had seen dipped down a winding course into a deep and wide valley, and about a mile distant was a building.

The flash died out and once more darkness enveloped them.

Bell felt her brother grip her arm.

"You saw it?" he breathed.

Crash, went the thunder.

"Yes, Phil, a house!" she answered as the rolling echoes died away.

"I thought so too. Come, we'll try and get there."

They caught at each other's hands, and, as the next flash came, plunged down the precipitous path. Stones rattled hither and thither under their stumbling feet and ever and anon at some unsheltered gap they encountered the full fury of the rain-laden gale.

"Shall we stop a moment and rest?" Bell heard her brother ask.

"No, no," she protested. "We shall soon be there now."

The thought of a house and shelter made her forget fatigue. Besides, she felt that if once she were to halt she would simply fall like a log.

Suddenly, a hundred yards away, a loud crack rent the air, a dazzling sparkle of light followed, and then a dull thud. Something had been struck by lightning—probably a tree. A succeeding flash showed a dark object lying across their path—a tree undoubtedly—but ere the flash died away they plainly saw an outline of a fair sized building just beyond.

To this haven of refuge they dashed full tilt.

CHAPTER II.

THE CRY IN THE DARKNESS

LOUDLY they knocked on the door. Their feet and knuckles rattled the panels.

The noise around was too great for them to hear any movements inside, and therefore it was with startling suddenness that the door opened a foot, and a man's head sprang into view.

"Who are you?"

The words were spoken in Spanish; the voice gruff, but not unkindly.

"Two travellers caught in the storm. May we shelter here?" answered Bell in the same language.

The man lifted the flickering light so that it shone on their faces.

"Ha, a girl and a man," said he, half to himself. "Well, I wouldn't turn away a dog on a night like this."

"My brother and I—we are English!" cried Bell.

90

And he opened the door another inch or so.

Something in his accent made Bell speak in her native tongue.

"My brother and I—we are English," she said.

At this the door opened to its fullest extent, and Bell and her brother were dragged inside.

"Wife! Wife!" shouted the man, in great excitement. "Come here—quick! A little lass and her brother from the old country! Ah, it does my eyes good to look upon you and my ears tingle at the sound of your voices. 'Tis many a weary month since I heard English spoken. Sibley is my name—Joe Sibley. My gracious, but you're soaking! What a storm! Wife!" he bellowed, striving to make his voice heard above the thunder.

Out bustled his wife, a broad smile of welcome on her face.

"And poor little lass!" she cried. "Right glad I am to see your pretty face. Quick, come to my room and let me give you dry things!" This and more did the good woman say as she slipped her arm about Bell's waist and started to lead her upstairs.

Bell quickly divested herself of her damp clothing and donned the garments that Mrs. Sibley raked out for her. Then downstairs they went, to find Phil had received the same kind attention from Mr. Sibley.

They sat down at the table, and quickly food and drink was placed before them. The sudden change from the raging storm outside to these peaceful quarters seemed like a dream to Bell.

Peaceful! It did not remain so for long. Hardly had she tasted the first mouthful of the plain, but welcome fare, when a louder crash than the thunder shook the house to its very foundations.

Bell laid down her knife and fork with a clatter, and started to her feet in imitation of the others.

"Joe, Joe!" cried Mrs. Sibley, all of a quiver. "Can it be an earthquake?"

Joe Sibley and Bell's brother rushed to a

window at the back, threw it open, and leaned out. Close behind them pressed Bell and Mrs. Sibley.

The lights in the apartment flickered in the draught, and the swooping rain beat in on their faces, as they peered into the blackness.

Once more came that ominous rumble, again the house shuddered in every beam and rafter, and then a vivid flash of lightning rent the sky, disclosing the distant mountain ridge and jutting peaks.

Even as they looked they saw one of these peaks detach itself from the ridge and—disappear!

Almost simultaneously the crash echoed far and wide. Hard on this came a series of nearer crashes, splintering sounds as if huge trees were toppling to the earth.

"My word!" breathed Joe Sibley, backing away from the window. " 'Tis a landslip. The whole valley may be buried—this very house——"

They huddled together for the moment, panic-stricken, uncertain whether to remain or quit the house.

For a moment there was a brief phase of comparative silence that was suddenly broken by a vague, wailing cry from the front. Twice it welled forth, and then the thunder dominated all other sound.

Bell happened to be nearest the door, and acting on the impulse of the moment, she darted into the entrance hall. The cry still echoed in her ears, and some curious intuition told her that it was a girl's voice that had given vent to it.

Often, in after years, she remembered how certain she was about this—remembered and marvelled!

"Bell! Bell!" she heard her brother's voice cry out; but even as he appeared, closely followed by the Sibleys, she had the front door open and had dived into the night.

Squelch! She found herself almost up to her knees in water. Strange! There had been no water here a quarter of an hour ago. She did not know that the mountain stream had been turned from its course and was now flooding the house and gardens.

An excellent sense of direction guided Bell to the track by which they had made their approach, and, reaching it, she became aware that somewhere close at hand animals were kicking and plunging.

Cautiously she waded in that direction, and, aided by the flashes of lightning, she made out the squat form of an overturned carriage. From the occupant evidently had proceeded the cry she had heard.

"Help is near!" she called out in Spanish.

No answer came from the carriage; but behind her boomed her brother's voice asking her whereabouts.

"I am here—this way—there has been an accident!" And as she cried out these words Bell clambered up on to the overturned carriage, and sought for the handle of the door.

She found it; but almost immediately another matter claimed her whole attention. Out from the open window dangled a limp little hand.

Bell grasped it with her right hand, and her other travelled up the arm until her fingers came in contact with a face—cold as stone.

"Phil! Phil!" she shouted frantically.

In a moment her brother and Joe Sibley joined her, and their strong arms tore open the door as if it had been made of matchboard. Then they groped inside and gently lifted out the limp form of a girl of about Bell's age and size.

"She breathes," muttered Phil. "No other passenger, eh?"

"Seemingly not," returned Sibley. "But where's the driver—he must be found."

"Mr. Sibley and I will search, Phil, while you take the girl to the house," said Bell.

"Nay, nay, lassie; you've done enough, and more, this night," broke in Joe Sibley. "You go with your good brother. This is no work for a young girl—besides, the wife will want you. Yon poor lassie, I fear, is sore hurt, and doctors don't grow in these parts."

CHAPTER III.
THE PRINCESS.

As is the habit of storms in South America, it died down as quickly as it had arisen. The clouds were now broken, and a sickly moon shone down on the scene of the tempest's havoc. One of its pale beams entered the bed-room and mingled with the yellow candle-light that flickered by the bedside. On the ceiling were two huge shadows cast by the heads of Bell Constantine and Mrs. Sibley as they stood regarding the still figure of the girl Bell had rescued.

On the white pillow, her dank hair, black as a raven's wing, spread its locks either side of the still face. Spanish in features, a beautiful face doubtless when animated, but now the eyes were closed and the mouth drawn. She breathed jerkily.

"She will recover—you think so?" whispered Bell.

Mrs. Sibley muttered a hurried "Yes," but clearly she had her doubts.

"At any rate," she added, "we've done all we could. Get you downstairs, my dear, and warm a bit by the fire. I'll stop here meantime. Ay, and please take the letter we found on the poor girl. The men folk had better read it."

Bell took the crumpled paper Mrs. Sibley handed to her and crept on tip-toe from the room.

"Well?" asked her brother when she appeared.

"She's still unconscious," said Bell, kneeling on the hearthrug between the chairs where Phil and Joe Sibley sat.

"Ah!" said Joe Sibley. "'Tis as I say. The horses took fright some distance from here, threw the driver off the box, and bolted. Bound for Campana likely enough. I wonder who the girl is?"

Bell unfolded the piece of paper she had brought down, and flourished it before their eyes.

"This," said she, "tells us! It is written in Spanish, and we found it on her when we undressed her. Phil, she is a princess!"

They sat up at this announcement and stared at Bell.

"This is what the letter says," went on Bell, and she began to translate:

"Your Excellency,—This is Donna Anna, daughter of the late King of Campana. You should find her in every way a girl likely to further your policy.—I am, your humble servant, ZALVA LEZARDO."

Bell stopped, and then she glanced at the heading.

"It is addressed to Don Pedro Carlos," she announced.

"Pedro Carlos!" ejaculated Joe Sibley in a tone of disgust. "Further *his* policy—another word for treachery. And that poor maid upstairs is the daughter of the late king whom Pedro schemed against, and eventually superseded two years ago? Well, well, she's better where she is than being mixed up in the plots of that scoundrel. Campana is a town to avoid these days."

Bell looked at her brother, and he, catching her anxious glance, turned to Sibley.

"For all that," said he, "I and my sister must go there to-morrow. Our father, Captain Constantine, of the trading ship Patrol, is there a prisoner. We hope to rescue him."

"We *must* rescue him," added Bell.

Joe Sibley's eyes nearly started out of his head.

"You have as much chance of rescuing him as you have of ruling Campana!" he protested. "A foreigner to put his nose inside the town is asking to be robbed and thrown into prison. No, no! Neither of you must go there. How came it that your father was captured?"

"He refused to undertake to ship arms to Campana," said Phil Constantine. "By a false message he was de-coyed from his ship a week ago, and we have certain information that he was taken to Campana."

"And you and your sister hope to rescue him?"

"Yes," returned Bell simply. "I can speak Spanish like a native, and, disguised, we thought there might be a chance to get father free."

"My word!" breathed Sibley, glancing at Bell with great admiration. "You're a fine-hearted lass and that's the truth. Still——"

He broke off and held up his hand as a signal for silence. Then he rose from his chair.

"I hear voices outside," he whispered. "More travellers for shelter?"

A loud knocking at the door echoed through the house. Joe Sibley strode into the hall, and they heard him withdrawing the bolts. Then voices arose—foreign voices—with a certain ring of command in their tones. Sibley could be heard arguing.

"Not very welcome visitors, I should judge," muttered Phil Constantine to Bell.

Bell thought the same, and when, a minute later, four swarthy-looking men entered, each with a rifle slung over his shoulder, her opinion was confirmed.

"You do not always speak the truth, my friend," said one, addressing Sibley in Spanish.

Then, before Sibley could reply, he turned to Bell.

"Help is near," called out Bell. But no answer came from the interior of the carriage.

93

"Donna Anna," he said, lowering his voice in a sort of rough respect, " you will please continue your journey to Campana, *at once !* "

CHAPTER IV.
THEIR " MISTAKE."

"THEY take me for the girl upstairs ! " These words buzzed through Bell's brain ; but, even as she was about to deny the statement, a wild thought came to her. Why shouldn't she enact this character ?

As "Donna Anna " she would have a far greater chance of helping her father than if she went to Campana, as was the original intention, in her guise as a poor native girl. And the real Donna Anna—surely it would be doing her a kindness to take her place, for a time, at any rate.

Joe Sibley had spoken to Donna Anna's father being deposed two years ago. Two years ! During that time Donna Anna had very likely been away from Campana, and in that case, thought Bell, the difference in her appearance to that of the real princess might not arouse any comment. Indeed, now Bell came to think of it, they were not so very much unlike. Bell was dark, and the recent exposure to wind and sun had turned her to the duskiness of a Spanish South American.

These varied thoughts only occupied the space of a fraction of a moment ; indeed, hardly had the man's voice died away than Joe Sibley was attempting to rectify the mistake.

"This girl is not the one you seek," he interjected. "She and her brother were caught in the storm, and——"

He paused, for one of the visitors had picked up the letter Mrs. Sibley had found on Donna Anna.

"Evidence here to the contrary," he observed, with a short laugh.

"Bell, what's all the jabber about ? " demanded Phil.

Bell opened her lips to explain, but at that moment the four men closed around her.

"Come, Donna Anna," said he who was their leader. "It will go badly with you if you attempt to disobey the orders of his Excellency Don Pedro. We have no wish to use force ; but if force is necessary—well ! "

He paused significantly.

Although her brother did not understand what was being said, the attitude of these men left him under no delusions. He sprang forward, his fists clenched, and with a flush of anger on his face.

They wheeled round on him, hands grasping their rifles.

"Phil," cried Bell in English, "they take me for the girl upstairs, and wish to conduct me to Campana. Why not let them do it ? Oh, don't you see how it will help ? "

Her brother's jaw dropped. For a second he stood dumbfounded—attempting to get hold of the situation.

"But—but—the risk ! " he muttered.

"Who is this man ? " demanded the leader.

"English," returned Bell. "He is a good friend——"

"Ah ! He travelled with you ? "

Bell nodded.

The man favoured Phil with a keen scrutiny for a second or so.

"Strange," he grunted. "Still, it is a matter for his Excellency to investigate. Now, your Highness, waste no further time in words, but follow us. Señor Sibley, his Excellency, Don Pedro, will doubtless see that you are rewarded for helping the princess. Adios ! "

Joe Sibley scratched his head in perplexity. He took Bell's hand in his, and all he could mumble was : " They'll find out the mistake, and then——"

"Ah, but it's *their* mistake," returned Bell quickly. "They have only themselves to blame."

Out into the flooded garden they trudged, and made straight for the overturned carriage. The four men, helped by Phil, managed to right it, and, after harnessing a couple of horses, they moved off down the uneven track which led to Campana.

"Bell," said Phil, for they had allowed him to ride inside with her, "I don't know whether to shake you or hug you. How can you ever hope to play the part ? It's mad—magnificently mad, perhaps—but for all that quite mad."

"Phil ! " she breathed. "I know it is, yet it *may* succeed. After all, having put me in this position themselves, it will take a lot to convince them they have made a mistake."

Her brother gave vent to a doleful whistle, and to himself he muttered :

"Personally, I have no hope—no hope at all."

CHAPTER V.
YOUR " MAJESTY ! "

THE morning sun streamed down on the city of Campana, and reflected its bright rays on a thousand windows, penetrating into squalor and splendour with fine indifference to poverty and riches.

Many things it disclosed, from poor Captain Constantine in his bare prison to his Excellency Don Pedro at breakfast in the gilded banqueting hall at the palace. In the courtyard, overlooked by both prison and palace, stood a ramshackle, mud-bespattered coach, the latter an object of great interest to the soldiers on guard. Rumour had it that the vehicle had brought to Campana none other than the late king's daughter, Princess Anna.

94

Rumour, as we are aware, was only partly right, but his Excellency Don Pedro had no idea of this. The girl who was now being robed in the rich attire befitting her rank was the princess without a doubt.

That she could be otherwise he never gave a thought.

"A pretty, silent child," he remarked to the tall, lantern-jawed person who shared his breakfast—his right-hand man, General Sandoval. "She was, of course, over-awed by my presence. Well, in name she shall be ruler of Campana, and so satisfy those who still give allegiance to the old king, her father; but in reality it will be I who will rule."

The other nodded in approval.

"She must continue to remain in awe of your Excellency," he said.

Don Pedro smiled a thin, cruel smile.

"I fancy there will be no difficulty about *that*, my friend. Now, as to the coronation, it must be mainly a military ceremony. I rely upon *you* to see to that, Sandoval."

"The whole army shall be present, sir."

Don Pedro and his general exchanged a meaning smile.

"The matter of the English

"Father! Father!" cried Bell.

Bell, with as regal a demeanour as she could muster, passed through the ranks of the guard of honour.

prisoner still awaits your decision," said General Sandoval after a pause. "It is a pity we can neither speak his language nor he ours. An interpreter would be invaluable to make him understand *exactly* what will happen if he refuses to bring us those guns on board his ship."

Don Pedro bared his gums, which was apparently the nearest he ever got to a laugh.

"An interpreter has fortunately arrived," he said. "The princess during her stay in San Juan has apparently picked up a smattering of English. Selim told me this. Also, the man sent with her is an Englishman. I think, therefore, before many hours are over we shall be able to make this Captain Constantine fully understand the perils of defying us."

A tap at the folding doors caused Don Pedro to wheel round in his chair.

"Enter!" he called out.

The doors swung open, and an official appeared.

"Your Excellency," he said, with a bow, "the Princess Anna awaits without. Is it your will that I admit her?"

Don Pedro nodded a curt assent.

A minute later there was a clamp of footsteps, and a dozen soldiers with drawn sabres filed through the doorway. They lined up by the entrance, with swords held at the salute. Then, Bell, with as regal a front as she could muster, passed through their ranks, and dropped a curtsey to Don Pedro.

Fine feathers, they say, make fine birds, yet the fact remains that Bell was in no way a discredit to the real princess. She wore her fine flowing robes to the manner born, and she was as pretty a little princess as ever stepped out of a fairy story.

95

Don Pedro returned her salutation with a fine bow. He took her hand in his, lightly kissed it, and led her to the seat of honour.

"Her Highness—shortly to be Her Majesty—and I would be alone," he announced ; and instantly the soldiers and attendants withdrew.

"Now!" breathed Bell to herself. "Now——"

For some moments Don Pedro paced the apartment. Then he turned on Bell. No longer was there the fawning smile upon his face. His features were fixed grimly and threateningly.

"Listen, signorita!" he snapped. "I have had you brought here, not for your own personal glorification, but for the good of Campana. You have to understand that!"

Meekly, Bell bowed her head.

"The good of Campana is in my hands," continued Don Pedro. "A maiden like you must regard me in the light of a father ; in other words, to be obeyed unquestioningly. Go contrary to my wishes, disobey my commands, and you will be punished—punished severely. You hear me?"

Once more Bell submissively inclined her head.

"You will be crowned Queen of Campana so as to satisfy the noisy rabble who still uphold your family. In public I shall treat you as a queen, but in private I am the master, you the pupil. Well?"

He eyed her fiercely. He had no doubt in his mind that she was thoroughly cowed ; ready to burst into tears ; ready to swear to obey him in everything. Men had trembled before his anger ; how much more so this girl!

Outwardly, Bell fell in with his expectations ; inwardly, however, quite a different state of affairs was going on. Bell's spirit was not to be shaken by all this bullying.

"You have seen this palace," resumed Don Pedro. "A beautiful place to live in, eh? But there is another side to the picture—the prison. Remember it is better to be ruled by me in the palace than to be under my rule in the prison. I will show you this prison. Ah-h, you shiver!"

It was a shiver of expectation on Bell's part. Visiting the prison would mean, perhaps, seeing her father!

"I hear that those who have been looking after you have taught you some English," said Don Pedro.

"I can speak some words in that language," returned Bell.

Don Pedro nodded with satisfaction.

"One of the prisoners is of that nation. I shall require you to make a certain statement to him. Listen very carefully. You will tell him that he is to sign an order to the first mate on board his ship, the Patrol, at San Juan to bring the vessel to Campana. If he refuses to do this—make

note of this—if he refuses he shall pass the rest of his days in the smallest cell in the prison—a cell so small that he will neither be able to stand upright nor lie out straight."

Bell drew a deep breath.

"Can you speak English well enough to say all this?" queried Don Pedro.

"I'll—I'll try," muttered Bell. She was gaining confidence now as the minutes went by and her impersonation remained undetected. "But — but — if that Englishman who accompanied me here could come with us and — and help me with the words, I think I could manage it."

She broke off and eyed him with feverish anxiety. Had she ventured too far in suggesting her brother's presence, she wondered? Would her words arouse suspicion?

Two years ago, at the time when Don Pedro was scheming to get his present position, he would probably have smelt a rat. But now security had blunted his wits. He was so powerful, so successful, that he had grown careless.

"Ay, if it will help, you can bring the man," he replied, with a shrug.

And Bell naturally *did* think Phil's presence would help—help immensely.

———

CHAPTER VI.

IN A DUNGEON CELL

SOME two hours later Phil Constantine was given to understand by means of various signs that his presence was required by her Highness the Princess Anna. Two soldiers then conducted him to her.

Bell received her brother with carefully studied indifference. Her personal attendants were all within sight, and although presumably ignorant of English—one never knew. Don Pedro was the sort who would have spies everywhere.

Therefore, Bell motioned Phil to follow her without saying a word, and the big brother, alert at reading signs, strolled after her, hands in pockets and humming a soft tune.

Before they had proceeded many paces this tune gradually had words added to it.

"Any—news—of—father?" he sang.

Bell gave a swift nod.

"Where — is— his — prison?" hummed her brother.

Bell suddenly stopped as if she had dropped something.

"We are going to pay him a visit," she muttered.

After that Phil sang no more. His mind became solely occupied with trying to imagine what was going to happen.

Down a gloomy passage they proceeded, and then Don Pedro, muffled in a long cloak and accompanied by a couple of soldiers, joined them.

"Has this man helped you to put the words into English?" he demanded.

"Not yet, your Excellency," returned Bell.

"He shall do so now."

She turned to Phil, and, speaking some words, in Spanish and some in her own tongue, said:

"I am to ask the prisoner to sign an order to the first mate of his ship, the Petrol, at San Juan, to bring the vessel to Campana——"

Bell paused.

"Repeat that," she said. "Repeat it as if you were teaching me to say it in English."

Phil did so.

Then Bell gave the rest of Don Pedro's words that person listening all the while with bored interest to the meaningless sounds they uttered. It struck him that the princess was singularly slow in absorbing this ugly foreign language.

Needless to say, however, that Bell's talk with her brother had a wider range than Don Pedro imagined.

"I am ready, Your Excellency," said Bell at last.

Forthwith they proceeded down a number of passages and stairs until at length they arrived in a dark and gloomy stone corridor. Don Pedro halted at one of the doors, took out a key, turned the lock, and, beckoning Bell and Phil to follow, entered the cell.

"Wait within call," he said to the two soldiers.

Phil nudged Bell. The fates were surely fighting on their side.

From the corner near the iron-grated window a form arose. He stumbled forward to where the thin shaft of light fell, and then halted. A fine, tall man was he, muscular, and in the prime of life. He stood firm and erect. Round his chest thin ropes were bound, binding his arms tightly behind him. He said not a word, but his eyes burned like living coal, and conveyed anything but a flattering opinion of Don Pedro.

Don Pedro realised this.

"Quick!" he snapped to Bell. "Give the dog my orders!"

Bell stepped forward. As her father's eyes met hers, the gleam in his gradually evaporated, giving place to a look of blank astonishment. His mouth opened to speak, and Bell, fearing that by an ejaculation he would disclose everything, half raised her hand in caution.

Then, to her surprise, he suddenly swung his hands from behind him, the cords slipped from his body, and with a bound he was by her.

Like lightning Bell turned, fully expecting to hear Don Pedro's voice bellowing for help. It was to find, however, Phil's arm encircling the Don's head in such a manner as to form an effective gag. Muffled grunts were all he could utter, and quickly they, too, were stifled as in Phil's muscular grip he was bent back and back until he suddenly collapsed on the floor in a limp heap.

Bell clutched her brother's arm.

"What has happened?" she whispered.

"Hush!" he warned her. "He'll come round in a couple of seconds. We must act quickly. Father, those ropes!"

Captain Constantine bore them forward.

"*I* will do the binding"—he nodded grimly —"as tightly as he had me bound—though *more* securely."

And so when Don Pedro recovered his senses it was to find himself as fast a prisoner as any of the others in that gloomy prison of his. He was bound hand and foot, a skilfully twisted cloth across his mouth prevented him from crying out, and the only things free were his eyes.

The things he saw did not serve to lessen his annoyance or his surprise. His erstwhile captive was decked out in *his* long cloak and hat, and the little girl—the *princess*—the girl who was to obey him in everything, was unlocking the door and leading the way to freedom!

The door opened, then shut with a bang, and he was alone—a prisoner in his own prison.

Outside the cell, Bell walked calmly down the corridor and ordered the two soldiers to withdraw to their quarters. They obeyed the command without question — naturally! The "Princess Anna" would shortly be their queen, and as the tall cloaked man, whom they took to be the all-powerful Don Pedro, nodded confirmation of her orders they had no suspicion of what had happened.

"What next, Bell?" asked Phil and her father. They were grown men, strong and swift of action, but they thought it no shame to consult their young companion and act upon her advice.

"When will they next visit the cell?" asked Bell.

"Not until to-morrow morning," said her father.

"Then we have twelve good hours," observed Phil. "Ample time to get well on our way back to San Juan."

As they approached the open air, shouts and the firing of guns reached their ears.

They stopped short, uncertain what to do, and at that moment the figure of General Sandoval—although they had no idea who he was—came rushing towards them.

"Your Excellency," he cried, addressing Captain Constantine, "a revolution has broken out against us. The army has deserted. They are chasing our friends. Quick—you and the princess must escape! You can hold her as hostage——"

Bell's father, knowing no Spanish, could not make head nor tail of these frantic words. Bell, however, caught the drift of them, and it was she who answered.

"How can we escape?" she asked.

"Follow me, your Highness, and I will show you!"

And with this the general led them along several corridors and passages until they emerged by a back exit, which showed the seashore a few hundred yards away.

"There is a boat awaiting us," he muttered. "It will take us out to yonder English vessel that rides at anchor. You, Your Highness, being able to speak English, can doubtless persuade them to allow us to remain on board."

"It may be I can," returned Bell, with an inward chuckle. "What is the name of the vessel?"

"The 'Patrol,'" answered the Spaniard. He turned to Captain Constantine. "Your Excellency," he continued, "it is the boat which your English prisoner commanded. They have doubtless come here to seek him. If you offer to disclose his whereabouts, pretending that our enemies have imprisoned him and *not* you, they will surely prove generous in their dealings."

Her father's boat! Bell could contain her laughter no longer at the complete way the general had disclosed everything. She laughed delightedly.

"I have made a joke, Your Highness?" asked the Spaniard, with a great show of offended dignity. "Perhaps Your Highness will please condescend to explain?"

"Ha, ha, ha!" laughed Bell. "Oh, yes, it shall all be explained—presently."

. . . . . .

The unlucky general received his explanation some ten minutes later, but he did not evince any mirth. On the contrary, the only emotion he displayed was one of the keenest apprehension as Captain Constantine and Phil stood over him, with Bell close by, acting as interpreter.

"Then you are *not* the Princess Anna!" he faltered at length. "How came it that you managed to do all this? It—it smacks of magic; it—it is amazing!"

But when Bell condescended to enlighten him admiration absorbed all other feelings.

"Signorita," he said, bowing, "I am proud to be defeated by so gallant and fair an enemy. Though you are not the real Queen of Campana, you are fully worthy to be so."

An opinion to which both her father and brother enthusiastically subscribed.

In other words, little Bell Constantine was the heroine of the hour.

And the real genuine princess—what of her?

A month or so later Bell heard rumours of a great coronation ceremony in Campana, in which a girl queen had been placed on the throne amidst general rejoicings; so it can be assured that, thanks to Sibley's care, Donna Anna recovered, and lived to rule the people who, under Don Pedro, had dethroned her father.

Indeed, a year later it was proved to be so without a doubt, for a mysterious package, containing a beautiful diamond bracelet, was sent to Bell. With it was a note containing these words:

"From a queen to a queen.—ANNA OF CAMPANA."

THE END

98

CYCLING HINTS

PUNCTURES IN TYRES

As a cyclist who is continually popping about on my machine, with a lot to do in a little time, I am astonished at the way girls look after their bicycles.

I ought, rather, to say do not look after them. Girls, who are so particular about their own personal appearance, very often do not seem ever to give a moment's thought to their bicycles. They allow them to be smothered with dirt and grease and mud from one year's end to another.

If they only knew how grit helps to wear out the bearings of their machine, and how much easier a cleaned and oiled bicycle runs, they would not begrudge the little time spent in this way.

And then again there is that annoying mishap—a puncture. Far too many girls, and guides, too, rush off to the cycle shop when their tyre becomes flat and the pump won't keep it up for any length of time.

Now, for ninepence you can buy a good outfit, and not only have sufficient material for mending a dozen punctures, but you can repair one yourself in five minutes if you use a little gumption.

On every outfit box there will be found complete instructions for mending punctures. Let me help you, however.

First of all, you have to find whether it is really a puncture or whether there is something wrong with the valve. To discover this, pump up the tyre, and then hold a cup of water so that the nozzle of the valve is immersed in the water.

If air bubbles are to be seen, all you need to do is to unscrew the valve nozzle, pull out the valve-pin, and tear off the tiny rubber tube you will find upon it. Replace with another tiny tube, insert the pin, and your trouble is over.

INNER TUBE TROUBLES

Supposing, however, there are no air bubbles, what is to be done next ?

I am afraid we must assume that there has been a puncture. Turn the wheel carefully round and examine the outer cover. Very often a thorn or a nail or a piece of flint can be seen sticking out from the rubber.

When you pull it out mark the spot with a lead pencil, for it is probably at this place where the inner tube has been pierced and allowed the air to escape.

Now let us take out the inner tube. To do this we must remove one side of the outer cover. Choose that side which is farthest away from the chain wheel and the gear-case.

If you haven't a tyre lever, get two or three dessert spoons. Insert the handle end of the spoon under the bead or wire of the outer cover and pull it forward. With another spoon, getting to work a few inches away, pull another section of the outer cover over, when it will be easy to run the fingers round the rim and to pull out the inner tube.

If you know where the puncture lies it can soon be repaired. If that is a mystery, fix the valve-pin in the tube and inflate the tyre. Immerse the inner tube in sections in a bowl of water until you see the spot where the air bubbles out.

MENDING THE PUNCTURE

Now we will mend the puncture. Rub round the spot with the little sulphur stick supplied with the outfit to remove the vulcanising on which the solution and the patch will not stick. Having cleaned a place, say, as big as a halfpenny, smear this spot with solution and do the same with the patch. Leave both till they are sticky to the touch. Place the patch then over the puncture spot and press firmly till it adheres all round.

Dust with French chalk, when the tube can be replaced and cycling will again become a joy to you. If the outer cover has been cut, a small patch of canvas should be stuck over the place so that no fresh piece of flint can work through.

In replacing the inner tube be careful not to get it twisted, and, when the outer cover is once more in the rim, see that the wire or bead does not grip the tube. This is very important, because if it is badly gripped and you start riding upon it a tear of at least an inch long will appear on the tube, and you will have something that will be a far worse trouble than a mere puncture.

WINTER CYCLE HINTS

Cyclists, somehow, seem to find more trouble during the winter months, with loose roads and mud and wind, than at any other time of the year. That, at any rate, is my experience.

If the tyres are old, for instance, the wet state of the roads gives a lot of trouble. I have found it a good plan to take out the inner tube and then, through the valve-hole, to pour about half an ounce of glycerine into each outer cover. Let the glycerine run round the cover and soak into the fabric.

On a windy night, if your lamp keeps blowing out, tie your handkerchief round it, fixing it by the four corners to the lamp bracket. The wind cannot get through the handkerchief, while the light can be clearly seen.

Lubricating the bearings of a cycle is even more necessary in muddy weather. A good and cheap lubricant can be made from five parts of olive oil, mixed with one part of paraffin. This will not clog the bearings.

To remove rust, a sequel to wet weather, make a paste of fine sand and paraffin. Apply the mixture to the rusted parts, and allow it to remain there for a few minutes. Rub off, and polish with a clean, soft rag.

Ordinary furniture-polish, applied with a soft flannel, makes a good polish for enamelled parts.

SUMMER CYCLE HINTS

Never pump your tyres " board " hard in dry summer weather. The compressed air may expand a trifle, and burst a tyre where it is weak.

Try not to let your machine stand for a great length of time on deflated tyres. Suspend it somewhere, if you are not able to pump up the tyres when they get flat. Owing to the weight upon them, the tyres will crack at the sides at the spot where they touch the ground.

Many girls have no suitable place in which to hang their bicycles. It is quite as good for the tyres if you turn your bicycle upside down, and leave it standing on the saddle and handle-bar. Do not forget to place a sack, or a piece of paper, under it, to prevent scratching.

REMEMBER

Never allow oil to get on your tyres. It rots them.

When mending a puncture remove the inner tube on the side furthest away from the chain.

When you replace a wheel, see that the cone for adjustment is on the left-hand side.

The easiest place to remove a wired-on tyre is opposite the valve.

HOW TO READ A ROAD MAP

This is the information that every applicant for a cyclist's badge should know, but it is such useful general knowledge that I recommend all guides to read, mark, learn, and inwardly digest it.

First of all, what is the object of a road map ? It is to show you the roads to certain places, to indicate landmarks and objects of interest you will pass on the way, how far those places are apart, and to tell you whether the roads are up-hill or downhill, and whether good, bad, or indifferent.

Supposing now that we had an ordinary road map stretched out on the table before us, just as we should have if we were enjoying a little chat in our drill-hall.

It will probably be a coloured map and will have a number of double lines stretching out all over it. Those double lines denote good roads, or first-class roads, as they are termed, and by this we can assume that they are fairly broad and possess a good surface.

Double broken lines are used to denote second-class roads. This does not mean that the roads are bad, but that they are not so good as the first-class roads.

A dotted single line on a coloured map is known as a third-class road, and is likely to be cut up, narrow, badly looked after, and therefore to be avoided by the cyclist, unless no other road is available.

Be careful to distinguish between these doted lines and a still fainter dotted line which merely indicates a footpath.

YOUR BICYCLE LAMP

Of course, you would like a smokeless light. Next time you get a new wick, soak it in vinegar and thoroughly dry it. Another good tip is to half fill the oil-tank with cotton wool. Keep everything very clean.

MUD SPOTS

At certain times in the year mud spots crop up about our clothes, when cycling, like mushrooms in a marsh. They quickly spoil a costume if not properly erased.

In the first place, you must see that the spots are perfectly dry before you attempt to remove them. With the edge of a coin break the crust of each spot, and brush rather lightly to avoid driving the dust into the material.

Any marks that remain will vanish if a little weak ammonia is rubbed on them.

Melita of the South Seas.

A STIRRING ADVENTURE
STORY OF SCHOOLGIRLS
ON A PACIFIC ISLE

By JULIA STORM

CHAPTER I.

INTRODUCES THE GIRL CRUSOES.

THERE was great excitement on the smart inter-island steamer, Southern Cross, as she steamed across a calm, moon-lit sea at half-speed.

For early on the morrow, it was said, she would raise the bank of trade wind cloud that enveloped the peaks of the famous Diamond Island from the straight blue horizon of the Pacific.

At sunset Captain Gale had slowed the ship to half-speed, for he was travelling over an almost uncharted sea.

In the cosy little deck saloon, a party of merry British school girls were gathered, listening to a letter that one of them was reading. They knew the contents almost by heart, as Josephine Hardy (the reader) was well aware. Quite a dozen times since they had left Australia Joe had read it aloud, but it was so wonderful, *so* thrilling and opened up such marvellous possibilities, that they were never tired of listening to the magic words.

Thus it ran :

"Dear Miss Joe, — You and your young lady friends will find Diamond Island pretty well set to rights by the time you get here. I haven't been idle since your father dumped me here to get things shipshape, and I ain't let the natives be idle either. We've run up a tidy school home and other houses for you and your mistresses to live in ; constructed roads ; made a small railway, built a pier and landing-stage, and generally made a job of the concern. I don't say as you'll ever get any skating here, nor will you want fur coats, for the old sun works overtime in these parts 'cept when there's a typhoon knocking around. Howsomdever, there's most other sports for the asking, and if you and your young lady friends ain't as happy as the day is long, I'm a Dutchman, and that's that.

"I beg to remain,
"Your obedient servant,
"JIMMY PIPES."

"Faith!" cried Pat MacDermott, the Irish girl. "It makes one's mouth water, so it does! It's meself that never thought I should look forward to going to school, but *this* school——!"

She laughed for sheer joy.

"It's three cheers we ought to be after giving for your father, Joe," she went on. "Yes, every night we ought to give them, for his splendid idea of getting Miss Strong to agree to take the school to Diamond Island. So hip-hip——!"

"Hurrah!" shouted the others.

But not all. No, there were two who did not cheer. Edith Forster, known amongst the girls as "Lady" Edith, on account of her airs of superiority, was one; and the other was languid Lily Parsons.

"What a perfectly illiterate and vulgar letter!" drawled Edith, in a die-away voice. "Who is this person—this James Pipes? And what an awful name!"

She sighed, and fanned herself with a large black lace fan with a languishing grace.

Joe flushed.

"If you want to know, Lily," she replied, "Jimmy Pipes is my father's coxswain. He served with dad all his life, and he's going to look after our requirements on Diamond Island. He is dad's oldest friend and my oldest friend!"

"Put that in your pipe and smoke it!" added Pat.

Edith sighed and fanned herself.

"You—aw—really are too vulgar, Patricia MacDermott," she answered. "There is nothing patrician about you; in fact, you and Joe and Hilda, and that young person, Dumpling Davis, seem to think that you can do as you like and set what tone you like to our new school."

Lily Parsons chimed in in support of her friend.

"And let me tell you, Patricia!" she exclaimed. "You and your friends are not going to have it all your own way at the Island School. There are new girls of good family coming from London and Edinburgh—girls who have been to schools where a good tone is set by daughters of the very best people, and they will not allow you and your rough friends to dictate your tone to the school!"

"Arrah now!" exclaimed Pat. "Phwat's all this about?"

"Why," put in "Lady" Edith, with a snap, "Lily means what she says! You and your set

are not going to dictate your tone to all of us because Miss Strong has been weak enough to make favourites of you."

Pat's eyes twinkled.

"What's that you say about the weak Miss Strong, 'Lady' Edith?" she asked.

"I say that Miss Strong has been weak enough to make favourites of you and your set, and, because she has done so you think that you can put upon the rest of us and dictate the tone to the whole school. But you will find that you are mistaken!" replied Edith Forster angrily.

"You are such an awful bad form, you see!" added Lily Parsons. "You behave more like rough boys than girls!" she said with a snigger. "And your clothes are awful. And we are not going to mix with that horrid black girl, Melita. You treat her just as though she was our equal. That is where Miss Strong is quite wrong in her management of this new school. She is going to open it to the daughters of chiefs. But what is the daughter of a chief? We don't want to mix with black girls?"

"Very well!" replied Joe. "There's room enough in Diamond Island for all of us. But there's one thing you will have to learn, and that is to treat old Pipes with proper respect. He is my father's old friend, and he is Governor of Diamond Island!"

"Aw!" sighed Lily. "He is only a common sailor! And I don't like common sailors!"

And lifting her eyebrows disdainfully, she waved her fan gracefully as though to wave away all discussion.

Joe was about to answer hotly.

But there was a sudden interruption in the discussion.

In at the door of the deck saloon there stepped a gorgeous figure.

CHAPTER II.

THE "EXCLUSIVES"

IT was Melita of Malaita, the Solomon Island girl, who had developed in the most extraordinary fashion during her residence in the civilised circles of Melbourne, Adelaide, and Brisbane.

Melita had come away from Diamond Island with all her worldly goods in a handkerchief.

She was returning there with a large trunk full of clothes—not, perhaps, very fashionable clothes, but precious possessions in the eyes of Melita.

A cry of delight went up from the girls as Melita entered the little saloon.

Miss Strong had never been able to prevent Melita from dyeing her frizzy wig of hair, for this was the custom of her island, and she knew that native customs must be observed.

At the end of the schoolroom there was a rush, and a rending of wood and plaster. Then the wall opened, and through the great hole came the engine, "Puffing Billy," followed by its train of jolting trucks.

W. TAYLER

103

But instead of the dull red dye of native henna or betel mixed with lime, Melita was now dyed with the brightest golden hair dye of civilisation, which had turned her hair to the shade which is greatly affected by the Somali tribesmen.

And to-night Melita, who had long been admiring the style and tone of Edith Forster, had thrust a huge comb into her wig, and had mounted on it in the form of a mantilla a whole tablecloth.

In her hand she held a huge fan.

Now, there is no mimic in the world so acute in observation as the native of the Solomon Islands, though all savage races are quick and clever in this respect.

And Melita's imitation of Edith's airs and graces had been closely studied, not in mockery, but in sincere admiration.

There were also traces of Miss Strong and Mdlle. Touch, the French mistress, in her speech and bearing as she entered the door of the saloon.

"Yaw-ah! Deah girl!" sighed Melita, rolling her eyes in imitation of Edith Forster's most languishing glance. "Deah girl, good-evenin'!"

She sighed, fluttered her fan, shrugged her shoulders inimitably in the style of mademoiselle, and laid a large white gloved hand on Joe's shoulder.

"Ha, ha!" she exclaimed. "My leetle Josephine! You sit up ver' late to-night. Be'old you shall lose um liddle roses in your cheek if you do not go early to your roose-box!"

Edith Forster sat up and scowled darkly at this black caricature of herself.

"Pouf! It am too 'ot!" sighed Melita, with a slow wave of her fan, enjoying the sensation that her new mantilla was creating. "This long ship travel is too much—aw!—bore!"

Pat was giggling with delight.

Melita had made tremendous strides in her studies of English, and loved nothing better now than mastering the longest words she could find.

"Pat, my dear chile!" she exclaimed, in Miss Strong's voice, fanning herself gracefully. "What you t'ink along o' dis creations belong me? Awfully jollie, don't you think? Me swell girl, don't you tink?"

Then, with a sudden change in the note of her voice, Melita unconsciously mimicked Lily Parsons to the life.

"Aw-yaas!" she sighed. "Aw nevah, nevah mix-ah!—with vulgar people! They—aw—gib one—aw—such a mos' twemendously bad—aw—tone!"

Lily Parsons leaped to her feet.

Her eyes were blazing with fury.

She snapped her fan together with such force that she broke half a dozen of the sticks, and strode over to Pat.

"You horrid girl!" she exclaimed. "You have been teaching this nigger girl to imitate me, and to make caricature of me. I won't stand it! I'll complain to Miss Strong. I'll—I'll——"

Lily Parsons said no more.

She burst into tears, and dashed out of the little saloon, whilst Edith Forster rose, eyeing Pat and Joe and Dumpling Davis with supercilious eyes.

"We don't want to speak to any of you again," she muttered spitefully, as she paused for a moment at the door. "If you choose to mix with that absurd black savage you can't expect us to know you!"

And with this Parthian dart she followed her friends.

Pat whistled under her breath.

"My word!" she said. "That was a declaration of war. The Belles av Di'mond Island have shown their hand with a vengeance. They are going to start a new set of their own, which is going to control the island school, and we are to be sent to Coventry with our poor old friend Melita."

Then Pat turned to Melita, who, fan in hand, had seated herself on the nearest settee.

"Do you hear that, ould Queen av the Cannibal Islands?" she exclaimed. "We are all sent to Coventry by the Exclusives!"

"All sent to Coventra by de Explosives?" asked Melita, fanning herself gently, and arranging her mantilla over her shoulders with the greatest care. "Why for Lilee so cross? Why for Edit' so cross?"

"Why," explained Pat, "they think that we take too much room in this school, so they are not going to speak to us again."

"No speak? No look?" asked Melita, her eyes rolling.

"No. They are going to send us to Coventry," persisted Pat. "They won't have anything to do with us at all. They'll just look as though we were so many shop windows with nothing behind the glass. They won't know you."

"Oh!" murmured Melita. "I tink dey like to know me—someday. Sposen dey get lost on *my* island?"

"True," said Joe. "I forgot you were the daughter of one of the chiefs of Diamond Island."

"Ay, me chief girl," returned Melita proudly. "Me heap swell."

At that moment there sounded a sudden jangling of bells in the engine-room. The engines stopped and the ship quivered through its length with a queer bumping movement and the screw of propellers were set hard astern.

The engines came to a stop, and the Southern Cross took a list to port.

104

"Pat gave a gasp, for she knew she had hooked the gamest and hardest fighting fish in all the seas—the jumping tuna of the Pacific!"

Joe peeped out through the moonlit porthole. She saw the boatswain running forward with a lead-line and sounding-lead in his hand, and she heard the word passed to get all the boats ready for lowering.

"Pat!" she called out to her chum. "We've struck something!"

CHAPTER III.

AN OLD FRIEND

THERE was no doubt about it. The Southern Cross had run on one of the many uncharted reefs that lay under that calm, treacherous sea for many miles round the coast of Diamond Island.

Though her engines were still, the dynamos down in the engine-room were still purring, and Joe switched on the electric light in her cabin.

Soon she heard the voice of Mrs. Howlett, the kindly stewardess of the ship, in the passage-way outside her cabin.

"Captain says that you young ladies are to come up on deck at once," said Mrs. Howlett calmly. "The ship has run on a coral reef, but there is no immediate danger."

Joe and the others lost no time in obeying the command, and quickly everyone was mustered on deck and served out with lifebelts.

The sea was as calm as a millpond and for once in a way the Pacific Ocean was living up to its name.

Luckily for the Southern Cross there was no rise and fall on the ocean.

She had touched the sunken reef lightly, and the carpenter, who had just come up on deck, announced that her hull was apparently undamaged, since no water was finding its way into the well.

The girls were marshalled on the moonlit deck in little anxious groups.

The boats were swung out at their davits, but were not yet lowered.

Each boat was provisioned and supplied with small beakers of water, together with a lighted binnacle-lamp and compass.

But the chief officer, who was in charge of getting these ready, said that there was no need for the girls to go to their boat-stations till the ship's whistle sounded.

And in the meantime, Tomkins, the deck-steward, was going round the groups with a tray of sandwiches and hot coffee, reassuring the more timid of the girls, and urging them to take coffee.

Tomkins was a great favourite with all the girls.

He was a little Londoner with a ready wit and a great eye for chalking out the deck for deck-games.

And it was to Tompkins that Mademoiselle La Touche, the French mistress, flew for comfort.

"Ah, Monsieur Tompkin'!" she exclaimed. "Ze sheep—does 'e sink?"

"Not a bit of it, Mademoiselle!" replied Tompkins. "You've lots of time for a cup of corfy an' a few sandwiches afore the boats are lowered."

"Ah, you Eenglish!" she cried. "You 'ave so much sangfroid. You are so cool in dangaire. And where are we?"

"There's a bit of a mist on the sea, Mademoiselle," said Tompkins, "but it's my belief that the old man 'as been set down by the currents nearer to Di'mond Island than he thought he was, and this 'ere reef on which we are perched is not far off the island. I—— Hallo! 'Ere comes Miss Strong to tell you that there's nothing to worry about!"

And this was just what Miss Strong had come to tell them.

The ship was safe where she was unless the sea got up, and in the meantime their wireless was trying to get the small wireless station which the sailors had installed on Diamond Island.

Mademoiselle was reassured, and retired to her cabin to sort out her boots and shoes.

Then Mr. Wright, the first officer, came bustling along the deck with a couple of rockets.

He seemed quite cheerful.

"It's all right, young ladies," he said. "We sha'n't want you for the boats yet awhile. We are going to try a few rockets to wake them up ashore."

The girls looked on with interest as he fitted a rocket in the socket that was set in the rail of the ship, and affixed the lanyard.

Then, standing back, he jerked the cord, and away roared the rocket, leaving a long trail of sparks behind it.

It lit the sky with a burst of bright stars that eclipsed the brilliant light of the tropical moon that turned the surrounding sea-mist to a veil of gleaming silver.

The answer was not long in coming.

Far away, but showing over the low-lying banks of sea-mist, a burst of red light showed an answering rocket.

The girls could hear the wireless instrument sending forth its queer whipping sounds, and soon the glad announcement came through that the reef on which they had stranded was but ten miles from the entrance to their own lagoon, and that two schooners in the harbour were coming to their help at once.

Rockets were sent up at intervals, and Melita, wearing two cork lifebelts and one of her largest hats of black velvet, trimmed with ostrich feathers, made her appearance amongst the groups on deck.

Melita was received with delight by the girls.

"We come 'long to Di'mond Island?" was Melita's first question.

"Well, we've hit some part of it!" responded Pat cheerfully.

"Now we go in liddle canoe?" asked Melita, who seemed to have no idea of the gravity of the ship's situation.

And she looked up at the boats which were swung out on the davits ready for lowering.

"Not yet," replied Pat. "As a matter of fact, Melita, we are run on a reef, and here are some ships coming to help us!"

And as Pat spoke she pointed into the clearing space between two banks of the moonlit sea mist.

There showed the shape of a large island schooner, which was evidently fitted with an auxiliary engine, for she came over the calm, windless sea in style.

Soon she came to a stop a hundred yards or so from the stranded steamer, towing several large shore-lighters behind her.

A boat was lowered from her side and came rowing alongside, the moonlight glittering like diamonds at every stroke of her oars in the water.

And no sooner was she alongside than an elderly man, with a short, white chin-beard and bronzed, weather-beaten face, ran nimbly up the side-ladder, and climbed over the rail.

He looked round on the little group of girls, and came to a stop before Joe.

"Why," he exclaimed, "it's my little Miss Josephine, grown out of all knowledge, and Miss Hilda, too!"

And Joe gave a cry of delight.

They had reached the shores of Diamond Island, after all, for here was her father's old friend come to greet them.

"It's Jimmy!" she exclaimed. "Jimmy Pipes!"

"Mr. Pipes, my dear Josephine!" corrected Miss Whiffen, Miss Strong's second in command, who was standing by.

Mr. Pipes gave Miss Whiffen a pleasant smile.

"The little maid always called me 'Jimmy,' madam," he said, "ever since she could speak at all. I nussed her in my arms when she was only a few weeks old. That was when we'd just come home from the China station in the old Astarte, and Miss Hilda, too, she was a babby in arms when we finished up on the East India station in th' Charybdis!"

"How did we get aground, Uncle Jimmy?" asked Joe.

"Easy enough, Miss Joe!" said Jimmy Pipes, shaking his head. "Easy enough in these waters, where the currents alter with every tide, and run sometimes as strong as mill races. You are a bit ahead of your time, otherwise I'd have met the ship farther out at sea, and piloted her into the lagoon. But you need have no fear. The tide is rising, the night is calm and she'll float off on the rising tide when we have lightened her of a few hundred tons of cargo. But I must be off now to see Captain Gale!"

And Jimmy went off to the bridge, leaving his boat with its Kanaka crew alongside.

Mademoiselle now made her appearance on deck again.

She was delighted when she saw the schooner laying to, with the big shore-boats in tow, only a hundred yards or so from the ship.

"Ah! We 'ave at las' come to our belove' Di'mond Island!" she exclaimed, clasping her hands.

"We have not exactly arrived there yet, Mademoiselle," answered Pat; "but it's somewhere yonder hidden in the sea mist. This schooner and the boats have come out from the lagoon, and Mr. Pipes is on board. He has gone up to the bridge to see Captain Gale. They are going to take some of the cargo out of the ship, and she will float off the reef on the rising tide, and then all ashore on Diamond Island. Huroo!"

Soon a second schooner showed like a fairy ship in the mist, and the two vessels were warped alongside the Southern Cross with their tow of boats, to take some of the cargo out of her to lighten her.

Then the decks of the steamer fairly buzzed with activity. The hatch covers were taken off, gangs of shouting, cheerful natives came tumbling on board, clutches of working lights were rigged,

An ugly black triangular fin of a large shark was heading straight for Melita.

and the derricks swung backwards and forwards, the winches rattling and hissing with steam as case after case of cargo was hoisted out of the holds and lowered on to the decks of the assisting vessels.

With such a racket going on, sleep was out of the question.

A steamship discharging cargo from every hold with every derrick and winch working with feverish haste is one of the noisiest places in the world.

So the girls, greatly to the amusement of the Kanaka crews, commenced to assist in handling the cargo.

So the strenuous night passed, and at length the mist on the sea turned rosy pink in the rising sun. Soon the engines of the Southern Cross began slowly to move astern, sending a big white wash of broken water streaming forward over the blue sea as she strove to fight her way back from the coral trash that held her bows as though in a trap.

The tide had risen, but the breeze was already springing up with the sun, and with the breeze would come the long ocean swells which would break the dead glassy calm, and start the ship pounding her life out on the coral.

In those few minutes it was touch and go for a ship's life and a captain's reputation.

But, of a sudden, there was a tremendous cheer from the men who were clustered at the sides looking down into the water.

The Southern Cross was coming astern.

She was coming off the rocks unscathed and unharmed, thanks to the labours of the night.

The crew cheered again and again, and mostly they cheered Miss Strong and Mademoiselle and the girls who had worked so staunchly, and had set such an example to the natives.

Back the ship moved, and a new life came into her. She was afloat.

And as they all stood there the curtain of pink mist rose from the sea as though by magic, and there on the horizon showed Diamond Island, sparkling and glorious in the morning sun.

CHAPTER IV.

"ALL ABOARD THE TRAIN"

SURE enough, it was Diamond Island itself that rose from the morning mists, glittering with a thousand tints of mother-of-pearl in the early sunrise.

It was one of the wonder pictures of the South Seas, and even the crew of the Southern Cross stood spellbound as they watched the curtain of pearly mist drawn slowly from the sea by the increasing rays of the swift-rising sun.

These men had made many a Pacific landfall, and had seen many a fairy island slide past their ships like the islands of a dream.

But they had never seen any scene to compare with this mystery island of the Pacific, with its rugged coastline and its tree-crowned hills and valleys, wrapped above in their eternal shroud of trade-wind cloud.

And now the Southern Cross was moving in slowly towards the land, and bit by bit they could see their old landmarks shaping in the pearly mists of the morning.

The girls' eyes were turned hungrily on the lagoon as they neared the entrance.

Through the clear water they could look down and see the wonderful coral gardens of green and pink and turquoise-blue sliding beneath the keel of the Southern Cross, whilst, over these, brilliant shoals of fish flitted like so many gorgeous butterflies.

There was a neat little pier of coral blocks built out as a landing-stage for boats, and along the shores of the lagoon the thick wall of cocoa-palms rose unbroken, and the great white stretch of coral beach was livened only by the presence of a few white-painted whaleboats.

At length the anchor went down with a crash in the deep turquoise waters of the lagoon.

Suddenly into the still air cut the shrill scream of a locomotive engine.

There was a puff of white steam amongst the shafts of the cocoa-palms a half-mile along the shore, and Pat gave a cry of delight as, looking through the glasses, she saw a tiny little engine dragging a train of jolting trucks behind it, which were piled high with copra, or the dried kernel of the cocoanut.

There was a sudden jolting and jarring of the train when it had reached a point on the lagoon shore opposite the spot where the Southern Cross was anchored.

The engine leaned in a disreputable fashion against the tall shaft of a cocoa-palm, which showered down nuts on the head of the driver as it was shaken under the impact.

Then the following train of iron tip-trucks jolted solemnly off the rails, turning over and emptying their contents by the side of the line.

"There! There!" exclaimed Jimmy Pipes' voice behind the girls, as they leaned upon the rail watching this scene. "There's that nigger Quashy has run the engine off the lines again! Lend me your glasses, Miss Pat, and let me see if he has damaged the engine!"

Pat handed the glasses to Jimmy Pipes.

"Faith, Mr. Pipes!" she said. "Do ye have a railway accident on the Di'mond Island Railway every day?"

"Every day?" echoed Mr. Pipes. "Why, that nigger manages to run the train off the line every hour. But he's better than the other driver, who forgot to put any water in the boiler, and who tied down the safety-valve, and came near blowing himself into the middle of next week. But Quashy has finished rubbing his head now where the cocoanut hit him, and he's getting out the screwjacks to lift his engine on to the line again!"

He closed the glasses and handed them back again to Pat, laughing.

"It's splendid!" gasped Pat. "A real railway! Where does it go to, Mr. Pipes? And may we drive the engine?"

"Well, Miss Pat, I think you'll make a better driver than Quashy," answered Mr. Pipes, laughing. "But you young ladies have come here to go to school, not to drive engines. You will find plenty of surprises waiting for you ashore."

Pat sighed.

"My word!" she exclaimed. "I think the surprise that we'll mostly get will be in the way av lessons. But we may drive the train sometimes on half-holidays, mayn't we, Mr. Pipes?" she added coaxingly.

"I daresay you will manage to get off from a lot of lessons, Miss Pat," he answered. "And I know that you are not going to have any school at all for the first fortnight you are on the island. Miss Strong told me so only just now!"

"There!" exclaimed Pat, wild with delight. "Didn't I tell ye girls that Miss Strong is the greatest schoolmistress in th' world. She knows when to start lessons and when to knock them off, and we'll be drivin' that ould train this afternoon!"

They could see Quashy getting the jacks under his engine and lifting it once more, hissing and spurting steam angrily on to the rails.

Then he set to work to shovel in the loads of copra which had tumbled out of the tip-trucks.

But Joe and her friends were soon far too busy in getting their belongings together to watch Quashy, and it was not until about an hour later that the engine driver once more engaged their attention.

This happened when they reached the shore.

Then there was a puff of steam and a whistling amongst the palm-groves, and the engine with eight trucks came backing noisily and fussily on to the pier, with Quashy grinning in the cab of the tiny toy engine.

"Here you are, Quashy!" called Mr. Johnstone. "These ladies and their luggage are to be taken up to the school at once!"

Quashy grinned from ear to ear, and glancing at Mademoiselle La Touche, whose name he had caught, he greeted her with as near as he could get to pronouncing the title "mademoiselle."

"Allee right, Missus Mammypoodle!" he said. "You jumpee in train. You putee bokkis (box) on train. We catchee school plenty quick!"

And, opening the firebox of his little engine, he piled in a huge mass of oily cocoa rubbish and shells, to raise the necessary steam to haul that huge load of boxes which the natives were placing in the little string of trucks.

There was plenty of room in the cab of the little engine, so the girls jumped in.

But Mademoiselle refused to join them. She waited till the natives had placed her boxes in the piled trucks, then she climbed up into that truck which would be rightly termed the luggage-van.

"Patreecia!" she called from her end of the little train. "You shall beg of zat black gentleman zat 'e shall not accelerate too much his engine!"

Quashy grinned.

His knowledge of English was imperfect, and he thought that Mademoiselle was demanding that she should be whirled away up to the school-house with all possible speed.

And Quashy, furthermore, was bursting with pride of his train, and burning to show how fast she could go.

"Allee rightee, missus!" he cried. "Me catchee school plenty quick!"

And the rest of his remarks and Mademoiselle's were drowned in the scream of the engine-whistle as he pulled off the quay with a sharp jerk that nearly threw Mademoiselle out of the luggage-van and the train started jerking and jolting in a most alarming fashion through the cocoa-groves.

"Goodness!" gasped Pat, as the little engine switched round a tree with a savage jerk, and ran down a little hill across the mouth of a small valley. "I was nearly out av the cab that time! Does your engine always jump like that, Quashy?"

Quashy smiled, showing a brilliant row of teeth.

"Yaas, little missy," he replied. "Engin' him get too cross sometime. Him jump too much. But, you see, we catchee school quick!"

Quashy seemed possessed of the notion that the girls were wildly and anxiously looking forward to getting to the school.

"Steady, Quashy!" said Joe, as the train dashed on to a sharp little made-up embankment of piled coral, which was built round the projecting lava cliff. "We don't want to go too fast round this bend. It looks dangerous!"

There was, indeed, a nasty take-off from this embankment, which rose full ten feet above the sand of the shore.

But Quashy shook his frizzy head.

"Sposum no go quick round corner," he said, "engin' him no stop along line!"

He opened the throttle, and the little engine, with a savage snort and a rush, made for the bend.

"Look here, Quashy!" said Pat severely. "If you ever went to a school for young ladies you wouldn't be in such a hurry to catchee school!"

But this remark was lost on Quashy. All his attention was taken up by the management of his train.

They were reaching the spot where the little railroad ran through one or two short tunnels cut in the face of the cliff, and whipped round the corner at an elevated grade, popping into the Happy Valley at an altitude of about eighty feet above the old native pathway or road.

Thence it ran down a gentle grade to the end of the big school-room, which had been built at the foot of the great pae-pae or stone platform where the natives of old had built their great speak-house.

It was a ticklish bit of driving, and Quashy was bent on bringing his little party and their luggage up to the school in his best style.

109

He was madly proud of his railway, and he wanted these white young ladies to see what he could do.

"You call Mammypoodle 'Hang on!' Me catchee school plenty quick!" he said, as he opened out the throttle of the little engine, and raced it at a sharp up-grade, leaping over a little bridge that spanned another little mountain-fall at a giddy height.

"Hang on, Mademoiselle!" screamed Joe, as the train shot up the steep little grade, nearly tipping Mademoiselle out of the guard's truck.

"Do hang on!" pleaded Pat. "Do hang on, Mademoiselle!"

Mademoiselle was hanging on like grim death now.

She clung to the edge of the truck as a drowning cat clings to the edge of a water-barrel.

Her face was set, and her teeth were clenched, and her smart Paris hat was tipped over her left eye at an entirely unfashionable angle.

"Please hang on, Miss Mammypoodle!" yelled Quashy. "We catchee school plenty quick now!"

"It strikes me that ye'll be catchin' somethin' else pretty quick, Mr. Quashy!" exclaimed Pat, through her teeth, as the train, in a shower of sparks from the engine, dashed into a little tunnel.

"Only one more liddle way!" yelled Quashy. "Den we catchee school plenty quick!"

. . . . . .

Now, whilst these happenings were taking place, most of the girls had reached the school, and had time to admire the spacious bungalow building which had been erected on the great stone platform, and the lesser buildings which surrounded it.

They did not admire quite so much the great Class-room building, which stood at the railway-terminus, and at the foot of the great pae-pae.

This was a true native building erected by native workmen in the very best style of the South Sea Islander's art, which is by no means to be despised.

It was a huge, cool hall, whose pillars were shafts, polished like marble, of the stately coc de mer, or the twin cocoanut palm—a hard wood which takes a brilliant polish.

The floor was of huge slabs of marble, cool, and clean.

Miss Strong had very wisely decided that this great schoolroom should be one which was best suited to the climate, and, therefore, she had been content to leave it in native hands.

The natives had built the desks on a European pattern from finely-figured woods, and as the forests of Diamond Island were rich in the rarer varieties of native woods, they had made these veritable works of art, for the arms of each desk were carved with native patterns.

It was in this stately native building, cool and spacious, that Miss Whiffen gathered the girls together, somewhat against their will, to make them a little speech and to give them a little lecture on the new schoolroom.

"Dear girls," she began. "In this spacious hall we shall pursue our studies."

The girls stared up dutifully into the great thatched roof, which, beautifully worked, was supported on great polished shafts of cocoa-wood.

They could have done without their schoolroom quite well.

"In this stately hall," continued Miss Whiffen, "we shall, dear girls, study the history of this remarkable valley—— Well, Poppy dear?"

Poppy Hayes, her simple face glowing with a new thought, had put up her hand for permission to ask a question.

"Please, Miss Whiffen," she asked, "will there be any cinemas?"

Miss Whiffen considered this question for a moment.

"Ahem! Well, perhaps, my dear Poppy," she replied, "we may have a cinema for the amusement and instruction of our native friends."

Miss Whiffen hastily switched off the matter of cinemas.

"We have, my dear girls, the greatest civilising influence already at work on the island," she said, holding up her hand. "We have the railway. Listen to the busy whistle of the locomotive, which crows like chanticleer over its cheerful toil!"

The girls listened dutifully.

They could all hear the whistle which Quashy was then blowing with all his might as the train shot through the little tunnels that were cut through the rock galleries at the side of the Happy Valley.

Miss Whiffen became ecstatic as she pursued this idea.

"Hark, dear girls," she exclaimed, "to what may be called the cockcrow which everywhere proclaims the dawn of civilisation. Our little locomotive and train, driven by the intelligent native gentleman, Quashy, rapidly approaches our secluded valley. Hark! The whistle grows nearer and nearer! Soon the brave and intelligent driver will bring his train to a standstill at the very end of this schoolroom, and——"

Miss Whiffen's lecture was cut short by a yell which went up from the natives who were working on the completion of some sheds outside.

It was followed by a shriek from the girls.

Melita had made up her mind that if she was going to be treated like a convict she could dress like one, and she had decorated her frock with broad arrows.

At the end of the schoolroom there was a crash and a rending of wood and plaster. The whole school building rocked under some great shock.

"An earthquake!" gasped Miss Whiffen.

The girls rushed inside as, with a crash, the wall at the end of the hall opened out in a fan of falling plaster.

And through the great hole thus made the engine, Puffing Billy, followed by its train of jolting trucks, skated over the polished marble floor, coming to rest, with a final shriek of its whistle, just in front of Miss Whiffen's desk.

Miss Whiffen stood in the desk paralysed.

She had been a schoolmistress all her life, and had seen many strange happenings in schoolrooms.

But she had never seen a locomotive and a train of goods trucks trying to get into a ladies' school before.

In the cab, white with plaster, were Joe and her chums, still clinging like grim death to the snorting locomotive.

From the last truck came the dismal screams of Mademoiselle.

Quashy's brakes had failed to act at the critical moment, and the engine, passing through the stop buffers, had burst through the wall of the hall.

But Quashy was not dismayed. It seemed to him to be all in the day's work.

He stepped down from the cab, his dark face wreathed in smiles.

"Dat ole engin', him gone and done it dis time!" he said comfortably. "But we catchee school plenty quick!"

CHAPTER V.
PAT GETS A "BITE."

A BULL in a china-shop creates a scene of excitement.

But the sensation of a bull in a china shop was nothing to the excitement caused amongst the girls of the Island School when, recovering from their surprise, they discovered that a full-length train of trucks, with a real puffing and steaming engine, had burst through the end wall in the great schoolroom.

And in the last truck of the train was Mademoiselle, her smart shore-going hat tipped over one eye, her umbrella broken, and the luggage and herself covered with the fine white dust of the fallen coral plaster.

"Ow!" exclaimed Mademoiselle. "Nevaire have I driven behind a driver so mad! 'E is lunatic, this Quashee!"

She descended from the truck, which the girls called "the guard's van," and waved her broken umbrella angrily at Quashy, whose face was still covered with smiles as he recounted again and again how he had "catchee'd the school all right!"

"Monsieur!" exclaimed Mademoiselle angrily. "You shall owe to me ten t'ousand apology. You 'ave precipitate my baggages on ze railway, you 'ave shake me mos' 'orrible, and you 'ave broke ze school!"

And Mademoiselle pointed majestically with her broken umbrella to the huge arch which the train had driven through the end wall of the large schoolroom.

The smiles faded from Quashy's copper-coloured face as he faced the angry French mistress.

He saw that Mademoiselle was really disturbed, and that she had not appreciated the record run from the pier to the school in the Happy Valley.

"Hoo!" he remarked, kicking the engine disconsolately. "Thou art the wicked one, oh engine! Thou hast put mud on my head and sorrow in my house. Mammypoodle is angered, and I have heaviness in my heart!"

Quashy made these remarks in his own Kingsmill Island dialect.

But the girls saw that he was upset.

They sympathetically helped him to clear away the fallen rubbish of plaster, and to unload Mademoiselle's luggage from the trucks.

Then, one by one, they pushed the trucks back through the hole in the wall of the schoolroom, and got them on the line again.

And, finally, they helped the disconsolate Quashy to push Puffing Billy, the engine, and to jack it up once more on its rickety little railroad.

"Mammypoodle she too cross along o' me! Me fright!" said Quashy.

"That's all right!" replied Pat comfortingly. "Mademoiselle is often cross with us. But her bark is always worse than her bite. She will get over it directly."

Quashy sniffed, and big tears came into his black eyes.

"She too cross belong me, and she big chief!" he said.

Quashy evidently had an exaggerated notion of Mademoiselle's importance on the island, which was probably founded on the smartness and splendour of her appearance as well as her French nationality.

"Look here, Quashy," said Dumpling Davis kindly, "don't you distress yourself. You just steam back along the line and pick up any of her trunks and boxes that you have dropped over on to the railway, and we'll soon pacify her. She won't be angry any more."

With this Quashy ambled off, apparently easier in his mind, and the girls started to explore. Arriving at the head of the steps, they gave a cry of pleasure when they saw the delightful home which had been built for them on the great stone platform.

They were not long in finding their dormitory— a long, cool room, floored with polished wood, and set with little white beds covered with mosquito curtains.

"I think it is a lovely room!" said Dumpling, looking round her. "And it's lovelier still," she added, "since we are all together, and are not shut in with Edith Forster or any of her friends! I should hate that!"

But there was one of their number who would not sleep on the neat, little white-enamelled iron bedstead which was provided for each.

This was Melita.

Melita could not get on with a bed at all, and, by a special dispensation, she was to be allowed to sleep on the floor according to the native custom, on a layer of mats.

And Melita was busy now arranging a huge roll of beautiful white mats, which were kept rolled up during the daytime, and only laid out at night. Melita was just arranging her bed to her satisfaction when the welcome cry of "dinner" sent them scuttling to the large dining hall.

Melita rolled her dark eyes, and nodded her head with approval as she seated herself at table.

"Ah!" she cried. "Plenty munchee-munchee, tray-bong food!"

Joe laughed.

"I hope you'll make a good meal, Melita," she said, "for I've got permission to go exploring this afternoon along the lagoon, and we may be away a long time."

"Your explore-parties, zey make too much excitements for me!" observed Mademoiselle, who was seated at the head of the table. "You say to me, 'Come, Mademoiselle, for nice quiet afternoon,' and you at once get making ze most exciting adventure! I am fatigued! I do not want to tumble down cliff or to turn ze capzise in ze boat! I would sooner stop at 'ome an' read ze nice book!"

"Do come, Mademoiselle!" urged the girls.

"We'll promise you we won't look for any adventures," urged Pat.

"We have got a lovely whale-boat," said Joe; "and you shall just drift along over the lagoon, reclining on cushions and reading your book."

Mademoiselle hesitated, and gave way.

But Mademoiselle nearly backed out of the excursion when the girls stopped at the terminus of the little railway, where Quashy and his train were waiting for them.

"We 'ave to go in ze train?" asked Mademoiselle. "I do not want to go in ze train! I will not be kill by zis mad boy Quashy an' 'is mad te-rain!"

Quashy looked very repentant.

"Me no catchee too quick, young missus!" he urged. "Me go 'long too quiet. Engin' him go too quiet now."

And he patted Puffing Billy, his tiny engine, as though it were a horse.

Mademoiselle allowed herself to be persuaded, after many assurances that Quashy would be careful in his driving over that rickety mile or two of miniature railway.

So she climbed gingerly into the truck which Quashy had lined with white tappa-cloth of the snowiest colour and the softest texture.

Facing page 112   THE BLACK GIRL'S HEROISM

Quashy opened the throttle of his engine, and off they went, rattling on their way to the beach.

Soon they were skimming along the base of the cliffs and the edge of the shore, and before Mademoiselle had time to get nervous of the serpentine dance of the little train through the groves of coco-palms, Quashy had brought his train to a standstill close by the little coral pier, where a neat white whale-boat was waiting for them.

They soon discovered that Mr. Pipes was not going to allow them to sail about the lagoon without some escort, for Quashy pointed with great delight to a huge Kanaka giant who was standing by the whaleboat, ready to hoist the sails when his passengers should arrive.

This islander stood full six feet four inches in his rope-soled slippers, and was neatly dressed in a kilt of snow-white tappa cloth and a white drill jacket with brass buttons.

" Him Nareo ! " exclaimed Quashy. " My li'l brother ! "

" Oh, he's your little brother, is he ? " asked Pat, looking at the native, who sat shyly in the boat. " If he's your little brother, what are your big brothers like ? "

" Him bery good boy ! " said Quashy earnestly. " But s'pose you no talk too angry to him. Him too shy ! Him cry ! Him too much baby ! "

Nareo hoisted the sails, and soon the whaler was skimming away over the blue waters of the lagoon, heading along the shores towards the spot where the Volcano Valley opened out to the sea.

The girls gave a great sigh of delight as they settled themselves in the boat and watched the long lines of the coco-groves sliding past them.

Between patches of coral and weed the channels of the lagoon were plainly marked by deep channels of turquoise blue water, and it was through these that Nareo was steering his course.

It was evident that though Nareo was dying of shyness, he was intensely proud of his charge, and of the smart new whaleboat.

" Ohe, Nareo ! " began Joe, with the intention of ordering the giant to steer ashore.

But, greatly to her horror, Nareo, covering his face with his hand, commenced to weep.

" Good gracious ! " exclaimed Joe, regarding the giant with wondering eyes. " Whatever is the matter with him ? "

Melita pondered over the question.

" Him come from long way off," she said, after a while. " Him too much fright along white people."

" He'll get used to us presently," put in Dumpling Davis. " Tell him to cheer up and try to look on the bright side of things, Melita."

" I try," agreed Melita patiently. " Him too silly nigger, dis one ! "

But presently the intent of the soothing messages was conveyed to the huge giant, who, after all, had but the brain of a small child, apart from his dexterity in handling a whaleboat.

As soon as they were out in the channel of the lagoon, Nareo hoisted the sail, and away they skimmed over a surface that was as brilliantly coloured as the interior of a pearl shell.

And the girls, looking over the side of the boat, simply gasped in admiration at the wonders that slid like a film under the keel of their boat.

Nareo was pleased by the girls' cries of admiration, and forgot his shyness, eager to show the wonders of the lagoon.

" S'posee you likee catchee big fiss, missy ? " he asked.

" Rather ! " replied Pat, to whom this question was addressed.

Nareo nodded and, stooping, produced from under the thwarts of the boat two sections of a powerful, shortish rod of lancewood, to which was attached a huge reel, on which was wound a tremendous length of the strongest oiled silk line.

This he fitted together and handed to Pat.

" Goodness gracious ! " exclaimed Pat. " Are we going to catch whales, Nareo ? "

" Catchum big fiss," urged Nareo. " You wait ! "

He sailed along the lagoon for a while till he came opposite the spot where the river from the Volcano Valley ran out into the lagoon.

Here, as always happens where there is a flow of fresh water into a lagoon, the wall of the coral reef enclosing the lagoon broke off in a wide, deep-water passage leading straight out into the open sea.

This was because the coralline insect, though it builds its tremendous walls of limestone in the face of the roughest breakers and the never-ending beat of the Pacific swells, cannot live in the presence of any volume of fresh water.

And out through this opening Nareo steered the whaleboat.

Soon they were beyond the reef, the whaler rising and falling on the long, low ground-swells of the calm Pacific, which this day was living up to its name, though it is by no means the smoothest or most peaceful ocean in the world.

The whaler, steered seawards by Nareo, headed out for the fishing grounds, where they might expect to catch a jumping tuna.

The girls had heard about this great fish, but never had they seen one of these gigantic fish caught with a rod and a line ; and they were all full of excitement as Nareo proceeded to fix up a large and powerful hook with a bait formed of a shining red mullet.

All their attention was then turned on Pat, who held the stout rod as Nareo dropped the mullet and hook into the sea and allowed the long length of line to run out till nearly a hundred yards of it was trailing behind the boat.

They could see the bait glittering and twisting close under the crests of the great, low swells.

Then the line tightened like a banjo-string, thrumming and singing as it was ripped sideways through the water.

" Oh ! " gasped Pat. " Shure, I've hooked a whale at last ! "

It was not a whale she had hooked ; but there was a great swirl in the sea eighty yards away, and a huge fish, gleaming in a bar of living silver in the sunshine, broke through the water, hurling itself high in the air and shaking its head savagely.

Pat gave a gasp, for the fish was eight feet long, and she knew she had hooked the gamest and hardest fighting fish in all the seas—the jumping tuna of the Pacific !

Crash ! The fish fell back into the water, sending up a fountain of foam, tightening the line like a piano-wire till it fairly sung as it whirled off the great fishing reel.

Nareo gave a shout of triumph as he lowered the sails of the whaler hastily.

Presently the line slackened, and Pat gave a sigh, partly of relief and partly of disappointment.

" There now ! " she exclaimed. " He's broken the line and gone off ; an' I'm not surprised ! He was pulling strong enough to break a rope ! "

But when she had wound in about eighty yards of the line, there came another savage jerk, and again the line tightened, humming off the reel with a droning sound.

" Goodness ! " exclaimed Pat. " He's not gone, after all ! "

CHAPTER VI.

IN DEADLY DANGER

AGAIN the huge fish broached, leaping twelve feet into the air in a magnificent curve, and plunging into the water again with a splash that left a great white swirl on the smooth sea.

At first he headed seawards. Then, with a sudden turn, he shaped a course for the land, and Nareo began to look anxious.

The tuna is a cunning fish, and the intention of this one was to get amongst the outlying reefs, and to break the line amongst the rocks.

And where the rocks were the low swells were breaking in sheets of white water.

Though there was no great sea running to-day, there was enough swell on the face of the smooth

ocean to make short work of the whaleboat if she were dragged in amongst the sharp points of coral that lay close under the water.

In a few minutes she would be broken to matchwood.

Of a sudden on either side of the boat a huge mile-long swell, that was running in towards the reef, seemed to rear up its head and grow transparent.

The sapphire sheen of it turned to pale emerald as it stood up in a breaker.

The tuna was towing them over a shallow patch.

Nareo leaped to the tiller, and cried out to Pat to let go the rod.

But Pat did not understand him.

Her whole will and soul was intent on sticking to the rod and in landing her fish.

She had made up her mind that nothing should force her to let the rod go from her aching hands.

And she was still sticking to the rod when the whaler met the breaker as it raced over the shallow patch outside the reef.

Mademoiselle gave a scream as suddenly, from out of the smooth sea, there rose a long wall of water six feet high, standing up steep and straight, as though it were going to overwhelm the boat.

And for a moment or two it was indeed a question as to whether the comber would break before the whaler had passed over it, or whether it would crash down over the boat in a welter of tumbling foam, capsizing her and filling her with water.

But the staunch little craft breasted the steep hill of water, standing on its crest for an infinite space of time, with both ends of its keel well clear of the water.

Then the wave, having passed, crashed down in an acre of white foam, and the whaler was safe.

Mademoiselle gave a great puffing sigh.

" Pooh ! " she exclaimed. " What did make ze sea jomp like dat ? "

" We passed over a shallow patch ! " said Joe. " But it's all right now, Mademoiselle ! "

" I call zis mos' dangerous ! " exclaimed Mademoiselle. " If zat wave did break two or three yards sooner, we should 'ave been returned upside down, and drowned ! "

" ' A miss is as good as a mile,' Mademoiselle !" gasped Pat. " And the wave has finished my old fish. I can feel him slackening now. He is beaten ! "

" Fiss him too sleepy now ! " cried Nareo exultantly, meaning that the giant tuna had had about enough of it.

And, bit by bit, Pat reeled in her line, bringing the great misty shape close alongside the boat, when Nareo, with a movement quick as lightning, gaffed it, and made it fast.

The wonderful dress of old rose lace and silk was absolutely ruined!

It was certainly a noble fish, and when it was secured and towed into the lagoon, Melita gave a shrill cry of triumph, which was near enough to the savage yell to bring a reproach from Mademoiselle.

"Melita!" she exclaimed. "You must not make zose shouts. It is not comme il faut for a young lady to yell like Apache."

Melita grinned ruefully.

"Me too glad, Mammypoodle!" she exclaimed, holding her hand apologetically over her mouth.

"You will be too sorry if I give you an imposition to write in French!" said Mademoiselle severely.

At this Melita's face lengthened.

Melita as yet had not made much progress beyond pothooks and hangers.

She was learning to speak both English and French, but the art of writing was a horror to her, and her fingers cramped and ached when she tried to hold the unfamiliar pen.

And as Mademoiselle seemed greatly disturbed Melita's face grew longer and longer till, picking up a silk scarf, she threw it over her frizzy wig and commenced to weep.

"Boo—hoo—hoo!" sobbed Melita. "Me be good! Me no shout! Me no wantee write splimposition! Yaw—wow—hoo!"

And Melita broke into a desolate howl.

Then all of a sudden Nareo, who was rowing stroke, started to weep in sympathy.

Nareo was not exactly certain what was the trouble in the boat, but he gathered that punishment of some sort was threatened, and he thought that the dreaded Mammypoodle was going to punish him as well as Melita.

"Boo—hoo—hoo—hoo—hoo!" yelled Nareo, the giant tears running down his copper face in showers.

"Goodness gracious, Nareo!" exclaimed Joe. "What on earth is the matter with you now? You cry-baby! What are you crying for?"

"Me ky 'cause Missy Melita she ky," sobbed Nareo. "Mammypoodle she too cross. She going to gib Nareo impasplaition!"

The girls burst out laughing at this.

Evidently Nareo thought an imposition was some drastic form of punishment as bad as a thrashing.

"Now, look here, Nareo!" said Joe, in impressive tones. "If you'll stop crying, you shall have this mouth-organ, and I'll promise you that Mammypoodle isn't going to punish you. You are not going to put little Nareo in the corner, are you, Mammypoodle?" added Joe, turning to

Mademoiselle, who, barely able to restrain her laughter, shook her head.

And never was a child more delighted with a gift than this native with his mouth-organ.

" You too kind ! " he exclaimed, taking the coveted instrument ; and, rowing with one hand, he breathed through the instrument, puzzling out little snatches of plaintive native tunes which quite charmed Mademoiselle.

And, playing on his new treasure, Nareo pulled them to the shore, where they were going to land and to have tea.

Nareo had stopped tootling on the mouth-organ, when he was sent away with the kettle to a little cascade of water that came tumbling out of the lava cliff in a fairy bay to get water.

Joe gave him instructions in his own tongue.

" Nareo," she said, " s'posee you takee kettle and catchee water belong tea—savvy ? "

Nareo understood perfectly.

" You wantee makee tea soup, missy ? " he asked.

" That's right ! " replied Joe. " Hurry up ! Water him close up," she added, pointing to the fall.

Nareo nodded, and, taking the kettle, walked towards the scrub and bush which surrounded the fall.

And presently he returned, tootling merrily on his mouth-organ.

By the time tea was finished it was high time that they should be returning to the coral pier.

So the tuna was hoisted into the boat, and Nareo was told to get the whaler ready for sailing.

The afternoon breeze was now coming in fresh from the sea with its refreshing breath, causing the coco-palms ashore to wake their long, graceful fronds, and rippling the lagoon into a million tiny dancing wavelets.

Soon they were all ready, the tea-basket was packed up, and Nareo, pushing the boat off from the beach, hoisted the sails.

Off they flew in fine style, heading back along the lagoon at racing speed.

All at once the boat gave a lurch, and in this lurch Melita, who was sitting on the side, suddenly lost her balance and fell overboard.

Everyone gave a cry ; but as they knew Melita could swim like a fish they were not very alarmed.

Suddenly, however, Nareo brought the whaleboat racing round in a wide circle, which left a wide streak of foam on the blue waters, and, crying to Joe to take the tiller, he leaped into the water, swimming away from the boat.

He had whipped out his knife as he dived.

For a moment Joe thought he had gone mad.

But, rippling across the lagoon, she saw an object which explained all.

It was the ugly, black, triangular fin of a large shark, and it was heading straight for Melita.

The girls crouched in the whaler, horrified, as they watched that sinister, triangular fin rippling to the spot where Melita's frizzy head was bobbing through the water.

They knew that it was a shark of the largest size, making across the lagoon, intent on his prey.

" Row, girls, row ! " cried Mademoiselle, standing up in the boat, which was now heading the wind with her sails shaking.

The girls were slipping the oars into the rowlocks, and soon they were rowing with all their strength after Melita.

But Melita had suddenly dived.

Melita had seen the shark, and she bobbed below the surface like a diving duck.

For a moment or two the huge brute slowed in its approach.

Though the great white shark is known as the sea tiger, it is the most cowardly brute in the world, and suspicious of the slightest splashing sound.

Nareo, like Melita, had disappeared under the water.

He was swimming like an otter, knife in hand, heading between the shark and the spot where Melita was swimming.

Melita had dived deep, and from her frock had snatched a knife.

Looking up through the green, clear water, she could see the great shape of the shark, hanging over her like an airship.

The shark was about to turn on his back to attack, when suddenly Melita saw, swimming close under him, the giant shape of Nareo, who simply, and without waiting, attacked the huge brute.

With a terrific blow of its powerful tail, it turned and strove to get at its adversary.

But Nareo, attacking it from below, could not be caught by those terrible jaws.

Then Melita, having taken in the situation, struck out, and joined in the fray.

The giant shark, which was full eighteen feet long, writhed and twisted, endeavouring to avoid those deadly knives.

But both Melita and Nareo had grabbed him, and were sticking to him as two dogs might tackle a wolf.

At last, with a prodigious swirl and lash of his tail, the shark broke away from them, and the girls were delighted by seeing the heads of Melita and Nareo bob up to the surface close by the boat.

" Goodness ! " gasped Pat, throwing Melita a line. " Come on board at once, you naughty girl ! What have you been doing ? "

"Me fightee shark!" replied Melita stolidly, as though tackling an eighteen-foot shark in his own element were quite an everyday matter. "Me fightee shark along Nareo! Shark, him pretty sick!" she added, as the girls, leaning over the gunwhale, dragged her into the boat.

Nareo, grinning all over his bronze-coloured face, paddled round to the rudder of the whaler, and, climbing up by it, dropped aboard.

"Melita!" exclaimed Mademoiselle. "You are 'urt!"

But Melita shook her head and grinned.

"Me no fright along shark. Shark, him no bitee me!" she responded, speaking of the shark with great contempt.

"You are 'urt, Melita!" exclaimed Mademoiselle, her face very white, as she pointed to Melita's arm.

And, sure enough, Melita's forearm was badly scraped where it had come in contact with the rough hide of the shark, which is like so much glass-paper.

And Nareo's shoulder had been scraped in a like fashion.

Not that Nareo was hurt, but the stout drill shirt he was wearing was quite torn where the shark had ripped past him, rubbing his shoulder with its terrific hide, which, throughout the South Seas, is used by the native carpenters for rasping and rubbing down woodwork.

Luckily, Mademoiselle was always thoughtful enough to carry a few bandages and first-aid appliances.

She insisted on bandaging up Melita's arm and wrist there and then, whilst Nareo looked round the calm, blue surface of the lagoon for his defeated enemy.

The girls could not help gazing at Nareo with a new respect.

They could not understand this simple native, who, although he was so shy and timid that he would cry if anyone stared at him, had showed not the slightest hesitation in tackling that terrible shark.

CHAPTER VII.

MELITA'S BAD BEHAVIOUR

As the boat approached the shore, Melita, apparently intent on showing her further prowess as a swimmer, suddenly stood up and without a word dived overboard.

"Melita!" cried Mademoiselle. "You shall come back! I do not geeve you permission to go!"

"Me wantee catchee more sharkee, Missy Mammypoodle!" exclaimed Melita.

Mademoiselle would not have been so dictatorial if her nerves had not been upset.

It is certainly enough to upset any schoolmistress when one of her pupils jumps out of a boat to indulge in shark-infested waters.

"Melita!" exclaimed Mademoiselle, standing up in the boat and sternly addressing the black girl. "I do insist that you shall once more enter ze boat!"

Then a very regrettable incident happened.

Melita lost her temper, and was guilty of an unpardonable rudeness.

She put out her tongue!

Two dull red spots showed on Mademoiselle's pale cheeks.

"Good! Mademoiselle Melita!" she muttered. "I must instruct you zat it is not comme il faut to make ze prolong tongue at your schoolmistress. It is not ladysome!"

"Now you've done it, Melita!" called out Pat as they saw her reach the shallow water and wade ashore, to march along the beach. "What d'ye mean by behaving like a horrid little gutter girl, not like a young lady and a princess?"

Mademoiselle was speechless for a while.

"Do not speak to her, Patreecia!" she exclaimed at length. "I shall punish her severely when we get back to ze school. Nevaire again shall she come out wiz us until she has made much repentance for her bad conduct!"

They were close to the shore now, and Melita heard this. Her face lengthened and set in a sullen scowl.

She was perfectly aware that she had been behaving disgracefully, and she thought that she was going to be thrashed.

"You no whack me, missus?" she said to Mademoiselle, impudently enough. "You no whack me. Me princess!"

And she drew herself up proudly, pointing to her tribal tattooing.

But Mademoiselle vouchsafed no answer, and the girls did not speak to their black friend.

Nareo steered the whaler towards the coral quay which was now in sight, and when he landed he immediately started telling the story of the shark, and of Melita's bad behaviour to all the niggers who were assembled on the quay.

And Melita's scowl grew darker and darker when she found that her friends were taking no notice of her antics.

"Why you no talkee along me, Joey?" she demanded in an arrogant voice of Joe, as she steered the boat towards the quay. "Why you not talkee along me? Me princess!"

"I'm not going to talk to you, Melita, whilst you go on showing off, and behaving yourself like that," replied Joe briefly. "We are all perfectly ashamed of you! If you are a princess you should behave like a princess, not like a ragamuffin!"

Melita flared up at this.

"Why you shame along me?" she exclaimed. "Me friend along you. Why you shamed along friend? Yah! You am little friend—white girl missy."

Joe made no answer to this. Then Melita turned on Pat.

"Why you no talk, Pat?" she demanded. "You 'fraid to talk along o' poor Melita?"

"Faith, I may be Irish," replied Pat, "but I know when to hould me tongue sometimes. An' I'd advise you, Melita, to hould yours. Silence is golden, me girl!"

"Yes, do be quiet, Melita," pleaded Dumpling Davis, who had been anxiously watching the grim anger that tightened Mademoiselle's lips.

She made faces behind Mademoiselle's back, trying to indicate by signs that Melita was storing up tremendous punishment for herself by her conduct.

But Melita only mocked her, which was a very poor appreciation of her friendly warnings.

Melita followed the group along the paths beneath the tall cocoa-palms, throwing stones at the land-crabs that were routing about amongst the husks of the fallen cocoanuts.

She dragged along behind the rest, giving shrill cries in imitation of birds, and gathering brilliant scarlet berries, which she threaded on a coarse grass, and hung round her neck as beads.

She also wreathed the berries in her hair, and, as they contained a brilliant scarlet juice, used by the natives for dyeing patterns on tappa cloths, Melita rubbed her face with the dye, and started to decorate her frock with broad arrows, such as she had seen convicts wearing on their clothes when she had watched some prison pictures on the films.

Melita made up her mind that if she was going to be treated like a convict, she would dress like a convict, and she managed to cover her frock with these broad arrows as they marched to the school in the Happy Valley.

She looked a horrid sight now.

But as they neared the schoolhouse, with its atmosphere of dignity and discipline, the wild, savage spirit which had been making Melita so naughty began to die out of her.

Halfway up the long stairway were standing Edith Forster and her friends.

These glared at the unruly Melita and giggled.

"Goodness!" exclaimed Edith Forster, in audible tones. "Just look at that horried young savage those girls are so chummy with! Isn't she a perfect fright? I wonder what she's been up to?"

"I wonder they have anything to do with her," replied Gladys Knox, in a shrill voice that was meant to be heard. "But they are all tarred with the same brush! The savage is quite good enough for their company!"

At the head of the great stairway the party was met by Miss Whiffen, who, though the tropic twilight was rapidly falling, saw, by the dabbing of Melita's dress and by her defiant and sullen attitude, that something was seriously wrong.

"Goodness gracious!" exclaimed Miss Whiffen, staring at Melita. "Whatever does this mean? What has this child been doing?"

"She has been making revolutions," replied Mademoiselle severely. "Where is Miss Strong? I have to report that Melita has been a too naughty girl! I shall put her to bed wizout ze suppaire!" added Mademoiselle wrathfully.

And at this awful threat Melita began to howl.

Miss Strong was not to be found about the school building. But Mademoiselle's word was law in this matter.

Melita had behaved very badly, and she was to be put to bed without any supper.

With the tears running down her face, stained by the scarlet berries, Melita was led along the corridors to her dormitory by Miss Whiffen and Mademoiselle, who stood over her until she was undressed and in bed.

And Melita was there, sitting up in her white bed, looking very depressed, when the girls came in to prepare for supper.

It was bad enough to be sent to bed. But to be sent to bed without supper was what most rankled in the heart of Melita.

She started to weep when her friends entered the dormitory.

"Boo-hoo!" wept Melita, using a sheet as a handkerchief.

"It's no good crying over spilt milk, Melita," said Pat, perching herself at the foot of Melita's bed, and speaking in consoling tones. "Whatever made you so naughty all of a sudden?"

Melita shook her tousled head and rolled her eyes.

"Me put too much sauce along Mammy-poodle!" she exclaimed dolefully. "She too cross along me now! She say me no get kai-kai (supper)!"

And Melita, at this terrible thought, wept profusely.

"Cheer up, Melita!" said Joe. "We will smuggle you some supper later on. But to-morrow you will have to tell Mademoiselle how sorry you are for being so rude to her."

Melita mopped her eyes, and nodded in agreement. She was very repentant now.

"You will apologise, won't you, Melita?" pleaded Dumpling Davis.

"Yes," answered the sorrowful Melita, sitting up in her bed, looking like a sorrowful golliwog.

The girls having tidied themselves went to the dining-hall.

As they passed along the corridor from their dormitory they noticed that a string of the scarlet berries with which Melita had smeared her face and wreathed her head was scattered and broken.

They gathered these up lest they should be trodden into the snowy Japanese matting, with which the corridor was carpeted.

" Pick them all up carefully, girls ! " said Joe. " Poor old Melita is in enough trouble already, and the dye in the berries is awful stuff. If it gets on the matting it will dye it for ever, for nothing will take it out ! "

Her chums gathered up the berries.

Then they passed on to the great lounge which opened into the dining-hall, waiting till the gong should sound for supper.

CHAPTER VIII.

UNDER SUSPICION

SUDDENLY Mademoiselle appeared, and she paused as she saw the girls waiting in the lounge. Then she came towards them.

" Josephine ! Patreecia ! " she called out.

" Yes, Mademoiselle," replied the two, advancing towards her.

" I am so agitate and so late ! " said Mademoiselle. " Will you come wiz me an' 'elp me to dress for ze suppaire, or I shall be too late for anysing ! Ze gong will call directly, an' ze servants dey do not understand ze fastening of my costume ! "

She led the way to her rooms along the same corridor in which her own dormitory was situated, and opened the white door of her room. Then she and the girls stood back in horror.

There on the bed, laid out ready, was her wonderful dress of old rose silk and lace.

The bed and the dress had hardly been disturbed, but smudged all over the dress, in the indelible dye of the red berries which Melita had gathered, and over the dainty pillow-slips and the snowy counterpane, were huge broad arrows, scarlet and forbidding.

The dress was absolutely ruined.

The berries were those of the Marrap-en-chet, or " Bunchy Mary," as the white beachcombers call the tree.

And the dye was as strong and as permanent as that of the northern partridge-berry, which is used by dyers for giving a permanent scarlet tint.

All the boiling and cleaning in the world would never remove those sinister marks from the dress or from the bed-linen ; it would only fix it permanently in purple dye of the tint of black-currant juice.

The dress and its valuable lace were ruined.

Poor Mademoiselle !

All she could do was to give a gasp, and, sinking into a chair, she covered her face with her hands, whilst the two girls looked ruefully at this malicious ruin.

It was the savage spitefulness of the deed which had overcome Mademoiselle.

There was not a doubt in her mind but that Melita was to blame.

For a few minutes the girls were as much overcome as Mademoiselle. It seemed impossible to them that Melita could have done this. Yet there was the evidence plain enough — of spiteful and malicious ruin, deliberate and stupid.

The girls could say nothing. They were distressed beyond words.

It seemed to them that Melita

In the arbour, Joe and Pat discovered Melita sobbing her heart out.

119

had taken leave of her senses—Melita, who had always been so cheery and open-hearted a companion.

The gong for supper thundered through the corridors as the two stood, helpless and sorrowful, gazing at Mademoiselle, who, with heaving shoulders, was sobbing, crouched in the chair.

Presently Mademoiselle, with a great effort, dried her eyes and rose.

She smiled piteously.

" I am sorry, girls, zat I make myself baby ! " she said. " I am no braver zan poor Monsieur Nareo, who cry so much. It is no good to cry over ze spilt milk or ze stain dress. We will put ze dress away, and we shall say nozzings. Poor little Melita, she do not know what she 'ave done ! "

But just at this moment there was a tap on the door.

" May I come in, Mademoiselle ? " said the voice of Miss Strong.

Mademoiselle had no time to answer or to hide the dress and those disfiguring broad arrows of stain on the coverlet and pillow-slips.

She stood with the dress in her hands as Miss Strong entered the room and came to a standstill, surveying the ruin with horror.

" Oh ! " gasped Miss Strong. " Who could have done such a thing ! "

Mademoiselle's lips were quivering as she pronounced the word " Melita," but she drew herself up, blinking the tears from her eyes.

" It is great misfortune, Mees Strong ! " she said. " But we will say nozzings. Poor Melita, she do not understand what she have done ! "

Miss Strong shook her head.

" I am afraid we must take some notice, Mademoiselle ! " she answered. " Otherwise, Melita will not understand that she must not commit such acts as this. It is so barbarous and wanton ! "

Then she turned to the two girls.

" Go to your supper, girls," she said gravely. " I will look after Mademoiselle and help her to dress."

The two girls walked sorrowfully away from the room, closing the door on Miss Strong and Mademoiselle.

They had only got a few paces along the passage when Joe faced Pat.

" Pat," she exclaimed, " I'm pretty well certain that Melita could not have done such a malicious trick ! It's not in her nature ! Anything she would do, she would do openly. She would not have sneaked into Mademoiselle's room and wantonly ruined her favourite evening-dress like that ! "

Pat shook her head.

" I wish I could think so, Joe ! " she said.

" But there it is—the same berries used, the same marks as Melita put on her own dress. She had a row with Mademoiselle, and she must have crept out of the dormitory after we left it and got into Mademoiselle's room."

" But such an act is not a bit like her ! " exclaimed Joe. " Melita is as true as the day ! She might, in a passion, throw a stone at Mademoiselle's head. But she would not throw it from behind a bush. She would throw it in the open. She was rude enough and naughty enough this afternoon. But it was all open ! "

Pat shook her head doubtfully.

" You've got to remember, Joe," she said wisely, " that Melita is still half a savage, although she is a chieftainess in her own country. And you've got to remember, besides, that Mademoiselle ordered that she was not to have any supper. Now, what you have got to consider is—what are the feelings of a child who is half a savage when her food is stopped ? It has quite a different meaning to such a girl as it would have to us. If we were sent to bed on bread and scrape, or nothing at all, we should just laugh. But poor old Melita was probably labouring under some dim, savage notion that she was going to be starved. Such notions are well-founded in her country, for the chiefs have starved people there—and in quite recent years, too ! "

" Come along to supper, Joe ! " said Pat, pulling her by the arm.

But Joe pulled her arm away.

" You go on, Pat ! " she answered. " I'm feeling rather sick and upset. I don't feel much like supper, and I'm going to have a look round these corridors. I can't believe that Melita did it ! "

Pat shook her head and went on.

" Whether she did it or not, we'll get her some supper," she said. " We've got to stand by her. She'll be in awful disgrace over this ! "

Joe nodded and turned.

She made her way softly past the closed door of Mademoiselle's room, and a few yards further on turned down a side-passage to one of the bath-rooms.

Here she turned on the light and examined the three spotless wash-basins.

They had all been recently used, as was evident by the beads of water which still lay on the porcelain.

There were no towels in the bath-room, for each girl kept her own towels in the dormitories.

And at the third basin Joe came to a standstill.

On the edge of it was just a tiny touch of scarlet. And then she picked up the cake of soap that was in the ledge and examined it closely.

There, clearly imprinted in the surface of the soap, were the marks of a thumb and forefinger, clear fingerprints embedded in scarlet stain.

Joe pocketed the soap and slipped out of the bath-room.

Then she made her way to the dormitory, where Melita was lying in bed.

The room was quite dark when Joe slipped in at the doorway.

But a stifled sniff from the bed showed that Melita was not asleep, and that she had been crying.

" Not asleep, Melita dear ? " asked Joe gently.

" Me not asleep ! " sniffed Melita. " Me too sorry ! Me wantee kiss Mammypoodle ! "

Joe nodded in the darkness.

Melita would hardly be in such a penitent frame of mind if she had, but a few minutes before, committed such an act as the ruin of Mademoiselle's dress.

" Me too sad ! " said Melita, sobbing. " An' arm belong me hurt now ! "

She lifted the bandaged arm, which had been chafed and rawed by the rough skin of the shark.

" Wait a minute ! " said Joe. " I will get a light and ease the bandages for you. Then you will be more comfortable, and later on Miss Strong will put it up in boracic ointment."

She lit a lamp and brought it to the bedside.

Then she eased the bandages round Melita's grazed arm with tender hands.

And at the same time Joe closely examined Melita's hands.

They were certainly stained with the juice of the tell-tale Bunchy Mary berries.

But they had certainly not been washed recently.

Who, then, had left that imprint of the finger and thumb-mark on that cake of soap in the bath-room ?

And another fact flashed into Joe's mind.

Melita and the girls of their dormitory did not use that particular bath-room.

Indeed, Melita was none too fond of washing her hands at all.

" Goodness gracious, Melita ! " said Joe. " How grubby your hands are ! I'll get a face-flannel and some water and wash them for you ! "

She performed this office and washed Melita's hands.

And it was plain from the exceeding griminess of the face-flannel when this operation was completed that, whoever had washed their hands free of the crimson berries and their stain, it was not Melita.

But, all the same, Melita's pillows were stained by the scarlet juice of the berry, for some of the crushed berries had remained in her frizzy hair,

and their marks had come off on the pillow when Melita, in her grief, had dug her head into it.

And Joe knew only too well that this further evidence would tell against Melita.

The graze on Melita's arm had made her feverish and fretful.

" Me too sorry ! " she moaned. " Me wan' to kiss Mammypoodle ! "

Joe nodded.

She left the dormitory, and in the corridor met " Lady Edith."

With a contemptuous glance, Edith swept by.

Joe gave a little start as Edith passed.

She was fanning herself with her handkerchief, and as the light fell on her right hand, Joe noticed that her thumb-nail was slightly tinged with scarlet—the scarlet of the Bunchy Mary berry !

CHAPTER IX.

THE COLD SHOULDER

MELITA was in disgrace !

The story of the wrecking of Mademoiselle's dinner-dress had spread round the school.

The native servants had got the story, and, by some mysterious means, Edith Forster, Gladys Knox, and their little set had discovered all about the staining of the dress and its lace with the indelible stain of the Bunchy Mary berries.

And the next day Melita, to her horror, found herself cold-shouldered in many directions.

Joe and Pat, descending to the gardens early in the morning, found Melita, who was always an early-riser, sobbing in an arbour of trailing bougainvillea.

" Hallo, Melita ! " exclaimed Joe, kneeling by their unhappy friend. " What's the trouble now ? "

" Me too sorry ! " wept Melita. " Me too sad ! Me met Gladdy Knock jus' now, little bimby ago. She go to wash 'erself all over ! "

" You mean that Gladys Knox was going to the bath ! " corrected Joe.

" Hi ! " agreed the sobbing Melita. " She goin' to wash 'erself up to 'er neck in big washee-washee basin ! "

" Bath, dear ! " corrected Joe again. " But I don't see why that should make you cry," she added.

" Me no cry along washee ! " answered Melita. " Me cry 'long Gladdy Knock. I say to Gladdy, ' Good-marnin', Gladdy ! Aloaha, Gladdy ! Love to you, Gladdy ! ' But she not take notice 'long o' me. She say dey girl put me under taboo along spoilin' Mammypoodle's number one dress ! "

" You mean her dinner-frock ? " said Joe. " But you didn't spoil it, Melita, did you ? "

"No!" sobbed Melita. "Me no do nuffin' along Mammypoodle's flock. Me spoil dress belong me. But me no go into Mammypoodle's room an' mark her flock along Bunchy Mary berry! Me told Mammypoodle so and head-mistress too, and dey say dey tink I not do it."

"Did Gladys Knox say anything to you?" asked Pat.

"Boo-hoo!" wept Melita. "She say ebbery-one put taboo on me for nasty, common, spiteful girl! Boo-hoo! Me no common, spiteful girl! Me princess!" wept Melita, who was almost quaking with fear at the thought of the taboo, which meant so much, according to her native customs and superstitions.

"Pooh!" exclaimed Pat. "That crowd can't put the taboo on you, Melita. We are not put-ting any on you, and if they taboo you they'll have to taboo us! And you shall see, Melita," added Pat, "which of us can best stand being sent to Coventry!"

"Send along Coventry?" echoed Melita. "What um mean?"

"Why it means the same as your old taboo!" replied Pat. "I've been sent to Coventry. Why I wanst went to a school where the girls sent me to Coventry and kept me there for a week. But, you see, I didn't take any hurt!"

And Pat hit herself proudly on the chest with her clenched fist to show that being sent to Coventry had not spoiled her health.

Melita looked at her friend admiringly and with envious eyes.

She felt that a girl who could stand being tabooed for a week must, indeed, be a girl of no common powers and health.

And the thought that Pat and Joe were her friends, notwithstanding the threats of Gladys Knox, cheered her up wonderfully.

"Come along, Melita!" said Pat, winding her arm in the arm of the sorrowful princess. "Don't take any notice of that taboo non-sense! And if that cat Gladys Knox doesn't want to know you—well, she sha'n't know us, either, and she will be kept out of a lot of fun. Now let us come and have a look at the Happy Valley, and see if we can find some fruit!"

Melita cheered up wonderfully as they de-scended into the beautiful valley. The rough walls of stone which had been built round the old orchards had been rebuilt again, with neat stiles and gates of dark brown koa-wood.

The underbrush and tangles of wild creepers and orchids had been cleared away, and the trees had been pruned and tended, till these deserted and neglected orchards looked once more what they had originally been — carefully-tended gardens.

There was no lack of fruit here.

The oranges and the lemons and the wild limes had boughs that were hanging low to the ground, heavy laden with golden fruits and blossoming at the same time, filling the air with their wonderful scent.

The side-shoots of the bananas had been cut away and replanted, greatly to the improvement of the trees, which were laden with huge bunches of the green-and-golden fruit.

And the paw-paw trees, or pai-pais, as Melita called them, were heavy laden with their great fruits growing rapidly ripe.

But the attention of the girls was suddenly attracted to the appearance of Edith Forster, with her inevitable satellites, Lily Parsons and Gladys Knox, coming arm-in-arm towards them.

They came first on Joe, who, seated on the low coral wall of the garden, was sampling pas-sion-fruit.

She nodded coldly to the three. She had not forgotten that patch of tell-tale scarlet on Edith's finger-tips.

The three girls drew up, facing Joe.

"Good-morning!" said Edith Forster. "We were looking for you. We thought it was only fair to tell you that we are going to send your black friend to Coventry."

"Why?" asked Joe steadily.

"Why," replied Edith, "we don't think it right in any case that white girls should be asked to mix with the niggers. You can see plainly for yourself how it is working out. You and your set have always taken up this nigger-girl Melita, and the result is that you have turned the girl's head. She behaved disgracefully yesterday to Mademoiselle—behaved like what she is, a savage. And when Mademoiselle punished her, she went and deliberately spoiled Mademoiselle's dress by rubbing red berries all over it, just as she had spoiled her own cotton frock. You may be able to stand that sort of thing and still be friends with the girl!" added Edith, with a sniff of self-righteousness. "But we—aw—belong to better sort of people!"

Joe eyed her deliberately.

"Why," she answered slowly, "before I take a hand in sending Melita to Coventry, I want exact and full proof that it was she who rubbed those Bunchy Mary berries on Mademoiselle's dress, and not three people who washed their hands last night in the bathroom!"

"Come along, girls!" snapped Edith, unable any longer to bear the steady gaze of Joe's eyes.

And, with a very artificial little laugh, she swung her friends round, and they walked off down the path.

"What did she mean about washing our hands?" demanded Lily Parsons, in uncomfortable tones. "Do you think she suspects anything?"

"It was you two who rubbed the berries on the dress!" exclaimed Gladys Knox. "I told you I would take no hand in it!"

"But you kept cave at the door!" sneered Edith Forster. "Don't forget that, my dear! You are as much in it as we are. No, girls," she added, "I don't believe that horrid Joe knows anything. She only suspects. And I did find some stain of those horrid berries on my fingers this morning. Perhaps she saw this last night. But it really proves nothing. So what's the good of bothering?"

CHAPTER X.

OFF FOR A CRUISE

"GIRLS!" cried Joe suddenly bursting in on Pat and Melita the following afternoon, "Miss Strong says that we may have a real picnic to-day, and Nareo is to take us out in the whaler, where we like. We can stop out till sunset."

Pat and Melita clapped their hands with delight at this news.

"No need to clap your hands till you have heard the rest of it," said Joe. "Miss Strong also says that we must ask Edith Forster and her crowd if they would like to come along with us."

Pat groaned at this addition.

"Faith!" she exclaimed. "That's the powder in the jam! I don't call it a picnic to sit all day in a boat with 'Lady' Edith Forster putting on airs, and with Gladys Knox eyeing us as though we were a lot of savages. Besides, haven't they sent us all to Coventry?"

"That does not matter a bit!" replied Joe. "We've got to ask them to go with us. Those are Miss Strong's orders. I think she has noticed that there is not much love lost between us, and that they are putting the taboo on Melita. And she wants us to be friendly."

"That settles it," replied Pat, with a sigh of resignation. "I suppose I'd better go and ask Edith Forster to come with us—she and her lady friends."

Joe nodded glumly.

"We do not care to mix with nigger girls," sneered Edith Forster.

"I suppose you'd better!" she said.

Pat immediately made her way to the verandah of the schoolhouse, where Edith Forster and her friends were reclining in long wicker chairs, fanning themselves with fans of palm-leaf.

Their cheeks were hot, and they all looked rather sulky, for Miss Strong had just been giving them a gentle lecture on the right treatment of Melita.

And this had resulted in a slight passage of arms between Edith Forster and Miss Strong, for Edith had tried to make capital of the fact that Mademoiselle's dress had been destroyed on the preceding evening, and that all the evidence pointed to Melita having done the deed.

But Miss Strong had replied to this almost sternly, telling Edith that there was not enough evidence to hold Melita guilty, and that Mademoiselle had overlooked the matter, and, further, that it was her duty to judge in such matters and not Edith's.

And with this Miss Strong had left the girls heated and sulky.

"I didn't come to this school," announced Edith hotly, "to mix with a lot of horrid nigger girls, or with that awful set of girls who surround those niggers. I don't care what Miss Strong says. I am going to cut the lot! And as for Pat——"

Edith broke off short as a shadow fell on the verandah, and Pat stood before her.

"Did I hear someone talking lovingly av me?" asked Pat, smiling. "Good-morning, Edith! Th'top av the morning to you, Miss Parsons. I've come to ask you if ye will like to go wid us on a picnic in the whaler."

Edith stared coldly at Pat.

"No," she replied; "we are not coming on your picnic. We have made up our minds that we don't want to mix with you, or with——"

Pat shrugged her shoulders.

"Very well, Edith," she replied patiently. "I don't want to press you to join us if you think we are low company. I suppose, now," added

Pat, "ye'll be goin' for a nice, exclusive little picnic av your own, a select party, all chosen from the highest av society?"

"Never mind where we are going!" snapped Edith. "It is no concern of yours or of your very unpleasant native friends. We don't care what anyone says. We are not going to mix with girls who do mean and underhand things. I should not be surprised if you didn't know something about the spoiling of that dress last night!"

For a moment Pat's eyes gleamed at this insult.

She already knew who was the culprit, for the fingerprints marked in scarlet dye on the soap which Joe had taken from the washstand proved beyond doubt that they were the fingerprints of Edith herself.

But she smiled with imperturbable good-humour.

"Then I understand that we are not to have the pleasure of your company?" said Pat, with a slight drawl.

Edith's eyes glittered.

"You can understand that you are not going to have our company at this or any other time!" she snapped.

Pat nodded and turned on her heel.

It was with something like a sigh of relief that she found herself on the wide, white coral steps that led up to the great stone platform on which the school was built where Joe was waiting to hear the results of her embassy.

"It's all right, Joe, my dear!" said Pat. "I have offered the young ladies a trip in the whaler, and they have refused, so there is nothing more to be said, and there is Nareo waiting for us in his best clothes, with the lunch-baskets, and—goodness gracious!—who is the golliwog friend of his wrapped in a bathing-towel, with his head wreathed in flowers?"

"That's Timeo, or Timothy," said Joe. "He is the crew of the whaler. Mr. Pipes says that we are not to go out with only one hand on board and Timeo has been made the crew. He is an Arru islander, and he talks English."

Timeo was grinning as the girls descended the glaring white steps.

He was wrapped in a snow-white sheet, and had a wreath of ginger flowers twisted in his hair, which was dyed brick-red.

"Marnin', missus!" he said, at the sight of Joe.

"Boat him all ready!" announced Nareo, who was not quite so shy this morning.

Pat nodded.

A quarter of an hour later, Joe, with her party, were at the pier. They found the whaler waiting for them, simply spotless in its white-scrubbed wood and gleaming brass.

In the South Seas huge ropes of sweet-scented flowers are used in farewell greeting, hanging from the sides of the ship to the wharf, snapping suddenly when the steamer moves away.

Joe gave a sigh of relief as the whaler moved away from the crowded little wharf.

"We are going exploring along the shores!" she said. "And we'll have a picnic on the beach round the headland."

Joe, who was sweeping the shore with her glasses, gave an exclamation.

"There!" exclaimed Joe, in accents of scorn. "There go Edith Forster and the rest along the shore."

"Where?" asked Dumpling Davis.

"Walking along there amongst the palms," replied Joe. "They are off for a picnic on their own account to the Golden Valley."

And Edith Forster and her satellites, who were marching along in the shadow of the tall coco-palms, waved their handkerchiefs, and a derisive shout from them floated across the smooth lagoon as they watched the whaler cut through the waters.

They sailed past miles of green coco-groves and dazzling beaches of coral, which were cut up by the great headlands of lava-rock, and which jutted out in great scarps from the shoulders of the tree-crowned hills.

The day was intensely hot, and the lava headland round which the whaler was now drifting on the current of the lagoon seemed to reflect back the sun's rays with increased intensity.

"Goodness!" exclaimed Pat. "If we could only get somewhere where it was cool!"

Joe sighed as she fanned herself with a palm-leaf fan.

"Can't you take us somewhere where it is cool, Nareo?" she asked.

"Waitee, missy," said he. "In little bimeby we come to nice place—not 'ot."

Dumpling looked up at the towering cliffs which were beginning to enclose them, and down at the deep-green malachite water which lay hot and sticky in the sunshine.

"I call this place the gas-oven!" she puffed.

But a few minutes later the cliff seemed to open before them as they turned a narrow corner where there was only just room to use the oars, so narrow was the crevasse which split the cliffs.

Then they pulled the boat forward as the girls ducked their heads instinctively under the low, massive keystone of lava-rock, which seemed to descend almost on their heads.

A moment later and they felt a sudden and delightful coolness, for the boat had passed into a huge cave that was full of a soft, greenish light from its almost submerged entrance.

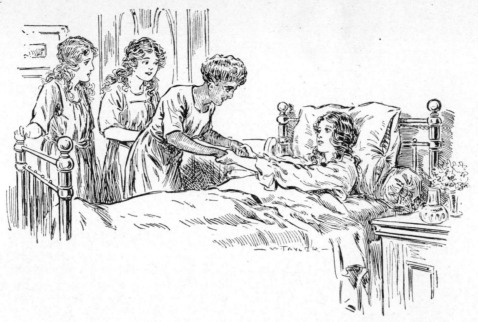

"I confess everything," whispered Edith. "I have been a wicked girl, Melita. Mademoiselle has forgiven me. Please! will you forgive me too?"

And in and out of the entrance of this cave flicked tiny sea-swallows, which filled the darkness overhead with their faint twitterings.

"Missy cool now?" asked Timeo, as he rowed the boat along through water that was as full of the strange blue light as that of the famous blue grotto at Capri.

"Oh, yes, Mr. Timeo!" sighed Dumpling, with relief. "This is lovely!"

They rowed the boat deeper into the cavern, and soon, round a bend of rock, they saw daylight again.

And the girls gave a cry of wonderment and admiration, for the whaler glided out of the cavern into the most wonderful and beautiful place they had ever seen.

It was a vast circle, or amphitheatre, sunk in the land behind the cliffs, and filled by a large pool of exquisite blue sea-water which flowed into it through the cavern.

But the cliffs which surrounded it were covered in trees and flowering creepers and ferns, and down from the top of the cliffs came falling three lovely waterfalls, which almost died away in a veil of spray, so high was their fall.

And in this beautiful hollow tall coco-palms, their fronds untowsled by the strong sea winds, from which they were sheltered, nodded over the turquoise pool, the edges of which were fringed with the whitest sand.

The girls at once called it Mermaid's Pool, and it was an ideal place for a picnic.

The whaler was rowed across the great pool, her keel grounding on sand that was of pink and white coral, and as fine as silk.

She was pulled up, and the girls landed spellbound and almost subdued by the exquisite beauty of this tropic fairyland.

"Oh!" sighed Dumpling. "I should like to live here always!"

"So would I," replied Pat, "if there was a draper's shop or two about, and you could go to the pictures once a week! And look at those glorious ferns and orchids!"

The two natives were not a bit impressed by the beauty of the scene.

They had set to work to make a fire, and Nareo was using the clear pool under the nearest waterfall to wash the birds'-nests to make clear soup.

They had seen so many beautiful scenes in their lives that they were scenery-proof.

The luncheon-basket was unpacked, and Nareo handed round glasses full of pink-tinted poi made from the bread-fruit.

The girls had lifted the crate of ginger-beer out of the boat, and had carried the ice-cream freezer up to the waterfall pool to keep it cool.

Now Joe requested ginger-beer.

"Nareo," she said, "will you open me a bottle of ginger-beer?"

"Yes, missy!" replied Nareo, with alacrity; and he took a bottle from the crate.

Nareo had never seen a bottle of ginger-beer before in his simple life, and he solemnly drew his knife and cut the strings that held the cork. Then, with his head bent over this mystery, he eased the cork, which flew out with a loud pop and hit him on the nose.

In a second Nareo had dropped the bottle, which, luckily, fell right side up, and was racing along the sands for dear life, followed closely by Timeo.

They ran a couple of hundred yards before they stopped, looking back timidly.

And, greatly to their wonderment, they saw Joe calmly pouring what was left of the ginger-beer out of this very explosive bottle.

"Don't take any notice of them, girls," said Pat. "They will come back. You would not think that grown men could be so silly, but you have to remember that they have come from the back islands. They believe spirits are everywhere."

"And yet they don't seem to think anything of fighting a shark in the water!" said Dumpling Davis.

"They are used to sharks," replied Pat. "They have been accustomed to sharks all their lives, but they are not accustomed to ginger-beer. Here they come. Don't laugh at them."

The two natives came back, looking rather shame-faced at having run so far for so small a matter.

"Look here, Nareo," said Joe firmly, "you and Timeo are so timid that you would run away from your shadows. We are not going to spoil our lovely picnic because you two are silly. Here is a big bun each for you, and if the spirits come and steal these, we will go. But I have never heard of an evil spirit stealing a bun."

The natives were reassured when they found that the spirits of the place did not snatch the buns from their hands, though their stubborn superstitions told them only that spirits did not fancy buns.

But well it was that Joe had refused to budge till the shadows were beginning to lengthen in the Mermaid's Pool, and the rising tide in the pool told them that if they wanted to get out through the cave they must go, or wait till the water had flowed and receded.

As it was, they had only just room enough to get out through the low arch of the cave, and they found that the tide had risen several feet since they had rowed in through the narrow cleft in the cliffs.

There was a fresh breeze blowing from the sea when they emerged once more into the lagoon.

The sails were hoisted, and away the whaler sailed for home, leaning gracefully under the press of her canvas and leaving a great track of white water behind her as she raced over the bounding waves.

It was a glorious sail along that beautiful coast.

The trade wind was blowing steadily, sending in great smoking blue billows that burst in clouds of white foam on the reef.

And at spots where the reef failed, the lagoon was quite rough, the whaler leaping over the long-backed blue seas which swept across the lagoon.

Timeo and Nareo were in the highest spirits, and Nareo was tootling away at a native tune on his beloved mouth-organ, when suddenly the plaintive music broke off short and he pointed excitedly seaward.

"What's up, Nareo?" asked Joe, who was sitting on the floor of the boat.

"Tide catchum missy along rocks," replied Nareo, pointing seaward through a mist of foam. "S'pose we no catchum missy quick, dey get drown."

Joe started up and gazed out to sea.

There, about a mile away, perched on a rugged island of rocks which projected from the sea by the reef, showed six figures that were waving wildly to them.

It was Edith Forster and her picnic party.

CHAPTER XI.

COALS OF FIRE

THERE were no signs of timidity now about Nareo and Timeo.

The business they were on was a dangerous one, for they had to sail the whaler through a labyrinth of reefs, over which the sea was now breaking in white sheets of foam.

To the girls it was a mystery how Edith and her followers had got where they were.

It was not till later on that they learned how they had been tempted out on that jagged mass of basaltic rocks more than a mile from the shore, when the low tide in the lagoon had left a causeway of rock exposed in dead calm water at low tide.

Over this they had passed, hunting for seaweeds and shells, and so absorbed had they been in their search and in the treasures they were finding, that not till too late did they discover that the tide had made and they were cut off from the shore by a mile of racing currents.

And the tide and the wind had come up together.

Now the girls were clinging to the pile of rocks, half-hidden by the sprays from the great rollers that were driving in from the sea, and bursting over the masses of water-worn basalt in great surges.

But Nareo and Timeo, for all their queer child-ishness and superstition, were superb boatmen, and though many a practised sailor would have held his breath to see them now, they betrayed not the slightest nervousness as they steered the racing whaler to the rescue of those six half-drowned figures on the submerging rocks.

They shaved death half a dozen times as the whaler beat out to the rock.

Then a chattering went on between them and Melita, who was crouching in the bow.

The whaler was drawing close under the lee of the rocks, where the girls were clinging now.

But Nareo dared not take her too close in the sea that was running.

Melita was overrunning a coil of rope, the bight of which she slipped over her shoulders.

Then, as the whaler came to a check, and Nareo dropped the anchor overside, Melita went overboard, swimming through the broken surf, taking the line to the rocks.

It was a dangerous swim with the undertow of that current.

But Melita bided her time, dodging and diving through the tumbling smoking seas, and at last crawled out safely, making the line fast to a pinnacle of basalt.

They saw her supporting Edith Forster, who was nearly paralysed with fear, and coaxing her into the water.

Then, holding to the line and supporting Edith, the brave, black princess brought her through the surf to the whaler.

The girls with eager hands dragged Edith into the boat.

Then back went Melita to bring Gladys Knox, who was in a state of collapse.

Six times was this dangerous passage between the tossing boat and the rocks made by Melita.

Then the line was cut and the sails were filled, and away went the whaler with her rescued passengers.

Nareo did not dare to attempt to run the passage of those dangerous reefs back to the lagoon again.

To tell the truth, he would not have run that passage a second time for all the tobacco in the world, which was his only standard of value and riches.

He sailed the whaler straight out to the open sea beyond the reef, and raced her over the great blue Pacific rollers, heading along outside the reef till at last he gained the entrance to the lagoon.

Edith Forster and her friends were utterly exhausted by the battering of the seas and the strain of their danger.

They lay in the bottom of the boat, white and fainting, notwithstanding the efforts of the girls to restore them, and when they reached the little coral pier they had to be carried up to the school, where they were at once placed in the hospital.

They were suffering from shock, and for two days no one but Mademoiselle and Miss Strong, who were nursing them, were allowed to see them.

But on the third day a message came to Joe and Pat and Melita that Edith Forster was asking for them.

They entered the hospital soft-footed, and there, propped up on her pillows, they found quite a new Edith Forster awaiting them.

Edith had been crying, and the tears were still wet on her cheeks, whilst Miss Strong leant over her, whispering comforting words.

She looked very frail and pallid, but at the sight of the three girls her eyes brightened, and two red spots of colour showed in her cheeks.

She held out her hands to the girls.

" I've confessed everything," she whispered. " I have been a wicked girl, Melita, and have wronged you. It was I who spoiled Mademoiselle's dress, but she has forgiven me; will you forgive, too? "

And Melita leaned over the bed and kissed her.

Her honest face had brightened as the shadow of suspicion passed away in good feeling and affection.

" Me forgive! " she said. " You get well plenty quick now, an' we come out and have some jolly times together—an' Gladdee Knox, too! "

And Miss Strong's face was radiant as she watched Joe and Pat stooping over the bed to exchange a kiss of peace with their old enemy, for she felt that a new and a better spirit had come amongst her girls, and that good days were in store for the Island School.

The End

127

OUT of DOORS with THE GUIDES

DISPATCH RUNNING

This is a great game for spring. It can be played by guides in towns as well as in the country.

The company play in this way. Their headquarters we'll call a besieged city. At a distance of three hundred yards the enemy take up their position. Then choose a girl adept at disguising herself at short notice, in dodging and hiding tricks, and who is a good runner, and pin a ribbon streamer to her shoulder.

She is sent off to a starting-place about a mile or so away. At a given time the dispatch-bearer, as we call her, is supposed to start and make her way through the enemy lines until she reaches the besieged city.

When she gets within three hundred yards of headquarters, a boundary fixed beforehand, it can be considered that she has crossed the lines and is with the defenders, and has succeeded in her task.

The enemy's object, of course, is to seize her and secure a victory by depriving her of her ribbon streamer.

The enemy may take any steps they think of to secure her capture. The dispatch-bearer, similarly, can exercise her wits and adopt any ruse that occurs to her to slip through the enemy's country.

TRAIL SIGNS FOR TRACKING GAMES

During the Spring months tracking games are in full swing.

In playing a tracking game it should be understood at the beginning what objects are going to be used for making the signs. Some companies use twigs, stones, grass, scraps of paper, as well as figures outlined on the ground with sticks, but it makes a game rather difficult for the average guide if she has to look out for signs of a miscellaneous nature like this.

If it is decided on before hand there can be no confusion, for trackers know exactly what to look for.

HOW TO SWIM

Every guide should be able to swim, and there are three reasons why.

Swimming is a pleasant pastime. It is an exercise which develops the body symmetrically and proportionately from head to foot. It is often the means of protecting and saving life.

The breast-stroke should be thoroughly mastered, as it is the foundation of all other strokes. It is quite easy if the move-ments are first practised on land. And when you start in the water keep to the shallows.

Do not be afraid to strike out in the water. You will never be a swimmer if you keep one foot touching the bottom for fear of leaving terra firma. You will be more likely to go under and get a nasty ducking and swallow a lot of water by doing this than by striking out and keeping calm.

So many girls in learning to swim splash about, but really do few movements in the water.

It is a good plan to practise swimming movements on land until you are thoroughly acquainted with the strokes, and when taking to the water it is well to have somebody with you to hold up your chin until you get your balance.

PRACTICE AT HOME

The following movements should be practised on a bench or stool, or, as I first learnt, on the lawn, in the garden, in a lying position, face downwards.

Start with the hands together, arms straight out in front. Keep the legs straight and close together, the feet touching, with toes stretched backwards.

On "One," sweep the arms round in a quarter of a circle, until they are in a line with the shoulders, the back of the hands facing the front. At the same time, open the knees out sideways, and keep the heels together until the soles of the feet touch.

On "Two," bring the elbows to the sides of the body, hands to the chest, fingers pointing to the front, and palms downwards, thumbs six inches apart, and at the same instant, by a backward and rounded flick, fling the legs wide apart.

On "Three," shoot the hands forward, and keep them together. At the same time blow, as if blowing your hands away from you.

GENERAL HINTS

Breathing is of the utmost importance in swimming, and must be done at the correct time. Inhale while the arms are sweeping backwards, and exhale when you are shooting them forward. A good plan is to blow as your hands shoot forward, as I have already told you. You are then bound to breathe in at the correct time.

Never attempt to swim after a heavy meal. Allow two hours to elapse before you enter the water after any sort of meal. On the slightest feeling of cold, or if you begin to shiver, come straight out of the water, have a brisk rub down, and drink a glass of hot milk if procurable. If not, go for a quick walk to restore the circulation.

THE ATHLETE'S BADGE

Every healthy guide should try for the athlete's badge. Its possession is proof that she is sound and healthy in wind and limb. Nor is it particularly hard to obtain.

A girl must be able to jump 2 ft. 6 in., or 3 ft. high, according to her age and her build, and also do the jump in good style, landing easily and gracefully.

She must show the examiner that she has a natural, upright carriage, and be able to walk and run well.

In three different sports she must show proficiency. She has her choice amongst relay racing, ice or roller skating, ball throwing, jumping the bar, ring catching, and balancing on a rail or plank.

She must also have performed breathing exercises daily for the past two months.

A guide must aim at attaining the standard measurements for a girl of her age.

ATHLETIC TIPS

In the high jump there are two things to be considered. A girl must jump high—that is, lift her head as high as she possibly can in clearing the bar.

When she alights she must bend the knees, thus reducing the jar and enabling her quickly to retain her balance.

When walking, press your shoulders back and your chest out. Try to make yourself as tall as possible without going up on your toes, and look straight in front of you.

In running, move from your hips, keep your head up, and your mouth shut. The last is necessary, unless you want to catch flies.

In the games don't be nervous. Do your best. You can't do more.

As regards standard measurements, a girl of ten should be 4 ft. 3 in. in height, and weigh 4 st 6 lb. A girl of fourteen should be 4 ft. $11\frac{5}{8}$ in., and 6 st. $12\frac{3}{4}$ lb. in weight A girl of eighteen's height should be 5 ft. $2\frac{1}{2}$ in., and her weight 8 st. 9 lb.

THE PIONEER'S BADGE

So many girls have been in camp, and have returned full of all the joys — and the pure air — of seaside and country camp life, that it is not surprising that many are interested about the pioneer's badge.

For, you see, one of the essentials to winning this badge is that a guide should have spent at least one week under canvas, or in a barn, or other entirely unfurnished building. If under canvas, a girl must know how to pitch, trench, air, and strike a tent. If she has camped in a barn or suchlike place, she must have passed the domestic service badge test.

In addition, the would-be winner of the pioneer's badge must possess the cook's badge, and have passed the test on a camp-kitchen and know how to collect, chop, and stack suitable firing.

That is not all. The guide must know how to construct a model of a single lockbridge and improvise some useful camp article, such as a candlestick and so forth. Of the following ten articles, she must be able to make three of them, namely : Camp mattress, washing cubicle, airing screen, refuse pit, haybox, camp larder, flagstaff, palliasse cover, and a shelter.

Finally, she must be able to tell the examiner how she would organise three scouting games.

THINGS NOT TO DO WHEN TAKING A PHOTOGRAPH

Most guides who have taken photographs at some time or the other have more often than not been disappointed with the results of their efforts.

If you remember the following hints, perhaps your photos will turn out better next time.

Never point your camera at any object or building if you cannot see it all in the finder when holding the instrument level. You must go farther away, for the picture will appear falling backwards if taken with the camera tilted up.

Never stand facing the sun with your camera. Always take a photograph with the sun over your shoulder.

Never hold your camera against your body when you are taking a photograph, for your breathing will move it and will render the picture blurred.

Never take a time-exposure with your camera in your hands. Always rest the instrument on a table, fence, or tripod.

WHY WE MUST TAKE OUTDOOR EXERCISE

Exercise in the fresh air assists all the functions upon which life depends. It quickens the circulation of the blood, and thereby nourishes every part of the body, causing the bones to become firm, and the muscles to become full and healthy.

It promotes breathing, by which oxygen is taken into the system and the carbonic gas is thrown off from the lungs. In this way it promotes a higher degree of organic life and strength that would not otherwise exist.

It promotes perspiration, by which, through the millions of pores of the skin much of the fluid of the body is changed and purified.

And, moreover, it induces that genial and diffused warmth which is one of the chief conditions of a high degree of vitality.

Finally, outdoor exercise keeps you well and makes you happy, and happiness is the most wonderful thing in the world.

POULTRY KEEPING FOR GIRLS

A FEW USEFUL WRINKLES FOR THE OUT-DOOR GIRL

The Poultry House

I HAVE heard some people say that they cannot find room in their gardens for fowls. That is only an excuse. You can buy poultry-houses at the big stores which you can hang against a wall like a birdcage. I have even been told of a man who kept fowls indoors, in an alcove on his staircase.

It would take up too much space to tell you how to build a small poultry house and run that could be put into a small garden.

The house must depend, of course, on the number of fowls you intend to keep. It is not advisable to begin with more than six hens. For these a house about five feet long, by three or four feet wide, with a sloping roof, will be ample. This will combine sleeping house and run. The perches should be placed at the back with trays under them to catch the droppings.

The house should be raised from the ground by bricks, as wet feet for fowls are as bad for them as they are for us. If possible, too, the house should face the south. Then it will miss bad weather and get the maximum sunshine.

Cleanliness is absolutely necessary to keep your fowls healthy and to make them pay. Their house should be whitewashed every six months. Scrape the perches every week and the floor of the house every day.

Feeding Your Fowls

ALWAYS see that your fowls have plenty of clean water. A jam-jar, stood away from the hens' scratching place, makes a good drinking vessel, for it does not become muddy like water in a dish.

The first meal should be a feed of corn, a small handful to each hen. Make them work to get it by burying it amongst their litter. At about one o'clock give them some green food, and a wet mash at about half an hour before they go to roost.

Fowls thrive, like we do, by having regular meals and a mixed diet. Don't give them scraps at any old time. In the spring and summer oats and wheat can be given alternately with the corn. In cold and wet weather maize, buckwheat, and barley are advisable.

To make a wet mash you boil household scraps till soft. Cut the mixture up small and mix with bran and barley meal in equal parts till like crumbs. During severe weather add a handful of green bone-meal, and occasionally add a teaspoonful of poultry mustard for each six or eight hens.

In addition, you want two boxes nailed to the wall of the house so that the hens can just reach them. In one keep a good supply of crushed oyster shells and flint grit. In the other, a more shallow box, put a quantity of dry wood ash. It does the hens good if they eat it, but it also serves as a dust bath for them and destroys any insects that infest their bodies.

Best Breeds for Beginners

THE best and most expensive breeds, though not always the best layers, are usually the most difficult to rear.

Strong, healthy birds can be found amongst the cross-breed class. Of these, Leghorn-Buff Orpingtons, Leghorn-Wyandotte, and Sussex-Faveroll can all be recommended. Other birds suitable for small gardens are White and Black Leghorns, White Wyandottes, and Rhode Island Reds.

A Land-worker's Kit

IT might not be out of place to mention here the sort of garments that are best suited for the out door girl.

A landworker's kit should be workmanlike, simple in cut, loose-fitting, fairly short, and quiet in colour. An old Guide tunic, with dark breeches or knickerbockers, and warm clothes underneath, is admirable for the purpose.

Wear woolly garments next the skin. It is often cold on a farm in the early morning, and woolly things will keep you warm. At midday you may be hot, but the wool will absorb the perspiration.

Whatever the material, it must be strong and not rub or tear. I recommend corduroy ; it does not show the mud or dust, which is easily brushed off when dry. Whipcord, jean, and good serge will also serve. Strong stockings, and stout water-tight boots are even more important.

INCOMPREHENSIBLE

By HILDA RICHARDS

A Farcical Playlet in One Act and Two Scenes, introducing the Girls of Cliff House School.

DRAMATIS PERSONÆ.

BARBARA REDFERN. Fourth Form girl, with long, wavy hair.
MABEL LYNN. Her chum. Bobbed hair.
BESSIE BUNTER. Fat, with a thick, cable-like plait, and round spectacles. Talks readily and complainingly, and proves to be a general "duffer."
(Study-mates in No. 4 Study. Aged about 14 years.)
CONNIE JACKSON. A spiteful monitress, aged 17.
MISS BULLIVANT. A prim, spectacled mistress.
BUNNY (Beatrice Barlow).
PIP (Priscilla Pacey).
TEDDY BEAR (Thelma D. Beare).
(Three Second Form girls, full of fun and excitement. Aged about 10 years.)

NOTE.—The Second Form girls can be reduced to two, if required, the additional lines being shared equally.

More Fourth Form girls can be introduced by making the Study the Fourth Form common-room, and sharing the parts of Barbara and Mabel amongst the additional players.

SCENE I.

(The scene shows No. 4 study at Cliff House School. It is a simply furnished room, the essential furniture being a table—with drawers—an easy chair, and three ordinary Windsor chairs. There is a fireplace at one side, with an electric lamp wrapped in red paper and embedded in coal to represent a fire. If this cannot be arranged, the fire may be assumed to be out of sight of the audience, a suitable curtain being in the way. There must be a door, or a curtain as substitute, used for all entrances and exits.

Properties required for the first scene are :—A frying-pan containing a yellow cardboard disc to represent a pancake, a fountain-pen, an empty ink bottle, an outline drawing with a black patch of ink in the middle, and the necessary impositions.

For the second scene : A jumper, a cushion, a flatiron, and a large, old book.

When the curtain rises, BARBARA REDFERN and MABEL LYNN are seen seated at the table writing, and BESSIE BUNTER is crouching over the fire with the frying-pan.)

BARBARA : Bessie, are you coming to get on with your lines ?

BESSIE (*over her shoulder*) : In a minute, Babs. Plenty of time. I'm just cooking a pancake. A girl must keep up her strength, you know !

MABEL : Gracious ! Cooking again ! Why, you ate a tremendous tea !

BESSIE (*peevishly*) : I wish you wouldn't keep harping on about that tea. That's half an hour ago. How can a girl write a hundred lines for Miss Bullivant when she's got such a dreadful sinking feeling ?

(BARBARA *throws down her pen and turns round in her chair.*)

BARBARA : Now look here, Bessie ! You really must come and get on. We three have got special permission to go to a concert with Miss Steel this evening, and you want to come, don't you ?

BESSIE (*eagerly*) : Of course I do !

BARBARA : Well, Miss Bullivant won't let you go unless her lines are finished.

BESSIE : They'll be finished. I'll dash them off in no time when I feel fit for it ! Besides, she's sure to forget.

BARBARA (*a trifle annoyed*) : It isn't good enough. Really, Bessie, I can't understand why you must start cooking like this. You know you want to go out, and we want you to go with us, and yet you're fooling about in this way. I can't understand it. It's incomprehensible !

BESSIE (*startled*) : Eh ?

BARBARA : I said that it was incomprehensible.

BESSIE : You're making that up !

BARBARA : Making what up ?

BESSIE : That word. There's no such word as in—incromdependible.

(BARBARA *and* MABEL *laugh.*)

BESSIE (*waving frying-pan indignantly*) : I'm blessed if I can see anything to laugh about. You're trying to show off. I call it jolly bad form to try and show off by using words that you've made up yourself.

MABEL : Don't be silly, Bessie. There is such a word. Everyone uses it at times.

BESSIE : I don't believe it. It isn't a word at all. No one ever says a silly word like that.

BARBARA : They do.

BESSIE (shouting) : They don't !

BARBARA : But I can prove to you——

BESSIE : Look here, Babs, I'll take you at your word ! Here's an offer for you. You say a lot of people use it. We'll listen all this evening, and if no one says it you'll stand me a good feed. Is that a bargain ?

MABEL : But what happens if someone does use it ? Will you stand us a feed ?

BESSIE (confidently) : No one's ever going to use it. Still, I'll tell you what I'd do if they did. I'd go just like this to them !

(BESSIE goes through facetious actions —suggest raising her hands to her forehead and then wave her arms three times. Giggles delightedly while she is doing it.)

MABEL : You'd never do that !

BESSIE (indignantly) : Of course I would ! Just to show anyone what I thought of them for using such a word. Look here, make it a bargain about that feed, you two, and if anyone does use such a silly word I'll either do that or—or stand you two a feed instead.

(BARBARA and MABEL exchange looks and nod resignedly.)

BARBARA : All right, Bessie, if it satisfies you. And now, will you leave that pancake alone and come and start writing your lines ?

BESSIE : But it's nearly done now. In another minute——

(A voice is heard off stage.)

VOICE : Is Bessie Bunter in there ?

BARBARA, MABEL, and BESSIE (together) : Miss Bullivant.

(BESSIE whirls round, seeking for somewhere to put the frying-pan. Tries to put it in a table drawer, but is stopped. Endeavours to put it behind a picture but cannot. Goes through various other actions and finally places it in easy chair, with an antimacassar over it. Just drops into a chair as MISS BULLIVANT enters the room.)

MISS BULLIVANT : Have you finished that imposition, Bessie ?

BESSIE : N-n-not quite !

MISS BULLIVANT : How much have you done ?

BESSIE : Well, the—the fact is I—I didn't think the colour of the ink was n-n-nice enough.

MISS BULLIVANT : You mean that you haven't started ?

BESSIE : Only the—the actual writing, Miss Bullivant. I—I've thought it all out—just what

I'm going to write. I—I'll dash them off in no time—that is, I'm going to start now.

(MISS BULLIVANT walks across room, turns, and seats herself in the easy chair. Gasps of horror from the girls. BESSIE looks painfully guilty.)

MISS BULLIVANT : I am very surprised.

BESSIE : I—I didn't mean it. I—I didn't think you'd sit there, Miss Bullivant.

MISS BULLIVANT : Whatever do you mean ? I am talking about your slackness.

BESSIE (relieved) : Oh, yes. Quite so. It—it's a rather nice chair that, isn't it ?

MISS BULLIVANT (sharply) : Bessie, at times you seem positively too lazy for words. I cannot make you out at all. You are incomprehensible !

(BESSIE gasps. BARBARA and MABEL nudge each other and chuckle. BESSIE hesitates and looks very uneasy, and finally commences to go through actions.)

MISS BULLIVANT (jumping up) : Goodness gracious ! Have you lost your reason, girl ?

BESSIE : No. Oh, dear, no ! I—I——

MISS BULLIVANT : Then, what is the meaning of those absurd antics ?

BESSIE (muddled) : I—I didn't want to stand them a feed.

MISS BULLIVANT : Goodness gracious ! Explain yourself !

BESSIE : I—I mean, it's nothing, Miss Bullivant, really. It's—it's just my high-spirited way —my little p-p-piece of girlish fun.

MISS BULLIVANT : Bessie, those lines are to be written immediately. You are a most foolish and disobedient girl. I sometimes feel that I shall never understand you. At times I feel that you are, as I said before, utterly in——

BESSIE : D-d-don't say it again !

MISS BULLIVANT : Girl !

BESSIE : I—I—I don't like that word. It—it makes me feel dreadful. Really it does, Miss Bullivant. S-s-say anything else you like.

(MISS BULLIVANT stares at the quaking BESSIE BUNTER and moves towards the door.)

MISS BULLIVANT : Those lines are to be written before you go out this evening. If they are not done I shall see that you remain in the school. Understand that ! (Exit.)

BARBARA AND MABEL : You duffer !

BESSIE : Oh, really ! I don't owe you a feed anyway. And I'm not going to count that one— she's always using words that no one else has ever heard of. 'Tisn't fair to count Miss Bullivant. (Goes across to chair and removes antimacassar.) Oh, I say ! Look at my pancake ! She's spoilt it !

MABEL : Are you going to get on with your lines, Bessie ?

(BESSIE lifts the " pancake " from the pan, and examines it critically)

132

BESSIE : I can't eat it now. It's absolutely spoilt. If you'd only let me put it in the drawer, as I wanted to——

(BARBARA *and* MABEL *rush forward and replace pancake in frying-pan. Pan is placed in hearth and* BESSIE *forcibly led back to her seat.*)

BARBARA (*angrily*) : Now, Bessie, if you won't get on with writing those lines we'll go out without you. Miss Bullivant's quite right. You *are* incomprehensible !

BESSIE : That's cheating !

BARBARA : What is ?

BESSIE : Saying that word ! But I sha'n't do it to *you*, so there ! I don't believe it's a real word now.

MABEL : But your impot—that's what we're worrying about ! You haven't even started, and you know what the Bull said.

BESSIE : I'll do it now—I will, really ! (*The door opens silently, and* CONNIE JACKSON *appears, but is not seen by the three girls. She stands still, listening.*) I say, jolly lucky I bluffed the Bull like I did, wasn't it ! You know, I've always got a way of getting over things. It isn't every girl who could carry it off, when she'd promised to wave her arms about whenever anyone said a stupid word like incom—inconde-prensible, is it ?

BARBARA : You were very lucky, dear. But do get on with your work now.

(CONNIE JACKSON *smiles to herself, and disappears again without having been observed.*)

BESSIE : Rather ! I'm going to ! Now you'll see how I write lines. (*Picks up fountain pen.*) Oh, bother ! There's no ink in this thing.

BARBARA AND MABEL (*anxiously*) : Let me fill it.

BESSIE : Pooh ! Think I can't fill a fountain pen, now ? Just you watch ! You take this little thing, and you just give it a push like this, and then—oh !

(BARBARA *and* MABEL *shriek, Mabel picks up the paper on which she had been drawing with a huge splodge of ink in the middle of it.*)

MABEL : Bessie, just look what you've done !

BESSIE : It—it went off wrong. The ink squirted out.

MABEL : Yes ; and now you've ruined my drawing. How can I show this to Miss Primrose ?

BESSIE : Well, it was an accident. I'm sorry.

I can't say more than that. And I really think you needn't make such a fuss when the stupid pen——

(*Enter* CONNIE JACKSON.)

CONNIE (*harshly*) : What is the meaning of all the noise in this study ?

BARBARA (*blandly*) : It's quite all right, Connie. It's all over now.

CONNIE (*aside*) : Is it, though ? I always suspect cheek in this study. I think this is my chance now to teach them something else. (*To others*) : What are you doing with that pen, Bessie ? What is the meaning of all this ink about the table ? Have you done it ?

BESSIE : Quite an accident, Connie.

CONNIE : Accident, indeed ! Bessie, you are a preposterous girl. (*With emphasis.*) I consider that you are quite incomprehensible.

(BESSIE *looks dismayed.* BARBARA *and* MABEL *exchange glances.*)

BARBARA (*aside*) : She'll never be so silly !

CONNIE : I said, Bessie, that you are utterly incomprehensible !

BESSIE (*in a nervous aside*) : I've got to stand them a feed if I don't !

(BESSIE *commences to go through her " actions " in a very half-hearted manner.*)

CONNIE : Girl, how dare you ! What are you doing ? What is the meaning of this impertinence ? Are you attempting to defy me ?

BESSIE : I—I—I——

CONNIE : How dare you ! Barbara ! Mabel ! Have you been urging this girl to do this sort of thing to a monitress ?

BARBARA : It's only a joke, Connie.

CONNIE : Joke, indeed ? Then I will teach you a better one. Bessie, you will write one hundred lines immediately ! Do you understand ? You will write them at once !

BESSIE (*anxiously*) : But I'm going to a concert with Miss Steel.

CONNIE : Not until you've finished those lines for me.

BARBARA (*hotly*) : Connie, you can't do it ! It's not fair ! We won't stand it !

CONNIE (*retreating to the door*) : That remains to be seen. Those lines are to be written at once.

There is plenty of time before any girls have permission to leave the school. I shall watch and see that you do not go out until they are finished. (*Exit.*)

BESSIE (*tearfully*): Another hundred lines! Two hundred to be written before I go out!

BARBARA (*angrily*): She must have known! It's Connie's spitefulness! I'm sure she knew all the time, and she's just made it an excuse to have her revenge on us!

MABEL: All our fault for ever letting Bessie be so silly!

BESSIE: Oh, really! I jolly well defied her, anyway!

BARBARA: But how can you possibly do two hundred lines now?

BESSIE: I'll try! I won't be beaten! I've got a spiffing idea! Just you listen! When you see it, you'll say that it's—it's—incomomprehendible!

(CURTAIN.)

TABLEAU. Curtain raised to show BESSIE *seated at table, with* BARBARA *and* MABEL *bending over watching her.* BESSIE *has four pens tied together, and is endeavouring to write with them all at once.*

The attempt fails, and she flings them to the ground in disgust.

(CURTAIN.)

SCENE 2.

(*Scene*) *same as Scene* 1. *Time, half an hour later.* BESSIE BUNTER *is alone in study, writing her hardest, and pausing constantly to hold her wrist, as though cramped. Great noise made by pen, which may, in reality, be scraping upon a piece of sandpaper.*)

BESSIE (*pausing in her work*): Ninety-five. Oh, dear, and I've got two hundred to do. Ninety-five from two hundred leaves a hundred and fifteen. It can't be done!

(*Starts work again, laboriously counting the lines aloud. Has just finished the hundredth, when the door opens. Enter* BUNNY, PIP, *and* TEDDY BEAR *looking ready for any mischief.*)

BUNNY: Hallo, Bessie. Busy?

BESSIE (*despairingly*): Yes, I'm writing lines for horrid old Connie Jackson, and the Bull as well.

PIP (*winking*): Writing lines, eh? I'll tell you a better way to do them, Bessie.

BESSIE (*eagerly*): What is it?

PIP: Why, do them with a ruler! (BUNNY, PIP, *and* TEDDY BEAR *shake with mirth.*)

BESSIE (*indignantly*): I'm blessed if I can see anything to laugh at in that. That's the worst of you Second Form kids. You're so ignorant. You don't understand how serious it is to be in the Fourth Form. (PIP *creeps behind* BESSIE, *and commences to tickle her.*) Oooh! Ow! He, he, he! Leave me alone! He, he, he! Oh, stoppit! He, he, he!

(*Bessie jumps up from chair and faces youngsters*).

TEDDY BEAR: We wondered if you'd like to play Red Indians with us this evening, Bessie.

BESSIE: I can't, Teddy Bear. I want to go to the concert. Besides, it's no good playing Indians with you—you always want to jolly well scalp me!

BUNNY: But you've got such a lovely plait!

BESSIE: Of course I have. But if you'd had your way you'd have jolly well chopped it off before now for a scalp. I say, do go away. I want to be busy. I've got a lot of lines to write.

PIP: Nonsense!

BESSIE (*severely*): You ought to know that it's very bad manners to talk like that to me. I don't know what they teach you kids in the Second Form. Really, I don't know what things are coming to at all. It's—it's—incom-com-prehendible!"

THE THREE: Ooooh!

What ever's that?

BESSIE (*triumphantly*): There you are! That shows how jolly ignorant you are! You don't know the meaning of a simple little word that—that everyone jolly well uses.

THE THREE: They don't!

BESSIE: Everyone *I've* met uses it.

BUNNY: What does it mean?

TEDDY BEAR: Spell it!

BESSIE: I-n-k-e-r-m-m——— No, I'm bothered if I will!

THE THREE: You can't!

BESSIE (*indignantly*): Who can't? Why, I knew how to spell that word when I was only half your age!

BUNNY: I don't believe it!

BESSIE: Why not?

BUNNY: It's incomprehensible!

BESSIE: I'll put you out of the study now!

(*Tussle follows in which* BESSIE *gets considerably the worst. Door opens abruptly. Enter* CONNIE JACKSON, *smiling triumphantly.*)

CONNIE: What is the meaning of this? Bessie! Answer me instantly! Have you written that imposition? Why are you playing about and bullying these youngsters?

BUNNY: She's not bullying us!

CONNIE: Silence! Where are those lines, Bessie? I want them at once!

(BESSIE *makes a clumsy attempt to hide the imposition she has been writing.*)

BESSIE: I haven't d-d-done them yet.

CONNIE: What is that under your hand?

BESSIE: Th-th-that's n n-nothing. Just a f-f-few——

CONNIE: It is an imposition!

BESSIE: Oh, dear! It's for Miss Bullivant, Connie. She—she won't let me go to the concert unless I give it to her first.

CONNIE: I have come for my own imposition.

(BESSIE *looks very uneasy, then opens one of the drawers and produces fresh papers which she hands to* CONNIE.)

CONNIE: You did not write these!

BESSIE: I've borrowed them. I—I mean I write better at some times than others—just like Babs, in fact.

CONNIE: These lines, written by some other girl will not do. (*Starts to tear them across.*)

BESSIE (*clutching her arm*): Stop! Don't tear them, Connie! Oh, don't do it! They're not m-m-mine at all. They're Babs' lines for Miss Steel.

(CONNIE *deliberately tears up the papers and strews them on the table.*)

CONNIE: You should have explained that before and not given me another girl's imposition. (*Laughs.*) You're so clever at explaining things that you'll be able to make it all right with your friend. Hallo, what is this? Why, you've written a hundred lines here!

BESSIE (*desperately*): They're for Miss Bullivant.

CONNIE: I shall take them.

BESSIE: But I can't go to the concert if you do. I was going to dodge you and do yours to-morrow—I mean, do them next!

(CONNIE *laughs again and crosses to the door.*)

CONNIE: You'd better hurry up and do your lines for Miss Bullivant. You'll have to be quick. The concert party's nearly ready to start. (*Exit, laughing afresh.*)

(BESSIE *sinks into a chair and starts to weep. The Three Second Form girls gather round her.*)

BUNNY: Bessie, I say, I *am* sorry!

PIP and TEDDY BEAR: So am I, honestly. We're both sorry.

BESSIE (*dismally*): I shan't be able to go to the concert now.

BUNNY (*dramatically*): It's all Connie's fault. We didn't understand that Bessie was in such a hurry. But if we hadn't fooled about Bessie might have got the lines done. Come on, we'll go and see Connie!

PIP: Oh, rather! We'll give her such a time of it!

TEDDY BEAR: We'll go up and tell her what we think of her!

BUNNY: Cheer up, Bessie. We're awfully sorry it's happened, and we'll make old Connie sorry for being so horrid! (*Exeunt Three.*)

(BESSIE *rises and examines the pancake critically, as though wondering if it is still possible to eat it. Returns it to the frying-pan in disgust. Enter* BARBARA *and* MABEL, *in hats and coats.*)

BARBARA (*cheerily*): Buck up, Bessie, it's all right after all. We've seen Stella Stone and she says Connie has no right to insist on her lines before you go out. So if you've done Miss Bullivant's hundred we can get off at once!

BESSIE (*dejectedly*): Connie's got them already.

BARBARA (*horrified*): Never!

(MABEL *steps to table and looks at scattered papers.*)

MABEL: Good gracious! What's all this litter?

BARBARA: My lines I wrote for Miss Steel!

(BESSIE *looks very nervous and worried.*)

BESSIE: Connie did that, Babs. I—I was just going to borrow them, you know. She—guessed that I hadn't written them, and jolly well tore them up.

BARBARA: Bessie!

BESSIE: I—I'm awfully sorry, Babs. I—I'll write you some more—better writing than yours, too. I—I'll do them in red ink as well.

BARBARA: I wasn't thinking of that. Connie's got your lines and you've nothing to show to Miss Bullivant. She won't let you go out now. I say, I am sorry!

BESSIE (*hopefully*): I say, suppose I defy the Bull?

MABEL: Don't be silly!

BESSIE: Oh, really! I could, easily. You know the way I can look at people when I'm angry. (*Strikes attitude.*) I'd say something like this to her : " Madam, I have stood all I kee-an ! You have dee-riven me to desperation. I have not done your lines, and for you to expect that I should is—is—is incom-om-prendible !

BARBARA (sighing) : It's no good. Connie's been too quick for us. She must have known that we had spoken to Stella, and she came down first.

(Bang at the door. Enter BUNNY, PIP, and TEDDY BEAR excitedly.)

THE THREE (shrieking) : We've got your lines back.

(BUNNY waves bundle of very crumpled papers.)

BESSIE : My lines.

PIP : Yes, we followed old Connie upstairs. She didn't tear them at all. She simply screwed them up and threw them in the paper basket. Here they are !

(BUNNY hands BESSIE the crumpled papers.)

BARBARA (doubtfully) : You can't give them to Miss Bullivant like that !

BESSIE (excitedly) : I don't care. I've got an idea. I'll make them all right again. I'll iron them !

BARBARA and MABEL : You'll what ?

(BESSIE darts to fireplace and gives a shriek.)

BESSIE : The iron's hot ! It jolly well burnt me ! (Grabs at jumper lying on chair.) This will do it. (Picks up iron.)

MABEL : My jumper ! Bessie, you silly noodle——

BESSIE : I say, don't be quarrelsome, Mabs. This is jolly important, you know. I'll iron these lines out in no time. (Dabs flat-iron on papers on table.)

BARBARA : You duffer ! They're scorching ! Take it off !

BESSIE (removing iron) : Oh, dear ! I—I think it must have been too hot. That top page looks rather brown, doesn't it. I—I'll have to put that one underneath. (Returns iron to fender and exhibits paper previously scorched with hot iron.)

BARBARA : It's impossible to do anything now !

BESSIE : Not at all. I'll get them smoothed out some way. The Bull never looks at lines, you know. I know what I'll do. I'll press them in this book !

(Puts papers into book and starts to squeeze it very hard and with a great amount of deep breathing. BUNNY, PIP, and TEDDY BEAR rush to help, and generally get in the way.)

BESSIE : Can't you leave a girl alone ? You'll jolly well tear the book if you're not careful ! A lot of consideration you've got for poor old Babs' atlas, I must say. I know what I'll do ! I'll jump on it !

BARBARA (feebly) : But my atlas——

(BESSIE places heavy book on floor and commences to jump excitedly on it.)

BESSIE : This'll make 'em flat in no time !

(Door opens quietly. Enter MISS BULLIVANT. All girls see her with the exception of BESSIE, whose back is towards the door.)

BESSIE (excitedly) : Jolly fine idea, this ! It'll take her in completely. She'll never guess anything now. My word, I would give her a look, too, if she asked any questions.

(Girls try frantically to warn BESSIE of MISS BULLIVANT's presence.)

BESSIE : I think it's mean of you to pull faces like that just because it happens to be your atlas, Babs ! Anyway, I'm not the sort of girl to be afraid of a mistress, just because she happens to be jolly suspicious. I shall simply smile at her and say——

MISS BULLIVANT : Bessie Bunter !

(BESSIE gives a cry of alarm and jumps off the atlas. She stands quaking.)

MISS BULLIVANT : I have come for that imposition, Bessie. Where is it ? The other girls are ready to start. Have you finished it ? What is the meaning of these extraordinary antics ?

BESSIE : I—I—I——

MISS BULLIVANT : Have you written it ?

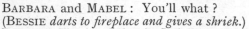

BESSIE : Oh, rather. I—I've done it beautifully.

MISS BULLIVANT : Then please give it to me at once.

BESSIE : Oh, dear ! I—I—I say ! Look at that picture over there, Miss Bullivant.

(Mistress does so. BESSIE snatches at the atlas, just as mistress turns again. BESSIE jumps to her feet and tries to look very unconcerned.)

MISS BULLIVANT (angrily) : What is the matter with you, you stupid girl ? Where is that imposition ?

BESSIE : I—I can't get it for the m-m-moment. I say, Miss Bullivant, if you—you'd j-j-just mind going out into the passage for a minute I'll tell you when you can come in again——

MISS BULLIVANT (breaking in) : I have stood as much of this nonsense as I can ! Where are those lines? Give them to me immediately. Are they in that atlas?

(BESSIE *looks thunderstruck.*)

BESSIE: Oh, dear! They—they might be in it. I—I can't understand how you guessed it. I—I'll just look and see if they are.

(*Examines atlas, and gives a very forced exclamation of surprise as she produces lines.*)

MISS BULLIVANT: These are very crumpled and soiled, Bessie!

BESSIE: They shouldn't be! I jumped hard enough.

MISS BULLIVANT: What?

BESSIE: I—I mean, it's the cheap paper. It's fearfully cheap paper. It—it gets a bit crumpled when you're writing quickly.

MISS BULLIVANT: And this bottom sheet—it looks as though it had been scorched.

BESSIE (*guiltily*): Oh, dear! So it does. I—I say, Miss Bullivant, that's funny, isn't it? He, he, he!

MISS BULLIVANT: I see nothing to laugh at!

BESSIE: Oh, no! Quite so. Barbara, what are you laughing about? I'm surprised at you! Miss Bullivant doesn't like you to laugh!

MISS BULLIVANT: You have not yet explained why these papers were in that atlas, Bessie!

BESSIE: H-h-haven't I? I—I put them in there to—to keep them clean, Miss Bullivant. That's—that's me all over. I—I didn't want them to lie on the table and get all dusty——

MISS BULLIVANT: Bessie, I cannot believe such a preposterous tale. You have been smoothing these papers out to deceive me.

BARBARA: It's true that they've been crumpled, Miss Bullivant, but it isn't Bessie's fault. She wrote them for you this evening.

MABEL: And someone took them away from here for spite.

BUNNY, PIP, and TEDDY BEAR: That's quite right, Miss Bullivant. We got them back.

MISS BULLIVANT: Goodness gracious! I am not deaf!

THE THREE: But it isn't Bessie's fault. We got the papers back for her, Miss Bullivant, and she did write them for you!

MISS BULLIVANT: Will you——

THE THREE: And we hope you'll let her go to——

MISS BULLIVANT (*shrieking*): Please be silent! You will deafen me. Bessie, I am very dissatisfied with the whole business, but I am willing to accept this explanation that you have not tried to deceive me intentionally. I will accept these lines, and you may get ready immediately. (BESSIE *beams.*) But I still cannot understand how you have written an imposition so quickly. Knowing your laziness so well, it really seems to me—well, quite——

BESSIE (*triumphantly*): Incomprehensible!

(CURTAIN).

First Curtain-call : BESSIE, in hat and coat, arm-in-arm with her two chums, waving concert tickets triumphantly.

Second Curtain-call : Full company.

(FINAL CURTAIN).

HOW TO RUN A CHUMMY CLUB

"MOTHER," said Nita, "please may I have the members of the C.C. here next Wednesday ? "

" Yes, dear," said mother, smilingly, and Cousin Dorothy pricked up her ears interestedly.

" What's the C.C., Nita ? " she asked.

" Don't you know ? " Nita was very fond of Cousin Dorothy, and never minded telling her all about her plans, and school friends ; in fact, about anything in which she was interested, in spite of the fact that Cousin Dorothy was a good deal older than she herself.

Forthwith, she launched into a long explanation of the C.C., which, of course, stood for " Chummy Club," and all its various workings, rules, and orders.

" The Chummy Club," said Nita, curling up in her favourite position in the armchair, " was started at our school some time ago, and we all belong to it. Its object is to make everyone friends of everyone else. Anyone can belong to it, provided they observe the rules and regulations of the club."

" Which are——? " prompted Cousin Dorothy.
And Nita told her.

You see, I happen to be Cousin Dorothy, and I was very interested indeed in the Chummy Club. It struck me as being such a thoroughly sensible idea, and when, as a special mark of favour, Nita asked me if I would like to come to the meeting to be held on Wednesday at her house, I was awfully glad to say, " Yes, thank you."

" Of course, we're all chums in our form," Nita explained to me, " but we used not to be. There were always some girls who were left out of the circles that were formed, partly because they were shy, or we didn't know them, or perhaps because no one particularly took to them. It isn't really ever fair to judge what a girl's like till you know her properly, and when you get the Chummy Club really going, everyone gets to know everyone else at once."

" And you meet at each other's houses ? "

" Yes, that's one of the rules of the club," said Nita. " Every member is obliged, unless, of course, there is some very definite reason for her not doing so, to invite the other members to tea, and an evening meeting of the club, at her house, once or twice, as the case may be, in a term. We have meetings every week, and everyone has to pay the "huge" sum of threepence. Threepence doesn't cover the expenses for tea always, of course, but it goes a fair way, and it's a jolly fine idea, don't you think so ? "

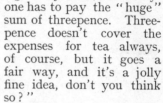

I did, and looked forward very much to the following Wednesday, to learn more about the "Chummy Club."

When I turned up at the house on Wednesday, just about tea-time, it sounded as though Bedlam had been let loose, and, when I got inside the house, girls seemed just—everywhere !

They met me on the stairs, they met me in the bedroom, and in *every* room. There seemed just swarms of them, in their short gym slips and white blouses.

Nita was there, supremely happy, and very busy, trying to introduce me to everyone, without performing an introduction twice. It was a job, I assure you.

Eventually we settled down at the table, and began tea. Nita stood up solemnly, and made a speech.

" Members of the Chummy Club," she said. Then, in a low aside to me : " The member at whose house the meeting is held has to make a speech, Doro." I made a mental note of the fact,

138

and listened eagerly for what should come next.

" Members of the Chummy Club," Nita began again. " This is our fifth meeting this term, and I want to welcome two new members to the Chummy Club, and hope they'll be real chums. Stand up, the two new ones."

One girl of about thirteen or fourteen stood up, but the other new member didn't. Nita nudged me.

" Get up and bow ! " she whispered in my ear.

I obeyed ! I was a member of the Chummy Club !

Tea then proceeded, amid much talk and laughter, and I had time to look around, and hear all the comments and talk about school, and about—well, practically every subject under the sun in which schoolgirls are interested.

Games, lessons, the horrors of Latin translations, as opposed to French, hockey, needlework — these were but a few of the subjects in which these thirty odd girls were interested.

I was interested, too—enormously so !

Tea over, everyone streamed out in perfect order, this time, I may say, and with a very little amount of noise, to the drawing-room, where a cheerful fire burned in the grate.

Everyone sat on the floor—crossed-leg style !

" There aren't enough chairs to go round," Nita told me, " and anyway, it's much more fun sitting on the floor, don't you think so ? "

As it apparently amounted to a rule of the club, and I was now a member, I too sat on the floor.

" Now," said Nita, getting up as far as a kneeling position, and addressing the assembly, " what's everyone got to do ? "

Not a girl there but had brought something. Stockings to darn, knitting, crochet, needlework of some sort, and I felt sadly out of place.

" You can darn some of mine," said Nita, generously, and I meekly took from her a very much damaged stocking, looking with no little apprehension at the gaping hole that must be filled up—somehow !

" Now "—Nita it was who spoke again—" shall we have someone to read aloud, or shall we talk ? "

" Talk ! " with one voice the company made answer.

I was glad. I had no end of questions to ask of the girls gathered together to-night, and I addressed a red-haired girl on my right.

" Do you always do needle-work ? " I asked.

" No ! " she answered emphatically. " We don't ! I don't think there'd be many members of the C.C. if we needleworked every week. We have sewing one week, one week we have a discussion of a book that everyone *must* read. Lately we've been reading one that might have been excellent, but which I found rather dry ! I waded through somehow, and I'm bothered if they didn't choose me to write the paper. We write a paper, and have it read, to start the discussion going," she explained.

" Then we have amateur dramatics ! That's fun ! " she went on. " Last time Biddy—Biddy's the girl over there with a long black ' pig '—wrote the play. It was awfully good. Biddy's going to be a writer one day."

She stopped for a minute to answer a question from someone else, and I turned to my neighbour on my left.

She was a tiny girl—ever so dainty and pretty. I found out her name was Muriel.

" Do tell me some more about the club," I begged. " I hear you have reading discussions and amateur theatricals—and sewing nights. Do you have anything else ? "

She gave me rather a shy glance. But Rule No. 6 of the Chummy Club says you must always answer questions.

" Yes," she said. " We have music nights. They're my favourites."

" What do you have to do ? " I asked

" Well, we nearly all learn the piano and sing-ing. Some learn dancing ; I do, for one. Everyone

has to do something, and do it as well as they can. No one is allowed to shirk. If they can't play, they have to sing ; if they can't sing, they dance or recite."

" Jolly good idea ! " I commented, knowing full well how often girls are rather foolishly reluctant to " perform " in public. Such an idea would rid them of that nervous self-consciousness that is often the cause of a girl growing up shy and awkward.

" Any other special nights ? " I queried, still anxious for information.

" Yes." Something evidently appealed to her sense of humour, and she chuckled. " One night that no one likes hardly. Cooking and housework. They like the cooking all right—that's fun—but

the housework doesn't appeal to anyone. You see, on housework nights we have either the mother of the girl at whose house we are, or an elder sister, to instruct. It means harder work than any other night. We have to guarantee if we are allowed the use of the kitchen, that we'll leave it as spotlessly clean and tidy as we found it. Not all mothers like the  girls working about in the kitchen—in fact, there are some who don't like it at all, and we occasionally have to give it up, and have another night instead. There's always rejoicing if that happens."

I laughed, too.

Needlework. Music. Reading discussions, Cooking, Housework, Amateur Dramatics—all these useful and amusing things were taken in, in the programme of the Chummy Club.

Its rules were that you came—you brought all your chums, and made them members! The idea was that every girl at school, or out of it, for that matter, should be friends with everyone else. There was no distinction—rich girls and poor could join the Chummy Club, under the conditions set down in the rules, which were comparatively few and simple.

You had to attend, and take part in every meeting, unless illness, or something else equally important, prevented.

You had to obtain the consent of your parents to your being a member, and you had to promise to do all in your power to give no trouble to the lady at whose house the meeting was held, week by week.

You had to extend your honest friendship to every member of the club, to refrain from tale-telling, unkind gossip, and quarrelling. Any quarrel was keenly sought into, and judgment passed at the meeting, and the quarrel patched up, if possible. Otherwise the two girls who quarrelled were expelled from the club, without any question as to which girl first caused the quarrel

No member of the club had any more prestige than any other member, except at given times. For instance, on the night of my becoming a member of the club, the meeting was held at Nita's mother's house, therefore, Nita for the time being took matters in hand, and became, for the one meeting, the " President."

I think I have seldom met a jollier, chummier, happier lot of girls in all my life. Everyone was " chummy " with everyone else. A spirit of the utmost good comradeship existed, and no girl, I was assured, would miss a single one of the meetings of the Chummy Club through their own fault.

A good idea, eh, girls ? And one that can easily be carried out.

No mother who had an interest in her girl's happiness and well-being, could possibly object to a meeting occasionally of the club that you could form, at her house.

But my schoolgirl's cousin and her friends were not content even with all they had achieved through their branch of the Chummy Club.

A little while ago, I heard frequent murmurs about " Sale of Work," " Bazaar," etc., and, on inquiring further, found that Nita and Co. were planning something really ambitious.

They had worked steadily and well for some time, and the net result was a collection of gollywogs, dolls, dressed well or indifferently well, pin cushions, calendars, workboxes and baskets, tea cloths, and the hundred and one things that go to make up a bazaar. I was invited, as an honorary member of the Chummy Club, to do " my bit," and contributed one or two little oddments to the stock.

The bazaar—and the concert that was held when everything had been " sold out "—was quite one of the most amusing and delightful things I had ever attended.

I haven't told you, either, that the result of their labours was close on ten pounds, which went to the district hospital.

So you see, the Chummy Club, of which I am an exceedingly proud member, has done wonders. It will do more wonderful things yet, for, as I have already told you, the girls are such absolute chums.

Think of the fun—think of the jolly chumship with countless girls who are friendless, who want chums of their very own. You'd have a friendship with as many girls as you wanted—all jolly, all united in the same bond of " chumminess."

Your chummy club can be a real thing—why not form it, now ?

BESSIE LISTENS IN

An Amusing Little Episode at Cliff House School

CHAPTER I.
AN EXCITING SOUND WAVE

"Bessie! Look out!"

"Keep back, duffer!"

"Hi! Mind where you're a-goin'!" a boy's frantic voice added to the sudden outcry.

"Oh, you—— Yooop!"

Clatter-clatter!

Crash!

Bessie Bunter, the fat girl of the Fourth Form at Cliff House School, blinked about her in short-sighted amazement.

Quite a large crowd of girls, chiefly Fourth Formers, had collected about the woodshed near the porter's lodge, and were staring upwards. Bessie Bunter, whose curiosity was, next to her appetite, her strongest point, rolled rapidly towards them, with the object of ascertaining what was "up."

The short-sighted junior did not notice the ladder which reclined against one of the elms a short distance from the shed; nor did she notice the round, youthful form of Boker, the page, in the act of descending the ladder.

One of Bessie's ample feet collided violently with the foot of the ladder, and she jumped with amazement as both Boker and the ladder prostrated themselves before her.

"I sus-sus-say, you girls!" she exclaimed. "Where's young Boker just come from?"

"Ha, ha, ha!"

Boker, unhurt but ruffled both in body and in temper, scrambled to his feet furiously.

"There you go, clumsy!" he spluttered.

"Eh! What's that, Boker?" exclaimed Bessie indignantly. "Why, I'll jolly well box your ears!"

"Pax, my infants!" cried Clara Trevlyn, the tomboy of the Fourth, stepping between them laughingly. "'Tis sad to see such wrath in ones so young. Desist!"

"But he jolly well insulted me!" spluttered Bessie indignantly.

"She came along and knocked me off the ladder," Boker exclaimed bellicosely.

"Well, let bygones be bygones," said Clara cheerily. "Don't dig up the dead and buried past. Behold, Fatima! Herbert Wireless Boker has just finished putting up his aerials!"

Bessie Bunter blinked upwards through her thick glasses in the direction indicated by Clara's sweeping hand. And then she saw at what the crowd of girls had been so interestedly staring.

From one of the branches of the tree to the roof of the woodshed stretched two parallel lengths of wire—"aerials" which the enterprising Boker had just erected, with the rather unexpected climax provided by the blundering Bessie Bunter.

Boker had spared no pains to make his aerial of a business-like nature, for he had fixed "insulators" at the end of the aerials, from which points the joining wires passed down and through an open window of the woodshed.

A friend of Boker's had lent him a wireless set for a short time, and the enthusiastic page, troubling neither to obtain permission from the headmistress nor the Postmaster-General—two exceedingly important points—had commenced to experiment right away.

"Now then, fair Boker," said Clara Trevlyn, as the page, mollified by the attentions paid to his labours, was beginning to look very important indeed. "Let's see what messages you can pick up in the woodshed!"

Nothing loath, Boker led the way to the woodshed where, on a rough table, was set out his receiving set, at which the girls gazed, somewhat impressed by the mysterious jumble of wires, switches, "valves," and electric bulbs.

Bessie Bunter, in fact, began to bubble over with the new excitement.

"I sus-sus-say, let me have a go, Boker," she exclaimed, as the page importantly commenced to fix the receivers over his head and ears. "I'm a dab at wireless—I once sent a telegram to dad in the City, about a remittance, and he got it ! I may pick up all kinds of mysterious messages and things. Gangs of burglars nowadays send all their messages by wireless so that nobody will know about it ! They call it broadcasting."

"Ha, ha, ha !"

"Look 'ere, Miss Bunter, you clear hoff !" said the page emphatically. "I don't want this 'ere set broke by you before I've started with it."

"Half a minute, Boker !" It was Clara Trevlyn who again interrupted, and there was a twinkle in her merry eye.

Clara had noticed that, on the table, lay coiled a lengthy piece of old gas tubing, which Boker might, or might not, have intended to use in connection with his wireless operations. The sight of that, together with Bessie's fatuous remarks concerning "messages" and "burglars," had suggested an idea to the joke-loving Clara.

She whispered a few words in the page's ear, and that youth's face relaxed and then grinned broadly.

"Right-o !" he said, dragging the receivers from his shaggy hair. "Let's see what Miss Bunter can do !"

"Hurrah !" chirped Bessie delightedly. "You girls just watch me listening-in. You just put those things over your ears, and—er—there you are !"

"There you are !" agreed Clara, with a wink at her chums. "Come on, Miss Wireless !"

And Clara arranged the 'phones over Bessie's large ears. Perhaps even Bessie would have been suspicious had she perceived exactly how the japing junior arranged them, for between Bessie's right ear and the receiver she inserted one end of the piece of old gas tubing. But Bessie was far too excited to take heed of that little detail.

"Hullo, hullo !" she cried, at the jumble of wires and switches before her (Bessie, however expert she might be, had apparently overlooked the fact that the wireless set was merely a receiving, and not a transmitting, apparatus). "Hullo, hullo-a ! Exchange, please ! I mum-mum-mean, is anybody there ?"

A tittering arose among the girls, but Clara suppressed it with a warning look.

"Let's get outside, everybody, while Bessie's at work !" said Clara briskly—and as she spoke she pushed the disengaged end of the gas tubing through the open window of the woodshed. "Can't you see you're all standing in the way of the ether waves ?"

"Yes, that's it—that's why I haven't already got a message !" Bessie cried indignantly. "You make them all get outside, Clara."

Needing something of an effort now to suppress their merriment, the girls trooped outside the

shed. Once outside, however, Clara hurried to the spot beneath the window, from which protruded the length of gas tube—the other end of which, of course, was in close proximity to the unconscious Bessie's ear-drum.

Placing her hand round the end of the tubing and placing her mouth against her hand, Clara spoke in a low and altered voice.

"Hul-loo-ah ! Is that Station Double X, One, Two, Three ?"

"Hurrah ! A message !" came an excited cry from Bessie within the shed. "Hul-loo-ah ! What—what's your message ? Fire ahead !"

"Do you speak on behalf of the Chief of the 'Conspirators' ?" spoke Clara again, in the same low, strange voice.

There sounded a loud gasp from the inside of the shed.

"Wer-wer—what was that ?" stammered Bessie's voice.

"Ah ! I recognise the voice ! You are the secretary of the Chief of the Conspirators ! Does my voice carry, Miss Grubbins ?"

"I—I—Y-yes ! I'm—I'm Miss Grubbins all right ! Tell us all about it !" exclaimed Bessie, her voice quivering with excitement.

"It is good ! We have robbed the duke's mansion as arranged——"

"Mum-mum-my hat !"

"This is no time to discuss hats, Miss Grubbins," said Clara, her voice deepening. "Restrain your feminine instincts ! The duke's golden plate, the family jewels, the precious water-colour paintings—they are all ours !"

"Mum-my word ! Then—then you're a bib-bib-burglar !" chattered Bessie.

"I am, of course, a loyal servant of the Conspirators !" said Clara deeply—and in a voice which, to Bessie, seemed very far away. "We have hidden the swag in the old hut in the woods near Cliff House School. Do your men know the place ?"

"Y-y-yes !" cried Bessie, almost dancing now with delight. "I'll get it myself, you burg—I mum-mum-mean——"

"It is well, Miss Grubbins !" replied the deep, far-away voice. "I must now ring off, as the Exchange are asking for more pennies ! Don't fail to tell the Chief of the Conspirators that I have rung up !"

In a second Clara had dropped the tubing, and the whole party of girls, almost convulsed with laughter, were rushing back to the entrance of the shed. There was a violent collision in the doorway, for Bessie, radiant with joy and excitement, was already rushing forth, the receivers cast, as it were, to the winds.

"Hurrah ! I told you so—I've got a message ! I——"

" What is it, Bessie ? " asked Clara gravely.

But Bessie suddenly became mysterious.

" Never you mind ! You leave it to me ! " she said, with a wink. " I'm going off to see about something now ! "

" But what about tea ? " Barbara Redfern now asked. " It's already laid on the table——"

" Bother tea, Babs ! " ejaculated Bessie.

" Bother tea ! " repeated Babs faintly.

" Some girls have more important things than eating to think about, if others haven't ! " said Bessie stiffly. " There's such a thing as saving a fortune that's been stolen from a duke——"

" Ha, ha, ha ! "

The girls had to let themselves go at that. But Bessie, with her snub nose elevated high in the air, ambled rapidly away, leaving her chums convulsed.

CHAPTER II.

A DUKE'S FORTUNE !

" So this is where they've left the swag, as they call it ! "

Bessie Bunter had taken a short cut—or what she fondly imagined to be a short cut—to the disused hut in Friardale Woods. Little did she know that a small party of girls had, setting off shortly after her, taken a short cut that really was short, and had reached and left the hut just before her !

Bessie blinked eagerly around, and then she literally jumped for joy. There, in a corner among a lot of old brushwood, lay a well-filled, bulging sack !

" The duke's golden plate, and—and things ! " she gasped excitedly. " My wuw-wuw-word ! I ought to be a lady detective, or something ! Fancy me taking the message in such great style ! "

The bag was well tied at the mouth, and Bessie dragged it into the centre of the shed. Something rattled even as she let it sag down, and Bessie's eyes gleamed triumphantly.

" It's the old duke's property, right enough ! " she muttered. " What had I better do ? Those —those bib-bib-burglars may have got that wireless message as well as me, and—and they may be here any minute ! I—I'll jolly well drag it to the school at once ! "

And, grasping the tied mouth firmly, Bessie dragged the heavy sack out of the shed and through the wood.

It was hard work to reach the lane at the end of the footpath, but Bessie did it with much tugging, gasping, and perspiring. And then came the long, long journey along the lane.

How Bessie's unmuscular arms stood the strain she never knew. They were aching unbearably by the time the gates of Cliff House came into sight. Outside the gates stood a party of Fourth Formers, looking as if they were expecting someone—as indeed they were !

" What's that, Bessie ? " hailed Babs. " A stock of provisions ! "

" Grooh ! Never you mind ! " puffed Bessie, dragging the heavy and dusty sack through the crowd of girls. " Don't any of you dare to touch this ! You'll get a shock later when you learn that I've saved a duke's fortune from burglars ! "

" Is this the Duke's fortune, Bessie ? " asked Babs gravely.

Bessie stopped to blink at the leader of the Fourth Form.

" How on earth did you guess that, Babs ? I mean, never you mind what it is ! I'm jolly well going to drag this up to the study, and go straight to Miss Primrose ! I'm a girl the Fourth's going to be proud of jolly shortly ! "

" Going to win the eating championship of Kent for us ? " asked Freda Foote, the humorist of the Fourth.

Bessie ignored the question, but Clara Trevlyn, with a wink at the smiling, surrounding girls, came forward.

" These are the things we were expecting for our studies, aren't they, Babs ? " she asked, prodding the sack.

" Leave it alone, Clara ! " yelled Bessie frantically. " This swag—I mean this sack is mine——"

" Your mistake, Bessie— it's ours, a good share of it, anyway ! " said Barbara Redfern. " We may let you have one or two things. Lend

" Don't you dare call me clumsy ! " exclaimed Bessie indignantly.

a hand, girls! It'd take Bessie all day to draw this to the study!"

"Otherwise we'd let her!" chuckled Freda Foote.

Bessie spluttered as the girls lifted the heavy sack between them and carried it into the school, and she spluttered still more as Barbara cut the string that tied the mouth.

But Bessie was all curiosity as she peered into the interior.

Then her jaw fell, and her eyes gaped behind her thick glasses.

"All our things, as we said, Bessie," remarked Barbara Redfern calmly, drawing forth a large frying pan. "Your old frying pan, Bessie!"

"I—I—I——" stuttered Bessie.

"And your Mrs. Beeton!" added Babs calmly.

"You—you spoofers!" shrieked Bessie, even her dull brain beginning to get something of a grasp of the situation at last.

The girls chuckled merrily as Babs drew forth the articles from the bag. There were pans and kettles belonging to various girls, and the rest of the contents of the sack of "swag" were in the form of old books!

"I know—I know what you've been up to!" spluttered Bessie furiously. "You heard me taking that message and you deliberately left these—these things for me to find!"

"Bessie—here's your old saucepan!"

Bessie blinked furiously as a great peal of laughter went up.

"Look here, I'm jolly well going to get into touch with those burglars again, find out where they live, and jolly well give their address to the police! That's what I'll do!"

And, with a glare that almost cracked her glasses, Bessie rolled out. But she did not go alone. The whole party of girls accompanied her blandly. If Bessie were to receive any message, only Clara could supply it.

Boker was not in the shed at the moment, or perhaps he would have objected to Bessie using his set for a second time. As it was, Bessie picked up the receivers and dragged them over her head. And as she did so, Clara obligingly helped—and incidentally inserted the end of the gas tubing again!

Then Clara tiptoed out, leaving Bessie to receive "messages."

"Hullo—hullo!" cried Bessie importantly. "Anybody there—anybody there?"

"Pennies, please!" sounded a faint voice.

"Eh? What do you say?" asked Bessie, blinking. "Is—is that the gang of b-b-burglars who——"

"Ah! That is Miss Grubbins again!" said the deep voice, sounding clearer. "Did you locate the valuables?"

"No, because it jolly well wasn't there!" said Bessie emphatically. "What I want to know is—I mean what the chief wants to know is—who are you, and where do you live?"

"My name you should know!" returned the deep voice. "As to my residence, I live at Cliff House——"

"Cliff House!" exclaimed Bessie.

"And in Study Number Seven!" went on the voice cheerily. "Fancy you not remembering my name, Fatima!" And Bessie jumped up now, and, spinning round, blinked towards the window, where Clara's smiling face had appeared. Clara was still speaking with her mouth to the gas tubing. "Do you mean to say you've forgotten your dear old Clara, who gets you out of bed in the morning?"

"Clara!" shrieked Bessie.

"What's that?" asked Clara blandly. "Are you there?"

"Ha, ha, ha!" pealed the girls.

"Kik-kik-Klara!" stuttered Bessie Bunter. "You—you were speaking all the time. There, there aren't any bib-bib-burglars at all!"

"Go on!" said Clara.

"Ha, ha, ha!" pealed the girls again.

For Bessie's expression was too funny for words. She tried to speak, but her voice failed her. The sight of Clara and the gas tubing, the other end of which Bessie now dragged from between her ear and the receiver, were too much for the fat girl of the Fourth. And the girls left her blinking and gasping, and certainly not in a mood to receive more wireless messages—from Clara!

THE END

SHADOW SHOW

Shadow pictures have always been a great attraction, more so in latter years, owing to the use of cardboard and paper shapes held in the fingers. The addition of a shadow frame, *i.e.*, a frame of wood with linen stretched and pinned over it, is a great improvement on the shadows made with the hands against the wall. A frame of this kind can be easily made by placing the family clothes-horse against a table, with a sheet hung over the front, and the linen stretched with drawing pins; or, if you are using an old piece of linen, it can be tacked. Our heading will give you a suggestion of how to arrange the frame and candle. Of course, if the frame is a large one, a lamp must be used, as you will require more light.

The Runaway Rabbit

This is the usual type of hand shadow shown against the wall, but, in giving your performance, it is as well to show this kind of thing as an opening; the more elaborate shadows will then come as a novel surprise.

The figures above will show you how the fingers are interlaced. When moving your hands across the screen, also move the fingers marked with arrowheads, this will give your rabbit a life-like appearance.

The Old Lady

From a piece of cardboard cut the shape as shown at A; the size of which must be in proportion to your hand. Now hold this between your thumb and second finger, placing the first finger in the position shown in figure B. This finger forms the chin of the old lady, and is moved up and down.

To complete, place a handkerchief round the top of the hand, gripping it with the fingers not in use, and letting the folds fall as shown.

The Irate School Mistress

Cut a cardboard shape as shown at A, and place the pointed part at the top of same through a few strands of a ball of wool. Now hold the shape between your fingers, and place a small pair of scissors to form her eye-glasses; these you keep in position with your thumb. The first finger is again used to form the chin, and the handkerchief placed over the hand to form the body.

A Swan In Action

When making this shadow, let your left elbow rest on the table, first placing a length of cardboard across the lower part of your screen (*see diagram*). This cardboard can be shaped as shown, and will give a suggestion of water. Move the right hand and arm backward and forward, see dotted lines, and flutter the fingers of the left hand, that form the bird's tail.

A School Girl

TRY and make this figure as pretty as you can, so be careful when cutting the shape as shown at A. With the point of a penknife, cut the small openings that form the eye, and the oblong by the side of the mouth. Now cut the shape as shown at B, but in doing this you must remember that, as it forms the chin, it must therefore be in proportion to the nose and upper lip. The small part marked with an arrowhead is put through the oblong opening and the chin worked up and down by means of the tab; use the left finger and thumb for this.

Now take several strands of wool, and round them tie a piece of ribbon (see Fig. C.) Place one end of the wool through the cut curve, and hold the head as shown at Fig. D., with a handkerchief draped round the hand as before.

The Scotch Girl

TO prepare this figure, you first cut out the shapes A and B, and also use the same strands of wool as before, with its ribbon as previously described.

Grip the piece, A, in your hand, and place the strands of wool over the thumb, again using this member to hold the tam in position as shewn at Fig. C. To complete, you will require two handkerchiefs, one you roll up and place round the top of your hand to represent a muffler, and the other you drape underneath to form a cloak. The first finger of your left hand is used for the underlip and chin, also shown at Fig. C.

A Girl on Horseback

OUR last shadow picture is more ambitious, and though it may at first appear difficult, you will find that with a little care and patience it is really quite simple.

The sizes given in the diagram are for a hand that will take a 6½ glove. For hands larger or smaller you must allow accordingly. Cut from cardboard the shape marked with an A. Then the shape B, and with a penknife cut out the small circles on each. Through these circles pass about 4 ins. of lead pencil, see Fig. C. The circle on the Fig. B should be a trifle larger than that on the horse's headpiece, this is to allow the figure to turn easily on the pencil. You next cut a length of card 9 ins. long and ¾ in. wide, and fix this to the back of Fig. B by passing a pin through one end of the slip and the dot I, afterwards fixing a piece of cork on the point of the pin to keep the pieces in position. Now grip the pencil in your thumb, and the third and fourth fingers, the two latter being held up against the palm of the hand, with the joints bent; see Fig. D. The first and second fingers are used to form the front legs of the horse, and when showing, work the figure and hind legs by means of the long tab, also see D.

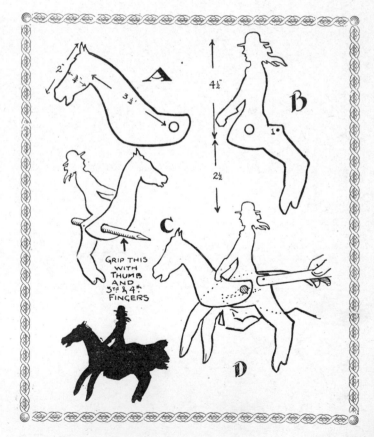

N.B.—All shapes must be in proportion to the performing hand, otherwise the shadows will be distorted.

146

The French Mistress

An Amusing Experience of Two Young Pickles

BY JOAN VINCENT

CHAPTER I.

A CAB, A COLONEL, AND A CONSPIRACY

"IT's really too bad!" said Marjorie Maddison.

"Far too bad—unheard-of!" agreed Mona, her sister.

The taxicab was purring steadily along the Edgware Road, and would soon be depositing them at Paddington Station. There they were to catch the Cornish Riviera express that would whirl them swiftly to Plymbury—and to all the fun of a new term at Castlebury College.

They had had a perfect summer holiday, and made no complaint that it was time for school again; yet it was obvious that there was a fly in the amber; an imminent development that neither of the Maddison Pickles, as they were usually called, awaited with any satisfaction.

"Let me see the letter again, Marjorie," said Mona suddenly.

Marjorie produced a letter from her handbag. The envelope was so creased that it indicated many previous perusals.

"Dear old Miss Tompkins means all right, of course," she said, as she smoothed the sheet of paper on her lap. "She's a dear for a Headmistress. But I wish she could understand how girls feel about—oh, this sort of thing!"

Mona took the letter and read what she should certainly have known by heart.

"My dear girls," Miss Tompkins had written in her old-fashioned hand, "the new French mistress I have engaged is travelling down from Paddington by the same train that will bring you, and I therefore wish you two to meet her and travel with her to Plymbury. I expect that she will be wearing a hat trimmed with red. Do not fail to look out for her on the platform—she is expecting to see you."

"A hat trimmed with red!" commented Mona. "We might have guessed that without Miss Tompkins being so careful to tell us!"

"Yes; and a dreadful parasol! She's sure to have a dreadful parasol," sighed Marjorie. "Mademoiselle du Fane always had one. And high-heeled shoes so that she can hardly walk."

"Lovely—the very last word, I am sure!" nodded Mona. "And she'll want us to sit in the train and jabber in French all the way down. Oh, Marjorie, we simply can't do it! Think how the people will stare at us!"

"Yes; and grin," said Marjorie; adding candidly; "Especially when we try and talk to her in French. Fancy a carriage full of people grinning at us all the way down to Plymbury!"

"Yes; and then Maisie and the others will see

us being trotted along by the dear, kind French mistress, and they'll laugh as well—oh, they'll simply die of laughter. And we sha'n't hear the end of it for the whole term. We've never had to be taken to school before! Never!"

The taxicab had stopped near to Praed Street; there was a jamb in the traffic.

A cab came to rest behind them with a squeaking of brakes. Hardly had it done so than a sharp and irascible voice was heard, apparently addressing the driver.

"Why are you stopping, eh? What's the matter? Why don't you go on? Think I can sit in this thing all day?"

Marjorie and Mona exchanged startled glances. They said, in one breath:

"Who's that?"

Then Marjorie was on her feet and peering through the little window at the back. The thin, flushed face and fierce grey moustache of the complaining passenger was visible as he leaned out of the window.

"Loitering, sir—loitering, that's what it is!" cried the indignant old gentleman. "I have been in this cab for hours! What's that? Police obstruction? Then why did you not hurry and get through first? No impertinence, my man!"

Marjorie bobbed back to her seat.

"Colonel Shunsnorth!" she said in a hollow voice.

"I thought so! I'd guessed it!" said Mona wearily. "I suppose he's going to Paddington as well. I suppose he'll be on the train. Oh, dear, what a jolly little picnic it's going to be!"

It was certainly not inspiriting to find their cab being followed by the most famous but unpopular of the school governors.

What qualifications the gallant Colonel Shunsnorth possessed to be a governor of Castlebury College for Girls no one had ever found out. But his opinions were frequently discernible in school orders; especially in physical drill. It was the general opinion that if Miss Tompkins did not happen to be a very firm and capable lady all lessons would be done to the accompaniment of physical exercises.

The colonel loved these exercises; he said they had made him what he was. The Maddison Pickles pointed out that that was a very strong reason why they should abolish "physical jerks" altogether.

"Off at last!" murmured Marjorie. "The dear colonel's said all he can think of for the moment, but I expect he'll fire a few more rounds at Paddington Station. And then—oh, gracious! What was that?"

A terrific report came from behind them.

"He's blown up!" remarked Mona, jumping

up. "Oh, no—not this time. It's a puncture, and the cab's stopping! Ha, ha, ha!"

They simply pealed with laughter as their cab sped smoothly along Praed Street, and they imagined the feelings of the irascible old gentleman whose journey had come to such a sudden stop.

Paddington Station was full of bustle when they alighted a few minutes later, and directed a porter to see to their luggage.

"It'll go from number one platform, I expect," said Marjorie. "We've got our tickets, so there's nothing to worry about—except the dear Mademoiselle. Now what are we going to do, sweet Mona?"

"It's unlikely that her cab will have a puncture, too," sighed Mona. "These things never happen in pairs. I really don't—— Oh, gracious! Just look!"

There was a flurry on the platform ahead of them.

Everyone was staring at a young lady who rushed up and down in a state of the most breathless excitement imaginable. She carried a brown bag in each hand, and contrived to hold a parasol of extravagant design under one arm and several books under the other. Her hat was trimmed with red; her costume was very *à la mode*; and her heels were dangerously high. Even as the two girls watched the parasol dropped, and the young lady gave a loud and unEnglish cry of dismay.

"Mademoiselle!" gasped Marjorie and Mona, horrified.

The books followed the parasol, to the accompaniment of shriller and more excited cries.

"Hide!" whispered Marjorie, clutching at Mona's arm. "We can't—we really can't be seen with her!"

"But—Miss Tomkins' wish, you know——" Mona demurred uneasily.

"She'll make you carry the parasol if you speak to her!"

"Oh, goodness!" said Mona, capitulating. "Let's get away quickly!"

They retreated to the doorway of the booking-office, while quite a number of people assisted the distressed Mademoiselle to regain her possessions.

"We can't go to Plymbury with her!" said Marjorie fearfully. "If the girls saw us trotting out of the station with anyone like that—oh, I'd rather miss the train and be late!"

Mademoiselle, in spite of the offers of help, had dropped everything in a frantic endeavour to rub certain stains from the parasol with a flimsy handkerchief.

"Let's get somewhere where we can think," said Marjorie. "I suppose we really ought to go and help her now. But if we've got to have

148

her company for about three hours, don't let us have any more than possible."

"We'll go to the bookstall—pretend we haven't started looking for her yet!" said Mona.

They drifted to the bookstall, noting with some satisfaction that Mademoiselle and her numerous possessions were more or less friends again.

At the bookstall they both made a discovery that they had made several times before, that they had packed almost all their money in their luggage.

"Never mind, I've enough for a couple of magazines," said Mona. "We'll get mags. and read them. It may be some relief. I wish I knew what to get."

"I wonder if I could make a suggestion—I read a lot of books," said a very sweet voice.

They turned to see a fair and beautiful young lady, with whom they fell instantly in love.

"Oh, if you know the mags.—we so seldom read them," said Marjorie. "It's really awfully good of you——"

"Not at all," said their companion very pleasantly. "Are you fond of adventure stories? Do you like something funny? No, I shouldn't choose that. You'd be horribly bored, and I suppose you're going a long journey?"

"Yes—to Plymbury," said Marjorie.

"Really. I am going there myself, and I have got my ammunition first!" laughed the young lady, indicating a plentiful store of reading matter.

She helped them choose, seeming to know the contents of everything included in the lavish display. The Maddison Pickles placed themselves implicitly in the hands of their pleasant helper. They felt, from her very words, a sympathy and understanding with her; they were sure they would like what she chose. And, really, she could not be more than eighteen herself — not more than three years older than they were.

"Perhaps we shall see you on the train," Marjorie suggested, when the purchases were made.

"Yes, very possibly," said the young lady. "Only, you see, we—we—that is, we've got a kind of duty we—we may have to perform," said Marjorie uneasily. "But thanks awfully for being so jolly and so helpful. We were feeling most frightfully depressed until you came along." The young lady smiled and went back towards the train, and they watched her regretfully.

In the distance they could see Mademoiselle still flustering and flurrying

about, and creating a greater fuss than ever. If Mademoiselle had been the only passenger for the West she could not have been more in evidence.

"What are we going to do now?" said Mona uneasily.

"Wait until the very last moment, that's certain!" Marjorie answered. "Miss Tomkins didn't tell us what time to meet the dear young thing. And if she gets in the train and doesn't seem to be worrying about us——"

"We'll give her a miss and travel by ourselves!" Mona agreed. "That's the idea! We can—— Oh, my best bonnet! Marjorie, has she seen us? Is she waving to us?"

The French young lady was certainly going through some extraordinary antics along the platform.

"Let's fade!" said Marjorie in alarm. "If she's too mean to have a porter, it isn't our business to carry her parasol about. Quickly!"

They turned to dart away.

A tall and very upright gentleman stood right in their way, and Mona

A tall and very military-looking gentleman stood in their way, and Mona unluckily collided with him somewhat violently.

149

unluckily collided with him somewhat violently.

The gentleman gave vent to a cry of wrath and indignation.

"Howitzers and horsemen! What do you think you are doing?"

Marjorie and Mona stared in unutterable dismay at Colonel Shunsnorth.

"Oh!" His expression underwent a change as he saw their badges, and a hat was raised with military precision. "Dear, dear, I did not notice that you were young ladies of Castlebury College!"

"We're awfully sorry, Colonel Shunsnorth," said Marjorie.

"You'll never believe it, but I have had to walk here through the crass idiocy of an idiot of a taxi-driver!" said the Colonel in a rumbling voice. "Really, I think Miss Tompkins would be very surprised to witness you rushing about in such a manner, young ladies."

Marjorie fielded the magazines that Mona had spilt, thus leaving Mona—rather unfairly—to reply to the Colonel. Mona rather tremblingly answered him.

"Really, Colonel, there was no need for you to be rushing for the train, either," she said. "There's plenty of time."

"I am not travelling myself!" the Colonel answered stiffly. "I am merely here to meet a friend. Good morning!"

They watched him stride away.

"We're not going to have the gallant Colonel criticising our manners all the way to Plymbury," sighed Marjorie. "But it's like his cheek to speak like that at all. He wasn't looking where he was going any more than we were."

Mona clutched her sister's arm and pointed excitedly.

"But look—look! See who his friend is!" she gasped. "It's the French Mademoiselle! See, he's taken off his hat and given her that dreadful bow. Now he's speaking to her!"

Marjorie could only gape for the moment.

"He's actually carrying her luggage," went on Mona.

"Mademoiselle—a friend of the Colonel!" breathed Marjorie. "Oh, my poor unfortunate sister, that only makes it ten times worse! He must have recommended her to Miss Tompkins, and he wouldn't recommend anyone unless she was a tartar as bad as himself!"

"It settles what we're going to do, anyway!" said Mona in a most determined voice. "You can parley-voo with Mademoiselle if you like. I'm going to travel without her delightful

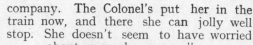

The "Pickles" were doubtful about this one, but—

company. The Colonel's put her in the train now, and there she can jolly well stop. She doesn't seem to have worried about us much, anyway."

The suggestion seemed good, and Marjorie was much relieved They walked up and down for a few minutes, and presently saw the Colonel coming in their direction. They rather feared that he would speak to them, and direct them to make themselves known to the young lady from France. But he gave them a stiff bow and passed.

"Perhaps he doesn't know that Miss Tommy told us to chum up with her," suggested Mona. "Anyway, we don't intend to do so now. Here's a nice carriage."

A surprising thing happened as they boarded the train. Hardly were they in the corridor than they found a very pleasant looking young lady near to them, and smiling. It was their friend of the bookstall.

"How is your duty—is it performed?" she asked.

Marjorie was momentarily confused.

"We're not going to—that is, we think it doesn't matter." And impulsively: "I say, are you travelling alone?"

"Quite."

"Then might we travel with you after all?" asked the sisters together.

"With pleasure—I should be delighted," said the young lady. "There is no one else in my compartment at present. Do come!"

They went very willingly indeed. The young lady seemed to have strayed some distance from her compartment, but as she did not comment they said nothing. When they were seated at last, she introduced herself as Muriel Verney, and they told her their names before indulging in general talk.

Both kept an eye on the platform during the last few minutes lest Mademoiselle should be dashing about in search of them, but they saw nothing of her. And their breaths of relief were genuine and heartfelt when the guard's whistle sounded at last and the train started to steam out of the station.

CHAPTER II.
PURSUER AND PURSUED

IT was Marjorie's suggestion that they should stroll along the corridor while the train gathered speed and clattered through the smoky environs of London.

Which of them saw the astonishing sight first is doubtful, for they both seemed to give a startled exclamation together. And then they remained outside the closed door of a compartment wherein a red-faced and grey-moustached gentleman was lying back against the cushions, peacefully slumbering.

It was Colonel Shunsnorth!

"I—I thought he said he wasn't travelling by this train!" said Marjorie, after a long and startled silence.

Mona began to chuckle suddenly and with great heartiness.

"But he is!"

"My dear, you—you surely don't think——"

Mona drew back and stuffed a handkerchief against her mouth. The same alarming symptom was suddenly visible in Marjorie. They shook, and their faces went very red indeed as the truth dawned on them.

"Oh, my dear! What a joke it'll be to tell the others!" Mona gurgled feebly. "It'll be the jape of the term! And he doesn't know anything about it yet!"

Marjorie tried to be more serious.

"But I say, Mona—he'll be furious!" she gasped. "What do you think we ought to do? Should we wake him up?"

"What! Raise a tornado of our own accord?" asked Mona. "Not for this child!"

"But——"

"Look where we are—and the train's doing forty or fifty by now!" said Mona, chuckling. "It'll never stop for the Colonel or anyone else. He's got to go to Plymbury whether he wants to or not. It'll be far better for everyone if he sleeps as long as possible."

"I—I suppose so, but—oh, dear! Come away!"

Marjorie clutched her sister's arm and dragged her away.

"He's waking up, I believe! Quick, Mona! If he sees us he's sure to say we knew all about it! Let's get away!"

They heard a gasp of military surprise.

The gasp was followed by a perfect roar.

They had just reached the end of the corridor when a door crashed open, and Colonel Shunsnorth started to bellow:

"Guard! Guard! Where's the guard? The train must be stopped! Guard!"

Marjorie and Mona made no comment. They were past it. They leant back against the woodwork, and shook with merriment.

Quick steps were heard in the corridor.

"The train—it must be stopped!" spluttered the Colonel. "I am not a passenger!"

—they absolutely adored THIS one!

"You look as though you were, sir," said the guard.

"Sir! Don't bandy words with me, sir!" roared the colonel. "I arranged to meet a friend in the last compartment of this coach. I must have dozed off while waiting. Apparently he has missed the train. But it must be stopped—I cannot go on!"

"We can't stop before Plymbury, sir," said the guard.

"Preposterous! I shall pull the alarm cord!"

"Very heavy penalty if you do, sir. You'll have to go to Plymbury. We can't stop the train because you've made a mistake. Every minute counts. There's a few hundred passengers to be considered besides yourself!"

Marjorie and Mona made their way back to their compartment.

In choking voices they told their pleasant companion what had happened. Muriel Verney shook with laughter.

"Oh, dear, how funny!" she murmured, wiping tears from her pretty eyes. "And this poor Colonel is being carried all the way to Plymbury? Dear me, I really ought not to laugh!"

"I don't see why you shouldn't!" chuckled Marjorie. "He's awfully domineering. It will do him good."

The speed of the train did not check; if anything it increased, as they slid through the open country.

Then, of a sudden, there came a sound that was effectually to check the merriment of the two girls.

In the corridor they heard a loud and excited voice, which they had heard at Paddington Station—a voice they were not likely to forget.

"I cannot find zem! I mos' find zem—I tell you I mos' find zem!"

Marjorie and Mona sat up in horrified attention. Then they ducked with one accord as a figure came suddenly hurrying along the corridor and passed the compartment. Out of the corners of their eyes they saw an excited and almost hysterical Mademoiselle waving her parasol.

"Oh, dear!" murmured Marjorie.

Muriel Verney was gazing at them in astonishment.

"Is—is anything the matter?" she asked.

Marjorie and Mona looked guilty and uneasy.

"N-no. Nothing much," said Mona. "It—it's someone we don't want to meet, that's all. We're going to see a lot of her before we're much older. Oh, how dreadful, Marjorie!"

Marjorie nodded. She had seen the wild, gesticulating figure. It was a glimpse of Mademoiselle that told more than volumes could have done. They could not dream of being " tacked on " to her for the rest of the journey.

Mona whispered to her sister.

" It's us she's after, I believe ! "

" Must be, from what she said ! " nodded Marjorie. " Her conscience has just pricked her. Perhaps she was too busy with her luggage before. Gracious, what's that ? "

In their agitation they quite forgot Muriel Verney as they rose and went into the corridor.

Two heated and excited voices were coming to their ears—it sounded like a violent quarrel that was taking place.

" Madam, I know nothing ! " boomed the Colonel's voice.

Excited and shrill-broken English answered him.

" Yes, you do, m'sieu. You were with zem ! You know vhere zey are ! I will 'ave zem—at once ! "

" Madam, leave me alone ! "

" 'Elp ! 'Elp ! " shrieked Mademoiselle. " À moi ! I will 'ave my rights ! I will find zem ! "

Marjorie and Mona were gasping.

" I thought they were friends ? "

" So did I," said Mona. " Now she's accusing him of not introducing us. Oh, gracious ! He'll be along, and we shall be planted with that woman whether we want it or not ! Whatever shall we do ? "

They went back into their compartment.

Hardly had they done so than a figure bustled past outside. It was the figure of Colonel Shunsnorth. They had never seen him look so uneasy, or move so quickly, as he did then.

Straight past their compartment—without one glance inside.

" I vill 'ave zem ! I vill ! " Mademoiselle's tearful voice was crying.

Doors began to bang open and shut. Marjorie jumped up gripping Mona's arm.

" She's searching every compartment ! Quick, we're not going to be caught like this ! We'll hide somewhere ! "

They emerged into the corridor just as the excited figure of Mademoiselle was seen flouncing into a compartment only two doors away.

Marjorie and Mona fled for their lives.

There was a restaurant car on the train, and just before it was reached there was a little kitchen. At the open door Marjorie stopped. Food was cooking, but no one was to be seen inside.

" We'll hide—under that sort of table," Marjorie murmured. " She'll never think of looking for us here. When she's searched

the train she'll conclude that we've missed it and everything will be all right."

" Good idea ! " nodded Mona.

They rushed into the kitchen and darted to the table. Then they halted—there was a figure already under the table.

Colonel Shunsnorth had " bagged " it first !

There followed the most horrifying pause that the Castlebury Pickles could ever remember.

The Colonel had been looking very hot and very red before they appeared. The sheer indignity of his position caused him to look as though he was on the point of exploding. Marjorie and Mona were too startled even to think of laughing at his grotesque and undignified attitude.

" Good—goodness gracious ! " spluttered the Colonel.

He extracted himself from the table and stood erect.

" Upon—upon my word—really—— "

But there were no words for Colonel Shunsnorth. His vocabulary was exhausted. He bestowed upon the two scholars of Castlebury College a terrific and infuriated glare and stamped out into the corridor.

The wild figure of Mademoiselle threw herself at him.

" M'sieu ! I find out ! I 'ave discover you ! Vhere are zey ? I vill make you tell me ! "

The Colonel fled, and in breathless pursuit followed Mademoiselle !

CHAPTER III.

THE COLONEL'S CAPTURE

MARJORIE and Mona Maddison were not enjoying their trip. The Colonel had disappeared altogether, but Mademoiselle had been seen several times wandering up and down the train in a disconsolate manner. Every time she appeared the sisters made themselves as small and as inconspicuous as possible.

Muriel Verney was obviously puzzled at their behaviour, but had asked no questions. Instead, she was being chatty and entertaining indeed. Now she had produced a very nice picnic hamper, and was inviting them to sample the contents.

" Oh, no thanks ! " protested Marjorie.

" Mona will not be so silly, I am sure," Muriel ventured.

" I—I can't. I'm not a bit hungry, thanks awfully ! " said Mona. " We—we can't rob you, really."

They felt that it was not fair to accept the stranger's hospitality when they had behaved in such an extraordinary way in front of her.

In their hearts they were really sorry that they had not made themselves known to Mademoiselle at Paddington, and risked a journey full

Then they halted and gasped——

of French conversation rather than what had actually happened.

Muriel had been so nice to them that they felt that they were not playing the game as they should have played it.

"We'll just have a little stroll and see if everything is all right," Marjorie announced suddenly. "You'll excuse us, won't you?"

"Oh, certainly—if you are sure that you won't help me to get rid of this dreadful pile of things!"

"We'd rather not—thanks awfully."

Out in the corridor they spoke their inmost thoughts.

"I'd just love a snack now!" said Marjorie.

"So would I!" said Mona. "But we couldn't sponge on her after the way we've been treating her. Can we get something in the restaurant car?"

"Where's the money?" said Marjorie. "I haven't got any. I spent it all on the magazines, which we haven't even opened as yet!"

"Bother! So you did!" said Mona. "But Marjorie, we can't go back to her now that we've refused. Could we get into the luggage-van? My purse is right in the top of the bag."

"I don't think they'd allow us," said Marjorie. "Still, we can try. Our things are at the back. They're using a sort of ordinary compartment for the luggage instead of the usual van."

They went hopefully along the corridor in quest of their money. A red-faced official was mounting guard over the van.

"No, certainly you can't go to the luggage!" he said gruffly. "Not on any account, young ladies! Better wait till you get to Plymbury!"

"But we want to get——"

"I can't allow anyone——"

"Not just to look?"

"Good gracious, no!" said the man in a startled tone. "You can't even peep inside. You'll have to leave it alone!"

They retreated disconsolately.

"Well, this is a horrid journey!" declared Marjorie. "And that man—why, he looked quite startled, Mona! Almost as though there was something in there that we shouldn't see!"

"Our purses—that's what it is!" said Mona gloomily.

They were almost on the point of going back to capitulate to the pleasant young lady when a voice called from the central part of the train. Within a few seconds the red-faced man who had been mounting guard over the luggage hurried past to obey it.

Marjorie gasped.

"See who it is, Mona? Now's our chance!"

They were off in a flash. The door leading to the impromptu luggage-van stood open and they sped past it, Mona jingling keys in her hand. In the piles of stacked luggage they saw, almost immediately, two familiar bags.

"There they are!" whispered Marjorie.

She stepped forward to get one of them down. It was necessary to move a light brown case that rested on top of it. Hardly had she taken a hold of it than there came a shrill cry of excitement from behind. Mademoiselle rushed forward and gripped her shoulders.

"I get you!"

Marjorie dropped the bag and whirled round.

"I 'ave get you—at last! At last I 'ave got!" cried Mademoiselle, dancing.

Marjorie was really angry at last.

"Well, supposing you have?" she said. "Do you think we want to travel with you?"

For "under the table" was already occupied.

"You 'ave got my baggage!" cried Mademoiselle.

"Baggage? But—but you've been chasing both of us——"

"Chase? What, chase two girls?" cried the French lady. "Indeed, nevaire! I chase my baggage! Now I 'ave found my baggage and you 'ave got it!"

There was a stamping footstep and the red-faced attendant appeared on the scene.

"Good gracious! What's happening here?" he cried. "You must leave here at once! No one's allowed in here at all!"

"My baggage——"

"Yes, everything's all right! You go back to your carriage——"

Mademoiselle gave a shriek and pointed to the side. Underneath a bag that was standing on its side was visible the toe of a boot!

"Whose foot is that?" she cried.

The foot disappeared!

"There's no foot, Mademoiselle!" cried the attendant. "You come along with me——"

"I see! I see for myself!"

The Frenchwoman sprang forward. With one swift movement she had dragged the bag away. A shower of luggage collapsed on the floor. From a chair in the ruins arose the towering, indignant figure of Colonel Shunsnorth.

"Zere! 'E is zere! The robbair that steal my baggage—'e is zere!" shrieked Mademoiselle dramatically.

Colonel Shunsnorth had never looked nearer to explosion than he looked at that moment.

"Guard! Take her away! Fetch a policeman—anything!" he thundered. "I—I will stand this no longer! I—a Colonel—a man in a highly responsible position—I am chased and hunted like this! I am not even allowed to ride in the guard's van! Preposterous! Not to be stood! I will not stand it any longer!"

"But my baggage——" wailed Mademoiselle.

"Your baggage! Bother your baggage! I am sick to death——"

"Can I be of any use, please?" asked a sweet voice.

Marjorie and Mona were startled to see that Miss Verney had unobtrusively joined them.

"I speak French," she explained. "Perhaps there is some little difficulty that I can clear up? I shall be only too happy if I can."

She commenced on Mademoiselle immediately.

Marjorie and Mona listened in an awed silence. They had never heard any Englishwoman who could speak such voluble and convincing French. Mademoiselle seemed to pour out her heart, and all its attendant troubles, to the quiet and self-possessed English girl.

"I fear there has been a misunderstanding,

Colonel," she said. "This lady has been searching for her luggage——"

"Yes! I know! I have tried to explain that it was all right!" spluttered the Colonel. "Everyone has tried to explain that it would be found at Plymbury! She would listen to no one."

"She couldn't understand—perhaps she was too excited."

"Excited! Huh!" gasped the Colonel. "And I have been accused before everyone of being a robber! Twice I have been driven to hiding to escape from her! And it all comes through helping a lady who was obviously in distress by seeing after her luggage, and then being brought on this idiotic train against my will!"

Mademoiselle listened to the explanations and abruptly burst into tears.

"Ze Colonel—oh, ze brave, brave Colonel! And I nevaire know!" she wept. "Oh, 'ow do I evaire apologise for all I 'ave said? Oh, ze brave Colonel——"

Colonel Shunsnorth tugged at his moustache, and moved uneasily from one foot to the other.

"Dear, dear, madam, pray do not distress yourself like that!" he murmured. "Perhaps I was—ah—unreasonable! Perhaps I was angry to find myself in such a position and—and refused to answer your questions. Please do not distress yourself!"

"But ze brave, brave officier—oh, 'ow I 'ave insult 'im!" wept the Frenchwoman. "I do not understand zat ze baggage is safe. I want to see 'im myself. And when ze brave Colonel run away——"

"Dear, dear!"

"When 'e disappear, and I 'ear 'e want to leave ze train—zat is why I am all so agitate, because I do not understand. Oh, sare, I 'ope you will forgive me!"

"Dear, dear!" said Colonel Shunsnorth again.

"If I feel that you nevaire forgive me——"

"Mademoiselle, I do! Vite! Beaucoup—I mean, very much——"

"But I was so vairy——"

Colonel Shunsnorth was completely out of his element, and looking more unhappy with every moment.

"Non, non, Mademoiselle. C'est—c'est bon, maintenant. That is to say, ca ne faire——"

Mademoiselle gave a cry of joy.

"Ze brave Colonel! 'E speak in ze French language!"

The Colonel went crimson.

"Certainly not, Mademoiselle. Just—just a few chance words——"

"Wiz ze accent of ze best Parisian gentleman. Vous-aimez la belle France?"

The Colonel gave a horrified gasp.

"Good gracious, really!" He turned an

agonised glance on Miss Verney. "Dear madam, if you would be so kind as to explain in this lady's language that I wish this incident to be ended, I—I should be very grateful."

"I will do my best, Colonel," promised Muriel Verney, smilingly.

She did so, and gently but firmly removed Mademoiselle to a compartment where she could calm herself in her own French way. It was a struggle for Miss Verney, but she was capable.

A heated and anxious Colonel made inquiries from the guard.

"A carriage, anywhere, guard!" he said. "I want to be locked in. Do not unlock it on any account. I—I have not the faintest wish to learn French at—at my time of life."

"Very good, sir," said the guard.

"And—and what train can I catch back to London? You say there is one a couple of minutes after this gets in? Then I shall catch it if I have to follow it along the lines. And, guard, I——"

Marjorie and Mona followed Miss Verney at a respectful distance. It seemed a suitable time to detach themselves from the conference. There was no knowing when the Colonel would start asking questions.

They watched their friend in awe and amazement.

"She's marvellous!" said Marjorie.

"Wonderful!" said Mona. "How anyone can jabber away like that and be understood beats me altogether. I could jabber, but if anyone understood——"

"They'd be still more marvellous," said Marjorie. "I say, it looks as though Miss Verney's worked the trick somehow. She must know a lot of French. But——"

Miss Verney came out of the compartment wherein she had deposited Mademoiselle, and smiled on them. The Maddison sisters returned

Marjorie and Mona listened in silent awe. Never had they heard such voluble French as proceeded from the lips of the two young ladies.

the smile and followed her along the corridor, and returned to their own compartment.

"I say, you got over that row jolly well!" said Marjorie, admiringly. "But who is that Frenchwoman? We thought she was our new French mistress!"

Miss Verney went into a peal of laughter.

"You did? Ha, ha, ha! I thought so!" She composed her face with an effort. "Forgive me for giving way to my feelings like that, please! I—I'm afraid that I owe you an apology. I've more or less guessed it all the time, and I thought it was too good a joke to spoil. You see, I was at school myself two years ago."

The Maddison Pickles stared.

"Yes?" said Mona bewildered.

"I didn't know what your arrangements were, and although Miss Tompkins had suggested —oh, well, I was a girl myself, and I know that girls aren't fond of coming back to school with mistresses. So I didn't like to press myself. And then— well, you can guess the rest."

Marjorie's eyes were wide with astonishment.

"You're pulling our legs, surely! You don't mean that you're going to Castlebury College?"

"I do!"

"As—as a French mistress?"

"Yes. You see, I've lived several years in France——"

The two girls pealed with laughter at the mistake they had been making.

"And now," continued Miss Verney, "I expect that you're really hungry, in spite of your denials. I brought a picnic hamper hoping to meet you two, and I haven't touched anything yet; I was sure you'd come along sooner or later! Please begin!"

And the Maddison Pickles needed no second invitation.

THE END.

155

BESSIE  BUNTER

At Cliff House School they say Bessie Bunter, the fat girl of the fourth, writes verse and worse! Still, Bessie's personality at least has the merit of promoting quite good poetry in others.

ODE TO A SKYLARK. By Bessie Bunter.

You pore bird, you do have to get up
Earlie in the morneing;
And then you sing sweete songes to me
When the day is dorning!
I orften wonder how you can climb
So highe up in the air;
The time that you have to get up
Is reely not fare.

Youre notes are bewtiful indeed;
I luv to hear yore mellerdy.
I lissened to you the other day—
I think it was larst Satterday.
I lissen to you, skylarke deer,
When you are in the sky,
And I wonder if you have a snack
Before you clime so high!

BESSIE BUNTER'S DREAM
BY BARBARA REDFERN.

Last lesson, girls, I could not keep
Myself from going off to sleep.
I dreamed that it had come to pass
That I was in a different class.

I noticed sitting next to me
The fattest girl you'd ever see!
She really was the largest size—
She hardly could see out her eyes!

" You poor, thin, skinny thing!" she said,
" This is the place where you'll be fed!
We're always in a happy mood
Surrounded by a lot of food.

" This school is fine, and I'll be bound
That it will suit you to the ground!
Because we do just what we please,
It's always called the ' School of Ease.' "

The mistress said : " We'll have a test
To see which girl can do the best.
Now, all join in, and make a start
On this tremendous treacle-tart!"

The other girls all seemed so small
That they had little chance at all.
The great fat girl just grabbed the lot,
And ate it up, although 'twas hot.

Arithmetic was splendid sport,
We counted food of every sort;
We ate the chairs—it was so funny,
I think they'd made them out of honey!

It really seemed quite like a fable
To find that we could eat the table.
They'd had the decency to make
The whole of marzipan and cake!

And, really, girls, what do you think?
We had ice-cream instead of ink;
I reached my pen to dig some out
Just when I heard a dreadful shout!

" Wake up, you idle, lazy thing!
One hundred lines to me you'll bring
Before you move outside the door!"
Now Bessie sleeps in class no more!

BESSIE BUNTER'S PROBLEM

By Katie Smith.

"I'd fifty twopenny cakes in town,
And sold off ten for half a crown;
I ate a dozen, gave one free,
And sold ten more for two-and-three.
I made a halfpenny profit, so
For what price did the others go?"
Poor Bessie Bunter's brow was glum.
She simply couldn't solve THAT *sum!*

The thought of eating cakes was nice;
She tried to work it once or twice.
But Bessie's efforts were not bright—
Her answers very far from right.
Arithmetic and algebra
Did not take Bessie very far,
And Bessie's brow grew still more glum.
How could a girl do SUCH *a sum?*

A sudden thought made Bessie stop.
She raced for Auntie Jones's shop,
And said that if she'd lend the cakes
She'd do it **in** a brace of shakes!
But Auntie's met our Bess before,
And firmly pointed to the door!
Poor Bessie's brow grew still more glum,
How was she now to solve the sum?

As Bessie went she stated that
She couldn't stand a jealous cat.
But Auntie Jones had nought to say,
So Bessie Bunter rolled away.
And, with an air of deepest gloom,
She joined us in the Common-room.
How could a girl be aught but glum
With such a very foolish sum?

"I say," said Bessie. "Half a tick!
Have all done your arithmetic?
Because I am the person who
Will solve that sum we have to do!
Just lend me fifty cakes, and I'll
Work out the thing in splendid style!"
Were Bessie Bunter's features glum
At that solution to her sum?

"See here!" said Bessie. "Listen, do!
I'm doing this for all of you!
I'll sell you twenty-two on trust,
And eat the dozen that I must!"
And then the pleased look left her face;
A roar of laughter filled the place!
Poor Bessie's brow grew dark and glum
To hear that we had SOLVED *the sum.*

The splendid offers Bessie makes
Did not produce the fifty cakes;
And, after having had her say,
She scowled at us and rolled away.
And then the kitchen she espied,
And, with a fat smile, rolled inside!
What need was there to be so glum
With SUCH *a means to solve her sum?*

In many things, I grieve to state,
Poor Bessie is unfortunate.
It was the Bull herself, in fact,
Who caught the fat girl in the act.
She took the cakes, gave her a fright,
    And several hundred lines to write.
    She left poor Bessie more than glum
    To think it was the Bull's OWN *sum!*

Now Bessie is a bit more quick
With problems in arithmetic.

ONLY A RUMOUR

By Mabel Lynn.

It was a winter's evening,
  And Bessie's work was done,
So she before the tuckshop door
  Was eating up a bun.

Although the bun was very plain,
  And looked so unexciting,
Her cash was spent on nourishment,
  And so—she kept on biting!

For you must understand that if
  You've got a splendid figure,
It's rash to fare alone on air,
  And think that you'll grow bigger.

But suddenly she gave a cry;
  'Twas heard by everyone.
The news went round that she **had** found
  A currant in her bun!

MIDNIGHT IN THE DORMITORY

By Clara Trevlyn.

What is this dreadful noise we hear,
That fills us with a trembling fear,
And draws from some a frightened tear?
  Sounds like a monster of the deep!

But stay! We are not near the sea;
'Tis something else, unknown to me,
Which roars in its ferocity,
  The while it waits to make its leap!

And yet, here in my quiet bed,
This thund'rous noise can rack my head;
Right near me is this thing of dread!
  I wish I had the pluck to peep!

In fear I've lain and listened while
It sounds in every noise and style.
Ah! Now I know, and I can smile—
  'Tis Bessie, snoring in her sleep!

A BITTER PILL, OH!

By Peggy Preston.

(*With apologies to " Tit-Willow."*)

A very fat girl is bemoaning her lot
  Of lessons, of lessons, of lessons;
She glares at her book and her unadded tot
  Of lessons, of lessons, of lessons.
She tries to subtract much from little, until
She feels she has had a lot more than her fill
  Of lessons, of lessons, of lessons.

A very fat girl, in a desperate state
  Of hunger, of hunger, of hunger;
Sketching poor victims all over her slate
  Of hunger, of hunger, of hunger.
She wishes in vain for some food for the brain—
Jam-tarts, cakes, or sweets to cure her bad pain
  Of hunger, of hunger, of hunger.

A very fat girl in a very low state
  Of money, of money, of money,
Is wroth that her pater's forgetful of late
  Of money, of money, of money!
She tries hard to borrow, but, much to her
    sorrow,
Her friends, too, expect a remittance to-morrow
  Of money, of money, of money!

THE

END

158

HOW TO MAKE
Dolls' Clothes and Furniture

ONE of the most fascinating pastimes imaginable is making dolls' clothes. For one thing, everything for dolls has to be made so tiny, and it is rather delightful, fashioning things on a small scale, isn't it, girls? And then, too, there is unlimited scope for the girl who would use her own ideas. Mother may not always let you have your own way with your own clothes, but you can develop original ideas that may occur to you, when you are making clothes for your doll.

There is nothing, perhaps, that is so disappointing as to find your dolly isn't dressed really nicely. Clothes that take off and on, eyes that shut, these are the two essentials, and really there is no reason at all why the former essential shouldn't be complied with. It may sound awfully hard, but in reality, all that is needed is a little patience, and you will find that buttonholing and button sewing will prove rather jolly, just because of the satisfaction you feel when you can take the things on and off.

To Make the Clothes

The little set of dolls' clothes illustrated below have clear diagrams that will enable you to cut them out correctly. First draw the pattern on a piece of paper, and get the proportions right, then cut out the paper pattern, and fit it on to the doll you are going to dress. By this you will be able to see whether you have cut the pattern large enough, before you actually cut into your material.

All three garments are easy enough to make. Join up the side seams of the tiny petticoat bodice, and edge the wee armholes and neck with a narrow scrap of lace, to give it a finish. The skirt is just a straight piece of material, edged with lace, or else a narrow embroidery flounce, simply gathered on to fit the width of the bodice. The fastenings should consist of the tiniest of tiny linen buttons, and loops also so that the little garment is easy to take on and off.

The frock is made in very much the same way, save that a tiny frilling

of your material will go round the neck, and at the end of each sleeve, in place of the lace, and also, the skirt of your frock is double flounced. The bottom flounce should be stitched on to the bodice first, and then the top flounce added, while a narrow width of velvet ribbon, in a contrasting shade to the material of which the frock is made, should make a pretty finish at the waist.

Last of all, you make the little cape. The little yoke diagram is given here, and the rest is merely a straight piece of material gathered on, with just the necessary fullness. Tiny slits should be made for armholes, and if possible edge these, and the yoke, as well as the bottom of the cloak with a narrow band of imitation beaver.

Millinery

Here is another dainty thing for a dolls' wardrobe, and really it is simplicity itself to make. Hats for dolls are always rather difficult to fashion, because they must necessarily be small, and on a small scale, it is hard to get a nice shape, but if you follow these directions, the charming little cloche shaped hat illustrated here will turn out very charmingly. It could be made up from one bundle of silk straw. Choose a soft pastel shade, and start at the top centre of crown, stitching the straw round and round until the crown fits the doll's head. Crown and brim are all-in-one, the latter being turned up or down from the face, as the taste desires.

Outline the narrow mushroom brim with tiny silken roses made from odd scraps of variegated silk, and finish at one side with a bunch of velvet bébé ribbon in the same shade as the straw. Allow the ends of this to fall on to the dress, and these will give the hat an added attraction.

If you are an ardent knitter, or are particularly fond of crochet, you may find that you would prefer to dress your doll in this type of garment, in preference to those made of ordinary material.

Here are some charming little ideas for knitted

Peter and I

TOLD BY ROVER THE COLLIE

CHAPTER I.

"I'LL TURN YOU INTO THE STREET!"

"COME on, Rover. Let's go and have a game in the garden!"

I put my ears back as I heard the merry tones of Ellen, my young mistress, and bounded off to obey her command. We had such a jolly game. The ball went over into the next-door garden several times, but I soon found it, though I rather think the lady who lives there was not very pleased at my frequent visits!

Lots of people think all animals are a nuisance. I'm quite sure none of you are like that, so I'll tell you a story.

First of all, perhaps, I had better tell you something about the family with whom I live and about myself.

My mistress is a widow—Mrs. Ferguson—and she has two children—Ellen, who is thirteen and a great chum of mine; and little Bobby, aged nine.

Bobby and I are very fond of one another, too, but we never play together, because—well, poor little Bobby is a cripple, and often, when other children are playing in the bright sunshine, Bobby Ferguson has to keep to his bed.

And what about myself? I'm just a collie dog. I'm a very lucky dog, I may tell you, for I have a good home and very kind people all round me, and what more can a dog wish for?

On the day when my story opens, little Bobby was not very well. His back had been hurting him a good deal, and he was lying quietly in bed while Ellen read to him.

I was sitting on the other side of the bed. Bobby had asked for me to be allowed to go into his room, as he often did when he was unwell.

"That's the end of the chapter, Bobby," said Ellen at length. "Would you like a change now? Let's have a game at something, shall we?"

Bobby turned his deep, blue eyes full on the bright face of his sister.

"I don't think I can sit up to play anything, Ellen," he answered her with a sigh. "I'm very sorry; it must be so dull for you sitting here with me hour after hour."

"I'd sooner be with you and mother than anywhere," said Ellen with a sweet smile. "Oh, Bobby, if only we were well-off so that mums could afford to send you to a great specialist to be cured. If daddy had not died——"

She broke off, and I noticed a tear stealing down her cheek. She turned her head hurriedly, so that Bobby should not see it, and resumed with a forced air of cheerfulness:

"Never mind, Bobby dear. Who knows? One day, perhaps, you'll be quite strong and well again and be able to run about like—like Rover!"

How I wagged my tail when I heard that! What sport Bobby and I could have, and what fine games the three of us could play!

But I sat down again when I thought how remote the prospect seemed. Little Bobby had been a cripple ever since I could remember, and many times have I seen Mrs. Ferguson come down stairs, after soothing him to sleep, crying bitterly when no one was there. Perhaps she thought I did not understand, but my heart ached for her and for the boy.

Let me tell you a little secret. Dogs, perhaps more than any other animals, can tell at once when a human being is sad, and it makes them feel sad, too, just as they bark and scamper and jump when they know that their human friends are happy.

At length, little Bobby dropped off to sleep, and Ellen and I went downstairs, being very careful not to make a noise.

"I'll get you a biscuit, Rover old boy," said Ellen softly to me; and I followed her into the kitchen, where my biscuits were kept.

Ellen got out the bag, and gave a little cry as she looked into it.

"Nearly all gone," she murmured to herself, "and I'm sure mums can't afford to buy any more at present!"

If only I could have made her understand that I could get on very well without biscuits! Instead of which, she turned to me with a wistful smile.

"Poor old boy," she said, "you don't get nearly enough nice things, I'm sure. But we really can't afford more, that's the reason."

I laughed, though probably it sounded to Ellen as though I had a cold. I've got the best home in the world, and I wouldn't change it for a king's palace.

The idea of her thinking that I needed more nice things seemed to me quite funny, though I appreciated her kindness none the less. However, I soon cheered Ellen up. I know one or two rather neat tricks that Ellen's father taught me when I was a puppy, and they never fail to make both Ellen and Bobby laugh.

I was in the middle of these when Ellen suddenly checked her mirth. She held up a finger, and, walking on tiptoe to the door, stood listening.

The sound of a man's voice came from the little drawing-room. It was not a pleasant voice. It was harsh and loud, the sort of voice that frightens little children—and little dogs, too!

Beckoning to me to follow her, Ellen led the way into the room where the man was seated, talking to her mother.

He was just the sort of man I expected to find there — very big and very fat. He looked about fifty and had scanty iron-grey hair. His face was forbidding and he seemed continually to be scowling either at other people or at his own thoughts.

He favoured me with a particularly black look as I walked quietly through the doorway at the heels of Ellen and sat down just against Mrs. Ferguson. Somehow, she seemed rather glad to see me there, for she stroked my ears—I like people to do that—and spoke to me in her customary gentle voice, so different from the grating tones of her visitor.

"Mother," said Ellen, crossing to her, "I must apologise to the gentleman for interrupting him, but I thought I had better tell you that Bobby is asleep and I am so afraid lest he should be awakened."

Mrs. Ferguson turned to the man.

"Bobby is my little boy, Mr. Isaacs," she explained. "He's a cripple and is not very well just now. He sleeps in the room above and is very easily awakened. I'm sure you'll understand."

The man's scowl deepened, if that were possible, as he answered Mrs. Ferguson.

"Sorry if my voice is a bit loud," he said. "But business is business, and I haven't much time to waste. Once again, Mrs. Ferguson, are you going to pay this debt, or aren't you?"

I looked up at my mistress, sitting very quietly there, and saw that her eyes filled with tears.

The man favoured me with a particularly black look as I walked through the doorway at the heels of Ellen

" I—I must ask you to wait a little longer, Mr. Isaacs," she murmured. " I'll pay you every penny as soon——"

" That's no good to me," interrupted the man, shrugging his shoulders. " I must have my money now, at once, or I'll have you sold up right away ! "

How I longed to nip his ankle. Half a word from my mistress and I would have done.

But she sat there as though stunned for a moment. Then she rose from her chair, her arms outstretched appealingly.

" Not—not that, please ! " she cried brokenly. " You wouldn't take what little I have left and turn me and my poor children into the streets without shelter—without a place to lay their dear heads."

The man rose suddenly to his feet, and, striding to the little table, banged his fist heavily on a piece of paper lying there.

" I can't help your troubles, ma'am," he snapped. " Your late husband owed me the money. This paper's proof of it, as I've already showed you, and unless you pay up I'll get the law's help to make you."

" But I can't pay now," began my mistress, tightly clasping Ellen, who had run to her, frightened by the man's threatening manner.

I didn't wait to hear any more, for an idea had suddenly struck me. I walked quietly from the room and sought out my friend Peter. I meant to spoil Mr. Isaac's little game, if possible !

CHAPTER II.

A SURPRISE FOR A BULLY !

PETER, I must tell you, is a very handsome black Persian cat. As a rule, I don't care much for cats, they seem to be able to do nothing but howl and scratch. But Peter's different. He's a real sport, and doesn't always want the warmest spot in front of the fire or the best bit of meat from the plate we share. Besides that, he's very intelligent, which is quite unusual in a cat— ask any dog, if you don't believe me !

Now, Peter and I have a little language of our own. Of course, human beings couldn't possibly understand us, but we get along very well with it.

" Peter, old chap," I said, when I came across him curled up in his box in the kitchen, " I'm sorry to disturb you, but there's trouble going on in the dining-room, and you and I can perhaps help Mrs. Ferguson and the children."

Peter was out of his box in a twinkling.

" What's wrong ? " he demanded, not even stopping to stretch himself.

I recounted the conversation I had heard between the strange man and Mrs. Ferguson.

" It seems to me that all the trouble centres round the piece of paper lying on the table," I added.

Peter looked at me and winked.

" Remove the cause and the trouble vanishes," he quoted sagely. " I've thought of a plan. Let's hurry, or the man will be gone—and the paper, too ! "

Without further delay we strolled back into the room as quietly as possible. Just as we crossed the threshold Mr. Isaacs was emphasising some remark with another thump on the table.

" Here's proof of the debt," he shouted, " and to-morrow the law shall be put in motion to have you turned out ! "

" That's the paper, Peter," I whispered. " Now's your chance."

" I'll waste no more time here," continued Mr. Isaacs, his face purple with anger.

" I'll—— Stop that animal ! " he yelled in the next breath, for good old Peter—I still laugh when I think of it—had sprung quickly and silently on to the table and, seizing the paper in his mouth, had bolted from the room as fast as he could run.

After him dashed the enraged visitor. Fat and heavy as he was, he might as well have tried to catch a fox in full cry.

" Come back, Peter ! " cried Mrs. Ferguson, as the Persian dashed out of the house.

We all followed, and just as we got to the back door there was Peter scrambling along the roof of an outhouse and well out of reach.

It was bright moonlight, or Mr. Isaacs would never have seen him. As for Mrs. Ferguson, I don't think she particularly wanted to catch him, nor did Ellen, whose blue eyes were bright with excitement.

" A ladder, quick ! A ladder ! " almost screamed the fat man, dancing with rage. " I must have that paper ! "

" There's a ladder in that shed," answered Mrs. Ferguson, " though I don't think it is very safe."

But, unheeding the warning, Mr. Isaacs rushed to the shed, and dragged out a long, rickety ladder which he found there. He reared it against the side of the coal-house and commenced to climb on to the roof after Peter.

At last the opportunity for which I had longed all the evening had come. I wasted no time, but rushed at him just as he had mounted the first three or four steps, and seized the leg of his trousers between my teeth.

Wildly he kicked out, and the additional strain proved too much for the ancient ladder. Crack ! went the half-rotten woodwork, and smack on the ground fell Mr. Isaacs, right in a puddle of water !

" I think you had better give up the chase,"

suggested Mrs. Ferguson quietly, as he struggled to his feet and shook his great fist at me.

Fortunately, he contented himself with that, or there would have been more trouble. I was just ready for a fight!

We returned into the house. There was nothing else to be done, for Peter had long since disappeared, and I guessed he would not return for some time.

"I'm very sorry, Mr. Isaacs," said Mrs. Ferguson, with just the suspicion of a smile about her mouth, when we got back into the dining-room once more. "I don't repudiate the debt, but again I must ask you to wait a little while for your money."

Mr. Isaacs turned angrily to her.

"You'll sign another paper to replace the one your cat has stolen before I leave this house," he blustered "or I shall fetch the police."

"I shall do nothing of the sort," answered Mrs. Ferguson with quiet dignity "I have promised that you shall be paid, and you must take my word for it."

"Your word! What good 's that to me," began the man sneeringly ; but Mrs. Ferguson checked him with a gesture.

"Stop, Mr. Isaacs!" she said, in such a tone that, bully as he was, he held his peace. "I will not be insulted by you, and unless you go at once, it will be I who will send for the police," she added, pointing to the door.

Peter, with the paper in his mouth, had bolted from the room

And, by way of emphasis, I growled my very loudest, and rose to my feet.

Mr. Isaacs knew he was beaten. All bullies are cowards at heart, and he was no exception to the rule. Without another word he snatched up his hat and umbrella, and a moment later the slamming of the front-door told of his departure.

Then my mistress, brave as she was, sat down and cried, while Ellen did her best to comfort her.

"Don't cry, mother dear," she pleaded soothingly. "Everything will come all right in the end. "We'll never want for friends while we've got dear old Peter and Rover."

And she kneeled down and flung her arms round my neck and kissed me. I felt very well repaid, I assure you, for my modest share in the discomfiture of Mr. Isaacs.

Mrs. Ferguson dried her eyes as she patted my head.

Just then a plaintive cry came from upstairs.

"Mummy, mummy, what's the matter? Do come upstairs."

It was little Bobby's voice.

"Oh, dear, how long has he been calling," Mrs. Ferguson exclaimed, starting to her feet. "That horrid man has wakened him. Come up with me, Ellen dear."

For once I invited myself into little Bobby's bedroom along with my mistress and Ellen. "What's the matter, dear?" cried Mrs. Ferguson, running to the bedside. "Are you feeling worse, my darling?"

"No, no, mummy," was Bobby's reassuring response.

"I was waked up by such a loud bang—I thought it was burglars, perhaps."

Mrs. Ferguson smiled wistfully.

"Nothing so terrible, Bobby dear," she said. "It—it was only a man who wanted some money, and I—I hadn't got it, that's all!"

The smile faded from her careworn face.

"And he threatened to turn us out of the house and sell our furniture!" exclaimed Ellen, in a voice full of indignation.

"Turn us out?" repeated little Bobby, who did not understand that such a thing was possible —that men could be so cruel. "Oh, mummy, whatever will happen to us?"

Ellen saw that she had alarmed her little brother, and hastened to comfort him.

"Don't worry, Bobby," she said, kissing him tenderly. "It's all right now. He'll have to wait for his money, thanks to Peter."

"Our cat, do you mean?" asked Bobby, thoroughly surprised.

"Yes, darling old Peter," answered Ellen; "he ran off with a piece of paper that the man has to have to prove that mother owes him the money. Oh, it was such fun!"

She launched off into an account of all that had occurred, and little Bobby laughed so heartily that Mrs. Ferguson began to think he would hurt himself.

' It almost seemed as if Peter knew exactly what all the talk was about," she said. " You know he has a habit of seizing anything if you point to it or bang your hand on it——"

" Daddy taught him that," interrupted little Bobby. " Didn't he ? "

" Yes, darling!" answered Mrs. Ferguson sadly.

The mention of her husband caused the smile to fade from her face. She pulled herself together—brave once more—for her children's sake.

" And now, dear, you really must go to bed," she said at length, turning to Ellen. " It's quite time we were all in bed and fast asleep."

" Right, mums," Ellen answered promptly. " I don't want to go one little bit, but I will, because I'd like to get up and go for a run with Rover in the morning."

Affectionate " good-nights " were said, and the house was soon in darkness. As I lay dozing in the kitchen I wondered what had become of Peter. What had he done with that important piece of paper ? I hoped he had hidden it so that it would never be found again.

CHAPTER III.

MORE ALLIES

NEXT day Ellen and I went early in the garden to play. First of all, Ellen fed her pet rabbits, of which she had four, and her guinea-pig.

Now, the only rabbits I care much about are those you see scampering about the fields. It's great fun to chase them, and I must admit they're very swift-footed, and very knowing.

However, Ellen seemed very fond of her pets, so I tolerated them for her sake. I rather liked the guinea-pig. He was such a sharp-looking fellow, and always very friendly in his manner towards me.

We were just moving away from the hutches, when Ellen saw a piece of paper lying on the ground near by. She picked it up, and looked at it closely. What she saw caused her to give an exclamation of surprise.

" Goodness ! " she said. " Here's a bit of the paper that Peter ran off with last night. I wonder where the rest of it is ? "

I'm almost sure I saw one of the rabbits wink at me as she said this, and as for the guinea-pig—he grinned quite openly. I looked carefully through the wire-netting of the hutch, and saw something that confirmed my suspicions. It was another piece of paper !

Ellen saw it, too, and quickly got it out of the hutch.

" Oh, " she cried, delightedly clapping her hands together, " they've eaten the rest ! Ha, ha, ha ! You dear bunnies and you, my darling piggy, you shall have something very nice for your dinners to-day."

I barked my appreciation, and Ellen, with a beaming face, turned to me.

" Come on, old fellow," she cried, " let's go and burn this piece, and tell mother all about it ! "

And off we scampered.

Mrs. Ferguson laughed heartily when she heard Ellen's story, and just then who should stroll in but Peter. He said " Good-morning!" in his quaint little purring voice, just as though nothing had happened.

And what a fuss they made of him ! At first he pretended that it was all a very great bore being hugged and kissed and petted like that. But I knew that was only his pose. Peter's an artful one sometimes, as I know from experience.

" You managed things very well, my boy," I said to him as soon as I got a chance to have a quiet word with him under the table.

" It was too easy for anything," he answered airily, leisurely smoothing back his somewhat luxurious whiskers. " The only difficulty was to know what to do with the paper when I had secured it."

" And the rabbits and Percy, the guinea-pig, helped you over that problem," I interrupted.

" How did you know that ? " asked Peter, pausing in the act of washing his right ear.

" They left one scrap of paper in the hutch and another bit fell on the ground," I said. " No good to anyone, of course, but just enough to let us know where the rest was ! "

Peter grinned until I thought his mouth would never stop widening, and when I told him what had happened afterwards to Mr. Isaacs, he just gurgled with merriment.

Mrs. Ferguson's voice came to our ears just then, and what we heard checked our mirth at once.

" It's no use, Ellen," she was saying very slowly. " I shall have to sell some of the furniture to pay Mr. Isaacs even part of the debt I owe him. The little I have coming in makes it impossible to put anything by. Perhaps, later on, when you're grown up, dear——"

" Oh, mums, let me go out and work now. I could earn something to help you, I'm sure," pleaded Ellen earnestly.

" No, no, dear ! " was the instant reply. " You do help me now both in the house and with my dressmaking. I do so want you to continue at school as long as possible. We'll manage—we must manage somehow, dear."

"It's a shame, mums, that you should be worried so," said Ellen, putting her arm round her mother's neck and giving her a resounding kiss.

Mrs. Ferguson smoothed her daughter's luxuriant golden hair. "I've much to be thankful for," she answered, "I've got you and little Bobbie, and you're worth more to me than all the gold in the world. Your daddy would never have owed a farthing if he hadn't been ill. One day, perhaps, our luck will change and all our little troubles will be ended."

And, curiously enough, Mrs. Ferguson's words were to find a strange response much sooner than she expected.

CHAPTER IV.

A WELCOME VISITOR THIS TIME!

IT was a few days later that the most interesting part of my story occurred.

I had accompanied Ellen to school, some distance away from her home. You've all read of a girl named Mary who had a pet lamb which went to school with her, haven't you?

Now, I often went to school with Ellen, but, unlike Mary's lamb, I did not go into the school and create a disturbance. I always said "Good-bye" at the gate, and made my way leisurely homewards.

On this particular day I decided to go through the park that lay between the school and Ellen's home. It was a glorious morning, and I thoroughly enjoyed my walk, though I felt quite sorry for Ellen having to stay in a room and do lessons.

Sometimes I'm rather glad I'm only a dog!

I was about half-way across the park when I noticed a gentleman sitting resting in the sun. He was well dressed and had such a good-natured face. Nothing of the Mr. Isaacs about him, I thought.

Just then he saw me, and called out to me.

"Hallo, old chap," he said, "whose dog are you?"

I knew at once he was a friend, and I wagged my tail. He stroked my head and patted me gently, and then I felt him touching my collar.

"Good gracious!" I heard him exclaim suddenly. "Ferguson! Surely it can't be—— Oh, if only dogs could talk!"

Dogs can't talk, but they understand what is said to them. I looked up at him and wagged my tail more furiously than ever, to try to tell him this.

"Where do you live, old fellow?" he said. "I will follow you home. I suppose I shall be disappointed, but it's a clue worth following up."

He got up and walked along with me, talking alternatively to me and to himself.

When we came to the cross-roads he hesitated and said, "Which way

"Hullo, old chap!" he called out. And as I went up to him he patted my head and said: "Whose dog are you?"

167

now, old fellow?" And he followed the road I took without question.

At last we reached Mrs. Ferguson's trim little house.

"It's very small," I heard him utter, "but so clean-looking. Just how I should expect Kate's house to be kept."

He walked up the little garden path and knocked gently at the door.

A moment later Mrs. Ferguson's step sounded in the tiny hall, and the door was opened.

For a second or two Mrs. Ferguson and her visitor just stared at one another. Then my friend flung out his arms impulsively.

"Kate!" he cried. "Is it—is it really you, my dear sister?"

He stepped across the threshold, and the next minute Mrs. Ferguson was sobbing in his arms.

"John!" she murmured. "How did you find me after all these years?"

They were seated in the little dining-room, where I had followed them, and John told his sister how he had come to England from South Africa a few weeks before, and had remembered the town where his sister lived, but had no further idea of her address.

"I determined to search until I found you," he said, "and this morning fate led me to you."

And he described how he had met me in the park and, seeing the name Ferguson on my collar, had followed me home in the hopes that he would find his sister.

"I'm a rich man now, Kate," he finished. "I've a splendid farm out in South Africa. I felt I should like to see you and Alec and England again before I got too old."

Tears came into Mrs. Ferguson's eyes.

"Alec died last year," she murmured brokenly.

"My poor Kate!" sympathised her brother. "I—I am indeed grieved to hear this. But you had some children, had you not?"

"Yes, two," answered Mrs. Ferguson, wiping her eyes, and endeavouring to smile. "Ellen's at school, and little Bobby is in bed. He—he's a cripple, you know."

"Do take me to the little fellow," asked the gentleman eagerly. "I am longing to see him, and Ellen, too."

We all went upstairs, and Mrs. Ferguson softly opened the door of Bobbie's bedroom.

"Bobbie," she said, "whom do you think has come to see you?"

"Dunno," said Bobby practically. "I hope it's not Mr. Isaacs."

Mrs. Ferguson had to laugh.

"Oh, no," she answered. "It's your uncle John from South Africa. I've told you about him lots of times."

"Uncle John!" cried Bobby, greatly excited.

"Oh, Rover, it's the uncle what lives among black men and goes hunting lions and tigers and—and ostriches!"

Uncle John stepped into the room and roared with laughter.

"The very same, Bobby," he cried, "though they are nearly always ostriches, and quite harmless."

And in a few minutes Bobby's face was shining with happiness, while Uncle John told him tales of his early days in South Africa and of his adventures "up country" on hunting expeditions. It seemed to me that South Africa must be a fine place for a dog to live.

At lunch time, Ellen came home from school, and Uncle John promptly hid in the kitchen.

"Ellen," said Mrs. Ferguson, when their greetings were over, "there's somebody wants to see you in the kitchen. Go in, will you?"

"Wants to see me?" said Ellen incredulously. "Whoever is it?"

"Go and see," repeated her mother smilingly.

"Come with me, Rover," Ellen called out as she walked slowly into the kitchen.

She looked round, but could see nobody there, and she was just about to walk out again when a deep voice hailed her.

She looked round, and saw a man's face, wreathed in smiles, peering from behind the pantry door.

"Hallo, Ellen my dear!" said the man, coming out from his hiding place. "Aren't you going to kiss me? I'm your Uncle John!"

I could see that Ellen liked him the moment she saw his beaming, kindly face, and now she did not hesitate.

With a glad cry, she ran forward, and was lifted right off the ground in a great loving hug that left her almost breathless. I barked so loudly that I got quite hoarse.

"Oh, uncle," she exclaimed at length, "I'm so glad it's you—I thought it was Mr. Isaacs at first."

Uncle John looked wonderingly at his sister, who had followed us into the little kitchen.

"Who on earth is this Mr. Isaacs?" he demanded.

"Only—only a man who came on business the other night!" stammered Mrs. Ferguson, going very red.

"A horrid man, he was!" chimed in Ellen; and, before Mrs. Ferguson could prevent her, she had told Uncle John what had happened.

Uncle John's face became very grave as he listened.

"Is this right, Kate?" he asked his sister. "Why didn't you tell me about it?"

"I—I didn't want to bother you with my troubles," began Mrs. Ferguson tremulously.

"Bother me, indeed!" interrupted her brother, crossing to her and placing an arm affectionately round her shoulders. "My dear, I'm very glad little Ellen has told me. I'm going to put everything right for you now."

I began to feel quite excited when I heard this, and so did Ellen.

"You darling uncle!" she exclaimed rapturously. "Stay with us always, won't you?"

Uncle John smiled.

"That's just what I was going to say to your mother, my dear," he answered.

Mrs. Ferguson looked at him wonderingly.

"What—what do you mean, John?" she asked.

"Just this," answered Uncle John. "I've got to go back to my farm in South Africa, of course, and I want all of you to come with me! I haven't a wife and family of my own, and I shall be very, very glad to have you, my dear sister, and the children."

Mrs. Ferguson hardly knew what to say at first, but a further talk convinced her that Uncle John's offer was too good to be refused.

As for me, I hardly knew whether to feel happy or miserable. I felt happy for their sakes, of course, but I wondered if it meant that Peter and I would have to say good-bye to them for ever.

"No," I said to myself, "I'll go to Africa, too, even if I have to swim all the way."

"The sea voyage will do little Bobby no end of good," said Uncle John, "and, when you have all settled down comfortably in your new home, I'll have the best medical skill in South Africa, and if he can be cured—he shall be!"

"Doesn't that sound fine?" I asked, turning to Peter, who had strolled into the room a few moments before.

And what a dejected Peter I saw!

His tail swept the ground, and his handsome whiskers drooped mournfully.

"I'm glad for their sakes, of course," he said miserably, "and you'll be all right; but who'll want to be bothered taking a cat all the way to South Africa?"

"Cheer up, old fellow!" I answered, though, to tell the truth, I had hard work not to share Peter's gloominess.

.   .   .   .   .

How happy they all were that evening! Ellen and little Bobby were radiant with excitement, and Uncle John kept them in roars of laughter with his tales.

"Uncle John," said Ellen at length, going up to his chair and putting her soft little arms round his neck, "I've got a question to ask you."

"What is it, dear?" said Uncle John, looking up.

"What about Rover, and Peter, and the rabbits, and—Percy?" murmured Ellen shyly. "I—I don't think I could go away and leave them here, uncle."

I sat very still and listened. What would Uncle John's answer be?

He looked at her affectionately.

"I'm glad to hear you say that, dear," he answered. "I like girls and boys who think of dumb animals. Well, supposing I say that they can come with us, too?"

"Oh, uncle!" cried Ellen and Bobby together.

And they hugged Peter and me alternately for the rest of the evening.

"I think they've earned a good home for the rest of their days," continued Uncle John, while Mrs. Ferguson nodded in hearty agreement.

"And they shall have one," he added. "I think they're——"

But modesty forbids my telling you what Uncle John said about us. I will just mention, in conclusion, that the happiness of our beloved mistress, and of Ellen and little Bobby, more than repaid us for the little we had been able to do to help them in their time of trouble.

THE   END

169

The "Lone" Guide!

An Amusing Little Story of a Camping-Out Party

"GWEN! Just a minute, please!"

Miss Sinclaire, standing at the entrance of the store-tent, addressed these words to Gwendoline Hutchings of the Fourth Form.

All the girls comprising the camping party from Grandcliffe School—with three exceptions—were clustered near the store-tent when the mistress called. They were dressed in Guide uniforms, and Gwen was mapping out the afternoon's programme for a guiding expedition across country.

The three absentees—Priscilla Havant and her cronies, Ailsa Lack and Henrietta Stubbs—affected a supreme indifference for the Grandcliffe Girl Guides, and "slacked" whenever possible.

It was seldom Ailsa and Henrietta moved far from their leader, but to-day Priscilla was deserted and had No. 2 tent to herself.

"Yes, Miss Sinclaire?" said Gwen.

"A little matter has arisen which necessitates Miss Green and myself spending the day in the village," announced the mistress. "The camp will consequently be under your command, Gwen, until we return. There are things we shall need while we are away"—Gwen followed the sweep of her arm, and saw some heavy-looking bundles lying about the floor of the tent—"and I must ask you to see that they are brought on to us this afternoon."

"Certainly, Miss Sinclaire."

"As these bundles are rather heavy," continued Miss Sinclaire, "I have arranged with the people at the farm to place a small dog-cart at your disposal. It will be round in half an hour's time. One moment, and I will give you our address in the village."

Gwen took the address and moved rather dejectedly out of the tent. The girls saw her emerge and clustered round her.

"Well, Gwen?" came the eager chorus.

"Off!" said Gwen briefly. "The guiding's off for me, at any rate."

And she explained. Everyone's sympathies went out to her at once.

"Well, we're not going off on any merry jaunt without you!" said Clarissa Smythe emphatically. "We'll stay and help."

"Now, Clarissa, don't be silly!" said Gwen quickly. "You go and enjoy yourselves."

"Gwen! I say!"

Martha Watson spoke. There was a twinkle in Martha's eyes, and it was clear that she had just been struck by something in the way of an inspiration.

"I say, Gwen, as the guiding's off for you—and, therefore, for me—could we lighten our burden by getting a little help? You know, there's Priscilla slacking the afternoon away in No. 2 tent."

Gwen looked at her doubtfully.

"If you mean that Priscilla would help us with the bundles——"

"She wouldn't!" said Martha promptly. "But I've got an idea for making her!"

"Go on, Martha. What's your idea?"

"Well, Priscilla hates us Guides like anything! We know for a fact she'd do anything to give us a set-back. But what she'd like most of all is to prove that she, who isn't a Guide, is of more use to the community than ourselves who are Guides."

"And your idea?" asked Clarissa.

"My idea," said Martha calmly, "is that Gwen and I should disguise ourselves as gipsies. We can borrow some clothes at the farm-house. Let Priscilla see us enter the store-tent, come out with those bundles, and drive off in the dog-cart. She will follow, naturally. We could take her ever such a long way round to the village—until she's tired out, in fact—and finally leave the bundles at their destination. It will be about the worst take-in Priscilla's ever experienced!"

"Jolly good, Martha!" ejaculated Clarissa, clapping her on the back. "However did you think of it? So you'll get some sort of guiding, after all, Gwen."

"But that's not all," said Martha hurriedly. "When we reach the house, we can still keep up the part of gipsies. Priscilla will be on the watch, and will at once jump to the conclusion that the house is a depot for stolen goods. She will call in assistance, and will finally find herself in the biggest bowl of soup she's ever known!"

Gwen shook her head at that step.

"We can't——" she began.

But Martha was all enthusiasm.

"It's just the thing—just the kind of thing I've been wanting!" she insisted. "Think of the part I'll have to play, Gwen dear! I'm badly in want of practice—you know how I love acting! Oh, do agree, Gwen, there's a dear!"

Imploring from her dearest chum was not to be resisted, and Gwen, with a laugh, gave way.

. . . .

"This way, Flo! Nobody about, there ain't!"

The cracked female voice floated in at the entrance of No. 2 tent.

Priscilla started up, the book she had been reading falling from her lap.

Peering out, her eyes blinking a little in the sunlight after the shadiness of the tent, she saw two stealthy forms moving away in the direction of the store-tent. Both were women, rather bent — apparently with age — and dressed in the gaudy, slipshod fashion of the gipsies.

"Good gracious!" muttered Priscilla. "They're going into the store-tent!"

She bit her lip, and was at a sheer loss as to what to do next.

As to getting help, she knew full well that the other two tents were deserted. She had seen the Guides set off across country, and, in secret, had envied them, though she wouldn't have admitted that for worlds. But, of course, she had not heard that the mistress had left camp for the day.

Priscilla was no coward, and, no doubt, had she heard anything like a shriek proceed from the store-tent, she would have darted at once to the rescue.

But there was no need for that. The two

Stealthily she followed in their wake

gipsies reappeared fairly quickly, staggering under heavy bundles.

"Lucky it was empty, Flo!" grated the same voice again; and nobody could have recognised the tones as Martha Watson's. "Saves a lot of explanation, don't it?"

"Yus; we can do the job quietly now!" husked the other "woman" carelessly.

"Ugh!" muttered Priscilla.

She felt rather sick after this, but her eyes showed a peculiar glimmer. As Martha had predicted, she was bent on scoring off the Guides, and would show them what a non-Guide could do.

She would be an unofficial Guide for the day!

Keeping a wary distance behind, Priscilla shadowed the laden pair across the fields to the main road, where they dumped their bundles into a waiting dog-cart.

She saw their faces as they mounted. They were yellow and lined. Priscilla shuddered involuntarily.

The dog-cart got going at a rattling pace. Priscilla had to run to keep it in sight. It appeared at first to be making a bee-line for the village, but it suddenly swerved to the left.

Priscilla, puffing and panting, contrived to keep the cart within sight as it travelled through a maze of country roads. She had completely lost her whereabouts, and, to tell the truth, it was taking Gwen all her time to understand the route she was following. Priscilla had already lost one of her shoes along the road, but, gritting her teeth, she kept on.

The dog-cart at last stopped, and the pair of gipsies hobbled down from it into the lane. In true gipsy fashion they seated themselves on the step, and commenced to talk, and Priscilla's eyes glittered with curiosity and exultation as she watched them from the distance.

"What are they talking about? Some further plans for robbing people, as sure as anything!" she muttered, nibbling her nails

"I am fearful of these paths, mistress!" murmured Judith, looking about her with timorous glances. "Those who travel to Nottingham have ever reason to be, for sorry tales have I heard of outlawry and violence in these seemingly peaceful glades!"

A ringing laugh echoed a-down the way by which they had come, and a sparkle of mischief came into the eyes of the girl who a few moments since had been addressed as Mistress Marian.

"By St. Boewulf, Judith!" she breathed through parted lips that showed her pearly teeth, "I do believe that you are afeared!"

She raised a mocking finger.

"Courage, Judith—courage!" she laughed gaily. "A truce to fear."

Judith flushed rosily.

"So many stories have been told of outlaws that infest Sherwood, mistress!" retorted the girl in respectful tones, "that I have learnt to fear the forest and those green jerkined hinds who infest it!"

Judith paused.

"In Nottingham they say that with their long bows they can split an apple in twain at fifty paces, and that they are even a match for any knight, however heavily armoured!"

Judith glanced down the forest aisles and then again at her mistress, whose fair hair the sun, streaming through the leafy awning above, was glorifying until it gleamed like gold.

"Ay, a match for Prince John's knights!" said Mistress Marian scoffingly. "I doubt that not; a match for stay-at-homes like Lord de Percy and Sir Bohun de Lys. Faint-hearted knights who remain to toady to a cowardly Prince while Richard takes the banner of England to the Crusades!"

The girl sighed.

"It is for King Richard's sake that I would fain find a way out of this maze," she added, "for in my wallet I bear a letter of warning to one who calls himself the 'Black Knight'—a knight who guards those interests of our King against the time of his return to guard that which is his own!"

Judith shook her head.

"They say he will never return!" she murmured gloomily. "And I was cautioned by

"Courage, Judith, courage!" cried Maid Marian

your father to haste ye to Nottingham because of that; he fears the consequences when Prince John is named for King!"

A shade passed across Maid Marian's face.

"Richard of England lives!" she murmured. "They have misinformed my father; it is a plan of Prince John's to snatch a throne he will so sadly fill!"

She had barely finished speaking when, with startling suddenness, the silvery note of a hunting-horn rang through the glade.

Judith's lips trembled, and she turned quickly to her mistress, and as she did so upon the ears of both of them there came a loud cry of rage and the heavy trampling of a horse's hoofs.

"The sound came from yonder path!" cried Maid Marian, nor did she hesitate now, but, turning her gentle palfrey's head, she urged the beautiful animal into a gallop.

The low hanging branches of the beech-trees brushed her hair as she rode, but of this she took no notice as she swung into the forest path that ran off at right angles from the one on which she had been travelling.

And as she came into that path, it was to see a sight that sent anger into her eyes.

Standing with his back to a tree, a fallen bow at his feet, was a youth of about her own age. His face was white, but unafraid.

It was not the sight of the lad that angered her, but of that other, a knight, who, seated on his war-horse, its sides as heavily armoured as himself, held his couched lance at the breast of the lad.

"The swan helm!"

A cry of indignation followed the words for in a moment she had recognised the helm of the mailed knight who, with vizor down, was preparing to pin the green-jerkined lad to the tree against which the lance had forced him.

"Say your prayers now, Saxon churl!" boomed a deep voice from behind the vizor. "How dared ye to shoot at a deer that crossed the path of a knight!"

The lad did not answer. A calm smile played about his lips, and it was evident that the smile annoyed the knight, for the lance was thrust forward until its sharp point pierced the loose green jerkin that the boy was wearing.

Marian had taken everything in at a glance— the green cap with the heron's feather in it, the fallen bow, and the steel-clad figure of the swan helm whom she knew to be none other than the Lord de Bercy, friend of the Sheriff of Nottingham, and a knight noted for cruelty to the harmless and cowardice in the tourney.

"Hold!" she cried as, raising her hand, she dashed towards the knight.

The sudden interruption caused de Bercy to turn and as he did so his lance, momentarily lowered, afforded just space enough for the lad to slip away from its threatening point, which he did with a gay laugh on his lips.

And so quick and agile was he that he found time also to retrieve his long bow and his quiver of arrows.

An angry exclamation came to the lips of De Bercy as Maid Marian laughed into his vizored eyes.

"The churl has gone—gone just as I was about to reward him for his insolence!" he fumed, raising his vizor with his mailed fist.

Marian laughed mockingly.

"One would think, my lord, that there was more valiant work to be done than that of attacking a mere lad!" she cried.

He glowered at her.

"It pleases you to scoff at me, Mistress Marian!" he said. "No doubt what you have said will interest my friend the Sheriff of Nottingham, into whose charge, so he informed me, you have been placed by your father!"

Maid Marian drew herself up.

"If my father follows the true Cross to the Crusades it is to teach a lesson to those who idle at home!" she answered.

De Bercy laughed sarcastically and, wheeling his horse, thundered away, crying mockingly over his shoulder as he did so.

"Good speed, Maid Marian, I go to prepare the Sheriff for your coming!"

Maid Marian watched him go, trying to determine the direction that he had taken; but he dashed off so suddenly, and now had come the interruption of Judith's precipitate arrival, that she could not follow the path by which he was returning. The fact was borne down on her that they were no nearer finding the right path than they had been before.

Judith's face was almost livid with fear.

"Did you not act too hastily, mistress?" she asked quickly. "De Bercy is powerful, you have made an enemy of him, and now we are alone in the forest his protection would have saved us from alarm!"

Maid Marian laughed softly.

"I want not the protection of such as he!" she said; and she would have spoken again had not a strange happening interrupted her words.

With dramatic suddenness the little glade had become filled with green jerkined figures, and, casting a timorous glance behind her, Judith saw that her mistress and herself were entirely surrounded.

"Why, the caitiff has gone, Robin!"

Now, as Marian, her eyes filled with

De Bercy's lance, momentarily raised, just afforded space enough for the lad to slip away from its threatening point

in the great hall there seemed to be triumph on the face of my Lord of Nottingham, and I saw De Bercy's eyes gloating with an expectancy of great honours in the near future!"

Marian lowered her voice to a whisper.

"And more than that!" she added. "Prince John is expected, and to-day five knights have ridden in with their men at arms. I know that something is untoward, but what that something is I cannot say!"

"It is not hard to imagine!" said Judith. "The mystery of King Richard's disappearance gives Prince John new hopes!"

"Yes, yes; that must be it!" said Maid Marian, almost impatiently. And she stepped back.

"Tell me, Judith, with the hood up, will they recognise me?"

Judith shook her head.

"We are of a height, mistress," she answered. "You should pass unobserved."

"Pray St. Boewulf that I may," said Marian fervently. "Now get ye to the door, Judith, and see if the passage is free of eavesdroppers."

Judith ran to the door, and, unlocking it, opened the heavy oak portal and looked without.

The corridor was empty, and the only sound that came to her ears was the distant tread of a man-at-arms. She waited until his tread had died away in the distance, and then she looked back at her mistress.

"Now!" she murmured. "Now."

Maid Marian did not wait. Slipping the hood over her head she ran out into the passage, along it, and to the stone staircase that led to where the portcullis exit and the drawbridge lay.

It was here that Judith's sentry would be.

On the last step Marian paused and glimpsed the erect figure of the sentry. He was standing resting on his spear, his eyes looking keenly over the drawbridge, which, to Maid Marian's relief, was still down, although dusk had fallen.

With one glance to either side of her she ran towards the sentry, her head lowered, her hood concealing her face.

"Now—ho, there—whither away?"

Marian laughed softly and, coming nearer to the man, whispered:

"It is my mistress, she complains of a megrim, and I go to an apothecary in the town to procure herbs!"

The man smiled.

"Then haste away!" he whispered, "Tell none that I let ye go, for we have had orders concerning your mistress."

Marian's face paled as she heard the words, but she did not show the surprise that she felt, nor did she hesitate. In a flash she was tripping across the drawbridge and making hot foot for the western bastion of the castle.

But keener eyes than those of the sentry saw her go, the eyes of a hunchback named Simon the Jester, but better known as Simon the Spy.

Slipping a cloak about his shoulders, and making sure that his sword was ready at his side, he darted to where, by the gate of the western bastion, lay the guard-house and captain of the guard.

And Marian recked not that she had been observed as she sped along.

To her left the green depths of the broad moat shone beneath the rays of the young moon, and in the distance she could see the fringe of the forest.

Now, as she ran, there loomed up in front of her the massive fortifications of the western bastion.

She paused, searching for direction. And now she saw, silhouetted out against the moonlight and the black forest behind it, a white and withered oak-tree.

"Will he be there?"

Loosening the letter in her wallet, she sped towards the ruined object, and now she was beneath its spectre-like branches—and she was alone!

There was no sign of the black knight, nor of any other living soul save herself!

But stay, even as she thought that her mission was fruitless, from behind her there came a rustle in the trees, and now, turning, she saw a tall and motionless figure standing at the edge of the forest.

The moon was full on him, and for the moment she fancied that this must be some ghost, for so still and solemnly he stood, and there was not a movement of either leg, arm, or head.

His suit of mail was as black as the riven night, and his helm possessed no feather or sign of his knighthood, although the golden spurs that he wore betokened his rank.

Belted to his side by a black velvet band was a great sword, that all but touched the ground.

His vizor was down, but Marian was conscious of keen eyes that watched her every movement.

And now, as she watched him, and with an impressive clank of chain mail, he came slowly forward.

"What want you of the Black Knight?" he asked in deep tones behind his vizor.

Marian trembled. But now, realising that this was the knight she sought and no spectral figure, she drew out the letter.

"I bear this letter to you," she said softly and quickly, "It is from Jaquelin de Henricourt to King Richard of England, and your mission is to bear it to our King!"

From behind the vizor there came a strange laugh, a laugh that died as quickly as it had come, and then the armoured hand folded like a vice over the missive.

"That command shall be obeyed," came the deep answer. "And you, fair maid, your name, and from whence you came?"

"From Nottingham Castle," answered Maid Marian, wonder in her tones, "I am known as Marian—Marian de Montfort."

"A loyal name!" came the deep words. "But you come from a strange castle. Stay," he added, "I will read this note!"

Opening the envelope, he read the few

Turning, Maid Marian saw a tall and motionless figure standing at the edge of the forest

words that the missive apparently contained, and then he turned again to her.

"It would be well for this to be destroyed," he said, "and for me to bear the message to King Richard!"

He came nearer to her.

"In the interests of Richard of England," he said, "tell me who rode in to Nottingham to-day. Who came armed for war?"

Marian did not hesitate.

"Sir Bohun de Lys, Sir Marechal de Chavannes, the Baron Lacy, Lord de Bercy, and Aladine St. Vrayne!"

The Black Knight nodded grimly.

"It is well!" he answered. "You have done King Richard a great service and you have taken a great risk, for times are perilous and danger is ahead, One service yet can ye do for Richard of England, an ye will, fair Marian!"

"I will do aught you ask me," she whispered, intensely.

For a moment he was silent whilst, with slow significance, he withdrew one of his steel gauntlets, and then, slipping off the other, took from his finger a small gold ring set with a single stone.

"Bear this to one Robin Hood," he said quickly. "Or, if you cannot bear it yourself, have it conveyed to him—he is of the forest, an outlaw. Send this ring or take it to him; he will understand the urgency of its meaning!"

Marian would have questioned him, for the mention of Robin's name had brought surprise into her face; but there was no time. With a bow, the tall figure in the black mail had turned, and now, as she looked, he was lost to view in the forest.

A moment later, and striking mysteriously upon her ears, there came the thunder of a horse's hoofs.

"Gone——"

She turned, and as she did so a cry of fear came to her lips, for there, rushing towards her, and led by Simon the Spy, were a dozen men-at-arms.

Marian sought to fly, but all her efforts were in vain. The men-at-arms were at hand, surrounding her, and now she found her arms pinioned behind her back as the sneering face of Simon looked into her white face.

"So, Mistress Marian!" he whispered cunningly, "what do you by this tree when so much is afoot, and men are marching and knights are riding?"

Marian flushed, but she did not answer him.

A cackle of laughter escaped his lips.

"Well, well," he muttered, "time will tell, and so will captivity—take her away, men!"

The next moment, and with soldiers ranged on either side of her, Marian was led back in the direction of the castle.

But, despite capture and her gloomy thoughts of the future, she had done what she intended to do. She would face what was ahead with fearlessness, knowing that, in her own way, she had struck a blow for Richard the Lion Heart.

CHAPTER III.

THE MESSAGE OF THE ARROW

"You may never see your father again!"

How those cruel words still rang in Maid Marian's ears!

It was some minutes ago since she had emerged from her ordeal of cross-examination by the Baron of Nottingham, and now, in this little cell just above the gap where the drawbridge fitted in, she had time to think of the dreadful significance those words conveyed.

To her it seemed that unless she spoke of whom she had seen by the tree and of the letter they would keep her prisoner here—and that would mean for ever, for never would she speak—never!

How different was this small stone chamber to the room in which she had been before! She could not help wondering why they had put her here, for the sentry had told her that it was an archer's room—the room that the archer who pro-protected the drawbridge gap used in the pursuit of his duty.

And as Marian looked about her she realised the truth of those words, for a long bow and a

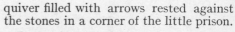

A strolling minstrel in Lincoln green

quiver filled with arrows rested against the stones in a corner of the little prison.

Parted from Judith even, alone and in this cold place.

Looking down, she could see the mist rising from the moat and the distant bastions of the great fortress.

If only she could escape!

But escape seemed hopeless.

There seemed no course that she could take, none at all. All that she could do was to be as brave as possible, and be prepared for the vengeance of the Baron of Nottingham to be meted out to her father, for that she felt sure was what would happen.

Her hands clasped and unclasped themselves, and now, taking from her blouse the ring the black knight had given her, she realised only too well that she would never be able to carry out that mission.

What aid could outlaws of the forest give? What help against a castle like this?

And now, turning moodily, she seated herself on the poor pallet bed that the little cell contained. It was just a sack filled with straw, and a smaller sack of straw had to serve for a pillow.

She seated herself on the sacking and gave herself up to thoughts, and into those thoughts something came stealing, something in harmony with her own sadness.

The notes of a song.

Maid Marian sprang to her feet and, dashing to the little window, looked down into the moonlit mead.

It was difficult to see at first. But now she did see, she started back at what she saw—and no wonder!

There, strolling along by the moat, strumming a harp as he walked, was a figure in Lincoln green.

"A forester!"

In a flash she remembered what Robin Hood had told her, of his talisman sent to any woodsman or outlaw, and as she fumbled for the talisman he had given to her the idea was in her mind to try a stratagem that had presented itself immediately.

Finding the little object, she hurried back into the cell, frantic lest the singer should pass from view, and finding an arrow, she deftly tied with ribbon the talisman to the arrow's shaft.

Picking up the bow she fitted the arrow to the strong cord, drew the bow, and winged the arrow over the head of the singer!

The bow dropped from her fingers, and frantically she watched, for fear that he might not have noticed it; but, to her joy, she saw the man stoop, and the song ceased.

He was picking up the arrow.

The next moment she saw him raise his head to the battlements and then, turning, he ran rather than walked towards the forest.

Marian's heart was beating furiously; but even as her spirits rose so did they fall again.

How could she make sure that the singer was of the forest?

For some little time she stood gazing out into the night, until at last, and tired out, she sank on to the bed and sought to sleep, but could not not.

It was not until the first grey shadows of morning began to peep into the cell that her eyes closed, and then not for long, for suddenly she was awakened by something falling on her face.

Maid Marian started up, and, as her eyes became accustomed to the light, she discovered an amazing thing.

Lying at her side was an arrow, and wound beneath the feathers was a piece of paper!

For a moment she felt that her heart would burst with excitement, and she hardly dared untie the paper from the arrow.

Her brain was awhirl with thoughts, and uppermost amongst those thoughts was the marvellous accuracy of the archer who had managed to send this arrow through the narrow slit that constituted the window of the cell.

And now, as with the gathering light she read the piece of paper, her heart leapt within her, for there, in just those few words, the wonder of the talisman was made clear. " Be prepared. I am at hand and with my men.—ROBIN HOOD."

With a cry on her lips Maid Marian started to her feet, and, brushing the straw off her dress, ran to the window.

There was no sign of a living soul!

She could see a tinge of red in the east, token of the coming day, and now, as she watched it, she saw a knight riding towards the castle.

He rode as one who has ridden far, for he seemed unsteady in his saddle and his helm was dinted and his lance was broken!

With excited eyes Marian watched him, she saw him draw in his foaming steed at the edge of the moat, saw him raise his vizor and place his horn to his lips, heard his shrill summons ring through the early morning!

And as she looked down she saw that the drawbridge was being lowered!

Its lip rested in a socket away below her, and, with interested eyes, she saw the great bridge go lower and lower until at last it touched the farther side of the moat.

" Make way there—make way for news from York—I have ridden hard—hoya!"

With a great cry on his lips, his lance resting on his shoulder, the knight galloped across the drawbridge and into the enclosure beyond, and as he did so Marian's amazed eyes saw a slim figure in green rise from the moat itself and, as the drawbridge slowly began to rise, she saw the slim figure, clad in the green jerkin of the forest, leap to the rising end of the drawbridge and hold fast.

Maid Marian saw the slim figure, clad in the green jerkin, leap to the rising end of the drawbridge and hold fast

She was held fascinated by the sight, but now she looked into eyes she had seen before and her heart leapt within her.

"Robin—Robin Hood!" she cried.

His eyes were raised, and now the draw-bridge was coming almost to the vertical, but, before it did so, the slim figure sprang to the top of it, poised himself a moment in giddy space, and then leapt!

Marian drew back as she saw that desperate leap towards her cell window!

To her it seemed an impossible hope that he could grip the stone, but, even as she thought thus, she saw firm fingers clutch at the stone and hold, saw a laughing face gazing into her own!

"Now! Come now!" he cried, and as he spoke he threw a rope into the cell.

"Make it fast to your prison door," he shouted.

Marian did not wait. She did not know if the alarm had been given, but she fancied that the boy had escaped notice in the mist of the morning.

Making the rope fast with frantically eager hands, she ran back with the end of it and passed it to Robin Hood.

"Into the opening, maid of the forest!" he cried. "There is not a second to be lost!"

She did as he bade her, and when she looked down into the moat that seemed so many, many feet below her, her head reeled.

"Courage!" he whispered, seeing how pale her face had gone. "Hold to the rope and follow me!"

Maid Marian grasped the rope, and as she did so Robin began to lower himself.

She followed, feeling that at any moment she might let go of that frail hold and fall into the moat, but no, her courage and his wonderful bravery held her up, and now—now she was touching the water, swimming to the side of the moat, to be drawn out by his strong arms!

Even as they scrambled safely ashore, with a thud the drawbridge came down, a flight of arrows whizzed above their heads, and cries came from the battlements!

"Hoya, hoya!" he cried. "We have been seen, maid of the forest—come!"

Clasping her hand, he ran with her in the direction of the dead oak-tree, and as they ran so across the drawbridge spurred horsemen and dashed men at arms!

The clash of accoutrements came to Marian's ears together with the hoarse cries of their pursuers.

Golden spurred knights, led by the Baron of Nottingham himself, were flooding from the castle, their whips were urging on the men-at-

arms, for the heavily armoured horses could not outdistance the fleet-footed archers.

Arrows rose in clouds, but only one found its mark, and that through the leather of Robin's jerkined arm.

"Better bowmen, better bowmen!" cried Robin, as they neared the trees. "Men of Sherwood, my men to me!"

And as he cried out the words the forest seemed suddenly to become alive with men in green.

From trees and shrubs, from the deep under-growth, through the aisles and clearings they came, and foremost amongst them was a monk with a great ash stave in his big fists.

Marian's face glowed as she saw hundreds of archers take up their positions on the fringe of the forest.

Turning, she saw the knights riding on. The pikes and staves of the men-at-arms glowed in the first rays of the morning sun.

Now they were to the trees and beyond them, and as they came to this temporary cover Robin Hood swung round.

"Men of Sherwood," he cried, "draw your bows now—draw them for Richard of England!"

Marian's hand was on the ring, and now she remembered.

"Robin," she cried — "Robin, this ring is for you; I have carried out the promise I made to the stranger knight!"

As she handed him the ring, in that second of tense excitement she saw the amazement that came into his eyes.

"The ring—the ring!" he said hoarsely, his boyish face lighting up with an amazing enthusiasm.

Dashing forward as those archers prepared to draw their long bows, he raised the ring above his head.

"Sherwood foresters," he cried, "the ring has come—strike—and strike now!"

Barely had he spoken than from every portion of the fringe of the forest the keen pointed arrows of the outlaws of Sherwood flighted towards the knights and men-at-arms who were advancing in serried array!

And now, as Marian watched the strange scene, she saw bowmen appear amid the ranks of the attacking men-at-arms, she saw the bows raised, and it seemed that every arrow was directed at the gallant lad who had befriended her.

Seeing his danger, she rushed forward and, as the bows twanged, she placed herself in front of him.

A cry came from Robin's lips, and the next moment Marian staggered backward, struck by some hard missile.

THING[S]

YOUR [...]

A girl's very own room should be her [...]
that are the work of her own hands. [...]
she has troubled to make it look char[...]
a pretty bedroom, but you can add [...]
Here are [...]

A Novelty Pin-Cushion

A NOVELTY pin-cushion is always a joy[...] cinating little fellow illustrated o[...] will do much to brighten your dre[...]

To make the novelty, take a piece of [...] and form it in to a bag, drawing up at t[...] a draw-string. Into this bag place a sma[...] of the type that can be p[...] any toy-shop for few pe[...] hold the doll in position s[...] with cotton-wool until qui[...] round. Draw up the bag [...] doll's neck, and cover w[...] of vivid orange or yellow[...]

To make the head [...] cone-shaped hat ou[...] strip of thin cardb[...] neatly paste over th[...] the covering silk [...] Gum hat into pos[...] round the edge, and [...] securely on the head [...]

To give a prett[...] touch to the quaint [...] make a small ruffle[...] encircle the neck and [...] the bag is drawn up. This frill looks m[...] against the orange when made out of a scr[...] silk. Embroider the hat and front of [...] with black spots, and the novelty is com[...]

It is always a good idea to sprinkle into [...] wool which stuffs these novelties a little p[...] a few drops of strong perfume.

A Dainty Hat-pin Stand

THERE is nothing, perhaps, that looks so untidy as to see hatpins lying about on the dressing-table. There is no necessity for it, either, for here is a charming little idea for a hat-pin stand that you can make with the greatest of ease.

Doubtless mother will have odd scraps of cretonne left over from something she has made, and you can utilise these.

"Robin," said King Richard, "Richard of England congratulates you. You have championed this fair maid as ye have guarded your country!"

But her surprise was only momentary, and now, as she recovered herself, the attacking bowmen had retired behind the shelter of the armoured horses of the knights.

As they did so Marian looked down.

It was to see an amazing thing.

The talisman that Robin Hood had returned to her, and which she had hung about her neck, was dented!

He followed the direction of her eyes, and there was a look of wonder in his own.

"You saved my life!" he whispered.

"Nay," she answered, with a smile, "had it not been for thy talisman, good forester, I had been pierced to the heart!"

As Marian spoke the foresters were sending their shafts at the advancing knights.

Before that cloud they paused and, during the pause, whilst fresh arrows were being fitted, the clear note of many a call rang through the forest.

Marian heard it being taken up by the other horns far distant, she heard the long away echo of other horns carrying the signal on.

The whole forest seemed to be sending that clarion signal forward, and now, even as she watched the distant aisles, they seemed thronged with fresh reinforcements that were coming flooding towards Nottingham Castle.

What could it all mean?

For a moment she had turned, but now she was again at Robin's side, watching with apprehension the preparations that were going on among the Baron of Nottingham's hosts.

It was obvious that he was going to make a desperate attack.

Now, as she watched, as those archers prepared grimly to meet the more heavily armoured knights and soldiers, from the distance there sounded the thudding of horses' hoofs.

War horses plunging ahead, lances drawn, swords loosened for war.

Marian trembled.

It seemed that fate had turned against them, that new forces had come to help the Baron of Nottingham!

Robin Hood turned to her, his eyes were points of glowing fire!

"The call of England!" he cried. "It has been heard!"

She did not understand for the moment; but as she watched, as from the distant trees there broke a bright and shining cavalcade, her heart leapt within her. For there, at the head of that gleaming body of knightly riders, so strange by contrast with their tossing plumes and silvery mail, was the mysterious knight, he of the coal black armour and the plumeless helm!

"Draw your bows for England!"

As Maid Marian's fascinated eyes watched the sun turning that bright array into something that was almost a picture in a dream, the foresters of Sherwood advanced, their bows drawn.

And now, with many a cry and a clattering of hoofs, some fifty knights spurred between the Baron of Nottingham's men and the castle itself.

He who led this brave company spurred towards the Baron of Nottingham, and now, to Marian's view came that short and lame figure who sat his horse so unsteadily beside the Baron.

"Prince John!" she whispered, amazed. "King Richard's brother and would-be usurper!"

With a cry on his lips, Robin Hood dashed forward, followed by his men, and Maid Marian found herself hurried along in the press.

With upraised eyes she saw that black mailed knight draw his horse in beside Prince John, saw Prince John's face pale with fear.

But the fear was momentary!

" Who comes in battle array
England ? " said the prince cold
to Nottingham as men ride to w

" Someone who has the right !
response from the Black Knight

" And who might you be, st
asked Prince John, his tones full

For answer there came a grea
next moment the Black Knight l
helm.

A gasp of astonishment cam
Prince John, a cry of alarm fro
and then a mighty cry from Rob
merry men.

" Richard come again ! " they
Richard of England ! "

" My brother ! " gasped the
John.

" Ay ! " came the answer, a
hardly believing that this Black
ruler of the land, came closer to
steed.

" Ay ! " he said again. " C
frustrate your plans, brother—ju

He turned, and his eyes found
Marian—and the eyes of the Li
very soft at that moment as he lo
that sweet face.

" Just in time, through the bra
this maid they call Marian ! "

" And through the help of Robi
forest of Sherwood ! "

He paused.

" Come hither, Robin ! " he sa
spoke he drew his great sword.

Robin Hood, his head bowed,

" Kneel, outlaw of Sherwood !
Richard, with a gay laugh.

And as Robin Hood knelt, Ki
England touched him lightly on
with the accolade.

pressing with a fairly hot iron.
Stitch securely three of the four
points together, and attach a
button of the ribbon to them.
This button is made by padding
and covering a wooden mould
with a scrap of the ribbon. Add
a loop to the fourth point, and a
smart bow of ribbon to finish off.

An attractive idea, when making these sachets,
is to sprinkle sprig lavender on the cotton-wool, or
a few drops of strong perfume, before joining the
handkerchiefs.

This type of sachet is always welcome at bazaars
and finds a ready sale.

A Pretty Nightdress Case

A NIGHTDRESS case always proves an acceptable
gift, and is a charming addition to any bed.

An odd length of coloured sateen forms the
foundation of the pretty case shown in the illustration, but should you wish to buy material specially
for the making of the case, half a yard of 36-in.-wide
satin, in a soft shade of pink, blue, rose, or lemon,
will meet the purpose.

No cutting at all is necessary for the making of the
case, the pocket being formed by folding back the
material and neatly stitching up the sides, leaving
an equal length of the satin to come over and form
the flap.

Finish off your case by turning back the flap and
in the top corner attaching a bunch of fruit. This
fruit is made from odd pieces of ribbon, and in this
way : Cut a circle of the ribbon, pad this tightly
with cotton-wool, and draw up. In the centre of
your stiff ball embroider two or three French

knots in brown or black silk to
give the effect of an apple. When
a little more ornamentation is
desired, stamp " Nightdress " on
the case, and embroider this in
the same colouring as your fruit.

For the Fancy-Work Girl

H ERE is a novel idea for keeping your silks tidy, and
one that will be welcomed
by the girl who is keen on fancy
work. So much depends on the
freshness of one's work when
finished, as when it has to be
washed owing to untidy handling
it never has the fascinating gloss
and newness about it that the
well-taken-care-of piece of work
has.

And isn't it more satisfactory
to yourselves, girls, to take a
pride in keeping your silks all
neatly arranged, than to have
the never-ending work of hunting all over the place for them,
only when found to have to
waste time in the very trying
and irritating process of straight-
ening out tangled skeins ?

This pretty little hold-all for silks is very simple
to make, and when rolled up neatly occupies very
little room.

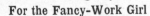

Use $\frac{1}{4}$ yard of linen. Cut a
piece 12 inches long and 8
inches wide ; then cut a smaller
piece 8 inches long and 6 inches
wide. Place the smaller piece
in the centre of the larger and
stitch down at each end with
coloured thread, and at 1-inch
intervals along the strip place a
row of stitching, as illustrated.

Slip through your different-coloured skeins of
silk, having, of course, cut them at one end. Thus
the top row is formed of loops of silk by which you
draw it out.

Buttonhole the outer edge of the hold-all with
coloured thread to correspond, and roll up. Then,
in your own hand-writing, write the word " silks,"
and stitch over in the same colour. Finish by
attaching a small piece of ribbon to match at the
back of the hold-all, and tie with a neat bow in
front.

A Dainty Dressing-Table Cover

T HERE is nothing, perhaps, that gives your own
room so fresh and sweet an appearance as a
pretty white cover to the dressing-table.

The sort you can buy in the shops are very nice,
but they are not really nice enough if you aim at
making your own room really characteristic of you.
You should make one yourself.

Does it sound a dreadfully long and tedious task ?
I assure you there are few things more fascinating
than making things for your very own room.

Make your dressing-table cover in linen, if you
can afford this. A strip of plain, rather coarse
linen, the length of your dressing-table, and about
seven or eight inches in width will do splendidly.
If you cannot run to linen, holland will make a
very attractive cover, though personally I prefer
the touch of whiteness that linen gives.

Now, do you prefer that charming broderie
anglaise, or drawn-thread work ? Either is very
easy to do, and both look simply delightful.

Suppose you choose broderie anglaise.

First turn in an inch of your material all the way
round, and tack it roughly down. Then commence
drawing threads for the necessary hemstitched
border. Draw as many threads as you think fit,
and do a neat, simple hemstitch all the way round.
That done, you can turn your attention to the
actual embroidery.

You can buy a pretty open broderie anglaise
transfer at any art needlework shop. You will need
white embroidery cotton, and needles.

Be very careful about stamping the transfer
on to your cover. It is the easiest thing in the
world to get the transfer crooked, and you will
regret it always if your pattern is not on straight.
Tack it on, and make sure it is correct before
stamping on.

Use a moderately hot iron for stamping the
transfer and only press once, otherwise you make
your transfer very faint through the heat of the
iron.

When you commence working, be sure that you
run round every open petal or leaf, so that you
make a firm foundation for the actual embroidery,
which is done in ordinary close " oversewing "

one of t...
the little...
match w...
winter.

On its...
challeng...
played...
honour f...

Now,...
available...
their ri...
sportswo...

" No,...
presentl...
honour...
think of...

" Oh,...
" Yes,...
answer.
not to b...
down !"

Grudg...
to the i...
the two...
Celia to...

Quick...
form fro...
with m...
being he...
her bro...
from the...
Regis n...
problem...
sensitive...

She l...
telling h...
of being...
Frank h...
bringing...
match.
spoilt b...
pected...
Holman...

Well,...
not be h...
thing w...
vent F...
his chu...
making...

stitch. Don't finish off your cotton if you can help it, carry it on to the next hole.

Drawn thread work looks equally as effective, and is, as you know, quite simple to perform. The real difficulty about this is drawing the thread. After that is done, it is simplicity itself to do the stitches, which of course, for a thing of this sort, should not be elaborate.

You can make little mats for the dressing-table in the same way; and, if you are particularly energetic, you could make a nightdress-case to match your dressing-table covers and mats. This could consist of a straight strip of the same kind of linen, with a third of the length sewn up to make the " bag " and the folding over piece embroidered or drawn thread worked in the same way.

It is things of this sort that make your bedroom look distinctive, and out of the ordinary, and really you will find the finished result more than compensates for the labour of making. Of that I am sure.

A Home-Made Waste-Paper Basket

THE pretty waste-paper basket shown on this page would make both a useful and charming ornament for the sitting-room or your own bedroom, and is a welcome change from the usual wicker affair.

The basket illustrated is merely a cylinder of cardboard, with a stiff circle sewn in for the bottom.

Chintz or cretonne is used to cover the outside, and a plain material, or good quality wallpaper, is pasted inside for lining.

When covering cardboard with material, always apply your paste to the cardboard, never the material, or you will damage the pattern irrevocably by giving a blurred, faded effect.

Should you merely wish to " do up " a basket of the wicker variety, thoroughly scrub with soap and hot water. When dry, line with cretonne or a plain material, and place a large bunch of fruit at one side.

THE ever-useful cretonne is again to be the chief material employed for the making of a highly necessary etcetera to your own room ; that is, your boot and shoe ottoman.

First of all you want a good, strong wooden box, not too large, or it will become ungainly. And it must have a lid. That is essential for this ottoman.

Get your brother to fix the hinges on for you, and if you can manage it, also have tiny wheels affixed on the under side of the box. This will not cost you very much, even if you have to get it done at an ironmonger's.

Your next job is either to line with pretty wallpaper, or else give your box a coat of varnish or white enamel on the inside. You will probably find that either of the latter two will be easier to accomplish than the wallpaper lining, and certainly the white enamel would have a far daintier appearance.

Start, of course, with the lid, and pad that before you attempt to tack on the cretonne. Use the very smallest tacks obtainable, and remember that it is

better to take your time before you start tacking on. You must take care that no rough edges or sharp nails and corners are left, which might tear the material, or injure anyone who chanced to knock against the box. If you find the wood is inclined to be rather rough, it is a good plan to sandpaper it before you commence operations.

A variation of this idea is the little boot and shoe cupboard, with the cretonne curtain. For this, there need be no lid to the box. Line in the same way, and cover, too, as when making the ottoman. The curtain should be made with a little heading at the top, and fixed, on a wooden rod, on hooks fixed on either side of the box.

There is another idea for cretonne that charmed me when I saw it in a friend's bedroom lately.

I saw a little cretonne-covered pot on her dressing-table, and as I picked it up, from it came a delicious perfume. I inquired eagerly the " hows " and " whys " and she very kindly told me. So I'm passing the little idea on to you.

My friend got a glass jar. Hers, to be precise, was one which had contained potted tongue, and she made a cover for it from cretonne. Then a pad of cotton-wool at the bottom and her " pot pourri " were placed in the jar. Then the " lid " was affixed. This took the form of a circular piece of cretonne, hemmed all round and run round with double silk about two inches from the hem. Before it was put on, three little holes were embroidered in the top of the lid, in the same shade of silk as the running, and the lid was then drawn up and put on to the jar. A dainty little idea, I think, don't you ?

A Novelty " Slipper " Hair-Tidy

A DAINTY addition to your dressing-table is shown in the " slipper " hair-tidy given on this page. The novelty illustrated was made up in pink and mauve—always a pretty combination for the bedroom—sateen, and the embroidery on the toecap was carried out in a soft shade of blue mallard floss.

To make the tidy, first cut out your sole from a piece of stiff, white cardboard ; this can be large or small, as the taste desires. Pad the sole lightly with cotton-wool, and cover quite flatly with the mauve sateen, by overstitching round the edge of the cardboard, or pasting on the material.

The toecap, too, is cut from the cardboard; it is padded with cotton-wool and neatly covered with pink sateen before attaching to the sole. To the toecap is stamped a flower or butterfly design, and this is outlined with the blue mallard floss, a pretty idea being to introduce into the design a few pink and mauve beads.

The sole of the slipper is then outlined with blue cord, the same shade as the embroidery, and this cord forms the loop at top with which to hang on to dressing-table or wall.

When a really elaborate hair-tidy is desired, stamp a design to the sole of the shoe, and embroider with mallard floss and beads.

made for the boys. In horror, Celia suddenly remembered there was to be a party, even quite a large party, half in honour of Celia having played in the Shield match !

Poor Celia went scarlet as she remembered that. She put the telegraph form down. Certainly she could not wire to her brother, asking him to stay away, without first consulting her mother.

And there could be no consulting Mrs. Riley until much too late in the day for the sending of telegrams, as her mother was away shopping in Lincoln.

In something like dismay Celia turned from the post office and commenced her walk home along Mere Road, positively miserable about matters. A girl like Lottie would have been merely disappointed.

"It has been no one's fault but my own," she thought more than once. "Vere couldn't do anything but choose Lottie to play, and Lottie wouldn't be playing the game to stand down for me. It's just that I have been silly and conceited in ever saying I should be chosen, and—and it serves me right ! "

But, oh, how she dreaded the coming of tomorrow ! How she dreaded the thought of meeting her brother as he came up to see the match, amazed to find his sister one of the spectators and not a player ! And those boyish words of sympathy that would come so naturally from him, the : "Hallo, Celia, old lady, what's this mean ? Why aren't you playing ? Oh, I say, what a shame ! "

And Frank had such a loud voice, too, and was just about the greatest athlete for his age at his school. Yes, it would be horrid for her !

She had trained so hard for this match, too, harder than anybody else, for it had seemed her one chance of living up to the reputation the Rileys, both boys and girls, had always had on the playing fields. No one but herself knew how hard she had trained.

All for just nothing, though. That was one of the parts that hurt so, and Celia walked on towards the home the Rileys were so soon to leave, unhappier than she had been for many a long day.

CHAPTER II.

THE SAVING OF GYP

JUST as Celia Riley was nearing her home, something happened which put all thoughts of ice hockey out of her mind. A rabbit scurried past her over the frosty ground, and fast after it came a puppy terrier.

Both animals were travelling at such a tremendous pace, that Celia had no time to recognise the dog, and then, in the failing light, a dreadful thing happened.

The rabbit dashed through some railings which fenced in the mere, and the dog was after him, travelling faster than ever. Then the rabbit swerved away to the right while the heavy little puppy dashed straight on, right on to the ice !

He yelped in sudden fear which Celia did not understand at first, then sprang forward, and the next moment was in water.

Instantly Celia understood now.

The mere was constantly being drained of its water, and so what ice there was could never be used for skating purposes. In fact, the ice existed only in patches, and there was the puppy swimming round in a frantic little circle, utterly unable to scramble back on to the ice.

As quickly as she could, Celia climbed the railings, but even when she had reached the edge of the mere, it seemed impossible that she could do anything. Certainly she could not walk over the intervening four or five yards of ice to where the puppy swam, for it could never have borne her weight.

She set her foot on it to make quite sure and instantly there was a loud crack !

No, it was impossible for Celia to think of reaching the dog that way, and for a moment the horror of it all rather numbed her.

She knew only too well that the mere was tremendously deep, even close to the edge, and she could see perfectly well that the puppy could never get to land unaided. He was completely hedged in by ice and his desperate, pathetic little attempts to clamber up were heart-breaking to watch.

He must be nearly frozen, too, and yet it seemed that Celia could do nothing but stand there and watch, waiting for the dreadful moment when the dog would drown right in front of her eyes.

But Celia Riley could not do that.

She racked her brains in a frantic effort to think of something that could be done, and she remembered suddenly that she was very close to Vere Rankin's home.

Surely she would be able to get help there, a plank, perhaps, which could be laid on the ice. Yes, if Celia could find a plank that was long enough, she believed she could reach the puppy !

But there was very little time to spare. That was horribly plain, for the dog was rapidly exhausting himself in his wild attempts to get on the ice. Already those efforts had grown quite feeble so Celia did not waste a single second.

She clambered over the rails again, and flashed away to Vere Rankin's home, but she dared not spend the time it would take to run all the way up the long carriage drive to the house itself.

Besides, there might be no need for that, for just in the grounds there was a large outhouse used by the gardener for storing tools and the like. It was *just* possible that a plank of some sort might be in there.

A little gasp of relief left the girl's lips when she found the shed door open, and then it did seem as if luck was to favour her, for there were several planks of wood lying in a heap against the wall.

They looked as if they would be just long enough, too, and everything depended now upon whether Betty would be able to carry or drag one to the mere.

How eagerly she caught at the first of the planks and how her heart thumped with relief when she found that she could just lift it. Still, Celia scarcely noticed the weight of the plank as she half-carried, half-dragged it to the mere, and she could have cheered aloud when she saw that the puppy was still swimming.

His strokes were so dreadfully feeble now, though, that Celia couldn't help the horrible thought that she was too late. She really thought the dog would sink and drown before she could get the plank out on the ice !

Using every bit of strength she had,

with her teeth clenched together, she stepped on to the plank and at once there was an ominous crack. The ice was giving.

Yes, but it might only be at the edge. If Celia walked very carefully and trod as lightly as possible, there was a chance that she would be successful.

But, oh how nerve-racking that short journey was, for at every step there was a fresh crack, and more than once Celia was conscious of the horrible feeling that she was losing her balance, that she was about to stumble off the plank.

The moment she did that, then disaster must follow. She knew that and she steeled herself to the ordeal.

Step by step she approached the puppy, and when at last she reached him, his little yelp of gratitude was reward enough for anything. And the return journey was not nearly so bad for, as Celia neared firm ground, Vere Rankin, the captain of the ice hockey team, came rushing to her assistance.

" Oh, Celia, whatever are you doing ? " Vere gasped. " I saw you take the plank from our shed and—oh, you went out to the water to save a dog ! "

Celia made no answer, but the drenched puppy in her arms was reply enough, and Vere's face flushed with admiration.

" Oh, how ripping of you," she exclaimed. " Why—why ever didn't you call for our gardener, though, to help you ? "

" I—I didn't think I had time," faltered Celia. " It was just too awful the way the dog swam round and round quite helpless. Oh, Vere, it is Lottie Holman's puppy ! "

" Yes, so it is ! " answered the other girl. " Gyp, you little rascal, you have escaped from the house and you haven't got your collar on ! Celia, it would nearly have broken Lottie's heart if Gyp had been drowned ! "

" Well, thank goodness he hasn't been,"

Using every bit of strength she had, Celia pushed the plank towards the struggling puppy

she pushed the plank out towards the puppy, and again the luck was splendid. The strip of wood reached the patch of water !

But could Celia walk along it and so reach the dog herself ? She thought she could if the ice were strong enough, but suppose it were not ! Suppose it broke up beneath the plank the moment she set foot on the wood ?

That was possible and more than possible, but Celia did not shrink from the risk. Very white,

answered Celia, shuddering. " Will—will you take him back to Lottie's house ? "

" Oh, but you must come, too——"

" No, I would rather not," answered Celia quickly. " Do please take him back, Vere, and don't tell Lottie what happened ! I—I would much rather she didn't know ! "

Vere's amazement can be imagined at that, and she was very emphatic in her reply.

" What nonsense, Celia," she cried. " Of course she must be told."

" No, please don't say anything," pleaded Celia. " Well, at least don't let Lottie know until—until after to-morrow. After the match, I mean——"

Poor Celia floundered away into embarrassed silence, and Vere's lips set a little.

She thought she was beginning to understand.

Celia was thinking of the fact that Lottie Holman's return to town had brought about a change in the Lydmouth forward line, perhaps, although Vere could not quite see how that affected Gyp's fine rescue. Still, she could not very well do anything else but fall in with Celia's wishes.

" Of course, I will do as you like," she conceded. " No, don't touch the plank. The gardener shall see to that. Shall I take Gyp home now ? "

" Yes, and you promise not to tell Lottie anything ? "

" I won't tell her to-day, if you like," was all Vere would answer. " She must be told sooner or later, though, for it was just fine of you, Celia, just fine ! "

She picked up Gyp as she spoke those few words, and ran with him to Lottie's home a little further along the road.

There she met Lottie, just back from her shopping, and Vere did her best to keep Celia's little, secret.

" Here is Gyp, found straying without his collar," she exclaimed. " The next time it happens there will be a fine ! "

" I am expecting to be fined every day," laughed Lottie, as Gyp scampered off to dry himself. " Thanks, awfully, Vere ! "

Vere half turned to go, then something made her face the other girl and ask a rather curious question.

" I say, you and Celia Riley haven't had a squabble about anything, have you ? " she said, quite on the spur of the moment. " I mean, there's no ill-feeling over the change in the hockey team ? "

" Oh, dear no ! " answered Lottie hastily. " Celia isn't a bit like that, only—well, I think she was disappointed."

" Yes, I suppose so——"

" You see, she was very keen on playing and had been training ever so hard ! "

Vere nodded.

" Yes, I know, but these things cannot be helped," she replied. " There would be no sportsmanship left if the best possible team weren't picked every time, would there ? One has to think of one's club before personal friends, you know ! "

" I suppose so," Lottie had to admit. " All the same—well, Celia is dreadfully sensitive, isn't she ? "

" Yes, and it must be horrid to be like that," nodded Vere, who wasn't the least bit sensitive herself. " Mind you are punctual at the station to-morrow, Lottie ; train leaves one-fifteen, you know ! "

And Vere departed, quite sure now that Celia had refused to have Lottie told about Gyp for the sole reason of not making her feel uncomfortable over the team change.

" Which goes to show that Celia Riley is a jolly sort," was Vere's final summing up of the affair. " I only wish she had been good enough to get her place in to-morrow's team ! "

And the matter rather slipped from Vere Rankin's mind.

CHAPTER III.

THE WINNING GOAL

ALL the Lydmouth team were on the station by one o'clock the following afternoon, armed with bags and hockey sticks, with Celia completing the round dozen, for she was first reserve.

She was a little quieter than usual, perhaps, because a telegram in her pocket told her that her brother and his chums would go straight to Beaton Regis and travel back with her after the match.

Still, Celia's quietness passed unnoticed by all except Lottie Holman. Generous-hearted Lottie always had the seeing eye.

" She's just about as unhappy as possible," ran through Lottie's mind. " Wish I hadn't come back to Lydmouth until after the match, I do really ! "

Still, it seemed too late to think about that now, for the train was in and Vere was busy finding comfortable compartments.

It happened that Celia and Lottie sat next to each other for the first portion of the journey, and then something that someone said about Frank Riley made Lottie flash quite an unexpected question to her companion.

" Why, is your brother coming to see the match, Celia ? " she exclaimed. " You never told me ? "

" Yes, he is coming, with Jack Cook and Tom Marsden," answered Celia hastily. " They—they've gone straight to Beaton Regis ! "

Not another word was said on the subject, but Lottie knew all she wanted to know now.

" And Frank Riley won't know she isn't picked to play," was one of Lottie's thoughts. " Oh, what a shame ! " And that thought remained with her all the way to the junction where trains had to be changed.

Vere was the first to leave the compartment at the junction, with Lottie Holman last, and then rather a curious thing happened. Lottie stopped dead and stood looking after the other girls, with eyes only for Celia.

And again generous, good-natured thoughts were flashing through her mind, thoughts which had all to do with this hockey match.

" I ought to have insisted upon standing down," was one of them. " After all, Celia is going away and this is her last chance of ever playing, perhaps. . . And her brother and those other boys are to be at the match ! Of course, they are only coming because they think she is playing ! "

Vaguely Lottie watched the rest of the team running up the steps of the overhead gangway, and found herself listening to a porter hurrying noisily along the platform.

" Cross by the bridge for Beaton Regis. Anybody here for Beaton ? "

Some one stepped forward and was told to run, and Lottie turned, too. Then, right on the spur of the moment, she did another curious thing. She hurried forward, but not towards the gangway ; instead she made for the waiting room, and slipped quietly through the doorway, to *sit down in the most comfortable chair* she could find in front of the fire.

And instead of being out on the ice with the rest of the team Lottie sat down in front of the waiting-room fire

CHAPTER IV.

AT THE LAST MOMENT!

" WHY, where ever is Lottie Holman ? " It was Vere Rankin who asked that question, just as the Lydmouth girls reached the beautifully prepared stretch of ice.

No one answered, of course, for no one knew where Lottie was. They all remembered seeing her get out of the train at the junction station, but no one remembered her boarding the Beaton Regis train.

" In fact, I am certain she wasn't with us," Vere went on anxiously. " Suppose she got into the wrong train at the junction. . . Good gracious, I believe that is what she has done ! "

Again there was no answer, but, presently the captain of the Beaton Regis team, looking very pretty and workmanlike in her blue jumper, came up to say everything was ready.

" And we ought to start just as soon as we can because it gets dark so early," she added.

" Yes, of course ! " nodded Vere, and a last frantic search was made for the missing Lottie. No trace of her could be found though, and Vere did the only thing left to be done. She turned anxiously to Celia Riley.

" Celia, you will have to play after all," she exclaimed. " You will take Lottie's place . . . She must have missed the train at the junction and cannot possibly get here until the game is half over ! "

Celia made no answer, but a very few minutes later she had joined the other girls on the ice, and it was just at that moment boyish cheers raised an echo in the still, crisp air.

" Play up, Lydmouth ! "

" Altogether, the visitors . . . "

Quickly Celia glanced to where the shouts were coming, and saw her brother and his boy chums waving frantically. Then the game started, and poor Celia promptly developed a fit of nerves.

The very first thing she did was to fumble a pass from Vere, and Beaton Regis were famous for making the best of their opportunities.

Brilliantly they got away, and some clever work in front of the Lydmouth goal ended with the home centre forward having a difficult chance.

She flashed in a splendid shot, but somehow the goal was kept intact, then Vere was in the picture again. Always a tower of strength at centre half, she intercepted splendidly, sweeping the ball ahead to Celia Riley.

Much too over-anxious, Celia fumbled again, then made amends and managed to get the ball out to her left wing.

Finely the game was carried up the ice, and a perfect centre presented Lydmouth with their first real chance of doing big things.

A quick pass by the inside left put Celia in possession, then she slipped, and the chance had gone.

" Oh, no luck, Celia ! "

" Hard lines. . . Better luck next time ! "

Frank Riley and his chums were shouting the most encouraging things they could think of from the touch line, but Frank did not look specially pleased. He could not help seeing that his sister was doing anything but shine.

Still, the game was young yet, and perhaps Celia would steady down. Frank and his boy chums hoped so sincerely, anyway.

Beaton Regis were monopolising the exchanges now, their forwards playing wonderfully well together. But for Vere Rankin they would have scored on several occasions, and there were plenty of cheers for the Lydmouth captain.

The scoring was still blank when half-time came in sight, then the Beaton Regis girls crammed on the pace.

Skating brilliantly, their forwards swept over the ice, and for once Vere was unable to stem the rush. She tried valiantly, but the home forwards were right on the top of their form.

Quick, flashlike passes ! A fine burst ahead, and the ball was in the danger zone.

Desperately Vere tried to save the situation, and she all but succeeded, but not quite. A Beaton Regis girl was in possession, and she had a splendid chance of opening the scoring.

She skated forward. She screwed round and her chance seemed to be almost a certainty.

" Shoot ! " screamed the spectators. " Oh, do shoot ! "

And the Beaton Regis girl took the advice. She swept the ball into the net and the home side were leading by one goal to nothing.

Three minutes later the same girl was through again, and amid the greatest enthusiasm, added a second goal within a few moments of half-time.

Because of the failing light no " breather " was taken, the restart being made straight away.

Quickly the home forwards were at work again, Vere nipping a dangerous looking movement in the bud just as Lottie Holman came on the ice.

Vere saw her and she could not keep her disappointment out of her face. If only Lottie hadn't been so silly as to miss her train at the junction ! What a difference she would have made to the game !

Others thought the same for Celia Riley was still woefully uncertain, until the game was was nearing its end.

With something like a quarter-of-an-hour to go, Lydmouth looked a beaten side and yet Frank Riley and his chums were still shouting encouragement. Lottie's voice, too, was constantly ringing out, and it was always Celia's name which was on her lips.

" Now you have a chance, Celia."

" Through on your own, Celia. Oh, hard luck ! "

As for Celia herself, she was painfully conscious of failure.

She knew she was playing weakly, and she just longed to make amends. She would simply have loved to have had the confidence to skate through on her own as Lottie would have tried to do again and again, but somehow she just could not do it.

She was much too over-anxious, and the luck was not with her. Time after time she experienced that.

And then, suddenly, Lottie's voice rang out once more.

" There's still time to win, Celia," echoed the words. " It's your last game for Lydmouth, remember ! "

The hot, sensitive blood rushed to Celia's face, but those words stirred her strangely, for it was true this must be the last game she would ever be able to play for Lydmouth—perhaps the last game she would play at all !

In three weeks' time she would be down in sunny, " tropical " Devonshire, far from all these girls who had been her good friends ! Never again would she have a chance of helping to win back the shield which Beaton Regis had held for so long.

But that chance was still with Celia Riley !

There were over ten minutes left of the match, and, as Lottie had said, there was still time for a win. Celia clung to that knowledge as if it were something wonderful.

It happened, too, that Vere got in a lovely forward pass just then, a pass that Celia could not have fumbled if she had tried to.

Quickly she transferred to her inside right, then back the ball came and Celia Riley became a new girl.

She whipped up the pass, then skated through the home defence in a manner which was well-nigh unstoppable.

Only for a second or two did that " run " last, and by that time Celia was right in front of goal before the Beaton Regis girls realised their danger. A moment after that the ball was in the net !

In bewilderment the spectators stared across the ice, with only Frank Riley and his boy chums and Lottie cheering. Then Celia was doing wonderful things again.

This time there was no pass out to the wing, for she obtained the ball almost from the re-start.

Brilliantly again she skated ahead, feinted to transfer the ball, then went right through the home defence single handed.

Breaths were held as a girl in a blue jumper came skating desperately to the rescue, but really there was no chance of stopping Celia. She had the goal at her mercy and equalised the scoring with a quick but sure shot !

Instantly there was something of an uproar, with unstinted praise for Celia for the first time during the match.

"Oh, well played !"

"Splendid, Celia !"

"Just one more, Lydmouth," cried Lottie. " There are five minutes left ! "

And a bewildering five minutes they proved to be, too, for Beaton Regis made tremendous attempts to regain the lead.

But for Vere Rankin they must have succeeded, for their forwards rose far above their usual form, then Lydmouth had a chance again right on time. Celia Riley had the ball and was skating at a terrific pace !

Close behind her was Vere, and again breaths were held.

A home back made a splendid attempt to tackle, but Celia was ready for that. She slipped the ball to Vere, then back it came, and Celia was through. The girl who had been able to do nothing right for three-quarters of the game had the goal at her mercy once more.

Wildly excited, of course, she shot and there was an instant of suspense. Then a tremendous cheer, for the ball was in the net and the shield was won and lost !

Everybody was just wild to congratulate Celia

. . . . . .

The scene which followed rather defeats description, for everybody was just wild to congratulate Celia and no one so anxious as her brother and his boy chums.

His eyes sparkling with delight, Frank rushed helter-skelter on to the ice, but before he could do more than shake Celia's hand, a young man with a notebook in one hand and a pencil in the other, hurried up. He was quite well known locally as the representative of the " Lydmouth and District Times," and it was Celia he wanted to see.

"I spent nearly all this morning trying to find you, Miss Riley," he said eagerly. "I want to hear full particulars of how you saved that dog which fell into the mere yesterday afternoon ! "

"The—the dog ? " rather faltered Celia, flushing up as usual.

"Yes, for the rescue was seen by someone from the other side of the mere," answered the reporter. "I —er—may mention that a certain society interested in the welfare of animals are anxious for details as well ! Now, do please tell me all the details."

After that, of course, everything had to be explained, and Vere Rankin did the explaining. When she told them all whose dog it was Celia had saved, Lottie's face went quite white, for this was the very first that she had heard of Gyp's narrow escape.

As for Frank Riley, he was openly enthusiastic.

"Good old Celia," he cried, with the boisterous enthusiasm that brothers are in the habit of adopting. "You'll get some sort of jolly old medal for this, you see if you don't. You deserve one too. 'Twas a real plucky thing you did."

"Yes, and she won the match for Lydmouth," said someone else. "Lottie, it was almost a good thing that you missed the train at the junction ! "

But Lottie Holman made no answer, in words. To herself, though, she made a little vow, and it was that no one in Lydmouth should ever learn that the train at the junction had been *missed on purpose*, to give Celia Riley her chance.

THE END

HOUSEHOLD HINTS FOR GIRLS

AT home, as every girl knows, not a day passes but some little problem crops up; problems that, with a little knowledge, can be easily mastered. Here is a portion of this "little knowledge" clearly set out which will be of inestimable value to the girl who aspires to become the handy girl about the house.

HOW TO STAIN A FLOOR

BEFORE a floor can be stained, it has to be thoroughly scrubbed. This should be done the way of the grain. Rinse the boards with a liberal supply of water, and allow them to dry slightly before starting on the staining.

There are many kinds of stain on the market. An oil and colourman will show you several, and you will be able to make your choice. Nearly all of them fail in one respect—they are difficult to apply to the floor because of the varnish that is mixed in with them.

It will be found a better plan to make your own stain, and varnish the floor afterwards. It has the added recommendation of being cheaper.

The principal ingredient of this stain is permanganate of potash, which can be obtained at the chemist's. To half a pint of water add a teaspoonful of the potash. This makes a liquid the colour of mahogany. It can be applied to the floor with an old nail-brush. Rub it well into the boards, taking a survey every now and then, to see that the colour is evenly distributed.

It will need to be sized over within twenty-four hours, or the sunlight will cause it to fade.

You can make the size by dissolving two ounces of glue in half a pailful of boiling water. Spread this evenly over the floor and allow it to dry. After this, when it is completely dry, it will require polishing.

FLOOR POLISH

To know how to make a good floor polish, which, by the way, can be also used upon furniture, is useful as well as economical. Dissolve two ounces of pure beeswax in a pint of turpentine, and then add to the mixture one pint of boiled linseed oil. Put the beeswax and the turpentine in an old earthenware jam-jar, and stand it in the oven, and it will be thoroughly dissolved by the morning.

Care should be taken that the oven is not very hot, as the mixture may boil over, and even catch fire.

Remember that in polishing you want a little polish and a lot of elbow-grease. That is the secret.

If Brunswick black is dissolved in twice its own quantity of turpentine, it makes an excellent dark brown stain and will take a polish when dry without the use of size.

PUTTING WASHERS ON TAPS

NOTHING is more annoying to the average housewife than to discover that one of the taps cannot be turned off properly.

When one knows how, it is quite easy to unscrew the tap and to put on a fresh washer in place of the old one—the cause of the trouble.

Washers can be obtained at the shop of any oil and colourman. The next thing to do is to turn the water off at the main.

Every girl should know where the main water tap is to be found in her house, and be familiar with the manner by which it can be turned on and off.

After the water has been turned off from the main, and the remaining water in the pipes has been allowed to run away, obtain a spanner and unscrew the nut below the movable portion of the tap. It will now be found that the top can be lifted out.

Take off the old, worn-out washer, wipe away with a rag any grit that is to be found there, and then fix on the new washer. Replace the parts

screw back the top into position, and then the water can be turned on at the main again.

TO REPAIR CHINA

THE white of an egg forms quite a good cement for fitting the broken pieces into cups and saucers.

Care should be taken when mending china that it is not used for twenty-four hours afterwards, and, if possible, a bandage should be tied tightly round the broken part to keep it in place.

For ordinary broken earthenware, where a piece has come cleanly out, a good plan is to make a paste of some plaster of Paris and to fix in the broken piece at once with it.

Some of the cements on sale at the shops for mending crockery require heating. Very often a failure only results because the mender forgets to heat the parts required to be put together. Do not put the cement on thickly. This also applies to mending wooden articles—furniture, for instance. Obtain as much pressure on the glued parts as possible by tieing them together for several hours.

HOW TO REMOVE STAINS

HOW aggravating it is to find ironmould on the linen. Ink is one of the causes, but damp clothes, left in contact with tin or iron, often make a bad stain.

The best and safest method to remove such stains is to cover the spot with the juice of a fresh lemon and allow the sunlight to fall upon the linen. The operation must be repeated if the first application of the lemon juice does not remove the stain.

Mildew is invariably caused by clothes being put away in a damp state. Lemon juice, again, will often remove it if the stain is not too bad. In this latter case, cover the spot with soap, and over this put a layer of French chalk and place the linen out in the sun. As it dries sprinkle a little water over the place.

It is best to remove tea and coffee stains immediately they are made. Put the stained part of a tablecloth over a basin and pour boiling water upon it. If the stains have dried, soak the stained part in a mixture of cold water and borax for a few hours. Borax and boiling water will also remove grease stains.

Fruit stains can be removed by covering the spots at once with powdered starch. Let it remain for an hour or two, and then rub off. If the stain has become ground into the material, cover the place with soap, sprinkle powdered starch over it, and expose to the air.

Turpentine is as good as anything for removing paint and tar stains. Smear it over the part with a clean rag, leave it for a time, and then wash off.

DISTEMPERING WALLS

HALF a pound of whitening has to be dissolved in a pailful of water. If the mixture is too thick, the whitewash will crack and fall off in scales. Size must now be added. Sometimes you can get this ready-made at an oil and colourman's shop. If you cannot, dissolve two ounces of glue in half a pail of boiling water. Stir into the whitewash while it is still hot.

Next the colour must be added. Stir it in until it is thoroughly mixed. Don't forget that when it dries the colour will be lighter than the stuff you put into the whitewash. Don't have too much liquid on your brush when you apply the distemper to the wall. The best plan is to put a thin coat on first and add another when it dries.

Distemper made this way costs much less than the tins of stuff that can be purchased already prepared for use.

It is the handling of the whitewash brush where skill can be shown. Don't have the brush too moist. Take long, firm sweeps down and across the wall.

WHITEWASHING A CEILING

THIS should be done really before you begin distempering the walls. The whitewash is made in the same way as described above only that you add a little blue to the mixture.

First of all, you remove all dirt and smoke from the ceiling with water in which a little lime has been dissolved. When it is dry you can get to work with the whitewash.

Use a large flat brush, tie a cloth round the handle to prevent the whitewash running down your arm, wear a cap over your hair, and a washable overall.

STAINS ON A CARPET

TO remove an ink stain from a carpet rub with a cloth wrung out in a little milk. Repeat till the stain has disappeared.

For a sooty stain, cover the spot with salt, and then brush off with a stiff brush.

To remove paint, rub the spot with a cloth dipped in turpentine.

For oil or grease, put powdered chalk on the place, and brush off with a stiff brush. Fuller's earth or flour will do just as well.

When candle grease is discovered, scrape off as much of the grease as possible with a blunt knife. Place a piece of blotting-paper over the spot and pass a warm iron over it. A hot iron and heavy pressure will make the grease sink more deeply into the carpet. If lightly done with a warm iron, the grease will come off on the paper.

SHARPEN YOUR SCISSORS

How annoying it is to find that your scissors are blunt just when you want to cut a piece of material in a hurry. Get a small glass bottle, and work your scissor blades as if you were trying to cut the neck off the bottle. Do this a few times vigorously, and you will find the blades will become quite sharp.

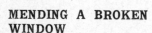

MENDING A BROKEN WINDOW

First of all, knock out all the broken glass, and then, with your guide knife, cut away all the old putty till the window frame is absolutely clear.

The next thing to do is to measure the window to see what sized piece of glass you will require to fill it. This needs care, for if the glass is only a quarter of an inch too short or too long it will be difficult to make the job a successful one.

Then go to the oil and colourman and buy the glass and a pound of fresh putty. To make sure that you obtain glass of the right thickness take a piece of the broken pane with you.

Put a layer of putty round the inside of the frame into which the window fits. An old, strong, broken knife will press the putty neatly into place. After that the glass is put in the frame and should fit exactly. To keep the glass in position fix tiny tacks, two on each side of the glass.

Drive the tacks in carefully, or you may need a new pane of glass.

Then another layer of putty must be pressed into the edge of the frame with the knife in such a way that it has a bevel all the way round. The odd scraps of putty are then wiped away with a rag.

A CUP OF TEA

Everyone appreciates a nice, hot cup of tea, but it is surprising how people get into the habit of regularly spoiling this favourite beverage.

We have all had the cup of tea with which there is something radically wrong. It is too strong or too weak, it is stewy or lukewarm and lifeless, and too seldom hot and refreshing.

The water must be really boiling first of all. Rinse out the teapot with some of the boiling water, which also warms it. If you are making three cups of tea, say, put in tea accordingly and only water sufficient for your requirement. Let it stand for a minute or two. Before pouring the tea into the cups put in the milk and sugar. That is the simple and only way to make a good cup of tea.

THE CARE OF UMBRELLAS

Always turn an umbrella upside down to dry. The reason is to prevent the rain water running into the part where the ribs and the covering meet. When this happens the ribs rust and the silk rots. By turning an umbrella upside down the water runs from these parts.

It is a good thing to put a small quantity of vaseline into the hinge portion of the frame. Vaseline does not spread like other oil, and so will not spoil the covering. For another thing, it is a sure preventative of rust, to which the ribs of an umbrella are liable.

Never tightly roll an umbrella. If you carry it through the streets like this, always allow it to stand loose at home. The covering will last ever so much longer.

Should you have the misfortune to make a small hole in the cover of your umbrella, it can be patched with some black sticking-plaster.

Cut a piece slightly bigger than the hole or patch you are repairing, and let it float in cold water, dull side down, until soft. Then very neatly place it inside the cover and over the hole, and allow it to dry.

A BLACKLEADING HINT

A good thing to save time and trouble when blackleading a stove is to moisten the blacklead with ammonia. This will give a most brilliant and lasting polish.

A stove or a grate never looks grey after being done in this way, and the polish will keep bright for weeks with an occasional brushing-up.

TO KEEP MOTHS FROM WOOLLENS

A pound of alum dissolved in four quarts of water. Dip the woollens in this liquid, and leave them to dry. It is a permanent protection from the devouring clothes-moth.

HOW TO CLEAN VELVET

THE best and quickest process is to get a piece of velvet, of as near the same colour as the dress, and, having smeared it with butter, to wipe it gently over the dress, particularly on the part where it is discoloured or stained.

If all the butter is afterwards carefully wiped off, the dress will look as fresh as when new. I would warn my little friend, however, that this remedy is only suitable for dark velvets. It would cause a light shade of velvet to change colour.

SAVE MOTHER'S COAL BILL

FILL the back of your stove with chalk. It gives out great heat, and it does not burn to ashes, and therefore lasts a very long time. One ton of coal will last as long as a ton and a half when chalk is used.

TO CURE BURNS AND SCALDS

SOME people have the habit, when any little accident occurs at home, of rushing off to the doctor, and, more frequently, to the chemist, for a remedy, wasting valuable time and money, when a cure is under their very noses.

Supposing you burn or scald your hand while helping mother in her cooking. The best method anyone can give you is a mixture of common whitening, such as is used for the hearth, mixed with water. Make it into a cream.

If it is used at once it will prevent blisters forming. As the heat dries up the moisture in

the whitening, it should be wetted again.

Similarly, pure butter forms an excellent ointment for all sorts of bruises, cuts, chaps, or roughness of the skin. The cream used in the manufacture of the butter has great soothing qualities.

THE SICK ROOM

A SICK-ROOM should be clean, airy and dry. If you have the choice of a room for the patient, select one with a south or south western aspect. This will protect the patient from direct sunlight for several hours in the day and yet obtain a soft, subdued light.

The room should not be too big. Quietness and good ventilation are essential. One on the top floor is best in the case of infectious diseases, for then it can be more easily isolated.

All the contents of the sick-room must be kept scrupulously clean. Keep it as cheerful and as bright as possible. Many young nurses make mistakes with flowers. They are often kept too long in the sick-room. Those with a strong perfume are not suitable.

Flowers should be taken from the sick-room at night-time, and until they are faded their water should be changed every night and morning.

In the sick-room every piece of furniture should be taken away except what is actually needed. The carpet, for instance, should be taken up and rugs put in its place. The reason for this is that the rugs can be removed easily for the purpose of cleaning the room, and that if it is necessary for them to be disinfected this can be done with the least possible trouble.

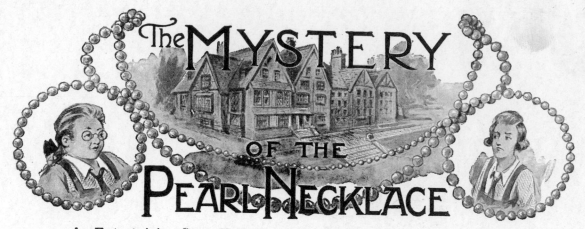

The MYSTERY OF THE PEARL NECKLACE

An Entertaining Story Telling of a Very Curious Series of Incidents at Cliff House School

By Hilda Richards

☾ ☾ ☾ ☾

CHAPTER I.

THE START OF A MYSTERY

CALLERS descended suddenly, and in a rush, upon Augusta Anstruther-Browne of the Fourth Form at Cliff House School.

Madge Stevens and Doris Redfern of the Third were the first. They tapped on the door, and popped two cheeky faces into the room before any invitation was given.

"Oh, Augusta——" began Madge.

"Sorry, but I'm busy!" said Augusta, without looking up from her preparation.

"We only want to borrow your violin," said Madge breathlessly. "We're getting up a jazz band. Fanny Tibbitts says she can manage a violin. So——"

"For a Third Form jazz band? Oh, my goodness!" said Augusta, in that really "crushing" voice that she could command when she liked. "I suppose you don't want to cut it in half so that two of you can use it?"

"Oh, no, nothing like that," said Doris Redfern persuasively. "Madge and I will look after it. I say, do lend it to us!"

"I'm far more likely to lend you all my dresses than the violin!" said Augusta. "Fancy thinking I would! Toddle off and try someone else—Connie Jackson, for instance. I want to be busy!"

She escorted the youngsters to the passage, closed the door, and returned to her seat. Hardly had she picked up her pen than there was a tap and the door started to open again.

"If you think——" began Augusta.

And there Augusta broke off, as she saw that her visitor was none other than moody-looking Marcia Loftus, the most unpopular girl in the Form.

"I've brought you up a letter," said Marcia, tossing an envelope sulkily on the table. "It was on the floor, and the kids were treading on it."

Augusta looked at the envelope with its foreign postmark, and an eager light leapt into her eyes.

"Oh, thanks, Marcia," she said, commencing to tear open the flap. "I think I know whom it's from."

Marcia lingered, a curious expression on her face.

"Yes, I thought——"

Marcia broke off as there was an ejaculation from the passage and the third batch of visitors broke into the study.

There was no time for Marcia to get away from the doorway.

Bump! bump! they went. And Marcia staggered back against the wall and gazed with glittering eyes at Barbara Redfern, the captain of the Fourth Form, and her chum Mabel Lynn.

"Sorry!" said Babs and Mabs, in one breath.

"Idiots!" snapped Marcia, rubbing her shoulder. "Flying into a study like mad girls. Why can't you look where you're going?"

"We didn't know you were standing just inside the door," said Babs.

"Well, look next time!" sneered the ill-tempered girl. "Jolly Babs and Mabs—always so full of spirits, always such dear, excited little girls!"

200

"Better than always sulking!" said Mabs with cheerful candour.

"Swankers!"

Augusta intervened.

"It was an accident, Marcia! No need to quarrel——"

"Oh, no! Friends of yours!" sneered Marcia. "All so jolly together—he, he, he! I'll bring your letters up to-morrow to see if I can get knocked about again!"

And Marcia flounced out of the study and banged the door in a very bad temper.

Babs and Mabs, not half as "squashed" as they ought to have felt, each grabbed one of Augusta's arms.

"Come on! We came to fetch you!" said Babs merrily. "It's Bessie Bunter! You simply must see her!"

"But I've got a letter——"

"Never mind! That can wait!" said Mabs. "All the fun will be over in a minute if you don't come along."

Augusta dropped the opened letter to the table.

"It's Bessie dressing up!" chuckled Babs, as she and her chum piloted Augusta eagerly to No. 4 study. "Ever since her people wrote saying they wanted a photo of her she's been doing it!"

"And talk about screams—oh, this really is the limit!" laughed Mabs. "Just a minute while I peep. Yes, it's all right."

The door of No. 4 study was opened very cautiously, and the three girls peeped at Bessie Bunter.

The fat girl of the Fourth had a mirror propped up in front of her, and was beaming with great satisfaction as she fumbled in a curious way with her ear.

Augusta saw that Bessie was trying to adorn herself with ear-rings of the type that are held by a small screw!

Bessie Bunter, quite unconscious of the presence of onlookers, was proceeding to turn

Bessie Bunter, unconscious of onlookers, gazed admiringly into the mirror as she fixed the ear-rings

the screw of one gaudy-looking ear-ring with her fat fingers.

She gave one brisk, good hard turn.

"Ow-wow-wow!" she ejaculated.

"Ha, ha, ha!"

Bessie started away from the chair. Something fell immediately, and went scrunch under her foot!

"Duffers! Now you've made me do it!" fumed Bessie.

Babs and Co. pealed with laughter.

"I've gone and pricked myself with one and trodden on the other!" hooted Bessie. "All through you startling me! Look at it! It can't possibly be straightened out!"

Babs and Mabs shrieked afresh as they gazed at the ear-ring that had felt the weight of Bessie Bunter.

"I'm blessed if I can see anything to cackle about!"

"You can't see yourself!"

"Rushing in on a girl, and startling her like that—you'll have to pay me compensation, anyway!"

"Fourpence!"

"Fourpence, when they cost sixpence-halfpenny—I mean, six and sixpence——"

"Ha, ha, ha!"

Bessie Bunter removed the one sound ear-ring from her ear and flung it on the table.

"It's jealousy! That's what it is!" she declared. "You're wild because I think of things that you don't. Ear-rings are awfully becoming, especially to a girl like myself. Don't you think I've got a rather Spanish type of beauty?"

"It certainly isn't English!" murmured Mabs.

"Oh, really——"

"African, I should say, Bessie," said Augusta very seriously.

"Yes, African, perhaps," said Bessie thoughtfully. "It might——"

"You only need to black your face—that's all!" finished Augusta.

Bessie sniffed. It was a most emphatic sniff, and it was followed by the banging of the door as Bessie sailed away.

Augusta recovered from her laughter and turned to Babs and Mabs.

"Poor Bessie!" she exclaimed. "Now let's get back to my study and see what my letter says. It may interest you girls."

"Who's it from?" Babs asked.

"Lorna Grey, I believe."

"Lorna!" said Babs. "My word, how long it seems since she left the school and joined her aunt on the Continent!"

"Yet I often think of her, and the times we had," Augusta replied. "She writes occasionally, and seems to be enjoying herself. Come on!"

She hurried back with them to her study.

But once there Augusta paused, amazement replacing the eager expression on her face.

"Why, it's gone!" she cried.

It was true! There was certainly no letter on the table, although they had seen Augusta drop it there.

"Perhaps it's blown down," suggested Babs; and they started to search.

They hunted everywhere, but without any result.

"What an extraordinary thing!" said Babs.

"Surely no one would take it?" said Mabs.

"I can't think of anyone who would want to read a letter from Lorna Grey," said Augusta. "Perhaps it's a jape."

She ran to the door as she heard a footstep outside. Marcia Loftus was just passing.

Peggy Preston, the cleverest girl in the Fourth

"I say, Marcia, you haven't seen that letter from Lorna Grey, have you?" Augusta asked.

Marcia's eyes glinted in sudden anger.

"Do you accuse me of taking that letter?" she demanded. "Saying such a thing, when I troubled to bring the letter up to you!" Marcia continued passionately. "How dare you insinuate such things! If the letter's gone it's where you left it! If you can't look after your own letters, don't you dare to come to me!"

And Marcia whirled round and hurried away.

There were startled looks in the study.

"My word! She can fly into a temper!" said Babs. "And why? There was nothing in what Augusta said to make her reply like that."

"Oh, Marcia all over!" said Augusta. "Let's have another look!"

They had commenced to search again when a loud and discordant noise came suddenly from outside the study.

"Ow-oooooh! Oh-oooooh! Yooooowl!"

Bang, bang, bang!

Trrrrrumpitty-trump, trump!

"Gracious! What ever is it?" cried Babs.

Augusta smiled.

"I should say it's the Third Form jazzband come to annoy me because I wouldn't lend them my violin. We'd better go out and clear them off!"

She opened the door.

Madge Stevens was outside, in charge of a dozen cheerful-looking and very noisy youngsters. The "music" stopped abruptly.

"Grab hold of Augusta!" cried Madge. "We'll make her listen to the band!"

A rush was made at Augusta.

"Rescue!" cried Babs and Mabs, running to Augusta's aid. But twelve Third Formers were far too many for three of their old rivals of the Fourth, no matter how determined they might be. Babs and Co. were seized and held against the wall while Fanny Tibbitts prepared to treat them to a solo from the terribly battered bugle that she had adopted on failing to borrow a violin.

Trrrrrmp! Trumpitty-trump!

"My hat! What a giddy rumpus!" cried a voice, as the door of the common-room opened. "Gee whiz! It's the Third! Come and send the cheeky kids away!"

The speaker was Clara Trevlyn, known as the "Tomboy of the Fourth."

Clara led a rush of girls from the common-room.

The members of the Third had not come prepared to deal with such a situation at all. They were simply swept off their feet. The offending musical instruments were seized and treated as such things should. Clara set the lead by rolling the battered-looking drum down the stairs.

"Send them after their things!" ordered Clara.

Madge Stevens took alarm.

"Clear!" she ordered; and her followers "cleared."

They were followed by cheery voices from the triumphant Fourth.

"Come back, and we'll roll you down like the drum!"

"We'll make you sing quite a new tune!"

"Give us a solo from down there!"

The Third Formers had descended hurriedly. They looked ruffled and far from happy. They knew that themselves.

So Madge Stevens gave a defiant glare on behalf of the whole party.

" Bah ! " she said. " Cheeky Fourth Formers ! Think you're clever ! "

" We know we are ! " said Babs blandly.

" We'll have our revenge ! " said Doris Redfern. " You think you've scored, but it wasn't your business to interfere at all. We were only japing Augusta."

" And it didn't come off ! "

" No need for you all to butt in ! " declared Madge Stevens. " We'll make them sorry for it, eh ? What do you girls say ? "

" Rather ! " cheered the Third Formers.

They little guessed the far-reaching effects that were to come out of that resolution to revive the ancient " hostility " between the Forms ; little guessed the mystery in which they were to be involved — the mystery that had started with the strange disappearance of Augusta's letter.

CHAPTER II.

WHOSE NECKLACE ?

MADGE STEVENS AND CO. returned rather more quietly than usual to the common room that served youngsters who had not attained to the dignity of studies.

Certain low-voiced remarks, however, showed that their calm was only the prelude to action. A chorus, which usually consisted of " Oh, rather ! " indicated that the Third were unanimous. It was part of the joy of life for these cheeky, irresponsible youngsters to be "at war" with someone.

Barbara Redfern, the Captain of the Fourth Form

" We'll work some ripping jape on them ! " declared Madge Stevens.

" Oh, rather ! "

" If we could make them come to us and beg for mercy ! " chuckled Doris Redfern, taking a great flight of fancy.

" It would be ripping ! " said Iris Marshall, one of the Two Blossoms.

" Oh, rather ! "

Then they fell silent again, wondering what great and crushing scheme might be hatched for dealing with the Fourth. It seemed easier to hope than to think of the idea, but they made a good effort.

That was why a figure lurking in the Third Form common-room did not hear their unusually silent return.

An unusual figure she was, too, to be seen here at all. There was something mysterious and uneasy in her movements. And what a start she gave as the door suddenly opened, and the first of the youngsters entered !

" Marcia Loftus ! " ejaculated Madge Stevens. " I say, girls, just look who's here ! A Fourth Former ! "

" Cheek ! " said Doris Redfern. " What's she doing ? "

Marcia was standing over by the window, a spot of colour in her cheeks, her thin lips twisted in an uneasy smile.

" I—I came down to see you," she announced.

" Us ? "

" Yes. About a—a book. You were asking if anyone could lend you a nice book. I've just read a rather decent one."

Madge Stevens stared.

" Not you ! " she said. " Whew ! Fancy you ever troubling to tell anyone anything ! You've been down here trying to rag us ! "

" I haven't ! " cried Marcia, starting to move to the door. " I —I wondered where you were. I've only just got here."

Marcia made a sudden rush for the door.

" Here ! Not so quickly ! " cried Madge, hanging on to her. " We never invited you down. Lend a hand, Blossoms ! She's struggling ! "

" Let me alone ! You sha'n't bully me ! Let me go or you'll be sorry ! " This and much more yelled Marcia Loftus.

" Marcia, if you dare to kick you'll be sorry ! " cried Fanny Tibbitts. " Madge, catch hold of her legs ! "

Madge Stevens boiled with youthful indignation.

" I sentence the cheeky Fourth Former to go Under the Table at Sea ! " she cried. " Pull her along, all of you ! We'll make her sorry for coming here ! "

" Don't you dare ! Leave me alone ! I'll report you ! " shrieked Marcia.

The reply of the Third Formers was to roll her on the ground. Experienced hands towed her along and helped to thrust her under the common-room table. The whole assembled company formed gleefully round the sides.

" Now, Marcia, you're going to stay there until you apologise ! " said Madge, with revered serenity. " Understand ? Off to Sea, girls ! "

The table began to joggle and bump about.

" Under the Table at Sea " was one of the specialised " punishments " that resourceful Madge had invented for dealing with unruly Third Formers. There were many of these weird and wonderful ways in vogue in the Third.

" Stop it ! Let me go ! " shrieked Marcia in muffled tones.

The table joggled on as the Third Formers moved it all round the room—with Marcia underneath.

If she stopped for a moment the table was sure to descend on her, or else someone would tread on her !

" Had enough ? " asked Madge.

Marcia made a sudden dash on all fours as the Third Formers unwisely paused, and in another moment she had scrambled out from under the table and was rushing for the door.

" Capture her ! "

But Marcia was out of the door. Marcia may have been very furious, but she also showed wisdom. Under the table was the most uncomfortable place that Marcia had discovered for a long while.

The Third Formers stopped in the passage, yelling with laughter.

" Poor old Marcia—what a shock for her ! " chuckled Madge Stevens gleefully.

She led the way back to the common-room, where their further merriment would probably take the form of another of Madge's ingenious inventions—this time the Third Form Dance of Triumph. But hardly were they inside than the door opened again, and a fat face and glimmering spectacles appeared.

" Come in, Bessie Bunter ! " invited Doris impishly ; and Bessie obeyed.

Poor Bessie was always a very unlucky girl. Through her little tiff with Babs and Mabs over the ear-rings she did not know that a " state of war " existed between Fourth and Third !

" Just thought I'd come along and see you," said Bessie blandly. " I'm having my photograph taken next week, you know."

" How dreadful for the camera ! " said Madge.

" Cheek ! " exclaimed Bessie. " Better be careful, young Madge, or I shall talk to you severely ! I really came down to see if you could lend me one or two things to wear when I have my photograph taken. You know, I'm a girl who looks rather well in jewellery."

" There's plenty of room to put it ! " chuckled Doris.

Bessie Bunter gave her a dignified blink.

" I think I'll let you lend me your brooch, Doris," she said. " Of course, it isn't the sort of thing that I'd wear in the ordinary way. But in a photograph people won't see that it's only brass, will they ? "

Doris Redfern started.

Bessie's way of putting things was not tactful, to say the least.

" Then I'll borrow two or three bangles—just for the day," Bessie went on blandly. " There's

that one that Madge must have got at a fair or somewhere—it's rather tinny, but it may look like silver in a photograph."

" Cheek ! " gasped Madge, astounded.

" Yes, cheap, of course," nodded Bessie. " It's only coloured glass in it, but it'll only be just in the corner of the picture. Then I think I'll have that celluloid hair-slide that Jessie calls tortoiseshell—it will look like it in the print. And I'll have—— I say, what are you doing, Doris Redfern ? "

Doris looked as though she was hugging Bessie.

" I—I say ! Ow ! " shrieked the fat girl. " What have I done ? What are you trying to do ? "

" You're going Under the Table at Sea for your sauce ! " said Madge. " Kim on ! "

Bessie shrieked with alarm. She knew all about it. Bessie was quite an experienced " voyager " so far as that punishment was concerned.

" Help ! Rescue ! I won't go under the horrid old table ! Let me alone ! Ow ! You're pinching ! "

Bessie Bunter was fat, but they still knew how to get her under the table. Skilled hands did it quickly.

And then came a yell that startled even the Third.

Bessie was shrieking—with excitement !

" Pearls ! I say, there's a string of pearls under here ! "

" Where ? " cried Madge.

Bessie crawled out backwards from under the table, holding a very pretty string of pearls in her hand.

" My hat ! " ejaculated Doris. " Wherever did they come from ? "

Everyone was clustering to look at Bessie's discovery.

" They were under the table ! "

" Never ! " cried incredulous voices.

" They were. I saw—— Oh, dear ! Hooray ! " Bessie Bunter gave a yell of delight. " They're mine—my missing pearls ! Those I lost some time ago ! I recognise—— Oh, I say, what are you doing ? "

Madge Stevens had grabbed the treasure.

" Give me my pearls ! " cried Bessie Bunter.

" I don't believe they are yours ! "

" They are ! I tell you I've recognised them ! My missing pearls ! I shall want them for my photograph ! "

Madge held the pearls behind her back.

Bessie struggled in tremendous indignation to get possession of them, and at that moment the door opened and two cheerful faces looked in. It was Babs and Mabs.

Babs and Co. were held against the wall by the Third Formers, while Fanny Tibbitts performed a solo of triumph on a battered bugle

"Hallo!" said Babs. "What's all the racket?"

"They've got my pearls!" cried Bessie desperately. "Those I lost some time ago. They won't give them to me!"

"They're not her pearls!" retorted Madge. "She's trying to bag them for her silly old photograph!"

Babs and Mabs asked for an explanation. It was given in a very noisy manner. Bessie insisted on saying as much as everybody else until seized for a fresh "trip to sea."

"Queer that they should be found there," murmured Babs. "Doesn't anyone in the Third claim them?"

"No," said Madge. "No one's got a string like them."

"I tell you they're mine!" squeaked Bessie hotly.

"They don't look like them," said Babs. "Be-

sides, you lost yours months ago, and you weren't sure whether you dropped them in the school or in the village."

"I'm sure now! I—I dropped them in here!" declared Bessie. "They must have been under the carpet all the time!"

Madge Stevens gave an exclamation.

"I know! They're Marcia's. She probably dropped them. See if you can find her, Doris."

Marcia was quickly found and brought somewhat reluctantly along the passage.

"Are these yours, Marcia?" asked Madge, holding the string aloft.

The Fourth Former shook her head emphatically.

"No," said Marcia. "Why should they be mine? I haven't got any pearls like those."

"There you are!" yelled Bessie Bunter, "That proves they're mine!"

"It doesn't! And you're not going to have them!" said Madge Stevens.

Babs intervened.

"They might be Bessie's, Madge, if she's so sure," she said. "She's as much entitled to them as anyone else. I think you'd better hand them over."

"No fear!" chuckled Madge. "Fourth Form advice! Thank you for nothing. We don't want it! We're going to keep these pearls as Third Form Treasure until they're claimed."

CHAPTER III.

LOST AND FOUND

THE discovery of the pearls in the Third Form common-room was the talk of the school that evening.

A Fifth Form girl examined them and pronounced them to be good artificial ones worth a couple of pounds. Now Bessie Bunter's had certainly not been worth anything like that!

But the strange thing was that, although the whole school heard of the discovery, no one with the exception of Bessie made any claim to them. And while the Third Formers advanced wild and most extravagant theories about burglars dropping them, the majority of the Fourth really considered that the fat girl was entitled to them.

She had certainly had pearls, and lost them, at an earlier date. No one else in the school seemed to have lost pearls.

Augusta Anstruther-Browne, the Fourth Form violinist

Fourth Formers, considering the matter gravely and judicially, told Madge Stevens that she had no right to keep the treasure. Madge and Co., being "at war" as they termed it, turned the position into a "score."

"We've got them, anyway!" they taunted the Fourth. "Get them if you can! Pearl snatchers. Any way's good enough for the Fourth! Ha, ha!"

In consequence of such boastfulness there were quite a number of skirmishes between the two Forms before bedtime, and it was therefore not surprising that there should be a dormitory raid that night.

Madge and Co., who went to bed earlier than the Fourth, laid their plans with great care. They crept from their dormitory as soon as the Fourth had gone to bed. With one yell they swept upon the foe.

"We'll show them who can guard pearls!" Madge Stevens cried. "We'll show them what we're made of!"

"Oh, rather!" came the Third Form cry. "At them!"

But the Fourth were not caught as unprepared as they might have been.

"It's the Third!" sang out Babs. "Quick, girls—back against the beds and get the pillows. Mabs—you and I for the bolster!"

Merry cries, and the thud of pillows, echoed through the dormitory when Babs and Mabs put into effect an idea that they had long considered.

Swinging a bolster between them they charged upon the Third Formers.

"Hurrah! They're going!" cheered Bessie Bunter, who had taken up her station on a distant bed. "Look out! I'm going to rush at you in a mum-mum-minute, Madge! I shall hit jolly hard when I do. Go it, Clara!"

Clara and Dolly Jobling were wielding another bolster.

The effect of that second bolster was to strike dismay to the hearts of the daring youngsters who had relied upon a quick and surprising raid on the Fourth, and an equally quick return to their dormitory.

A frantic rush for the door was made by those nearest to it, and the leaders regretfully followed.

Babs chuckled as she and Mabs pursued them.

"Make them run for it!" she whispered to the others. "We'll chase them into a corner and let them think we're really wild with them, eh?"

"Jolly good wheeze!" grinned Clara. "Fancy them thinking they could pillow-rag us!"

Bessie Bunter had descended from the bed. She called a courageous message after Babs and Co.

"You hold them, and I'll come along with a pillow and jolly well lam them for pushing me under the table!" she directed.

But the Fourth were too busy to heed such advice.

Pursuers and pursued fled rapidly.

Madge and Co. had unwittingly blundered into a corridor from which there was no escape. They drew up at the end, panting. The Fourth Formers came on, looking very determined indeed.

"Peace!" gasped Madge.

"Surrender?" asked Babs, in a stern and commanding voice.

"Oh, rather!" said the unfortunate members of the Third.

"All right," Babs said. "We'll pardon them this time, girls. What are the conditions? Supposing they solemnly declare that they are very sorry—a hundred times!"

"Oh, rats! We sha'n't say anything like that!" declared Madge cheekily. "We'll say that we'll make you sorry for yourselves to-morrow, if you like!"

"Poor misguided infants," chaffed Babs. "As we are strong so will we be merciful. Go in peace or else you'll go in pieces."

And the Third adopted the former policy.

Hardly had the Fourth returned and started to undress than Madge and Co. were on them again.

"Hallo! They've come for some more!" sang out Babs, moving for the bolster.

"It isn't that!" Madge answered excitedly. "Someone's taken the pearl necklace! It's missing!"

"Missing?" cried Babs, in amazement.

"Yes. Have you got it, Bessie Bunter?"

Bessie gasped.

"Of—of course I haven't! I—I never thought a word—"

"Well, it's gone!" said Madge. "'Tisn't fair to take it when we are ragging, is it, Babs? I mean, a jape's a jape. That's taking advantage."

"Quite true!" admitted Babs. "But — but — it's one of the girls who wasn't ragging — one who stopped behind here!" declared Madge. "We're going to search and see if we can find it."

"Steady on!" Babs exclaimed. "You're not going to search Fourth Formers. Here—keep them off! It's like their cheek! We'll do any searching that needs to be done!"

The Third Formers rushed for the beds of those who had been non-combatants.

Hardly had they started than a yell came from Fanny Tibbitts.

"I've found it!"

Everyone—Third and Fourth alike—turned in amazement as the girl stooped to the carpet in front of the fireplace and held a pearl necklace aloft.

"Right at the foot of Bessie's bed!" Fanny piped.

"Pearls!" shrieked Bessie in tremendous excitement. "They were underneath the table — and — and I believe they're the ones I lost some time ago!"

"I didn't see it there, anyway!" exclaimed Bessie. "I'd jolly soon have had it if I *had* seen it!"

Madge and Co. closed round the figure of Fanny and backed, with their precious "treasure," towards the door.

"We're going to keep it, anyway!" announced Madge. "Jolly mean trick taking the necklace when we were ragging."

And the Third departed, leaving an air of profound mystery in the dormitory.

"Bessie, did you have it?" asked Babs.

"No, I didn't!" shrilled Bessie. "And I don't think you're much of a chum to let them rob me of my necklace before my very own eyes!"

"But, Bessie, no one believes it is yours!" said Babs. "You'd really better leave it to the Third, now they've found it."

"I won't!"

"Then you must have had it!"

"I wouldn't have thrown my own property on the carpet if only I'd had it!" declared Bessie; and that certainly sounded convincing enough.

"Then where did it come from?" asked Clara Trevlyn.

No one answered. No one could. For if Bessie Bunter was not the girl who had stolen into the Third Form dormitory and taken the necklace during the commotion, who was?

CHAPTER IV.

BY WHOSE HAND?

"Where is it, Madge? In bed?"

"Under my pillow, and safe as houses!" answered Madge Stevens.

It was more than half an hour later, but there was still some excited whispering to be heard in the Third Form dormitory.

Madge Stevens and Co. were considering two important matters. One was the Fourth Form, and what manner of "return jape" should be played. The other was the necklace.

And really the necklace seemed the more interesting of the two, for at least a dozen times Madge had been asked to make quite sure that she still held the Third Form " treasure."

The fact that it should disappear and then be found in such a dramatic manner made it a far more interesting object in Third Form eyes. Somebody wanted it. It was exciting to hold something that someone else wanted, especially when they could not decide who that someone was.

For the members of the Third were, now they came to talk it over, not quite sure that Bessie was the culprit.

Just as they were dropping off to sleep Madge Stevens heard Fanny Tibbitts softly call her by name.

" Madge ! "

" Oh, what is it now, Fanny ? "

" Can you feel a wind—as though the door's open ? "

No answer came.

" Madge, I believe you can ! And I'm positive the door's open ! " said Fanny, her bed creaking as she sat up. " Someone strike a match ! "

Madge's chuckle sounded rather forced.

" No good trying — you simply won't scare me ! " she said. " I'm guarding the necklace, and I'll see it stays under my pillow——Oh ! "

The last sound was a gasp of alarm.

Suddenly Madge saw it—a black figure in the darkness. A hand grabbed at her and threw her roughly to one side of the bed—she almost fell out. Then her pillow jerked smotheringly across her face.

Madge wriggled free, and yelled.

" Help ! Help ! Someone in the dorm—some-one's stolen the necklace ! "

She heard a swift pattering footstep, a bump—then silence.

Everyone leapt out of bed and blundered towards the door.

" Someone's stolen it and rushed off ! " Madge Stevens cried. " But I'll catch her, whoever she is ! I'll—— Oh ! "

Doris gave a gasping cry, and there came the sound of a heavy thud. Someone at last switched on the electric light. Madge was sprawling in the doorway, and under her feet was the pillow that had caused her fall.

The bed that she had left was in scattered and wild disorder.

" Hurt ? " they cried, running to help their chum to her feet.

" No. Someone left that pillow. I fell over. It doesn't look like one of ours. Some girl must have dropped it. We'll find her, this time."

She was already hurrying into the corridor.

The Two Blossoms, Fanny Tibbitts, and Minnie Jerome—famed as being of a most inquiring turn of mind, and always in everything—pattered across the dormitory and followed.

" Some Fourth Former for a certainty ! " Madge muttered. " My word, it's all in darkness. But it must have been one of them. If we're quick we may see."

She spun open the door and clicked on the electric light. Their eyes took in a long line of slumbering figures—and one empty bed. That bed was near to the fireplace.

Clara Trevlyn, the Tomboy of the Fourth Form.

" Hallo ! What ever's the matter ? " asked the sleepy voice of Babs as she sat up and rubbed her eyes.

" It's Madge again ! " gasped Clara. " My hat, if that bolster——"

" I say, we've been robbed ! " Madge interrupted breathlessly. " Someone's just stolen the necklace. She came this way. Who's out of that bed there ? "

Babs looked, and gasped.

" Bessie Bunter ! But—but——"

" Is this her pillow ? " asked Doris.

" I don't know ! " said Babs, more bewildered. " But there certainly isn't one on her bed. It looks—— Oh, my goodness ! "

There was a patter of footsteps. The fat figure of Bessie Bunter, clad in slippers and dressing-gown, whizzed into the dormitory.

" Oh, dear," she gasped, " what ever is it ? Bib-bib-burglars ? "

The Third grabbed her, bringing a further yell from her.

" Where's the necklace ? "

" I—I don't know ! " stuttered Bessie Bunter. " I—I've looked everywhere."

" What ? "

" But I—I couldn't find where you've hidden it——"

" And you were the burglar ! " said Madge grimly. " It's no good pretending, Bessie Bunter. You've been in our dormitory. Where have you hidden the pearls ? "

Bessie stared at Madge in bewilderment.

" I—I haven't been near your dormitory ! " she cried.

" Fibber ! "

" It's a fact ! I've been down in the common-room. I thought you might have hidden the pearls there ! ”

“ Then how did your pillow get in our room ? ” asked Madge, exhibiting that article triumphantly.

Bessie blinked from the pillow to her bed and back to the pillow.

The sleepy voice of Marcia Loftus chimed in at that moment.

“ What ever's all the noise about ? I wish you kids would go and argue somewhere else ! ” she said peevishly.

“ Bessie's taken our pearls ! ” said Fanny Tibbitts.

“ I—I haven't had them—— ”

Marcia sat up in bed, frowning sleepily and disagreeably.

“ Oh, don't listen to Bessie, Madge ! ” she said. “ You know what a story-teller she is—always full of excuses ! Make her show you where they are ! ”

“ I haven't been near your dormitory, Madge ! ” quavered Bessie. “ I didn't know the horrid old pearls were there at all. Oh, dear, I've had such a shock, too, thinking there were bib-bib-burglars ! ”

Babs interposed.

“ I say, you kids, pack it up now ! ” she advised the Third. “ We don't know anything about the pearls, and I'm sure Bessie doesn't ! Bessie would tell you if she'd hidden the pearls. Go away ! You'll find out who's got them when it's daylight. It's all through making such a song in the school that you've been japed about like this ! ”

Bessie Bunter, the fat girl of the Fourth Form

The general opinion supported Babs ; and Clara went further and offered Madge and Co. a good shaking if they robbed her of further “ beauty sleep.” And so, after a last protest, Bessie was allowed to take her pillow and return to her bed ; and Madge and Co. went.

The dormitory was in darkness. Babs had turned over to sleep again when a sudden thought struck her. She was quite startled.

No one had explained how Bessie's pillow came to be in the Third Form dormitory !

A mystery that — unless, indeed, it was positive proof ! And then Babs thought of Bessie. She was a blunderer in the general way. Was it possible for her to make such a daring and single-handed raid on the Third ?

It was a perplexing thought and enough to keep Babs awake for longer than she wished.

CHAPTER V.

THE THIRD FORM WAY

BABS woke on the following morning to hear the complaining voice of a girl who seldom complained in the ordinary way.

“ It's getting a bit of a craze—this taking of things that belong to someone else,” Augusta Anstruther-Browne was remarking. “ That letter of mine from Lorna Grey hasn't turned up. I don't see how it could possibly interest anyone, and yet it's gone ! ”

“ A very clever business that,” said Clara Trevlyn.

“ It would have been returned by now if anyone took it for a jape,” said Augusta.

“ You weren't out of the study for five minutes—that's what beats me,” said Babs. “ Someone must have gone in and taken it at once.”

Augusta gave a puzzled frown and went to wash.

Babs slid out of bed and cast an eye round for the slackers. As Form captain it was more or less her duty to see that everyone turned out in time for breakfast.

Bessie, as usual, was snoring.

But there was one vacant bed, and Babs cried out :

“ Where's Marcia ? ”

“ Gone down to do some prep. she didn't do last night,” said Clara. “ She was nearly dressed when I got up. Must have risen before rising-bell.”

“ Strange for Marcia to worry about prep ! ” ruminated Babs. “ Wish she would every morning. Now then, Fatima—awake, my fairy ! ”

Babs stooped and whirled the bed-clothes off Bessie Bunter's curled-up form, and “ the fairy ” abruptly straightened out and shrieked.

“ Ow ! It's cold ! ”

“ Time to get up, my sweetest ! ”

“ I'm going to have another five minutes ! ”

“ Yes, without the bedclothes ! ” smiled Babs, holding them tightly. “ Curl up peacefully. I'll tell you when the time's up ! ”

Bessie Bunter favoured Babs with an indignant glare and rolled discontentedly out of bed. Five minutes under those conditions wasn't good enough !

The Fourth Formers were still chuckling, when the door opened to reveal the cheerful faces of Madge Stevens and Co. Madge stepped into the room—wearing a string of pearls !

“ My hat,” cried Clara, “ have you found them ? ”

Madge Stevens chuckled delightedly.

" Of course! Trust the Third to get what they want!" she said. "We were up before rising-bell searching for them. You'll never guess where they were!"

"Under your pillow all the time?" suggested Babs.

"Wrong—so there! We found them tucked on top of a beam in the corridor. Only one of them was showing! We searched ever so long before we found them."

Bessie Bunter having just commenced her real ablutions, whirled round from the wash-stand.

"Have they found the pearls?" she gasped. "I say, Babs, grab them! Have they found the—— Ow! Ooooh! Where's a towel? A towel, someone!"

"But you haven't washed the soap off your face!" said Mabel Lynn.

"It's all gone in my eyes through trying to see the pearls!" wailed Bessie Bunter. "Oh, I'll be blinded! Give me a towel, quick!"

It was most unfortunate for poor Bessie that she would not even see the treasures!

"And we didn't find them with the help of the Fourth, either!" said Madge triumphantly. "We've had a helper from your Form—Marcia gave us a hand."

And with this surprising piece of information the youngsters departed as quickly as they had come.

"So they're back," said Babs in a puzzled voice. "Found on a beam in the corridor! Marcia helped them, too! Curious!"

Bessie raised a red face from the towel.

"Did you grab them, Babs?"

"Of course not, Bessie."

"Well, I've told you I'm going to have my photo taken——"

"Oh, bother the photo! I don't believe they're yours at all!" said Babs quite crossly. "I've had enough of those pearls!"

"I haven't had one of them yet, although I found them!" said Bessie morosely. "It's my necklace, too. I'll have it!"

Babs let it go at that, rather than argue. She was not pleased at the vanity that Bessie was showing over her forthcoming photograph. She wished that Bessie's people had never thought of the idea and given such long notice.

After breakfast the Fourth Formers were strolling in the quadrangle when Bessie Bunter came rushing up to them in a very breathless and excited state.

"Babs! Mabs! Clara! I'm being insulted!" she cried. "I say, come and go for them, girls!"

Clara tapped her forehead significantly.

"She's lost her reason at last!" Clara sighed.

"That's right—I mean, don't be so silly, Clara!" cried Bessie. "You come along and see what the Third are doing. They're making fun of the most influential girl in the Form. It's an insult to the Fourth! You come along and go for them! They're in the common-room. It's an absolute insult! I'd a good mind to go to Miss Primrose when I saw it! Oh dear, I do feel annoyed! You come and shake them, Babs!"

Babs sighed and followed Bessie. Quite a number followed Babs. They had an idea that there was something interesting.

And there was!

The Third Form common-room door was open. A crowd of gleeful youngsters were arranged around a queer dummy propped on the table. Babs and Mabs looked at it—and went off into shrieks of laughter.

The dummy was made from a sack, and was very fat. It had a very large head, and wore " glasses " made out of bent wire. Around its neck was a string of white turnips, evidently representing " pearls," and two carrots hung from its ears as ear-rings. And a notice pinned on the dummy read:

A Typical Fourth Former.

All Ready to be Photographed.

Isn't it Wonderful!

Clara Trevlyn, Flap Derwent, Phyllis Howell, and Peggy Preston looked at the dummy—and shrieked as well!

"Oh, I say!" exploded Bessie Bunter furiously. "You're laughing!"

"No—no," said Babs feebly. "It's only a rumour!"

"It's supposed to be *me!*" shrieked Bessie. "They say it's a typical Fourth Former. Don't you think it's an insult?"

"It is—to call you typical!" grinned Clara. "You're one on your own, Bessie! Ha, ha, ha!"

Madge Stevens and Co. were also pealing with laughter.

"One of the pearl-loving Fourth!" she chortled. "I say, Babs, aren't you proud of your old chum now?"

"There you are!" hooted Bessie. "They're still being insulting, and you're afraid of them. Yah! Afraid to go for them! Coward!"

"How about yourself, Bessie?" asked Mabs.

Babs turned to the others.

"It's very funny, but I suppose we'd better give these Third Formers what they're asking for, girls," she said. "Catch them!"

"If you can!" said Madge Stevens; and she headed a frantic rush for the passage, broke from Clara who grabbed at her, and fled, pealing with laughter, at the head of her followers.

Bessie Bunter rushed at the "guy," dragged it from the table, and jumped on it furiously.

"Now you can understand what we feel we'd like to do to you sometimes, Fatima," said Clara.

"Eh? What's that?" said Bessie, pausing.

"Why, what you're doing now! Jump on you!" said Clara.

Bessie Bunter glared furiously.

"You were afraid to go for the Third, anyway!" she said. "I wasn't! I called them all sorts of things when I saw this horrid old dummy. When they've got my missing pearls——"

Marcia smiled apologetically.

"I'm sorry. I shan't do so again. If it's your necklace you ought to have it. I see that now. If you like, I'll try and help you get your pearls again. And I think I've got a plan."

"It's supposed to be *me!*" shrieked Bessie. "This is an insult to the Fourth, and I call on you, Babs, to avenge it."

"Oh, for goodness' sake be quiet about the pearls, Bessie!" cried Babs. "Come on, girls, and let her talk to herself!"

Bessie Bunter saw her Form chums depart, with the Third unpunished. It made her so angry that she jumped on the guy again—twice. Even that did not relieve her feelings.

Marcia Loftus came along just then.

"Got the necklace yet, Bessie?" she asked.

"No, I haven't!" growled Bessie. "And I don't want to talk to you about it. You backed up those Third Form kids last night."

CHAPTER VI.

THE OTHER PEARLS!

BESSIE BUNTER was in quite a fever of excitement at dinner-time that Wednesday. She had just heard Marcia's "plan."

"The pearls," said Marcia, "were locked in a box in the Third Form common-room, and the key hung on the wall, concealed underneath a kettle-holder!"

Bessie would have rushed off at once to secure the key and try the box if Marcia had not stopped her.

"Not yet, Bessie!" she warned. "Take your time; pretend you know nothing. I believe they're going to carry out some jape on the Second. That will give you your chance."

And Marcia went away, chuckling.

Bessie hung about in the corridors, waiting her chance. She was very excited. Twice she nearly gave herself away when she was lurking near the Third Form common-room, and girls came along.

But at last her opportunity dawned.

Madge and Co. came out in a body and went cheerily up the stairs. Bessie watched the last of them go, and then moved to the common-room. She was inside—and alone! At last!

Her fat fingers trembled so badly as she took the key from its hiding-place that she dropped it twice on the floor.

But there was the playbox that belonged to Madge Stevens—a big wooden affair. Bessie turned the key in the lock. Her heart thumped at the creaking of the lid, and she threw terrified glances in the direction of the door. But no one seemed to have heard.

And there were the pearls!

She took them out of the box and put them round her neck. She beamed on herself in a looking-glass. Her pearls at last!

Bessie was so wildly excited that she almost forgot to lock the box and return the key.

But she did so. Then she took off the pearls and tied them up in her handkerchief. Looking a picture of guilt, Bessie crept away from the common-room and scuttled up the stairs.

Now that she had taken them, she certainly felt a rather uneasy conscience pricking her.

No. 4 study was empty when Bessie entered and banged the door with quite unnecessary force in her excitement. She gazed round for a hiding-place. The bookcase? Behind the dusty old cookery books with which she had long since dispensed—the very spot!

Bessie hid the pearls—and her conscience pricked her again.

Bessie was a very poor one at keeping a secret.

"I—I think I ought to tell Babs and Mabs," she muttered. "They're bound to be in the quadrangle. I'll go down and see them."

Bessie Bunter, trembling between admiration of her own daring and a queer uneasiness, scuttled off to the quadrangle.

Although it was a Wednesday afternoon, it was not a very promising day, and numbers of girls were still in the quadrangle, talking.

Babs and Mabs were in conversation with Miss Bullivant when Bessie sailed up.

Bessie had no wish to converse with the "Bull," as affectionate pupils called her. But something in the mistress's excited manner made it impossible for Bessie to keep away.

"I have just returned from Friardale," Miss Bullivant was saying in a jerky tone. "I am telling you as Fourth Form captain—a girl likely to be able to throw some light on the matter. For pearls to be missing is really such a serious thing that I could do nothing but return immediately."

Bessie Bunter's heart seemed to give a leap right into her throat.

"But, Miss Bullivant," Babs was protesting, "surely this has nothing to do with Cliff House——"

"It has!" said Miss Bullivant sharply. "Two days ago a string of quite valuable artificial pearls disappeared from the jeweller's shop. A Cliff House girl had been making purchases there when they went. The jeweller has made no accusation, but he has talked—talked to everyone."

"Then it's only talk——"

"Talk is worse than an accusation!" exclaimed the mistress. "I only heard it second-hand in the village. I was most indignant. That the common tradesmen should be saying such a thing about a Cliff House girl—no, that man shall apologise! I will have the whole matter thrashed out!"

Bessie Bunter's throat was dry as she listened.

"I will make him apologise for such scandalous talk in the village. He declared that the pearls were lost after a Cliff House girl had bought some cheap and tawdry ear-rings! The story was so absurd that I would not even go to question the man. It is ridiculous to believe that any girl at this school would purchase sixpenny earrings! I would like you, Barbara, to find out the names of the girls who have recently visited this jeweller and let me know. I am now going to see Miss Primrose."

Miss Bullivant sailed grimly away, intent upon clearing the honour of the school she loved in her own jealous and stern way.

Bessie Bunter shook like a fat jelly as Babs and Mabs looked at her.

"Sixpenny ear-rings!" Babs breathed. "Why, Bessie, are you the girl who has been to this shop?"

Bessie Bunter could hardly speak.

"Only w-w-w-once——"

"But you have been there?"

"I—I didn't steal the pearls!" gasped Bessie. Babs and Mabs stared at her.

"They—they're my mum-mum-missing nun-nun-necklace!" stammered Bessie. "I—I recognised them when I sis-sis-saw them in the Third. I—I haven't stolen them."

Babs was looking very serious, and her brow was puckered with thought.

"No, Bessie, we know *you're* not a thief," she said gently. "But this is really a very serious business—pearls missing from the village, and a stray necklace turning up at the school. I must tell Madge Stevens that it will be better for her to give the necklace to Miss Primrose at once."

Bessie Bunter clung to Babs and Mabs as they would have hurried away.

"She—she kik-kik-can't!" gasped Bessie desperately.

"How? Why not?" said Babs.

"I—I've got them myself—they're in No. 4 study!"

"My hat!" said Mabs.

Bessie Bunter shook with alarm.

"Y-y-yes. Marcia advised me to take them. I had the chance. I—I really thought they were mine. But I—I don't want the horrid old pearls now. I—I'm a particular sort of girl. I won't touch them if—if there's any kik-kik-question about them!"

Babs and Mabs took her arms and hurried her to the school.

"You're a silly duffer to have taken them when we told you they couldn't be yours," said Babs, as they raced her up the stairs. "But I'll take charge of them now and give them to Miss Primrose. We simply must, when there's such a question about them."

They hurried into No. 4 study.

Bessie Bunter was very upset and very sorry for herself.

She had no hesitation at all in revealing her hiding-place.

"Behind the old cookery books, Babs. I—I only put them there just before I came down. I'll get them."

She dragged the books out and they crashed dustily to the floor.

Behind them was a handkerchief. The fat girl grasped it and gave a shrill cry of amazement and dismay.

"They've gig-gig-gone!"

Babs and Mabs stared as she shook the handkerchief over the carpet to reveal its emptiness.

"They can't have gone if you put them there, Bessie!" said Babs incredulously.

Mabs began to drag the bookcase away from the wall.

"Of course not!" she said. "They've fallen down somewhere. I'll find them."

Bessie Bunter began to weep dismally.

Marjorie Hazeldene, the needlewoman of the Fourth Form

"I—I know they have gone!" she quavered. "I tut-tut-tied them in the handkerchief."

Mabs gave a startling cry.

"There are no pearls to be seen here, Babs! They haven't dropped down anywhere!"

Babs looked thunderstruck.

She was beginning to hate the very name of these pearls that could play such extraordinary pranks, apparently of their own free will.

"You hid them somewhere else, Bessie, and you've forgotten!" she declared.

"I—I didn't!" wailed Bessie. "They were tied in the handkerchief."

"Let's have a proper look and see!" cried Babs.

She and her chum started to ransack the study while Bessie stood by, tearful and upset. Marjorie Hazeldene and the chums from No. 7, who happened to look in, were pressed into service as well.

The search was at its height when the door opened to reveal the stern face of Miss Bullivant.

"I hear, Barbara, that a mysterious string of pearls has been seen in the school recently," she said. "I was told that it was in the possession of the Third Form, but Madge Stevens declares that it has been stolen away from her keeping."

There was a dramatic silence in No. 4 study.

"It appears from general conversation, Barbara, that Bessie Bunter may possibly know where they are."

"I—I—I don't!" stammered Bessie glumly. "I—I hid them in here."

"What, you admit taking them from the Third Form room?"

"Only for fif-fif-fun. But——"

"Then, Bessie, where are the pearls?"

"I—I don't know!" wept Bessie.

Miss Bullivant's voice resembled thunder.

"Good gracious! You admit having a string of pearls this very afternoon—a string not your own?"

"I—I thought they were mine!" said the fat girl desperately.

"Produce them instantly!"

"I—I can't!"

Miss Bullivant's brow was puckered in lines of wrath.

"Bessie Bunter, you will come with me to my study instantly!" she cried.

"But I—I'm innocent!" yelled Bessie. "I haven't sis-sis-stolen the pearls!"

"We will see," said Miss Bullivant; and dragged her away.

CHAPTER VII.

A MASS OF EVIDENCE!

MISS BULLIVANT was a grim and relentless questioner, and Bessie was one of the most talkative and blundering witnesses possible.

Within a minute the mistress had no doubt that Bessie was the girl upon whom the jeweller's suspicions had fallen, causing him to make such a scandal in the village.

When Bessie explained that she only bought the ear-rings because she wanted plenty of jewellery for her photograph, it only made matters worse.

Babs and Mabs, try though they did to protect their fat chum, were very soon silenced when the accused girl was giving such condemning evidence against herself.

"You say that the girls have said that the pearls did not belong to you, Elizabeth Bunter?" rumbled the Bull.

"But I was sis-sis-sure they were mine!" wept Bessie.

"You mean, that you insisted on claiming them, and did all you could to get the pearls by stealth? Wait a minute. I will find the first Third Form girl I can, and question her."

By the worst possible luck, Miss Bullivant found Minnie Jerome, famed for her talkativeness.

The youngster was scared by the seriousness of the scene in the mistress's study, and did not know how much was known.

Very soon she unwittingly betrayed how the pearls had disappeared twice in one night, and the suspicion had fallen on Bessie each time.

"As though this girl was trying to get them without anyone knowing that they were in her possession?" asked Miss Bullivant.

"Yes, Miss Bullivant," admitted Minnie; and she was told that that would do.

"But it wasn't Bessie who took them at night, we're all positive of that, Miss Bullivant!" cried out Babs.

"Then whom do you accuse?" asked the mistress coldly.

Babs could say nothing.

"I will see Madge Stevens, who seems the most important girl in the Third Form," said Miss Bullivant grimly. "Dorothy Jobling, you are not required here. You may fetch her."

Madge Stevens was fetched.

Miss Bullivant questioned her very sharply indeed as to how the pearls came into the possession of the Third Form, and Madge could only tell the true story.

"So they were found under the table by Bessie?" said the mistress. "No one had seen them before that?"

"That's true, Miss Bullivant," admitted Madge.

There was a very hard light in the Bull's eyes.

"In other words, Madge, it was possible for Bessie to throw the pearls under the table and then to pretend to find them?"

Babs nearly jumped with horror.

"Oh, Miss Bullivant!" she gasped.

"Silence!" cried the Bull. "Is that so, Madge?"

"It—it might be," said Madge. And impulsively: "But I won't believe *that* of Bessie, all the same!"

"You are not asked to believe anything," said the mistress coldly. "You are positive that no one else saw the pearls before Bessie?"

"Yes. But all the same——"

"That is enough! You may go."

Madge Stevens was driven forth.

"This is a very serious case indeed," said Miss Bullivant, again repulsing the frantic attempt that Babs and Co. were making to intercede for their chum. "Very serious! Elizabeth Bunter admits visiting the jeweller. She is gravely suspected of endeavouring to create a false impression about these pearls. They must be found at once. No. 4 study will be searched."

"We've searched it and found nothing!" burst out Babs.

"It will be searched by a monitress this time," said the mistress grimly.

Iris Bentley undertook to search No. 4 study—in the presence of Bessie and her chums, of course.

There were numerous other Fourth Formers outside the study, and prominent amongst them was silent Marcia Loftus.

Iris began to search quickly and methodically.

The bookcase sheltered nothing. Nor did the work-baskets. Then she came to the cupboard and looked there. Almost the first thing to hand was an apparently empty jampot and—it rattled!

What a thrill there was at that!

Not one pair of eyes failed to watch the flushed monitress as she took the jampot and turned it over on her hand. And then—what a simultaneous gasp as its contents were revealed!

The pearls!

There was the elusive string of pearls—there it was, gleaming on Iris's hand.

"I—I didn't put them there!" cried out Bessie, in a sort of shriek.

Marcia Loftus spoke in a sort of triumphant whisper.

"Fancy her thinking of a jampot!"

The screen swayed and fell against the wall, disclosing to Marcia the form of the girl she thought was hundreds of miles away

215

Babs wheeled round, with burning eyes.

"Bessie didn't hide them there, Marcia, and you sha'n't say such a thing!" she cried out.

"Silence!" rumbled the mistress.

"But, Miss Bullivant, this is the work of someone else——"

"Barbara!"

"While we've been out of the study! No one was left to guard it——"

"Enough! Elizabeth Bunter," cried Miss Bullivant, "you will come with me to the Headmistress instantly. Iris, of course, will be required as a witness, and also Barbara, Mabel, Clara, and Marjorie. At once!"

Sobbing and protesting, Bessie was almost dragged by mistress and monitress to Miss Primrose's study.

Babs saved her efforts now, preparing for a final desperate appeal to the Headmistress herself. Surely Miss Primrose would not be so harsh and ready to judge by circumstantial evidence?

But what course was there for the Headmistress?

She listened to Miss Bullivant's report, and it was certainly a very black case indeed against the fat girl. Babs knew that protests of innocence were useless against such an array of facts and suspicions. Tensely she whispered with Mabs before stepping forward to make her appeal.

"Miss Primrose, please!"

"Unless you have actual evidence in Bessie's favour, Barbara——" demurred the Headmistress.

"We think it's a mistake, Miss Primrose," Babs put in breathlessly. "We can't account for this necklace, but we don't think it's the missing one."

"How can there be any doubt?" exclaimed Miss Bullivant.

"For Bessie's sake, Miss Primrose," Babs begged, "will you let us go to the village and get an exact description of the missing necklace?"

"Why?"

"Because Mabs and I are both sure we've seen this one before—somewhere!" said Babs in a startling voice. "We can't be sure, but we're almost certain that we have seen it. May we go, Miss Primrose?"

Miss Primrose gave permission. They must only ask for details of the loss, and promise to say no word of what had transpired at the school.

Leaving tearful Bessie still in the study, Babs and Mabs slipped away, eager for their investigations. They found many Fourth Formers waiting anxiously for news.

"What's happening?" asked Peggy Preston anxiously. "Is it any better for Bessie?"

Babs explained their mission in quick sentences.

"What a splendid idea!" was the unusual comment of Marcia Loftus. "Well done, Babs! I believe you'll have luck, too!"

So unexpected was such a speech from Marcia that everyone stared.

"Thanks, Marcia," said Babs drily. "We sha'n't fail if we can help it."

They hurried down to the shed for the bicycles, and trotted with them to the gates. In the very act of jumping into the saddle Babs gave a cry of surprise.

"Puncture?" asked Mabs.

Babs laughed almost gaily.

"No. I've just thought, Mabs!" she said breathlessly. "You know how puzzled we've been over that necklace. I remember, now, the girl who used to wear one like it. She's away from the school—that's why we didn't guess before. That girl is Lorna Grey!"

"Lorna!" ejaculated Mabs. "My hat, Babs! Lorna Grey! Why, of course! She did have a necklace just like that once. It disappeared when —when Marcia Loftus was threatening to tread on it and smash it after a quarrel they had. I don't remember seeing it again after that!"

They rode on, their minds full of exciting thoughts. Both felt positive now. Did it mean that they were at last on the track of the explanation of what had been a baffling mystery?

CHAPTER VIII.

LOST AGAIN!

TWO very cheery looking girls rode up to Cliff House School, dropped their bicycles against the wall, and went running for the door. Marcia Loftus, who had apparently been strolling up and down by herself, intercepted them.

"Good news?" she asked.

But their faces showed that. Babs and Mabs were full of smiles. In the ordinary way they would not have been so courteous to Marcia, but they were in the mood to talk to anyone now!

"Rather!" said Mabs.

"Bessie—she's going to be quite all right, after all," Babs declared. "Sorry we can't stop, Marcia, now—we're in such a hurry to get upstairs."

On they raced, to be besieged immediately by a crowd of Fourth Formers who wanted to know everything. But the crowd had to be content with scraps of information. Babs and Mabs were bound for the Headmistress's study.

They found Miss Primrose talking to Miss Steel, the Fourth Form mistress, while Bessie sat in one corner, sniffing loudly. Boker, the page, was summoned to bring Miss Bullivant.

"And the necklace, Barbara?" Miss Primrose

asked. " You have a written description of the missing article ? "

" No, Miss Primrose," said Babs.

" But really—why not, may I ask ? "

" Because there is no missing necklace ! " Babs announced dramatically.

" Good gracious ! " ejaculated Miss Bullivant; and Miss Primrose puckered her forehead and gave Babs a harder look.

" You see, Miss Primrose, the necklace has never really been missing," Babs explained. " What Miss Bullivant reported was nothing more than village gossip ! "

" Gossip ? " cried Miss Bullivant. " But—I was told by Miss Tabitha Tenson, who considered that I ought to know——"

" It's quite true, Miss Bullivant, that the jeweller told everyone that he believed he had been robbed," said Babs. " But, as it happens, there was no robbery at all. The necklace was sent to a customer in error, and has been returned. He was ashamed to admit his mistake, but that is why he had taken no further action."

" Goodness gracious ! " said Miss Primrose.

She was giving Miss Bullivant the sort of look that said, very plainly : " Now, why did you not make further inquiries ? "

Miss Bullivant appeared to be quite as embarrassed as she must have felt.

" I—I am very sorry indeed, Miss Primrose," she stammered. " But I was quite impartial. You will admit yourself that the evidence was most conclusive. However, I—I must say that Bessie Bunter is entirely vindicated."

Bessie Bunter blinked, and wiped her eyes, and tried to grin as Miss Bullivant approached her.

" Bessie, I am very sorry, and I withdraw whatever I have said."

" Oh, dear ! " gasped Bessie. " It's quite all right, Miss Bullivant, as—as long as I'm not going to be expelled ! "

Miss Primrose was patting her back while Babs and Mabs shook the fat girl's arms.

" It is a mistake for which we are all very sorry," said Miss Primrose cordially.

Bessie Bunter began to beam.

" Oh, that's all right, Miss Primrose," she said. " I say, it's awfully good of Babs and Mabs to have made inquiries. I suppose they knew I was innocent from the courageous way I took it all, eh ? "

" The what ? " murmured Babs.

" My fearlessness," said Bessie, growing more and more like her own self. " You know, some girls might have been quite cut-up if they'd been in my position, even if they were innocent."

Miss Primrose looked away to hide a smile.

" But the necklace ! " she exclaimed a moment later. " The one that was found in No. 4 study —we have not yet decided whose property it is. Do you still claim it, Bessie ? "

" I—I don't know, Miss Primrose," said Bessie doubtfully.

Babs and Mabs exchanged a look and decided to say nothing of their own suspicions—at present.

" Bessie Bunter certainly found it," put in Miss Bullivant.

" And everyone in the school knows of it," nodded Miss Primrose. " You have it, Miss Bullivant ? "

" Yes, Miss Primrose. In the table-drawer in my study."

" Then, as Bessie is the only girl who has made any claim to the necklace, Miss Bullivant, I direct that it shall be given to her for safe keeping."

Bessie Bunter giggled delightedly.

Miss Bullivant reached her study and went straight to the drawer.

She pulled it open, and only paused when her hand had gone halfway towards it, to give vent to a startled cry.

" The pearls ! They are gone again ! "

If the ceiling had fallen in, the girls could hardly have been more startled.

Bessie Bunter jumped forward and peered at the papers that filled the drawer.

" Perhaps they—they've got pushed to the back ! " she gasped.

Miss Bullivant was breathing heavily.

" Nothing of the sort ! They were right in the front—— Bessie ! Girl ! How dare you treat my papers in that manner ? "

For Bessie Bunter was taking the matter into her own hands, and starting to search—as only Bessie could search !

Miss Bullivant felt at the back of the drawer to satisfy the clamouring Bessie.

" No. They are not here now ! " she declared.

Miss Bullivant dismissed them with a wave of her hand.

" I shall hold a very close inquiry into this outrageous offence ! " she declared. " This is not the last that will be heard of the matter. You may all go now."

" Bub—bub—but the necklace ! " gasped Bessie. " My pearls ! "

" Kindly leave the room, Bessie," said the mistress, with acidity in her voice.

Babs and Mabs seized hold of the protesting Bessie by either arm and marched her out of the study.

" I wish we had never seen the wretched pearls," said Mabs, as they walked back to meet the rest of the form, who, eager for news, were awaiting them.

CHAPTER IX

TWO AND TWO

BARBARA REDFERN and Mabel Lynn were taking counsel with the chums of No. 7 study.

Bessie Bunter was not with them. She was occupied in a zealous and indignant search around the school in quest of pearls. Bessie was most annoyed to think that, only when she had really been pronounced entitled to them, they should mysteriously and utterly disappear.

Babs and Mabs were looking for causes and explanations rather than pearls.

"It isn't Bessie!" Clara Trevlyn said, shaking her head. "Of course, this last disappearance proves it completely. There's some other girl in it. Who?"

Echo answered: "Who?"

"You feel sure that the necklace is really Lorna Grey's, Babs?" asked Marjorie Hazeldene.

Babs nodded.

"Practically," she said. "It's a long while since Lorna Grey was at school, and I've had time to forget it. But I think there was one flawed pearl in her necklace, and it was seeing a flawed pearl in this mystery one that has worried me all the time. But go on, Clara. You were going to reason things out. I've got an idea, but I'll keep quiet while you have your say."

Clara addressed the assembled company.

Mabel Lynn, the Fourth Form's leading actress

"If it was Lorna Grey's necklace," she said, "it was obvious why Bessie was the only open claimant. Now, Bessie's motives were transparent. Bessie wanted to look smart. She admitted that. She admitted that she was not sure. But, as no one else claimed the necklace, she wanted it herself. And someone else wanted it—secretly. Someone who has been cunning enough to work so cleverly that suspicion has always fallen on the girl everyone was likely to suspect—Bessie!

"The necklace disappeared while we were pillow-ragging, and was found near Bessie's bed. Why? Because the real culprit lost her nerve, and didn't want the necklace to be found on her. The same girl—obviously a Fourth Form girl—tried to get the necklace the same night. Again she threw suspicion on Bessie. Perhaps she was lying awake when Bessie got up, and really did go to the Third Form common-room as she told us. That made it easy for this girl to take her pillow—to delay pursuit, of course—and get the necklace. She hid it this time, so that there should be no danger of it being found on her."

"Good!" nodded Marjorie Hazeldene. "That's sense, anyway. And because this girl—whoever she is—doesn't want anyone to know that she had the necklace she's never claimed it openly."

"It's really getting very obvious," said Babs, with an enigmatic smile.

"Eh?" said Clara. "I'm afraid I don't see it. What happened next? The pearls were found, and hidden by the Third. Bessie found out where they were, and took them. Of course, anyone could find out where Bessie hid anything. So Miss Who-is-she took them. Then followed a giddy mix-up. The young lady who had them didn't want them any longer, so she put them back in Bessie's study. Then Bessie is cleared, and Miss Who-is-she wants them again. She has some urgent reason for that, I expect, because it wants a bit of nerve to visit the Bull's study and take them."

"Someone working behind Bessie all the time, someone who wanted to have the pearls, but not to let anyone know that she even wished to have such things!" muttered Mabs.

Babs said, very quietly:

"It's funny how careful Clara has been to leave out the name of Marcia Loftus all the time!"

And Mabel Lynn laughed!

Clara Trevlyn started.

"Eh? You've guessed it?" she said.

"You've guessed that it's Marcia?"

"Marcia and none other!" said Babs in the same quiet tone.

Clara smote the table with her open palm and gave a rueful grin.

"Well, I really did think I'd solved it myself," she said. "When did you guess?"

Babs smiled.

"I'm not sure. The idea's been in my mind longer than I realised. But I began to get suspicious this afternoon when I heard that Marcia had told Bessie how to get the pearls. Marcia never tries to help anyone—let alone Bessie—without some reason, and it's seldom a good-natured one."

"My hat, yes!" said Clara. "She told Bessie, you think, so that Bessie would get all the blame if there was any mistake?"

"Of course, Marcia's been careful all the time that she shouldn't arouse suspicion of herself," said Babs. "She's accused me of being afraid of the Third, and of treating Bessie unjustly. But we really might have guessed something this morning when Marcia got up so early to 'do prep.,' and pretended to help the Third look for the pearls. It was Marcia who knew they were hidden, and wanted to get them back off that beam."

"Marcia—and she must still have them!" breathed Marjorie. "But whose pearls are they really? How is it that we've seen them?"

"What was in that letter that Augusta lost?" countered Babs.

"What? The one from Lorna Grey?" cried Marjorie.

"Yes. Marcia brought it to Augusta," said Babs. "She flew into a temper when Augusta asked if she had seen it. Yet she had had a chance of slipping in to Augusta's study to read it."

"And if the letter was about pearls, that accounts for the letter disappearing when Marcia had read it—a mean trick that she's ready to do with anyone's letter," said Mabel Lynn.

Clara drummed on the table with her fingers—a habit she had when deep in thought.

"Lorna Grey's pearls disappeared because Marcia said Lorna had spoilt something, and she was going to smash the pearls to be 'even with her,' as she said," murmured Clara.

"Go on!"

"Where did they disappear? Lorna must have hidden them, and that letter probably told Augusta the hiding-place."

"The Third Form common-room, of course!" said Babs.

"Eh? How do you make that out?" asked Dolly Jobling.

"Because Marcia was found in the Third Form common-room, looking rather guilty. She'd taken the pearls from some hiding-place, I reckon,"

"I didn't put them there!" shrieked Bessie. "I'd no idea the pearls were in that jampot."

said Babs. "In that business of 'Under the Table at Sea' she dropped them."

"And she was spying about outside the door to know what was going to happen when we thought we saw a figure!" declared Mabs.

"It's growing as clear as clear, girls!" she exclaimed. "There's hardly anything to be explained now. Marcia dare not claim the pearls openly because everyone knows that she doesn't possess such things. She wanted to get them and say nothing about it. Probably, in her mean way, she's quite convinced that she's entitled to anything of Lorna's."

There was a long silence in No. 7.

Although there was still no proof, the evidence against Marcia was now ten times stronger than it had ever been against the unfortunate Bessie.

Clara rose suddenly to her feet.

"It wouldn't be a bad idea if we went and chatted with Marcia!" she exclaimed, with somewhat grim relish.

But there was no sign of Marcia in her study.

They inquired here and there, and finally went to the gates. Piper was able to give information. Miss Marcia had been out of the school nearly half an hour now.

"Gone—while we've been jawing!" cried Clara. "My goodness, what a sell! She must have bolted off as soon as she got the pearls!"

"And where's she gone now?" asked Dolly Jobling, in dismay.

They were standing in a group, looking perplexed and baffled, when a voice floated to their ears, and a figure came running towards them.

It was Augusta Anstruther-Browne, and she waved a buff envelope.

"I say, I've been looking for you everywhere!" said Augusta breathlessly. "I've got the queerest telegram imaginable. Guess whom it's from?"

"Lorna Grey!" said five voices in unison.

Augusta was startled.

"Right," she said. "But how did you know? And the message—I suppose you'll be telling me that, next? Is it a jape?"

"Not that we know," smiled Babs. "But what does it say?"

"Lorna asks me to meet her at the town hall instead of the railway-station at five o'clock, and I hadn't the foggiest notion that she was even in England."

Babs gave a yell of pleasure and hugged Augusta.

"Meet her at five o'clock?" she cried. "How splendid! And—ha, ha, ha!—I believe some-one else is going to be disappointed. Augusta, put on your things, and we'll all cycle to Courtfield with you."

"But—but what——" stammered Augusta, astonished at their excitement.

"We'll explain as we ride over," said Babs gaily. "We've got something to tell you—something that will take quite a long while. And I think our meeting with Lorna Grey is going to be more interesting still."

"'Twill be a lovely cycle ride!" quoth Clara; and she headed the rush of the chums of No. 7 study for their hats and coats and Courtfield.

Phyllis Howell, the sports-girl of the Fourth

CHAPTER X.
BLUFF AGAINST BLUFF

"COME in, Marcia! We'd like to speak to you."

Tea was over at Cliff House. There was almost a full muster in the common-room when Marcia Loftus poked her face round the door and received that invitation from Barbara Redfern.

"What do you want?" asked Marcia sulkily.

She had a dejected and somewhat hangdog air, but there was a touch of defiance in her tones. Babs seemed to answer quite cheerily.

"We'd like to have just a little chat," she said. "Something that concerns the Form."

"Oh," said Marcia, in a tone of relief, and entered. She took a seat near the fire.

"It is about a pearl necklace," announced Babs, in a more casual tone than ever.

"Yes-s!" murmured Marcia.

"Something that concerns the Form, certainly," nodded Babs. "This does very much, as it happens." She turned round and looked at Marcia. "The fact of the matter is, Marcia,

we'd like you to lay Lorna Grey's pearl necklace on the table!"

Marcia's cheeks had gone crimson.

Everyone in the room was staring at her.

"I—I don't know what you mean," said Marcia, in a thin voice.

"I think you mean that you don't want to know," answered Babs.

Marcia Loftus leapt to her feet.

"What are you insinuating, eh?" she cried, in a high-pitched, trembling voice. "I—I stand a good many insults from you, Barbara, but I won't stand this! Say what you profess to mean!"

"Cut it out, Marcia," advised Clara. "Where's the necklace?"

Marcia took a step back, defiant and at bay.

"I—I won't have this sort of thing said!" she cried out. "I don't know anything about a necklace. Who says I do?"

"I do," answered Babs.

Marcia whirled on her, her lips twitching, her eyes full of that curious greenish glint.

"Then prove it, Barbara Redfern!" she shouted. "Prove it! You shall, now! I'll go to Miss Primrose, and you shall prove it! Do you dare? I'll go to the Headmistress, unless you apologise at once!"

"It would be better for you to put the necklace down and go and tell Miss Primrose all about it afterwards," said Babs.

There was a sensation in the common-room, for half of the girls did not know the truth as yet.

The words seemed to strike a chill to Marcia's heart.

"Go—go and tell Miss Primrose afterwards?" she repeated.

Babs nodded.

"That's what it will come to, after all that's happened," she said. "There's no other way. Marcia, you've been scheming to keep that necklace, and Bessie has had to suffer. It's only fair that the Form should see the real culprit and know who's hoodwinked us all."

"You know nothing—nothing at all!" shouted Marcia. "You're trying to make a case against me!"

"Augusta would like her letter back as well," Babs said.

"Her—her letter?" repeated Marcia.

"Yes, please," came from Augusta. "You see, I haven't read it at all, Marcia. Besides saying where the pearl necklace was hidden, there must have been a lot of interesting things in it."

Marcia took a step back, standing as though dumb.

"It would be awkward if you were searched and a necklace found on you when you denied having one," said Mabel Lynn gravely. She saw that Marcia needed further frightening. "You probably will be searched if you don't give it up!"

"I—I don't care! You—you can't frighten me!" said Marcia. Her face twitched. "As—as a matter of fact, I've bought some pearls this afternoon. I—I suppose some of you clever little spies have been following me, thinking you could make a case against me!"

Babs stared.

She was astonished for the first time. Was Marcia making a desperate attempt to bluff even now? It seemed so.

"Yes, this afternoon I bought them!" Marcia went on, as though gaining confidence. "Here they here!"

She groped in her pocket and produced a little red case. It fell on the table, and she opened the lid with trembling fingers. Packed in wadding inside were strung pearls.

"My pearls!" yelled Bessie Bunter.

Marcia Loftus whirled round on her.

"Well, they're not!" she cried. "And you can see for yourself that they're new—that I've only just bought them! Someone's got to know I've bought them, and they're trying to get me mixed up in this other business. But I appeal to the Form for justice!"

That was the signal for Katie Smith to rise.

Katie considered herself to represent the Form when the justice of Babs and Co. was challenged.

"Can you prove that you bought the pearls this afternoon?" she asked.

Marcia nodded eagerly.

"Yes, in Courtfield. The girl assistant—she happens to be a friend of mine, unfortunately—but she will tell you that I bought them at her

"Marcia," said Babs sternly, "we'd like you to lay Lorna Grey's pearl necklace on the table"

shop. I—I've wanted some pearls of my own for a long while."

The silence in the common-room, at that statement, was dramatic in the extreme.

Marcia, emboldened by it, beckoned to Babs.

"You were clever enough to start on me, thinking I—I'd be scared by your threats," she said, a touch of the old venom in her voice again. "How about your story that—that they belong to Lorna Grey, who left the school terms ago?"

"I'm not sufficient judge of pearls myself," Babs answered.

"I should think not——"

"But Lorna Grey herself would be!"

Marcia turned on Babs, with a sneering, triumphant retort.

"Then fetch Lorna Grey! Tell her to come and identify her pearls—if you can!"

Babs smiled at last.

"Yes, that would be the best way, wouldn't it? Lorna, come and identify them!"

A gasp went round the common-room as a screen swayed and fell against the wall.

Marcia screamed out in horror, and hid her face.

Walking across the common-room from her hiding-place was the elegant figure of Lorna, who had once been a Fourth Former,

221

" Lorna ! Here—here ! " Marcia gasped, her face still hidden in her hands.

Lorna picked up the pearls with languid interest. " Quite right, Babs," she said. " The flawed one is still here. And here's the clasp, with that stupid dent I made when I tried to make it stronger one day. My pearls all right, Marcia, kindly placed in a new box provided by your friend."

Marcia shuddered, and looked up at last with horrified, tear-filled eyes.

" Lorna ! " she gasped. " We—we were friends once. Give them to me—give them to me now ! Make them mine ! Oh, Lorna—do ! "

" When you've tried to steal them ? " asked Lorna cuttingly.

" I—I didn't steal them. You said in your letter to Augusta that you had thought of writing and telling me of the hiding-place that you had forgotten all about——"

" So you admit reading it ? "

" Oh, yes, yes—I must," Marcia muttered. " But I felt justified. I brought the envelope up. It was very thin paper, and I could see my name, where you had printed it in capitals—it showed through the paper. I felt I was justified in seeing what you said about me. I had the chance when Augusta left the letter in the study. I didn't see any harm in reading a letter—from *you*, especially when it was opened."

" And not letting Augusta see it at all ? " asked Lorna sarcastically.

" You described where the pearls were hidden," mumbled Marcia. " You put it in such a way that I felt as much entitled to them as Augusta, who doesn't need them at all. I used to be more friendly with you than Augusta. I meant to return the letter to her when I had found the pearls, but there was such a fuss that I—I lost my nerve."

" And you were going to get over the difficulty of Augusta's meeting me to-night at the station by meeting me yourself, I suppose, and explaining that Augusta couldn't get away from school ? " asked Lorna.

Marcia trembled.

" I didn't mean any wrong by it," she said tearfully. " I've wished a dozen times I'd never touched the pearls. But I couldn't go back. And I couldn't sit and see Bessie have them when I felt they were mine—in recompense for that dress of mine you spoilt, when I said I'd smash the pearls if I could ! "

Philippa Derwent, the best horsewoman of the Fourth.

Lorna held the pearls in a delicate hand and toyed with them, looking no more at Marcia.

" Well, I find you as big a sneak as ever ! " she declared. " It isn't my business what happens now ; but I'm glad I came up to school when Augusta was so pressing. Babs'll have to decide."

" You can't do anything ! " said Marcia, through her teeth.

" We don't want to," Babs answered. " But we shall act if you don't, Marcia. You've let things go too far. We wouldn't have minded if you had just hood-winked us. But Bessie has suffered when you could have explained so much. The Bull won't let the matter drop. If you don't go and explain everything to her, we shall. Lorna, she needn't say that she's come near stealing, need she ? "

" No," said Lorna. " Let her pretend to the Bull that it was a mistake as to who was to have the necklace. I suppose, in her way, she did make a mistake."

Bessie Bunter gave a cry of delight.

" I say ! I've got it, girls ! I see it all ! "

" What ever do you see ? " asked Clara, interestedly.

" Why, I've guessed the whole mystery ! " cried Bessie, triumphantly. " I've just worked it all out in my head. Marcia dropped the pearls in the Third Form common-room when they ragged her."

" How clever of you ! " said Clara, with some sarcasm.

" Well, it's quite right, anyway," said Bessie. " And, of course, she tried to get them at night, and jolly well threw the blame on me. And she must be the girl who took them from my fine hiding place——"

" A very fine one ! " smiled Augusta.

" And then put them back, and then jolly well took them from the Bull's study ! " declared Bessie. " I say, I don't suppose you girls had guessed all that ! "

" I think you're wonderful, Bessie," said Clara.

" Well——"

" I can't think how you do it, really. That isn't a brain you've got at all. It's a gramophone record ! "

" Ha, ha, ha ! "

Bessie Bunter was not pleased by the merriment.

" Look here, Clara——"

" Oh, do give your poor little tongue a rest for a moment," said Clara. " Marcia's not going to get away as easily as she seems to think. Marcia, just come back!"

Marcia, half-way towards the door, stopped and glared.

"I suppose you're going to Miss Bullivant now, Marcia?" asked Babs.

"Why should I?" muttered Marcia.

"Well, you'll simply have to," said Babs. "You'll have to clear Bessie. Lorna says you can plead that it was all a mistake."

"And if I refuse?"

"The Form will have to explain the whole truth," Babs answered.

In another moment Marcia had turned and was going out of the common-room without a word.

A crowd thronged about Lorna, congratulating her, chaffing her, plying her with all sorts of questions. And Lorna laughed, and explained that she was really enjoying life very much indeed, and had only intended to pay a flying visit that would not enable her to come to Cliff House.

"But I wired to aunt, and here I am!" Lorna declared. "Jolly glad I came along, too—it seems just like lovely old times. And the necklace—I say, Augusta, you don't really want it, do you?"

"No, thanks!" smiled Augusta.

"Then why shouldn't Bessie have it?" Lorna exclaimed. "I don't want it, and I'm sure Bessie deserves something for all she's suffered."

Bessie Bunter gave an incredulous gasp.

"Wh—wh—what? Me have the necklace?"

Lorna Grey winked an eye that Bessie Bunter could not see.

"Still, of course, I don't know," she said. "When I come to think of it, I don't think pearls would suit Bessie's style of beauty. What do you girls think?"

The girls played up well.

"Most unsuitable!" said Dolly Jobling.

"They're lost on her!" said Mabs.

"Absolutely!" agreed Clara. "She's too big for little pearls. What Bessie wants is a string of young turnips!"

"Ha, ha, ha!"

Bessie Bunter was a picture of wrath.

"Lorna! Don't you listen to them! It's only because they're jolly well jealous!" she cried. "I look spiffing in pearls!"

"Don't you believe her!" said Clara.

Dolly Jobling, the Fourth Form cookery expert.

Bessie Bunter whirled round.

"That's just because you're jealous—you want them yourself, Clara! I call it mean of you. And spiteful!"

Lorna Grey laughed.

"Look here, girls!" she said. "Supposing we put it to the vote. Hands up those in favour of Bessie having the pearls!"

Two podgy hands shot into the air—only two.

They were the hands of Bessie Bunter herself.

"Ha, ha, ha!"

Bessie Bunter looked as though she could have leapt at her chums.

"It's those in favour—not those against!" she cried. "Put up your hands! You know you're all in favour."

"In favour of Bessie not having them—rather!" said Clara.

"Ha, ha, ha!"

"Really, you girls——"

Lorna Grey interposed, and beckoned to the fat girl.

"Never mind, Bessie—I'm only pulling your leg," she said. "Here they are! You can have them!"

Bessie Bunter gave a whoop of delight as she grabbed the necklace and hung it lovingly round her fat neck.

"Lorna, you're a brick—topping!" said Bessie, wild with excitement. "Babs—I say, just look! Don't you think I look spiffing in my pearl necklace? I say, Babs, have I told you I'm going to have my photo taken next week?"

There was a shriek of laughter.

"Are you really?" asked Babs, very solemnly.

"Yes. My pater wants it specially to hang in the Hall at Bunter Court, you know."

"To keep away the burglars?" asked Freda Foote; and there was a fresh yell.

But they did not worry Bessie, and she strutted proudly up and down.

"It'll be a spiffing photo now!" Bessie declared. "I think Lorna's a brick! They're lovely pearls—far better than the ones I lost!"

And that scene of gaiety was to mark the end of Bessie's troubles. For Marcia had indeed gone to make a cautious but incriminating confession of her part in the pearl mystery. And the large imposition she received as a punishment was voted by everyone to be thoroughly deserved.

THE END